In Her Mothers' Shoes

a novel based on three true stories

by

Felicity Price

www.felicityprice.com

ISBN: 978-0-473-219253

This book is dedicated to both my mothers.

Other titles by Felicity Price available on Amazon:

A Sandwich Short of a Picnic, 2010
Head Over Heels, 2011

Reviews of "In Her Mothers' Shoes":

"Sometimes when you read a book, you can't imagine why it has never been written before: it seems so self-evidently a story waiting to be told, and in just that fashion. This is that kind of book." – **Fiona Farrell, Author.**

This book is "social history as much as a study in character," written with "a style that is open, often funny and frequently affecting." - **Damien Wilkins, Author**

Part 1: Lizzie

Chapter 1

Wellington. Late June, 1950

The tram rattled slowly up the hill, lights blazing against the driving rain and eerie darkness. Through the window, Lizzie watched as the fractured shadows over pavements and parked cars flattened into the puddles at her school gates. She ducked her head, recognising someone; she didn't want any questions tomorrow.

The tram was almost empty, the after-work rush over. Up the front, Peter was joking with the driver, who kept ringing the bell and looking back in her direction, grinning like a manic monkey. What was so funny? Was it her?

Peter, tall and proud in his conductor's uniform, cockily aware of his attraction, smiled and winked. She smiled back, nervous, uncertain.

For a moment she thought of running to the back door and jumping off, joining the flickering shadows at the side of the road. But she stayed in her seat, felt the smooth, varnished wooden slats between her fingers, traced the grooves of carved initials, then turned away and looked out the window again.

What was she doing here?

It was Steven Davidson's fault; he was the reason she was chasing after this man who collected the fares and clicked the tickets on the Karori line. Peter might look smart in his fitted uniform; he might give her cheek and make jokes that sounded so clever and witty, even though she didn't really understand them; he might have the dark attraction of the other side of the tracks, with his rough accent and abrupt finish to his schooling at the age of fifteen; but he wasn't right for her.

Who *was* her type? Was it Steven Davidson, the Wellington College seventh former she'd met at Mount Ruapehu skifield last weekend? Although not as off limits as Peter, her mother wouldn't approve of him either; he didn't go to Scots.

She had little chance to meet boys. There were none at her all-girls' school, and there were none who'd caught her eye on the tram-ride home from trips to town – until that afternoon weeks ago when Peter had held onto her ticket for much longer than necessary then teased her when she tried to take it from him. He'd winked, made one of his unintelligible jokes, and the next time she made the trip had persuaded her to ride the tram all the way to the end of the line at the Karori Pavilion, where they'd talked, laughed a lot and, just as the driver had rung the bell for the tram to turn around and go back to the city, Peter had leant over and kissed her, lightly, on the lips.

She'd expected her first kiss – not counting the one with the boy in the sandpit at primary school – to bring some sense of excitement, of romance, but she'd felt little more than a slight fluttering in the pit of her stomach.

It was nothing compared to the jolt when Steven had fallen on top of her in the ski lodge just over a fortnight ago. She smiled at the recollection. Everyone had been sitting in the chalet's big common room, the pot-bellied stove burning furiously in the corner, the dinner dishes done and put away. The boys from Wellington College – all six of them – were drinking beer from brown quart bottles. They'd offered Lizzie and her friend Julia a swig.

No thanks, they'd said, a bit giggly over being singled out. But they hadn't said no to a hot mug of mulled wine that the group of adults had brewed up after they'd all come in from skiing, cold from the biting wind outside. She could feel the warm glow, could smell the aromatic spices and taste the thin slice of orange with its strong alcoholic bite. Her parents never offered her such delights; her parents weren't there.

She and Julia had caught the ski bus from town, along with a crowd of others their age, to stay at the club lodge without either of their parents for the first time. They'd both felt as if they were living a little on the edge, as if anything were possible.

'Let's have the indoor ski race,' one of the boys from their bus called out.

There was a scrabble for the door and soon four boys returned brandishing a pair of long wooden skis each, clumping awkwardly down the steps in their heavy ski boots. One of them was Steven.

Lizzie and Julia had stayed seated on the bench seat, leaning back on the sturdy wooden table, sipping at their mulled wine, laughing with the others, knowing what was about to happen. Indoor ski races had been a regular nightly occurrence at the lodge over the years after the boys – and some of the girls – had downed a few drinks.

Steven, who'd introduced himself to Lizzie while they were standing next to each other in the rope-tow queue that morning, was lining up with the other three at the far end of the room, a path in front cleared of clothing and bottles.

'On your marks… Get set …. Go!'

They were off, shuffling their skis with as much speed as they could muster, jockeying for position who could get up the stairs first, pulling themselves up by the handrails, poles flailing, and suddenly they were gone, outside into the snow, where Lizzie knew they'd be poling themselves once around the lodge. Inside, everyone was cheering, catching glimpses of the racers as they flashed past each window, until they burst back in the door, fighting to be first down the stairs and into the middle of the room.

Steven flung himself at the finish line, crossing just ahead of the next boy then toppled in a heap at Lizzie's feet, grazing her knee with his pole.

'Sorry, Lizzie.' He was bright red with the effort, sweat had broken out on his forehead, and he was grinning happily. He'd remembered her name! And as he brushed against her, she'd felt a huge thrill, almost as if he'd hit her in the stomach.

'You won, Steven! Well done.' Lizzie jumped up and started to help him up off the floor.

'I'll be all right. I just need to get these skis off.'

Lizzie helped release his bindings and their fingers met as he reached for the lever at the same time. Again, that thrill. She looked at him. By the expression on his face, there was no doubt he'd felt it too.

They'd spent ages talking around the table, with Julia and the other boys, then on their own. Later, as they'd walked to their separate bunkrooms, he'd held her hand, pulled her awkwardly towards him and held her close for a moment.

Then he'd said good night and disappeared inside the men's bunkroom door.

He hadn't kissed her. What was wrong with her that he hadn't kissed her? It was Saturday night – they had to get the bus home on Sunday, there would be no other opportunity. Maybe he didn't like her after all? Maybe she'd just imagined it. All the way home, she wondered, she dissected that moment in the bus with Julia: where had she gone wrong?

'Karori terminus. End of the line.' Peter was making his way down the aisle towards her. All the other passengers had gone.

'You coming, love?' That cheeky grin, that sparkle in his eye, daring her to follow.

Why not, she thought. Steven hadn't tried to make any contact with her since that weekend at Ruapehu. He knew her name, what school she went to. It wouldn't have been hard to find her, to give her a call. At first, she'd jumped to answer the phone every time it rang in the hall. But after two weeks, she'd given up. He wasn't going to call. He didn't care.

Peter cared. Peter carried an air of danger, of risk, and she liked that. She could tell by the way he talked he was from a rougher part of town, the other side of the tracks her mother would say, and that had its own appeal. He was very good looking, he was three years older than her – not a silly schoolboy who didn't know how to kiss – and there was something about him, about his uniform, his smile, his impudence, that was unaccountably attractive.

He pulled her towards him and planted his mouth on top of hers, kissing her roughly. She could taste tobacco and smell something raw and wild about him that made her respond just as roughly. In the pit of her stomach, something stirred, shooting right through her, burning, breathtaking. He knew how to kiss.

'Come on then.' He broke away from her and strode towards the pavilion without looking back.

She splashed across the road and the shingle carpark, trying to keep up. This time, instead of heading round the back, he veered to the left and stopped outside the men's toilets. She stopped, unable to move forward. This didn't seem right. The stench of ammonia was so powerful that Lizzie thought she would gag.

She knew it wasn't sensible, she knew her father wouldn't approve, but still she followed.

How often had she accompanied her father at weekends to watch cricket at the Karori Pavilion? She'd lost count. But that was in daylight, under the summer sun. This was midwinter, well after dark and so cold her bare legs were blotched blue and white. The Karori Pavilion was familiar. But the Men's toilets weren't.

Perhaps she should turn back. She was beginning to feel less daring with every second that passed. She hesitated, clutching the iron railing, wondering if she should make a run for it.

Peter turned the handle and pushed open the heavy wrought-iron gate.

'It's okay, love, there's nobody here,' he called.

She emerged from the shadow of the dripping bushes and walked cautiously up the ramp to stand beside him, half blinded by the vicious light shining in her eyes from above the Men's door. How had it come to this?

For the last few weeks, ever since Peter had been rostered as conductor on her route, catching the Karori tram from music lessons in town had been heaven on wheels. His jaunty grin as he clicked her ticket, his sarcasm when she climbed aboard – 'Here comes Miss Marsden College' – he'd turned journey into something to look forward to, so much in fact that she'd caught the tram on several occasions for no other reason than to see him again.

Now, here she was at the end of the line. Could she go back? Should she?

He took her hand and the touch, the smell of him released that burning sensation once more. Suddenly her courage returned; she let him lead her inside.

The stench was even more throat-catching. She coughed.

'You okay, love?' He looked down at her, his face unreadable in the dim light inside. 'Do you want to stay outside?'

'No. We'll get wet. I'll come in.'

Lizzie remembered how her flute teacher had shown her to breathe through her mouth, to take big, deep breaths from way down below her diaphragm. She opened her mouth and breathed deeply. The smell receded.

The bushes around the sprawling, white-weatherboard pavilion had sheltered several trysts with Peter, sometimes in broad daylight but, from the day that he first kissed her, their hasty, breathless, fumbling encounters had been after dark, outside in the wintry cold. A small nook on the far side of the pavilion, overlooking the cricket grounds, became their hiding place; but this was the first time he'd invited her into the Men's.

Even the dim light could not hide the peeling cream paint, names scratched on the wall – *Susie loves Dave, Sally & Johnny 1949, Griff was here* – dark splotches on the floor, and stains everywhere that didn't bear thinking about. There was a strange white oval porcelain fixture on the far wall with water squirting noisily down a brown-stained smear towards a plughole. The water stopped.

All she could hear was the rain rattling on the tin roof and the thud of her heart.

'Sorry, love, it's not exactly a palace,' Peter said with his familiar grin.

He pulled off his dark navy conductor's jacket and flung it on the floor under the hand basin. The silver metal buttons clattered on the hard concrete. 'Here you are love. A bed fit for a princess. Let's lie down.' He hastily closed the door to the single toilet cubicle to her right, took her hand and pulled her down beside him. Below her gym slip, unprotected by the rough serge jacket still warm from his body, her bare legs recoiled from the cold, damp concrete.

Lizzie and her friends had talked about doing "IT". One was rumoured to have crossed the threshold and done IT, but it later transpired IT was only heavy petting. A bra had been removed, pants had been pulled down, but nothing further had occurred. Try as they might, they'd been unable to discover anything much at all about IT and what was involved.

This time, Lizzie knew for sure that IT was happening. Pants were pulled down and soon afterwards she felt a searing pain between her legs so intense she screamed.

Peter said, 'Shhh, Jack will hear us.'

Lizzie couldn't care less about Jack. The pain was unbearable.

If this was IT she didn't like it.

The rest was a blur. Peter thrust up and down on top of her a lot then cried out 'Yes' very loudly, then subsided on her ribs, making it hard to for her to breathe. Everything hurt – her back, her thighs, her calves, her arms – everything that came into contact with the concrete floor. But most of all, it hurt just below her stomach and between her legs. He was breathing heavily, like her brother Jerry did after he'd run all the way home up the hill from the tram stop.

She studied the ceiling. The wire cage around the light had become a mortuary for dozens of moths and spidery bugs with long spindly legs. A large black splodge in the shape of Italy covered the patch between the light fitting and the wall. There was no Sicily.

An embarrassing wetness between her legs trickled down into the fabric of the conductor's jacket.

She wished she had a handkerchief. She wished Peter would get off. She wished she could get up and walk away. She wished the whole vile experience had never happened.

Perhaps she should say something? She couldn't think of anything that seemed appropriate.

Peter rolled off her and his jacket, pulled his pants up and produced a cigarette packet from his jacket pocket.

'Damn, it's been squashed,' he said, holding it up. 'You shouldn't have made me get so carried away, Lizzie.' He extracted a cigarette, not at all squashed, and lit it. 'You want one?'

Lizzie inhaled the familiar tobacco aroma. An hour ago, she'd have said yes. She'd always fancied herself with a cigarette in her mouth, elegant, sophisticated, just like in the advertisements. But she simply couldn't face another new experience.

'No thanks, Peter.'

'I'd better get back, then,' he said, blowing smoke all around her. 'Jack will have turned the tram around and be ready to head back to town.'

She studied his blue, blue eyes, his thick, sandy hair, his handsome, square-jawed face with its strong, slightly crooked Roman nose, his even teeth, his teasing smile. He'd once told her he was an athlete, a sprinter, a champion at the hundred yards' hurdles, a record-setter on the high-jump. A real athlete.

'Come on, Lizzie. Time to go.'

'Yes.' Sitting up, she grabbed her underpants, which had wrapped themselves, bright white, around her left leg. Acutely aware of her inelegance, she wrestled them across to her right leg, hooked them over and pulled them up. Horrified, she could see a red stain spreading across the crotch. Maybe she was getting her period? What a terrible time for it to arrive. Peter noticed it at the same time.

'Oh God, look at that. You're bleeding. A bleeding virgin. You might have told me.' He laughed coarsely. 'Bloody hell, you've bled all over me jacket.' He grabbed it from under her, opened the cubicle door and dashed inside, grabbing fistfuls of toilet paper, wiping away at the back of his jacket. The toilet paper turned pink.

His uniform was ruined, and it was all her fault.

'I'm sorry, Peter.'

'You should have told me. I had no idea you were a virgin.'

Neither did I, Lizzie thought, but didn't say. Why was he making such a fuss about it? There was the Virgin Mary they taught you about at school. Did she bleed between her legs too? Maybe it was something to do with not having done IT before? She tried to recall if one of her friends had said anything about bleeding virgins, but drew a blank.

Peter took his jacket over to the basin and splashed water on the stain. Lizzie escaped into the cubicle and shut the door.

'Don't take too long in there,' he called after her. 'We've got to go.'

She grabbed the toilet paper – there were just a few leaves of the coarse Jeyes paper left in the container – and stuffed them in her pants, pulled down her gym frock and did up her blazer.

Peter was hovering in the doorway.

'Come on, let's go.'

She followed him into the night. It had stopped raining. Hurrying to keep up with him, she splashed straight through the car-park puddles, getting her school shoes wet. They reached the tram. Its red and cream paintwork shone from the recent rain-washing; its blunt nose faced towards Karori and the city; its sign above the front window read Newtown Depot. Through the open front door she could see Jack watching her closely.

'You're still here, Jack? That's good of you.' Peter and Jack laughed like conspirators. Lizzie could hear a new tone in Peter's voice, almost triumphant, as if he'd won the hurdles. Jack nudged him as he jumped nimbly aboard and brushed past the driver. He was grinning.

'About time, Pete my boy. I was going to go without you.'

'You wouldn't do that. You're not allowed to.'

'Don't you believe it. I've driven without a conductor before and I'll do it again if I have to.'

Peter turned to Lizzie, hanging uncomfortably back from the tram's lights. 'You want to come back in the tram as far as your street? No charge, of course.'

'Yes, please.' She didn't want to be parted from Peter now, not for a minute and dreaded the moment when she would have to get down off the tram and say goodnight.

'Climb aboard then.'

She pulled herself up the steep, high iron step, trod carefully along the grooved wood floor, slippery from the rain, and perched uncomfortably on her usual wooden slatted seat. But this time Peter didn't come back to sit beside her. Instead, he was talking animatedly to Jack, stopping frequently to roar with laughter. Lizzie couldn't see what was so funny. She didn't feel at all like laughing. She wanted to be cuddled, to be told everything would be all right. She shivered. Jack usually left both front and back doors of the tram wide open, even at this time of year. She hadn't noticed until now, though, just how the wind whistled through.

She shivered from the cold and from fear. Fear of consequences. Would Peter lose interest in her now, like Julia had said? Would he try to avoid her next time she caught the tram? And why was he ignoring her now and cracking jokes with Jack instead? And why was she bleeding? Her period wasn't due for another two weeks.

Julia would know. Julia knew everything. Well almost everything. Julia had brought that book to school: *You and Your Body* it was called, with page after page of line drawings of girls with small breasts – not at all like hers, which only just fitted into her new Maidenform bra her mother had been so embarrassing about in the middle of Kirkaldies' ladies fashions.

'My daughter is growing so fast, she needs a new brassiere again,' she'd said to the saleswoman.

Lizzie had cringed, wishing she'd stayed in the shoe department trying on those baby louis heels. It was bad enough having the biggest-size bra in the class without having to go another size up.

The girls in *You and Your Body* didn't have to worry about getting an outsized bra. Their chests had two firm little semi-circles with neat dots for nipples, and they didn't have any unsightly hair between their legs like hers. She and Julia had giggled over that – over how unrealistic the pictures were.

'They don't look like us at all,' Julia said.

'I wish I was that slim.' Lizzie held up the picture.

'You are.'

'Not like that.' She pointed to the tiny semi-circles.

'You're lucky.' Julia looked down at her emerging bumps. 'Boys like them big like yours.'

Julia always knew that sort of thing.

Julia had said that once you'd done it, once you'd gone all the way, they didn't want to know you. Was that true? She stared at him, scared. She couldn't believe he wouldn't want to see her again now they were so close, now she'd done what he wanted of her.

Lizzie looked out the tram window at the wet street glistening under the street lamps. If only she knew as much as Julia. Would she have gone all the way with Peter? She doubted it somehow. Julia was good at talking about daring things like going all the way, but she lacked the daring to do it.

Like the time they'd met Steven and the other boys in the tramping hut. Julia had flirted with one of them, she'd been so obvious it was embarrassing. But when he'd called her bluff and asked to 'take a trip outside' with him, she'd backed down at a hundred miles an hour.

Steven hadn't been forward like that. Until the ski race last month, he'd been quiet, shy even; had looked at his thick black rugby socks with their yellow stripe round the top when Julia's flirting became too much to bear. But when they'd walked back to the bunkrooms together, she'd wondered if perhaps he'd be a better choice than Peter. Except he hadn't kissed her and the next day, he'd barely acknowledged her, looking away when it was time to get on the bus, sitting with his friends instead of her.

Lizzie had always felt that 'going all the way' would elicit feelings of elation and achievement; the way it had sounded during Julia's breathless delivery, the least she expected was fireworks and rainbows to appear. But there were no skyrockets, no pots of gold. She felt soiled and slightly foolish, her uniform grubby, her underpants bloodied.

They were getting near her corner. Annoyed, she stood up and walked down the front. She said, 'I'm getting off in a minute.'

'Oh, are we there already?' Peter looked surprised, though whether that was surprise that they were nearly at her stop, or surprise that she was still there, she couldn't tell. 'Better let her off then, Jack.'

Lizzie was sure she'd seen Peter wink at the driver. She could feel her cheeks go warm, the way they did when her father treated her like a child in front of his friends.

The tram squealed slowly to a halt. Desperate for some contact, she took Peter by the arm and gave it a slight squeeze.

'I'll see you tomorrow,' she said quietly.

'Yes.' He shook off her arm and grinned. 'See you tomorrow.'

She waited a moment for her usual kiss, but it was not forthcoming. She climbed down to the asphalt.

'See you then.'

He didn't answer. She stood on the wet pavement, desolate, as the tram trundled noisily up the hill out of Karori on its way into town. The last she saw of him was his arm waving out the door as the tram disappeared from view.

Trying to muster up some courage, Lizzie slung her schoolbag over her shoulder, looked to see the way was clear and crossed the deserted street. Lights from under the verandas of the familiar butcher's, baker's, shoe repairer's and corner store shone brightly but all were closed. She felt very alone.

She turned the corner into the street leading up to her home. Only a slight rise to start with, the pavement soon became steeper and she found herself a little out of breath. She paused to recover.

If I were as fit as Peter, she thought, I could run up this hill in no time at all. She choked back a sob. Just thinking of him hurt. 'See you tomorrow,' he'd said. But there was something in the casual way he said it, while not even looking at her, that made her anxious.

He'd been on the Karori route for the past three months; did that mean he'd be on it for the rest of the year? Or could he change his route like he changed his white shirt?

The what-ifs were swirling round in her head when it started to rain again.

Lizzie had no raincoat, no cover other than her school blazer. That morning, as she'd left for school, her mother had warned her rain was forecast and told her to pack her raincoat.

'Yes, Mummy,' she'd said, and promptly ignored her. A voluminous, school-issue raincoat would not be the right look for seeing Peter that night on the way home from town. She'd also hidden her school hat and gloves in her bag – she hated them.

She started up the hill again, quickening her step, thoughts of her mother now joining the other anxieties.

What would her mother say?

She'd gone into town after school and waited there until the appointed time when she was to catch Peter's tram; she knew she would be late home, but she had no watch and no idea how late. Peter had told her not to turn up until it was dark and after the evening rush-hour.

And what would her mother say about the underpants? Lizzie was so horror-stricken at the thought she stopped walking for a moment. Clearly she would have to get rid of the evidence, hide them somehow. She remembered the burner beside the kitchen stove. If she could spirit the panties in there when her mother wasn't looking she might get away with it.

Water trickled ran down her nose – her hair was dripping wet. She started up the hill again.

At last, drenched and cold, she arrived at the bottom of the long, curved drive up to their house.

Through the trees she could see the outline of the rambling, two-storey weatherboard mansion perched on the top of the hill, silhouetted against the sky. The upstairs curtains were closed. Downstairs, the sitting room lights were blazing, but the trees obscured the lower part of the big picture window so she couldn't tell if her mother was standing there, watching out for her wayward daughter to come home.

Both front and back door lights were on – not a good sign. She paused, scared and ashamed. Then she started to shiver.

She knew she had to get inside. Surely the lecture she'd get from her mother would be over in a few minutes and then she could get warm. Maybe even a hot bath?

This thought spurred her on up the drive, up the steps and in the back door, hoping to evade her mother momentarily. Her mother spent most of her evenings in the big formal sitting room, either entertaining or playing two-handed bridge with her father when he was home from his club.

She was right. The kitchen was empty, but there was a wonderful aroma coming from the oven. Mrs Mullen, who came in three times a week to help with the domestic chores, would have prepared the evening meal. And it was always delicious; Mrs Mullen clipped recipes from *Good Housekeeping* and took pride in discovering new tastes, even using fresh herbs from the garden.

Lizzie opened the oven door – an aromatic casserole and a baked potato lay within – and was tempted to seize the dish and devour it at once. Then it dawned on her that it was only a meal for one. Where was everyone else's dinner?

She looked at the clock on the mantel and gasped. Six-thirty. She hadn't realised it was that late. The family would have eaten, done the dishes and dispersed. Jerry would be in his room doing his homework – or pretending to – and Penny, just six years old, would already be in bed.

She put down her wet schoolbag, took off her soaked jacket, hung it on the back of the kitchen chair, and removed her socks and shoes, which had left a dark rain-stain across the top of her feet.

Just as she was shoving the second sock in the bottom of its shoe, she heard the tap-tap of her mother's heels in the hall.

'Lizzie, is that you?' her mother called as she rounded the door. 'Where have you been? You're soaked. You'll catch your death.'

Her mother was wearing her usual after-dinner attire – pearls, an elegant, tailored floral dress reaching just below the knee, matching heels and flawless stockings. Her hair, her clothes were always beautiful. Even now, even when Lizzie appeared before her like shipwreck flotsam, dripping all over the kitchen floor, her mother's demeanour gave the appearance of being unruffled, though Lizzie knew this could be deceptive. For a moment, her mother was poised in the doorway, as if waiting for a camera flash. Photographers loved Helena Hamilton; she was handsome, if not quite beautiful, and had been ever since her coming out party in 1926. These days it was the National Council of Women who gathered at their home for meetings and fund-raising events that captured the photographers' attentions. Lizzie loved studying the paper the following day, reading out any report that mentioned her mother's name, cutting out the photos with her in them and pinning them inside her wardrobe door. One day, she hoped, she would be famous like that.

Lizzie took a deep breath to quell the shivering welling up from within. 'I know.'

Her mother swooped on her, enveloping her in Shalimar perfume. 'We need to get you out of your wet things, you poor thing. You're frozen.'

Lizzie's teeth chattered in agreement.

'What happened to the raincoat I gave you this morning?'

Lizzie couldn't speak for her chattering teeth. And there was no answer to that, anyway.

'And look at the time. Where on earth have you been?' Her mother stood back, studying her. 'You were supposed to be home at half-past five.'

'The tram was late.'

'Late? The tram was surely not an hour late!'

'No, I suppose not.' She should have had a story ready. What was her story?

'So tell me the truth then, what have you been doing all this time?'

'Julia and I went into town after school and then I went home to her place. And then I had to wait ages for the tram.'

'I don't believe you, young lady. You can't have been at Julia's. Her mother would have phoned. She always does when you visit her.'

'Oh.'

'The truth, Elizabeth, please.'

'I don't know. I caught the tram home and it was late. That's all.'

Her mother pursed her lips. 'I can see I'm not going to get any further. Maybe your father will get some sense out of you when he comes home.'

Lizzie knew her father could be strict, but more than likely he wouldn't care. He involved himself with his children as little as possible, ignoring them most of the time he was home – which wasn't until late during the week, while at weekends he would be absorbed in the garden, disappearing into his vegetable patch for hours at a time.

The immediate confrontation over, she started to shiver uncontrollably.

Her mother's stance, annoyed after the dissembling and excuses, softened visibly. 'Come on upstairs and get those wet clothes off. I'll run you a hot bath.'

Chapter 2

Wellington. August, 1950

When the vomiting started, Lizzie could no longer block out the fear she'd kept locked away. What if she were pregnant? There'd been a girl at school in the upper sixth who was sick in the corridor and everyone said she was pregnant. That was the last day she'd ever been seen.

She remembered the girl in her class, Marjorie, who'd been so upset last year when she thought she was going to get pregnant because her boyfriend had taken her down to the beach one night, lain next to her on the sand and put his hands 'there'. But Julia had said hands were not responsible; Julia's big sister had told her a boy's penis (they'd laughed so much at the word 'penis') had to be produced for pregnancy to occur.

When Lizzie felt the initial queasiness, she wondered if there might be more to it, especially when the feeling returned day after day, first thing in the morning. She looked it up in the dictionary, the encyclopaedia, even her mother's crossword thesaurus. She tried the school library in the biology section and learned a lot about the procreation of frogs and mice, but nothing about real people. She borrowed Julia's *You and Your Body*, saying she wanted to read it properly, but the detail about what happened when the egg travelled down the fallopian tube was a bit vague. She pinched her mother's *Good Housekeeping* magazine, in case there was something in there, but she remained almost as ignorant as when she'd started.

In the end, she blocked it from her mind.

It was at church last Sunday that the queasiness became worse; throughout the interminable sermon she'd felt like being sick and only the total embarrassment of having to rush outside, with all eyes on her, prevented her from leaving.

Lying in bed now, staring at the ceiling and waiting for the nausea to diminish, she realised that she was actually going to be sick and rushed to the toilet, only just making it in time. As she passed the bathroom door, she could hear her father splashing in the basin, shaving. The splashing stopped.

'Is that you, Elizabeth? What's going on?'

She couldn't reply; another wave of nausea overcame her. Maybe she had a stomach bug. One of the girls in her class had been home nearly all week with an upset tummy. That would make sense. A bug. Or maybe something she had eaten – Mrs Mullen's curried chicken might have caused a reaction. That could be it.

'I'd better get your mother.'

As Lizzie heaved again into the porcelain bowl, she heard the bathroom door open and the pad of her father's slippered feet along the hall carpet to the bedroom.

A few minutes later came the flip-flop of her mother's heeled mules and a rap on the toilet door.

'What's the matter, Lizzie? Your father says you're not well.'

Wiping her mouth with toilet paper, she managed to reply through the bile, 'I've just been sick.'

'Oh dear, that's no good. I'd better get the doctor to call by on his rounds.'

The mules tap-tapped away again.

The doctor. She felt like throwing up again at the thought of him. Dr McQuilkin had a hideous blotchy face with a big bulbous red nose that sprouted long hairs. He always talked bridge hands with her mother and ignored the children if they were around. Once, when she'd had the measles, a drip had come out of his nose and landed on her forehead. She'd washed her face in scalding water afterwards to get rid of the feel of him. Ever since, she'd made a habit of being out of the room when he 'called by'.

But this time, his visit carried an even greater threat. If she was indeed pregnant, he'd know – and he'd tell her mother.

It didn't bear thinking about. Her mother would know, and what about school? If she was pregnant, she'd have to miss school.

It was her last year and she'd been working hard on all her subjects, but especially on her art portfolio. The art teacher, Miss de Lambert, had said her work was very good indeed;

she'd exhibited her painting of two pears on a plate at the school parents' day, along with her pencil drawing of Julia.

'You have talent, Elizabeth,' Miss de Lambert had said. 'You seem a natural.'

Lizzie had glowed; her cousin Freda had won the school art prize four years earlier and she aspired to win it before she finished school at the end of the year. Although she had no desire to be an artist; while scorning her parents' social extravagance, she did not plan on being poor, as she'd been warned artists inevitably were. She wanted to fulfil her artistic promise, she wanted to create things of great beauty, but she also wanted to earn good money. Her chosen career was therefore architecture. As well as Art, she was good at Maths and passable at Science. The things of great beauty she would create would be buildings.

But getting into Architecture at university was competitive; she would need to pass Scholarship to get in, so she had to get better and get back to school.

Missing school was unthinkable. Though she wouldn't miss catching the tram. She'd guessed right – Peter's conductorship of the Karori tram had been brought to an end; she'd not seen him since the night in the Karori Pavilion, despite trying different tram times. But she hadn't given up completely.

Unable to summon the strength to get dressed, Lizzie made it down to the dining room for breakfast in her dressing gown. But faced with the smell of tea and toast, she had to make a run for the bathroom again.

Her mother tapped on the door just as Lizzie heaved again. 'You poor thing.'

Another stream of bile came up.

'This is so unlike you, Lizzie. You're never sick.'

Of course not – not with the threat of Dr McQuilkin calling by and dripping all over her. How could she avoid him? She could hide in her room and refuse to come down. She could run away. Except she couldn't go too far from the toilet.

What was it about toilets? That awful concrete cell where she had let Peter do what he wanted to do with her had the dirtiest, smelliest toilet she'd ever endured in her life. Now, doubled over another toilet, filled with her own foul-smelling vomit and bile, she suspected the two incidents just might be connected.

She groaned.

'You do sound under the weather Lizzie. I'll telephone the doctor after nine and see if he can call by.'

She desperately wanted to say 'No, I don't want to see the doctor', but she knew it was inevitable.

'All right, Mummy.'

Another wave of nausea cramped her stomach but this time she managed to hold it in.

'You'd better pop back to bed until he arrives and I'll bring you some boiled water.'

Lizzie wanted to argue. She didn't want to go back to bed; she wanted to go to school as usual. Surely she would feel better soon. The cramps would have to stop eventually. She put all her effort into not throwing up again while her mother was still outside the door, but as soon as the footsteps retreated, another burst of evil tasting bile made its way up her throat.

The morning dragged by. She got out her English exercise book and tried to make a start on the essay due next week – 'Jane Austen is regarded as both a friend and foe to women: discuss'. She'd promised her mother she'd do better in English – her mother was forever complaining about her marks in English and Latin but never praised her for doing so well in Art and Maths. Julia had lent her notes to help with the essay, but whenever Lizzie put her head up from the pillow to write she felt dizzy.

By lunchtime, she felt better and asked her mother if she might have some soup and a piece of bread, but her mother said to wait until the doctor came because he might think eating the wrong thing to do. 'An upset stomach is best treated with boiled water and fresh air,' she said.

'But I'm hungry,' she protested.

Her mother won. There was no lunch.

Dr McQuilkin didn't arrive until mid afternoon; by then Lizzie was starving. She heard him come in but waited for her mother to call.

He asked her how often she'd been sick, at what time of the day, whether she'd been able to eat in the evenings then asked her to lie down on the couch. He knelt beside her, with some difficulty, on creaking knees, ran his hands over her abdomen, tapped and pushed and pummelled here and there, then asked her to get up again.

'Excuse me Mrs Hamilton, but I need to ask a personal question of your daughter.'

'Oh.' Her mother looked extremely uncomfortable.

'Can you tell me when you last had your monthly period, Elizabeth?'

She could have died of embarrassment. She never talked about her period, not even with her mother and she had a horrible premonition where this was heading.

'Er . . . I don't know.'

'Well think then. Was it anytime this month?'

Lizzie shook her head no.

'Last month then?'

'I don't think so.'

Dr McQuillin had a strange look, almost triumphant.

Her mother's face looked like she'd just read a bad write-up of one of their meetings in the paper.

The doctor opened up his bag, pulled out a small white box, produced a glass bottle with a cap and held it out to her. Then, to her horror, he asked her to take it into the toilet and hold it under the stream of urine she was expected to produce. Flushed with embarrassment, she left the room, did as she was told and returned, carrying the filled bottle in her much-washed hand.

'Thank you, Elizabeth. I will send that off for tests to confirm what I think has happened.'

Lizzie had no idea what he was talking about. 'Pardon?'

'The laboratory will inject this into a frog and if she produces eggs within the next twenty-four hours, then it will show if you are pregnant.'

She gasped. The poor frog!

'Elizabeth, I wonder if you could please leave the room for a moment while I ask your mother some questions.' She nodded and left, inwardly seething at the injustice of it. It was *her* stomach that was upset, not her mother's. If anything else was wrong, if the awful fear that gnawed at her proved to be true, she should be the first to know. So why couldn't they talk about it with her present? What were they saying behind her back? She waited outside in the hall, trying in vain to hear through the keyhole what was being said.

Moments later she was called back in. Her mother had retreated behind an armchair, gripping it for support, her mouth tightly drawn, as if confronted in her living room by the Wednesday gardener in his work boots.

The doctor spoke first. 'We will have to wait until the test results come back, Elizabeth, but it is possible that you are pregnant.'

Pregnant. It was such an ugly word, ugly and unbelievable. What would Julia say? And the headmistress? It was too awful to contemplate.

She pictured herself in class with a pregnant tummy, trying to fit behind the desk in the narrow space between the rows, her gym frock hitched up over the bump, the perfect excuse at last for getting out of P.E. She could hardly be expected to jump over the vaulting horse in that condition.

'Do you understand me, Elizabeth?' Dr McQuilkin was frowning.

She couldn't look at him any longer, the judgmental old poop.

Her mother kept her mouth clamped shut; all the lines around it deepened in disapproval, or was it disappointment? Lizzie didn't blame her.

The doctor continued in a measured manner. 'Have you had relations with a young man who could have done this to you?'

Her face was burning. How could she confess? She had never told anyone at home about Peter. She knew he was from an entirely different social class; her mother would be horrified. A *tram conductor*? She could hear her mother's revulsion. She couldn't believe she had been so stupid, so naive, to let Peter talk her into it without recognising the consequences. She'd just blindly followed him into the Men's and let him do what he wanted without a moment's thought of what it could lead to, what it had led to.

She remembered the headmistress telling her once that she had scant disregard for consequences. She'd wanted so badly to go to an exhibition in town last month; she'd just caught the tram to the gallery one lunchtime and, of course, had been late back. She had to admit it: she'd not once thought of the consequences, and she hadn't with Peter either.

Why had she let him do it? What had scrambled her mind so much she'd been oblivious to where it might lead? He had a mesmerising effect on her: he could have said follow me to moon and she would have gone. She thought about his cheeky grin, his blue eyes, his shiny silver buttons.

And how it had ended, on a cold concrete floor in the Men's toilets.

'Come on, Elizabeth. You have to tell us. Was there someone?' Her mother's tone was flat, sad almost.

She looked out the window and focused on the trees at the end of the lawn. Their branches bare and stark, their leaves long ago swept into neat piles and burned, emitting thick plumes of dirty brown smoke.

Not so long ago, she was out there with her little sister Penny, rolling in the leaves, throwing them at each other, shrieking with laughter. It was one of those rare still autumn days, the leaves falling on their heads like shreds of brown crinkly parchment. Mummy joined in, scooping up armful after armful and giggling with them as she let it drop on her girls. Lizzie could still smell the damp decay, the earthy mustiness as she burrowed into a mound of fallen leaves under the big chestnut tree, its harvest of prickly hedgehog balls scratching her skin. When she was a child, she used to collect the spiky shells, taking them up to her room to crack them open in the hope that the shiny hard conker would reveal the chestnut fairy from her favourite book *Fairies of the Flowers and Trees.* She could picture him still, an impish brown elf in tights and jerkin, his head covered by a hat of tiny barbs, his wings speckled with white like a moth's, his hands offering up the chestnut, 'silky within'.

'Elizabeth!'

Her mother never called her that. She was really in trouble. She swivelled her eyes from her mother to the doctor and back again. They were both looking at her sternly, waiting for her to tell on Peter. Well, she wasn't going to.

'I don't know.'

'This isn't like you, to be so wilful.' Her mother's stern expression belied the sadness in her eyes. 'You just don't think. You never think of the consequences.'

'Mrs Hamilton, perhaps I could have a word with her.' Dr McQuilkin's red nose flared, making it stand out even more than usual.

'Very well then.' Her mother left the room without glancing at her daughter.

Lizzie kept staring out the window; she didn't want to face the doctor and his questions. She hated him for his smugness, his superiority.

'You can tell me, Elizabeth. I'm your doctor. If you're in trouble, I can help you. You've got a boyfriend, haven't you?'

She wouldn't look at him.

'You don't have to tell me his name if you don't want to, just tell me what happened.'

He was so persistent. She glanced at him, annoyed, wishing he would just go away.

Dr McQuilkin was watching patiently.

She realised she had to say something or he'd just go on and on. Gripping the chair for support she said, 'I think I've done it with a boy.'

'Ah, I thought you had a boyfriend. Can you tell me more?'

The doctor's glasses glinted in the afternoon sun; his nose shone even brighter red; a drip hung on the end of one of its long whiskers. His uneven, brown-tipped teeth were bared in a greedy smile.

She hadn't told him she had a boyfriend. How dare he make that assumption? Was Peter a boyfriend? Not really, not like Julia's boyfriend at Scots. They went on dates to the movies, they met up at the milkbar on the corner of Julia's street, they wrote each other silly notes. Peter didn't do anything like that. And he wasn't a boy either. He was a man. All of twenty, and working in a real job. No, she didn't have a boyfriend. The doctor was quite wrong.

The trees continued to hold their fascination. She wasn't going to tell this man anything, not Peter's name, nor anything that might identify him; nothing about the tram or about the pavilion, and especially nothing about the men's toilets. Then her mother would never know.

She shook her head. She'd said enough.

'Did he use a condom?'

'A what?'

'A condom? A rubber sheath. To stop you getting pregnant.'

A rubber sheath? It sounded revolting. There hadn't been anything about rubber sheaths in *You and Your Body*. Perhaps there should have been; if it could have stopped all this – the creepy doctor, her mother's disappointment and missing school – it might have been worth it. Why hadn't Peter thought of it? Did he want her to get pregnant?

'No.'

The doctor asked her if she'd be able to tell her mother, or would she like him to tell her.

'I don't want you to tell her anything.' She was glad she hadn't given him much to tell.

He folded his arms and looked exasperated. 'Very well then,' he said at last. 'I'll leave that up to you.'

She stood to ready herself for the confrontation she knew would follow.

The doctor brushed past her on his way to the door to fetch her mother. His elbow touched her chest. 'My, you have grown up to be a big girl.'

He stopped and raised his hand - a huge hand ridged with dark veins and dotted with liver spots. She stood very still. But he didn't touch her again.

'I can see I'll have to keep an eye on you,' he said, wagging his finger at her like she'd been a naughty child.

Her tongue stuck to the back of her mouth; she was speechless. She nodded.

The rest of the doctor's visit went by in a blur, with a red haze covering her eyes. The doctor did most of the talking. Her mother was so upset her lips disappeared in a thin drawn line, like a mailbox snapped shut.

No sooner had Dr McQuilkin departed than Lizzie's mother ushered her into the kitchen and sat her down at the big wooden table.

'You foolish, foolish girl,' her mother cried – her mother who never usually raised her voice. 'I don't believe you can have been so stupid.'

Lizzie studied the marks on the table, the faint scorch from one of Mrs Mullen's casseroles, the dish so hot from the oven it had glued the cork mat to the wood; the watermark from teapots and jugs with no coasters, which almost constituted a hanging offence; the scratches from carelessly held knives; the deep score her brother Jerry had made when questioning his mother's ruling that he couldn't go away on a weekend camping trip with his friends – the table bore all the hieroglyphics of the Hamilton family's existence.

'Are you listening to me?'

'Yes.' Sullen, withdrawn; she continued to study the table.

'Well answer me then, who was he?'

The inquisition began. Did he go to Scots College? How old was he? Who were his parents? Where did they live?

Lizzie gave away nothing. She refused to say anything until the results came back.

Something must be up, she realised a week later, when her mother came running up the stairs to her room the moment she got home from school. She'd come in the back way, hoping to give her mother the slip, but the top stair always creaked, even when she tried to step across it. She'd flung herself down on her bedspread and was clutching her doll Jemima when her mother knocked briefly then came straight in, before she'd even answered.

'The doctor's letter arrived in the mail this morning and I opened it,' she said then continued on before Lizzie had time to protest at her mail being opened. 'It's positive. You're eleven weeks pregnant.' She sounded businesslike, matter-of-fact.

Lizzie held Jemima tightly, holding her breath, determined not to show a reaction.

Not that it mattered; her mother was fired up and nothing would stop her. It seemed she had been thinking it all through since the doctor's visit.

'You'll have to leave town of course and have the baby somewhere nobody knows you. You can't possibly have it here. The neighbours would soon work it out and then everybody will know. You'll have to go away. I'll make some phone calls and find a place for you somewhere a long way off, like New Plymouth or Christchurch, where you'll be looked after with other girls in the same situation until the baby's born. Then you can come back here.'

'Come back with the baby and live here?'

'No, of course not. You can't keep the baby. That's simply not possible. What happens when girls like you get themselves in the family way, they go away for a few months, give the baby up for adoption to a nice family, and then come back as if nothing's happened. Nobody except your father and I will know.'

‘A few months?’

‘Yes, what did you think would happen? We can’t have you growing fat and waddling around here. The Foster-Browns next door, everybody would know. You’ll be able to stay at school for maybe another two months if you can stop being sick, and then you’ll have to leave town before it starts to show.’

‘Before what starts to show?’

‘That you’re pregnant, you silly girl. Your pregnancy will start to show, probably in October, so that’s when you’ll have to go.’

‘October? But that’s only a few weeks away. What about my school work? I’ve got my final exams, and my art portfolio is due a month later.’

‘You should have thought of that when you got yourself pregnant.’

‘Then maybe I can take my schoolwork away with me? Maybe the school will let me take my exams in another town?’

Her mother sat back and looked at her incredulously. ‘You really don’t understand the consequences, do you?’ Suddenly, her expression softened. She sat next to Lizzie on the bed, put her arm round her shoulder and gave her a squeeze. ‘The school can’t know what’s happened, where you’re going or why because then everybody will know. We can’t tell anyone what’s happened, especially not the headmistress. Those things never remain a secret for long.’

Lizzie thought back to the girl who’d had to leave in her last year of school after she’d been sick in the corridor. Within just a few days, all the girls in her class knew why she’d gone. It remained a subject of gossip for months – sometimes of admiration, sometimes of horror. Why hadn’t she taken more notice, why hadn’t she realised she was putting herself at risk of the very same fate?

Her mother was right: she was a very silly girl incapable of recognising consequences.

She hung her head, defeated.

Her dream of becoming an architect was shredded in that brief and unhappy moment on the hard concrete floor. Her art portfolio would never be judged. Her Scholarship Maths exam would never be sat.

'What will I tell them? What will I tell Julia?'

'Nothing,' her mother said emphatically. 'You tell them absolutely nothing. Especially not Julia, nor any of your friends.'

'But what will they think when I'm no longer at school. I'll have to say something.'

'You let me handle it. I'll write the school a letter the day after you leave and say you're sick, or you've had to visit your grandmother in Auckland who's dying perhaps. I'll make something up. That's the least of your worries, what to say. You just say nothing.'

Lizzie ran her finger along Jemima's stiff black curls. Leaving school, not seeing Julia or any of her friends again, just disappearing one day without saying goodbye – it couldn't happen.

There was only one way of stopping this terrible chain of events and that was for Peter to marry her. She was sure he would, if only he knew. He could be such a gentleman, calling her love, making her laugh. True, he had been a bit offhand in the tram on the way back to Karori that night, but he was probably just nervous after what they'd done together. She started to work out how she would make contact with him, how she'd let him know.

She decided to try it on her mother.

'What if my boyfriend agrees to marry me? He's got a good job . . .'

'Has he? So he's not at Scots? He's a working man?'

Too late, Lizzie realised she'd given away more than she meant to. She put Jemima down and stuck her chin out defiantly. 'Yes, he's old enough to support me. He's not a schoolboy.'

'And just how old is he?'

She hesitated. His age was surely not the point? 'I don't know.'

Her mother drew back, withdrew her arm, and looked at her incredulously. 'You don't know? Surely you must have some idea?'

She wasn't going to tell. 'We never discussed it.'

'You're far too young to get married, Elizabeth. You're only seventeen.'

'But Nellie Stevens got married. You know, that girl at school last year. She married her boyfriend when she was in the upper sixth.'

'You're not Nellie Stevens. Your father would never agree to it. And neither would I.'

'But I know he can support me. He's got a good job.'

'And what does he do?'

'Look, it doesn't matter what he does. What matters is that he cares about me and if I told him about this he might . . .'

'You haven't told him?' Her mother's eyes were wide.

'No. How could I? I've only just found out.' It was too much. Lizzie felt intense prickling behind her eyes. A few moments later, she felt her mother put her arms around her again. This time, it made her cry, an overflow of self-pity and real fear.

Her mother took her white Irish linen handkerchief out of her pocket and handed it over; Lizzie accepted it and dabbed ineffectually at her eyes then studied the sweeping *HH* initials in the corner, now wrinkled and damp.

'You poor child,' her mother soothed, sitting down beside her and taking her free hand. 'It's a terrible time for you, I know, but let's just take some time to think it through. Whoever this Peter is, he has to be pretty special to deserve you, Lizzie. And I'm not sure marriage for you right now is the best thing.'

Lizzie sniffed and blew her nose.

'Would you like to bring him home to meet us?'

Would she? She couldn't imagine it would go very well, even if Peter agreed. And somehow she doubted it. 'I'll ask him.' Would she really? How would she get hold of him now he wasn't on the Karori route any longer?

'I'll talk to your father and see what he thinks.'

'What do you think he'll say? Will he be angry?'

'He won't be happy, that's for sure. But . . .'

The slam of the back door announced the arrival of Penny home from school.

Her mother held her fingers to her lips. 'It's our secret for now. Not a word.'

There was the stomp of feet up the stairs then Penny burst into the bedroom. 'Lizzie, you're home,' she cried, flinging herself on the bed in the space their mother had just vacated. 'Will you and Jemima play houses with me?'

At six, Penny was besotted with the game of mothers and fathers, tending to her many dolls as if they were babies. The youngest by many years, she was spoiled by everyone except her mother, and Lizzie was often chivvied into playing father. Big brother Jerry indulged Penny in other ways, but drew the line at playing with dolls.

'Not just now, Penelope, your sister is not feeling well.' Her mother crossed to the bedroom door and stood holding the handle. 'Come down to the kitchen and I'll get you milk and something to eat.'

'I'll play later,' Lizzie promised.

'Thanks Lizzie. What's that matter with you?'

'Just a tummy bug.'

'Did the doctor come?'

'Yes, he came. He says I might have to stay off school a bit longer.'

'Now that's enough, Penelope. Your sister needs to take it easy, not be hounded with questions.'

'When I was walking home with Sally today, she told me they're getting a puppy,' Penny said, neatly changing the subject. 'Can we have a puppy too?'

'No, we can't.'

'But Sally is.'

'Sally's house has got fences all around it. We haven't got any fences. We're on the top of a hill. It would be impossible to put fences up. No, a puppy is out of the question.'

Penny looked like she might cry.

'Go and have your milk, Penny, then come back upstairs and play.'

'Will I catch your tummy bug, Lizzie?'

'No, I don't think so. The doctor didn't say it was catching.'

He'd also said her morning sickness could last another month. How on earth was she going to pretend she had an upset stomach all that time? And did that mean she would be off school for a whole month? Her mother had asked the doctor and he'd said it depended on the girl – some girls were sick all along and some just had occasional off days. She hoped hers just involved occasional off days. She wanted to be at school.

Their father was not at the dinner table.

'Where's Daddy?' Jerry asked almost as soon as he'd sat down.

'He's at his club.' Her mother's lips were pursed. Arthur Hamilton spent Thursday and Friday nights at the Wellington Club and came home, only occasionally in time for dinner, reeking of tobacco and whisky. 'His dinner's in the oven. He'll be here soon.' She spooned onto their plates the mashed potato, peas and baked chops that she'd prepared – it was Mrs Mullen's day off.

'I thought Lizzie was ill this morning?' Jerry said. 'But she's having dinner.'

'Yes, well, that's a good sign then, isn't it? She must be getting better.'

Jerry clearly thought better of arguing with their mother and started to cut up his lamb.

Lizzie was so hungry she almost shovelled the food into her mouth. The nausea she'd felt this morning had disappeared. She let the dinnertime conversation about school flow over her as she ate, thinking of the future her mother had painted.

She couldn't bear not saying goodbye to Julia. Just leaving one day and not coming back, with no explanation, no farewells, it was just unthinkable. Perhaps Julia would guess. She hadn't told her about Peter, at least not his name or even that he was older than her. As far as she and the other girls knew, she was seeing a boy from Wellington College who lived on the other side of town. For as long as she could, she'd resisted their pleas and teasing to reveal much more but at Julia's intensive questioning, she had finally confessed they'd done IT.

Julia had an unexpected, sharp way of hitting home to the truth. It would be typical of her to guess that Lizzie was off school with morning sickness. How many days would it take her to work it out? Somehow, Lizzie had to get herself to school in the morning and prevent the rumour starting.

Or could she tell them and swear them to secrecy? Julia would keep it to herself, but would her other friends? Probably not. And then the whole school would know. Oh, the shame of it. Once the secret was out, even if she did as her mother said and went away for a few months, she could never come back and face seeing anyone from school again.

But if she could track Peter down at the tram depot, maybe he would understand, maybe he would marry her and everything would be all right.

Her mother would never approve but maybe if they had a quiet wedding, with just family present it would work. Would there be a space for Peter in the Hamilton family?

'Lizzie?' Her mother's voice broke into her thoughts.

'Yes?'

'I was saying would you like any more to eat? You seem to have finished your dinner remarkably quickly.'

'No thanks, Mummy.'

While they were doing the dishes, their father arrived home, pouring his bonhomie through the door, all smiles and whisky breath. Their mother retrieved his dinner from the oven and joined him in the dining room while he ate, closing the door behind them and giving them a fierce-eyed warning, forbidding them to follow.

Lizzie kept on washing, trying to ignore what she suspected was about to happen next door, joining in the chatter as if nothing at all was wrong. It remained eerily quiet in the dining room. Her mother had decided not to say anything to her father about the suspected pregnancy until it was confirmed, not wanting to upset him unnecessarily. Now it was necessary.

'What's up with you, then?' Jerry asked as he piled up the dinner plates ready for Penny to put away.

'Nothing, why?'

'You're so quiet,' Jerry said. 'Are you in trouble?'

'Me? Of course not.' She buried her face in the cupboard under the sink, putting away the dish cloths and soap.

Suddenly their father cried out something; he sounded furious.

'Well, somebody is. Glad it's not me.'

'What's up with Daddy?' Penny asked as she put away the knives and forks painstakingly slowly.

'Could be anything.' She tried to sound nonchalant. 'Probably something to do with his work.'

'I'm off upstairs,' Jerry said hanging up his tea towel and departing hastily.

'Come on, Penny. Let's go and play mothers and fathers. You go and set up the dolls' house and I'll be along in a minute. I need to go to my room first.'

Once there, Lizzie closed the door firmly behind her and threw herself on her bed, grabbing hold of battered old Mr Ted and Jemima, the only doll she'd held on to when Penny had begged to have them all. She held Jemima tight.

The way things had turned out, she wouldn't be playing with dolls anymore; she was going to have a real live baby.

Except her mother had said she wasn't allowed to keep it.

Why couldn't she decide for herself what she was going to do? No matter which way she turned, the decisions would be made by her mother, her father, Peter. She felt like a stick floating in the tide, pushed around without any say where she went. Her life was no longer her own.

Most of all, she wanted to be with Peter. But what if he didn't want to be with her?

There was a timid knock on her door.

'Lizzie.' Tap, tap, tap. 'Lizzie, can we play mothers and fathers now?'

Chapter 3.

Christchurch, October 1950

The night she caught the overnight ferry to Lyttelton, Lizzie's mother took her out to a big hotel near the steamer wharf and treated her to a slap-up meal. They were early and had the dining room to themselves.

'Anything you want, Lizzie,' she said when the waiter brought the menu. 'I'm paying. I won't tell your father how much we spent.'

That afternoon, her father had left the house just after lunch with the excuse of an appointment at his club. Lizzie knew he'd made it up – he never went to his club on a Saturday. It had fallen to her mother to supervise the packing and transport to Customhouse Quay.

Packing had been stressful, her mother wanting her to take warm, practical clothes and sensible shoes; Lizzie arguing for the skirts and dresses she liked best. The arguments, however, hid the real friction: the reason she was going. Lizzie suspected her mother might have been close to tears; she'd never seen her like that before, which had made her feel even worse.

'I'm sorry Daddy's not here with us,' she continued. 'He wanted to come, but he was just too upset. He'd have ruined the dinner for you, he said.'

Lizzie felt wretched – her father was so ashamed of her, he hadn't been able to face this final meal together.

'I know. I'm sorry too.' She studied her place setting, the gleaming silver, the cut crystal, the starched white table cloth. It was something special to be taken out to dinner, but the occasion had lost its shine. At first she'd been relieved her father wasn't able to come – he would have made it too formal, fussing over which knife and fork went with what, asking the waiter endless questions. But now she was missing him. Knowing it was her fault only made the sight of the empty place setting worse. The waiter had whisked it away quickly enough, but the white space where it had been mocked her.

When they'd ordered and the menus had been removed, her mother said suddenly, 'I hope you're going to be all right down in Christchurch. If there's anything I can . . .'

'I'll be fine, Mummy, don't worry.'

'But I do worry about you. If I'd met that heartless man who did this to you, I'd have given him a piece of my mind.'

'I know. You said.'

'You know your father and I would have done the right thing by you, don't you? We'd have put on a good wedding for you if you'd wanted.'

'I know.'

'But you said you didn't want that. And I think you made the right decision to go to Christchurch instead.' She fiddled with her fork as the waiter returned with a glass of sherry. 'Thank you.' She smiled briefly up at the waiter and as soon as the man disappeared, continued, 'When all this is over, you'll see, it's for the best. You can come back home and get a job. Or you can go to secretarial school like your father said. You can take your pick, a good education like yours.'

'I know.'

'It's all come as a bit of a blow you know, Lizzie . . .' She looked across at Lizzie, waiting for some acknowledgement.

She gave her mother a rueful smile. 'Yes.'

Her father had been furious after Mummy had told him. But she'd expected that. She knew she deserved it. He'd stormed out of the dining room, slamming the door, and driven back to his club, where he'd stayed until well after midnight – she knew because she'd been unable to go to sleep. She heard him come in and waited for his footfall on the stairs but it had never happened. He must have stayed in the kitchen or living room until after she'd fallen asleep.

It was her mother who'd borne most of the brunt of his anger. And like all his other outbursts, it had been followed by a long period of silence, when he'd refused to speak to his daughter for close to a fortnight.

'Your meal, Madam. Miss.' The waiter delivered their plates.

Lizzie had chosen the chicken. It came in a thick creamy sauce, with perfectly roasted potatoes and a pile of green peas and carrots, followed by ice cream and chocolate sauce.

It was the peas and carrots she recognised as she leant over the toilet in the bowels of the overnight ferry while the floor heaved up and down underneath her. She'd no idea she'd eaten so many pieces of carrot. She particularly wished she hadn't eaten so much ice cream. She could taste the chocolate sauce as it came up again. It was a foul night at sea, with not much sleep, and she didn't felt at all comforted when the purser told her it was a comparatively calm crossing.

As the ferry edged slowly towards the dock, she looked at the surrounding hills crowding down on the tiny port and felt a surge of sadness – she didn't want to be here. She wished she was back home, at school with her friends. She wished her mother was with her to guide her down that awful gang plank she had slipped on when boarding, and to make sure she found her allotted seat on the boat train. She even wished for a moment that her father was there.

Bells rang somewhere, the signal, they'd been told, to head for the big doors that opened to the gangway. She pushed the heavy iron deck-door open, hurried down to her double cabin and picked up her suitcase, which she'd crammed with as much of her past life as she could squeeze into it – all she would have for the next five months until the baby was born. There were so many things she'd had to leave behind, so many things that could have brought her comfort while parted from her family. She'd managed to find room for some of her paints and brushes, her pens and pencils, and her art book – and worn old Mr Ted. But by the time her mother had folded and refolded her clothes and underwear and made sure there were enough warm things – 'Christchurch is supposed to be very cold, Lizzie, you need to be prepared' – there wasn't room for anything else, not more than one of her favourite books nor even her thick winter dressing gown; she'd had to make do with the thin summery one. At the last minute, she'd grabbed a photograph of her family and forced the case closed again, and this morning she'd had even more difficulty repacking her nightdress. Her mother seemed to have a knack with suitcases, with anything that required organisation. Lizzie knew only too well she was hopeless at that.

The other overnight occupant of the cabin, a kindly woman much older than her mother, had already taken her bag and disappeared. Lizzie blushed, recalling the brief conversation they'd had as they'd readied for bed the night before. Lizzie had just returned from the lavatories, where she'd been ill and was still feeling fragile.

'You're all on your own, dear? I hope you'll be all right?' the lady had said after introducing herself as Mrs Parsons.

'I've never travelled by sea before,' Lizzie had said. 'I'm sure I'll come right.'

'Never been on the ferry before? Goodness, and all alone too. I hope you have someone to meet you at Lyttelton. Do you have relatives in Christchurch?'

Lizzie swallowed. She didn't want to lie to this nice lady but she couldn't see any other way out of it.

'Yes I'm going to visit my aunt. She's meeting me at the station.'

'Oh, that's good then.' Mrs Parsons fussed around with her spongebag, washing her face in the tiny basin and slathering a lot of white cream on her face.

Lizzie waited on her bed, wishing she could tell her the truth and go home with Mrs Parsons – she seemed homely, somehow, as motherly as her own mother would be if she were here. She bit her lip, pushing thoughts of her mother to the recesses of her mind. The intermittent sleep, interrupted by the thud of the engines and the shuddering of the ship, had heightened her yearning for some comfort.

She lugged her heavy case along the corridor and up several flights of stairs towards the exit. There was such a crowd she had to wait on the stairs then, when the doors were opened, she surged forward with all the other passengers, off the boat, onto the wharf and along to the boat train, which was whistling and spurting out a huge plume of steam.

The carriages were so full, she couldn't find her allotted seat and had to stand all the way through the tunnel and into

Christchurch, holding onto the overhead strap and balancing her case between her legs, terrified someone might make off with it and its contents, representing her entire existence for the next few months.

As the train steamed into the station, she craned her neck to see past all the heads in the way. She was to be met by a deputy matron of the home where she was to stay and had been told to look out for a tall woman in a tan coloured coat and hat. She was nowhere to be seen.

Alighting from the train at last, after waiting for all the families and other passengers in her carriage to go first, she found herself right in front of a tall, camel-coated woman.

'There you are Elizabeth, and about time too. I was beginning to think you'd missed the train.' The woman held out her hand. 'Miss Mayhew,' she said. 'I take it you *are* Elizabeth Hamilton?'

'Yes, Ma'am. Er, Miss Mayhew.' She shook Miss Mayhew's brown glove.

'Well, come along then. Bring your case. It's big enough. It must be heavy.'

'It is.' But Lizzie had no regrets – there wasn't a single thing she would have left behind. If she could, she would have brought a second bag, but her mother had been firm on taking just the one. She hefted the big case along the platform, hurrying to keep up with Miss Mayhew's bobbing brown hat disappearing towards the parked cars behind the station building.

She climbed into a large black car and Miss Mayhew drove out of the station and onto a big, wide bustling street. Towards the east, the sun was beginning to push through the low cloud but meanwhile the grey film gave the city an air of exotic mystery. She'd never been south before, never crossed Cook Strait even and a brief moment of exhilaration coursed through her as she realised neither of her siblings, nor her mother or father, had been this far south either. She was the first!

Avenues lined with towering trees, a winding river surrounded with drooping bright green weeping willows, a tall stone cathedral spire appearing from time to time between the city buildings, and so many buildings. They were different from the ones in Wellington, less formidable, not so big, not like all the government buildings around Parliament. And everywhere it was flat, unbelievably flat; she'd never seen anything like it. The massive hills between the port and the town had receded into the distance and now there wasn't a hill in sight, not at all like Wellington.

Miss Mayhew was clearly not a conversationalist, remaining silent for most of the journey except to exclaim occasionally at the state of the traffic or behaviour of other drivers and cyclists. Lizzie had never seen so many bicycles.

'Well, here we are then,' Miss Mayhew said at last. 'Fitzgibbon House.'

The car slowed and drew up at a semi-circle of gravel in front of a large, ugly, dirty-white weatherboard building. From the main door - a huge gaping hole like the mouths one of those fairground clowns - the building stretched the width of the section, its expanse interrupted at regular intervals by numerous, multi-paned windows. Its appearance reminded her, unhappily, of the Karori Pavilion.

'Leave your case in the hall,' Miss Mayhew instructed as Lizzie pushed through the heavy swing door and found herself standing in a high-ceilinged entrance, wood-panelled to waist height and painted above that in a sickly pale yellow, the colour of thin custard. Black-framed photographs of stern-looking women in flowing nurses' veils and short capes were the only adornment.

'Our matrons,' Miss Mayhew said when Lizzie paused to study them. 'Fitzgibbon House is an institution with a long history of caring for young women in unfortunate circumstances. There have been many wonderful matrons in charge over the years. You will meet Matron Waldron now.' She ushered Lizzie towards a wooden door, knocked and, when a reply came from inside to enter, opened it and indicated she should go in. 'Miss Hamilton to see you, Ma'am.'

Lizzie hesitated, wondering if perhaps she should curtsey, such was the formality of the introduction.

'Well, come in, child. Don't loiter in the doorway.'

Hesitantly, she approached the heavy-set wooden desk over by the window. Behind it, standing silhouetted against the light, was a large woman wearing a white dress topped with a white starched bib and apron; on her head perched a stiff white cap with small white wings either side, making her look as if she were about to rise heavenward. There was no welcoming smile. Her thin lips were clamped in a frown of disapproval, her eyebrows arched in censure.

'Do sit down,' she said.

Lizzie did as she was told. The last time she'd felt like this was after the lunchtime episode at school two months ago when she'd taken off to the art gallery without permission and received a lengthy dressing down from the headmistress. Her closing line still haunted her: 'Really, Elizabeth, we would have expected better from you.' The hard wooden chair in front of the matron felt very similar to the one in the headmistress's study.

'Miss Elizabeth Hamilton.' The matron was studying a white card on her desk with some details printed on it. 'Due date March the twenty-fifth.' She looked up and a thin attempt of a smile forced her lips apart to reveal a startling gold front tooth.

'Yes.' Lizzie couldn't help staring; she'd never seen a gold tooth like that.

'You'll find you get along here if you follow all the rules and don't cause any trouble,' Matron continued. She then proceeded to outline a long list of these rules, which included a strict timetable: up at six, communal showers, an early breakfast in the dining hall followed by work – in the kitchen, the garden, the laundry or the sewing room – lunch, more work, two hours of leisure and mild exercise before dinner, then quiet reading and board games until lights out at nine. 'And no talking after lights-out, we strictly enforce that.'

It seemed she was a prisoner – there was to be no walking to the shops without a permission slip and only limited supervised trips to town, mainly to go to the library. The rest of the time, she was restricted to the grounds of Fitzgibbon House.

She swallowed down the homesickness threatening to overwhelm her, longing for her room overlooking the chestnut tree in the back garden, the lawn sweeping to the edge of the hill before dropping down to the thickly wooded dell she and Jerry had played in before he decided he was too big to play with girls, even his sister.

She pictured her bed as she'd left it, neatly made with the fat eiderdown, its roses cascading down each side of the bed to reach the green patterned carpet. Her favourite pillow, feathery light, that somehow just knew how to smooth itself round her face each night, an empty space on top of it where Mr Ted had once reigned over his domain.

Now she knew how the third formers had felt at Marsden, coming in from the country and leaving behind all that was familiar. Now she knew for the first time how it was to be deeply homesick. She clutched the purse her mother had given her – one of her own, no longer needed, it was of dark brown leather, the same colour as her sensible shoes. Her mother was always insistent that shoes and bags should match.

'Pay attention please, Miss Hamilton.'

Hearing her name, Lizzie started. 'Oh, sorry.'

Visiting hours, Matron explained, were on Saturday and Sunday afternoons.

'I won't be expecting any visitors, Matron. My parents are in Wellington and I don't know anybody in Christchurch.'

'I see.' Matron Walden studied her notes.

'May I phone home sometimes?'

'You may only make phone calls after receiving permission, and any calls out of town must be made collect. You may write letters, but all incoming and outgoing mail will be checked first by me.' She studied the list on her desk then looked up again. 'Do you have any questions, Elizabeth?'

'Do I have a room of my own?' she ventured.

'Good heavens, no, you will be in a dormitory with five other girls. There are six dormitories, and they are all full. You were very lucky to get a place here, young lady. We're very busy.'

Matron rang a little brass bell on her desk and Miss Mayhew reappeared.

'I'll take you up to your room,' she said. 'Follow me.'

Lizzie lugged her suitcase up the stairs. Miss Mayhew opened the door to reveal two neat rows of perfectly made high iron beds, each covered with sheets and two thick dark grey woollen blankets. At each bedhead was a neat row of pillows in cases so pristine they might have been soaking for hours in Mrs Mullen's Bluo whitener. The off-white walls were now smudged with grey; the woodwork chipped and worn. Beside each bed was a narrow set of cupboards, all but one covered with photo frames, books, brushes and combs.

'The girls are all at work now. You will meet them at morning tea, which is at ten on the dot.' She looked at her watch. 'In half an hour. I suggest you unpack your things then come downstairs to the front hall. I'll get one of the girls to meet you there.'

Lizzie looked around. 'Which is my. . .?'

'That's your bed there.' Miss Mayhew pointed to one at the end with the empty cupboard. 'That's your uniform hanging up beside it. You are to put it on before you come to morning tea. Is that understood?'

'Yes.' She studied the shapeless grey smock drooping from its hanger and couldn't stop pulling a face at it.

That brought a sniff of disapproval from Miss Mayhew. 'They come in one size only and are washed every Thursday. You get whichever one is allocated to you.'

Suddenly, the Marsden uniform, with its heavy gym frock and increasingly tight blazer, its ugly hat and ridiculous gloves seemed not so bad after all. If only she could be wearing it now, running through the corridors to classes, laughing with Julia, not a care in the world.

'You should unpack,' Miss Mayhew continued. 'You may put out your personal items as the other girls have, but there are to be no photos of boys. D'you understand?'

'Yes, Miss Mayhew.'

'Good.' Miss Mayhew nodded and disappeared.

She sat on her bed and surveyed what was to be her home for the next five months.

Where was Peter now she needed him? She flushed recalling the last time they'd met. She'd put on her newest dress, pulling the crossover top low to expose more neckline, and sneaked into her mother's bedroom to use her makeup. More than anything, she hated her freckles - they made her look so juvenile. Peter would think she was much older, much more sophisticated if they weren't so obvious and the only way to tame them was the application of a coat of her mother's Elizabeth Arden foundation, smoothed carefully across her cheeks, chin and nose, until the offending brown dots had disappeared. A smear of her mother's lipstick, a dab of her Shalimar perfume and all she had to do was slip out the back door while her mother was busy with her National Council of Women meeting in the sitting room. She borrowed a pair of her mother's shoes, which she'd carried in her bag all the way into town and on to the Newtown terminus, only putting them on as the tram pulled up at the last stop. Climbing down to the pavement in them had required considerable skill, involving clutching onto the handrail as she negotiated the steep steps.

She walked slowly from there to the tramway office, practising what she was going to say. The makeup and the shoes made her feel as if she were acting a part, as if she really were the sophisticated lady she was pretending to be.

'Yes, Miss?' The man behind the office window looked pleasant enough.

She plucked up all her courage and said, 'I'd like to see Peter Williams, please.'

'Is he expecting you, Miss?'

'No. Please tell him Miss Hamilton is here to see him.'

The man looked a bit taken aback, as if he didn't know what to do next. She smiled her most winning smile, pretending she was her mother asking a favour of the concierge at a posh hotel they'd stayed at in Auckland once.

The man fiddled with some papers on the desk below, scratched his head and said, 'Very well, then, Miss. I'll see if he's in.'

Lizzie was reasonably certain he would be. It was just before two in the afternoon, when she knew the conductors and drivers changed their shift. No matter what route he was on now, he should be in the big smoko room he'd talked about, chatting with his fellow trammies. She waited by the reception window, her heart beating loudly, trying to quell the uneasy feeling in her tummy.

A few moments later, Peter appeared, coming out of a door further along the tram shed and walking slowly towards her, stubbing his cigarette out under his foot. He looked annoyed.

'What are you doing here?' he said when he was close enough to be heard. 'You can't come and interrupt me at work. I'll never hear the end of it.'

'I had to Peter. I had to see you again.'

'Yeah?' He looked at her as if he was studying an irritating midge.

Lizzie faltered for a minute. 'I wanted you to know that I'm going to have a baby. Your baby.'

'Yeah? How do you know that?'

'Because the doctor said . . .'

'No, I mean, how do you know it's my baby?'

She looked at him earnestly. 'Because there's no one else, Peter. I've never done it with anyone else. It's your baby.'

'Yeah? That's what all the girls say when they're in the family way. Try to nail it on the nearest poor sod they can find.' He was looking away towards the door he'd come out of, his eyes flickering to her and back to the tram shed.

'But it's true, Peter. There's no one else. You know that's true.'

'No I don't.'

'But you were my first. You know you were.'

He shoved his hands in his pockets, his face hard set. 'Yeah, but that doesn't mean I was your last. For all I know, you've been off with others now you've had a taste for it. I bet that's what you done.'

'I wouldn't! There's only been you.' She reached out to him; he brushed her away.

'Look, Lizzie.' He spat out her name as if it was poisonous. 'I don't believe you. And I don't want to see you again. Do you understand?'

'But I thought we could get married and . . .'

'Forget it. Okay? It's not going to happen. I'm not accepting any responsibility for you getting yourself into trouble. You're on your own.'

And with that, he turned around, stomped off into the shed and slammed the smoko room door behind him.

She couldn't recall the journey through town and up the hill homewards. She couldn't even remember going through the tunnel, always her favourite part of the journey. It was going through the tunnel that Peter had kissed her for the second time, only stopping seconds before the tram emerged out the other side.

She remembered pausing at the back door and using a hanky to wipe off as much as she could of the lipstick and powder before taking off her shoes – her mother's shoes, which she'd unwittingly kept on the whole way home – hiding them behind her back and tiptoeing past the closed door to the sitting room, where her mother was chairing the council meeting. If her mother had caught her then, she wouldn't have known what to say; she was all out of excuses and all out of fight. But she needn't have worried; the door remained shut. Avoiding the creaky stair, she'd stripped off the dress – she'd never worn it again – returned her mother's shoes to the neat shoe tree in her wardrobe, and soaked herself under the hot shower, hoping to wash away the dirty feeling Peter had left her with. Then she'd crawled into bed and stayed there the rest of the day, missing dinner even, saying she felt sick again. She remembered the cool of the sheets against her hot, flushed cheek, the saltiness of the tears as she fiercely wiped them dry.

The sheets on the narrow little bed at Fitzgibbon House felt just as cool, just as crisp as her own, but the pillow was hard. She opened her case and pulled out Mr Ted, holding him tight. He looked cross; he didn't seem to like it here any more than she did.

Chapter 4

Christchurch. 1950

There was remarkably little to unpack when it came down to it.

Lizzie lifted her case onto the grey blanket stretched across the bed and began to take out her few belongings. She set her one family photograph in its frame on top of her cupboard along with her brush, her well-read copy of *Wuthering Heights* – the only book she'd managed to squeeze in her bag – her felt-covered sewing kit and, presiding over it all, Mr Ted. She looked along the two neat rows of beds – the other girls had left soft toys on their bedside tables, so Mr Ted should be safe.

Out came the Cellophane packet holding the three pressed flowers she'd saved from the posy Peter had picked for her from behind a picket fence near the tram stop – but she hesitated before placing it on the dresser. Instead she slipped it to one side of the top drawer; it was too precious to expose to others.

She hid her paintbrushes and paints at the back of the cupboard and her art book under the mattress as it was too big to fit inside. Finally, she folded her clothes away into the drawers, placed her long nightdress under the pillow and was done.

She took off her skirt and blouse, packed them away too, then unhooked the ugly grey uniform and pulled it on over her slip. She didn't need a mirror to know that she looked a frump; it was shapeless and voluminous, with plenty of room for a bulging stomach as the baby grew inside her. The front hung down well below her knees and the sleeves reached her elbows.

Despite a weak sun streaming through the windows, the room was still chilly and she shivered. She would need to put on the spencer her mother had made her bring. She hated spencers, but she could see it might have a use here, where she didn't know anybody and it didn't really matter what she looked like.

She found the bathroom block, with row upon row of communal showers and poky little toilet cubicles. They were spotless – probably because the girls had to clean them daily.

The dining hall seemed vast – a great cavernous, high-ceilinged room panelled with light-coloured wood half-way up the wall, the top half painted the same sickly yellow as the hallway. It was empty, save for about half a dozen girls, wearing the same grey work-smock she'd donned in the dorm, behind a servery down the far end. One was holding an enormous teapot above row upon row of white cups and pouring a steaming brown liquid into them in a continuous stream, moving the teapot from one cup to the next without a pause. Following her was a girl with a second teapot whose continuous flow seemed to be hot water. This second girl looked up when Lizzie came in, said something to her companion, put down the pot and beckoned her over. As Lizzie approached, she could see both girls were heavily pregnant, much more advanced than she was.

'You must be the new girl,' the girl said, resuming the pouring. 'Welcome to Fitzgibbon House for Wayward Girls.' Both girls laughed at this and Lizzie smiled at the joke. 'I'm Drusilla,' she added, 'but everyone calls me Dru. And this is Patricia.'

'Pat,' the tea-pouring girl said, pausing from her duties.

'Elizabeth, but everyone calls me Lizzie.'

'Hello Lizzie. How far gone are you?' Pat said.

'Just four months,' she said.

'We're thirty-six weeks,' Pat said 'They put you in groups so you're with other girls at the same stage as you.'

'When you get more advanced, you get taken off the garden and the laundry and get lighter duties,' Dru said.

'Like the kitchen,' said a third girl approaching the servery with a large cardboard box out of which she proceeded to scoop a handful of biscuits then placed one on each saucer, rarely avoiding the slopped tea. 'It's a lot easier than the laundry, I can tell you.'

'They start you on laundry when you first come in.'

'I can't wait,' Lizzie said without enthusiasm.

A bell rang somewhere, a bit like the fire alarm bell they used to ring at school for fire drill.

'What's that?' she asked, alarmed.

'You'll see in about thirty seconds,' said Dru.

The three girls behind the counter continued their duties until all the cups were full and a biscuit sat on each saucer.

Suddenly the door behind them burst open and a high-pitched chattering, shrieking and clattering horde of young women – all dressed in grey smocks – burst into the dining hall and headed as one towards the servery.

'Here, take this.' Pat thrust a cup, saucer and biscuit at Lizzie. 'Take it up the front and they'll tell you where to sit.'

'Thank you.' Lizzie did as she was told, wondering who 'they' was. It proved to be Miss Mayhew.

'Ah, Elizabeth, I see you've found your way to the dining room, well done. You'll be with the new entrants, on the table up the front here.' She indicated the centre table in a row of three. 'There are six tables, one for each dormitory. You will take all your meals together at the same table. Each month, your dormitory moves to make room for newer arrivals. Is that clear?'

'Yes, Miss Mayhew.'

'Good.'

Lizzie slid onto the bench seat at the table Miss Mayhew had indicated and put her cup down in front of her.

'You can't sit there, that's Jessie's seat.' A tiny girl, dwarfed by her enormous smock, and much younger than her – fifteen at the most she guessed – was looking fiercely at her.

'Oh, sorry. I didn't know.' She picked up her cup and went to move to the next place. 'Is this all right here?'

'Yes, that'll do. That's Anahira's place. She won't care.'

'Oh no, really, I don't want to upset anyone. Just tell me where to sit.'

By the time she'd got up and moved to the other side, the bench seats were all full except for the empty space which was clearly where she was supposed to be.

'Raisin biscuits. Yum.' One of the girls seized the biscuit and wolfed it down.

The tiny girl inspected her biscuit and pulled a face. 'There aren't any raisins in mine.' Quickly, she snatched a biscuit from the girl next to her and put hers in its place. 'There are now.'

The girl whose biscuit she'd stolen started to snatch it back then stopped. 'Poor Pearl,' she said, pulling a mock-sympathy face. 'We can't have you feeling disadvantaged, can we?'

Pearl punched her on the arm, making the other girl wince.

'You're so sensitive, Pearl,' one of the other girls said.

'Yes, take it easy Pearl,' another girl said, wagging her finger across the table at her.

Pearl looked sulky and turned away.

'So who's the new girl?' the tallest one asked.

Tripping over her name, wanting to make a good impression and aware that she was coming across as shy and hesitant, Lizzie introduced herself to the others and tried to remember who was who as Jessie recited their names. She had the most trouble trying to pronounce the name of the Maori girl, Anna-something – she'd never met a Maori girl before, though didn't want to admit it. She remembered Jessie easily – Lizzie's maternal grandmother had been called Jessie – and warmed to her at once. Jessie, the tallest and the oldest, at nineteen, was from Dunedin where she'd been doing her first year of medical studies and was desperate to return as soon as her baby was born. To her, this place was a temporary impediment in a promising career, whereas Christine – who wasn't at morning tea because it was her turn to stay behind and mind the laundry – wanted to be a nurse and loved babies, Jessie told her. Margaret, or Meg, a year older, was from a farm near Geraldine but had been at Teachers' College in Christchurch when 'it' happened; Anna-something, the Maori girl, came from a well-off farming family up Gisborne way; and little Pearl, the prickly one who'd been so insistent about where everyone sat, was from Wellington, like herself, but from near the top of the Hutt Valley, where Lizzie had to admit she'd never been.

'You've never been over our side of town? You haven't lived!' Pearl said, coming out of her sulk. 'I can see we're going to have to educate you.'

Lizzie hoped being 'educated' didn't mean being subjected to the sort of treatment the girls meted out to newcomers at boarding school.

She'd already been appalled at the lightning speed with which the girls had devoured their single biscuit and slurped at their tea, although she had to admit she was starving herself. All she'd had on the boat was the sweet dry biscuit the ancient stewardess had brought before dawn with tea in a cup so thick there was hardly any room for the milky tea. With no breakfast, Lizzie felt like scoffing the extra biscuit herself, but held back, mindful of her mother's words about first impressions. She'd reminded her how much it had cost to send her to the home – 'so you'll be with girls your own class, no riff-raff'. Despite their shameful circumstances, all these girls must be from families who were comfortably off – even Pearl and the Maori girl, whose presence surprised her considerably. If her mother could see her now, sitting next to a Maori girl. She'd be so shocked. Lizzie permitted herself a smirk as she finished her tea. There'd been no Maori girls at Marsden that she knew of. In fact, Lizzie didn't even know what they were until she was about six and her mother said to her one day in the tram, 'There's a Maori woman getting on.' She'd stared at the woman and her unfamiliar brown skin until her mother had told her it was rude. It wasn't until she was in an older class at primary school she'd seen two other Maoris and they'd been so unusual the other kids had laughed at them.

The alarm bell rang again.

'Come on, back to work girls,' Jessie called, clambering off the bench-seat. She looked across at Lizzie. 'You too, Lizzie. It's time for you to find out what you're in for.'

'Yes, to be inducted into the mysteries of the Laundry for Wayward Girls.' Meg sniggered and took her arm, leading her behind Jessie through a maze of corridors to the far end of the building.

'All the girls here call it Bleak House.' Jessie pulled a face. 'It is too.'

'Do we do all the washing for this place?' Lizzie asked innocently as they walked.

'Yes, and the rest.'

'The rest?'

'Fitzgibbon House's laundry is just the beginning,' Meg said. 'Most of the work is the laundry from the maternity home and hospital over there.' Meg pointed out the window.

'That's where the good mothers go,' Jessie said on her way to the door. 'The ones with husbands.'

'The father of the baby – we don't want any of those around,' Pearl said.

'Not likely to see them either,' Jessie said, putting her arm round Pearl.

They trailed behind Jessie and Pearl on the way out.

'Do you know about Essex Hospital, Lizzie?' Meg asked.

'Yes. It's where we go to have our babies.' It had been a morning of unpleasant revelations, but her mother had at least told her that much.

'Well, it's over there, behind the washing lines and through the back fence.'

Lizzie looked out the window where Meg was indicating. Behind a line of trees she could just make out another white building, smaller than the one she was in, equally plain and functional. 'Not far to go then when your time comes.' Lizzie smiled. It seemed a magical time way in the distance.

'No.' Meg laughed drily. 'Nice and handy. Meanwhile, we get to do all their washing. It's enough to put you off having a baby for ever – all that blood! Ugh!'

'Really?' Lizzie didn't want to show her new friends how squeamish she felt. She hadn't been warned about blood. She'd imagined having a baby would be a joyous experience, the arrival of a new life, your very own creation. That was certainly the picture painted in the few books she'd managed to find at the library about babies – a rosy glow hovered around the mother's head as she held the newly delivered baby wrapped tightly and smiling beatifically at her. There hadn't been any mention of blood. She shuddered. She didn't like blood.

Mind you, there had also been a doting father in all the pictures and she knew there wouldn't be one of those at the birth. What other unpleasant realities were in store?

'It's a bit late to be put off now.' Meg said, laughing at her own joke.

'I suppose so.' Lizzie didn't think it at all funny.

Meg's laugh turned bitter. 'In here,' she said, entering a room that was much warmer than the cool chill of the rest of the building.

She soon saw why. Through the steam she could make out, lined up against the outside wall, a row of laundry coppers, just like the one at home that Mrs Mullen presided over every Monday and Thursday morning. Each one was steaming away furiously, and a short, stout girl was running between them, stirring the contents with a long wooden pole.

'Here you are, Christine, I got you a biscuit.' Jessie handed over the tea-stained biscuit she'd saved from morning tea. It's got raisins in it.' She gave Pearl a taunting glance.

Pearl ignored her.

Christine ate it at once, continuing the incessant stirring with her other hand. 'I'll take that over now, you have a break.' Christine smiled gratefully and retreated to a corner near the door where she lowered herself, with some difficulty, onto a small, three-legged stool.

'Come on, Lizzie, I'll show you what to do.'

Lizzie, being the newcomer, was put in charge of stoking the fire under each copper, adding small pieces of wood through the firebox door, making sure the fire was drawing properly and the smoke was all going up the chimneys inserted into the side wall and not blowing back into the laundry. She was told not to let the fire get too fierce, nor was it to die down too low, so the water would continue to boil in the big vat above. Fetching and carrying the wood from outside, carefully opening each firebox with a thick cloth and feeding the flames took up the rest of the morning. It was hot work down by the fireboxes and she had to wipe her forehead all the time to keep the sweat from trickling in her eyes.

If the next month or so was going to be like this, she doubted she could cope. Were these the wages of sin the vicar used to talk about in his Sunday sermons? You committed a sin – like sex out of wedlock, she realised – and you paid for it stoking the fires of hell for all eternity. Or at least it seemed like eternity stretching out before her on day one. How would she make it to day thirty-one? A whole month of this before they got moved onto gardening.

She'd never been as relieved as when Jessie said she could let the fires go out it was time for the final cold-water rinse.

'I don't think I've ever been so hot in my life,' Lizzie said.

'You get used to that,' Jessie said.

'And not caring two figs for how you look,' Meg said, wiping her brow with her wet hands.

'My hair must look a fright,' Lizzie said, quickly rubbing a hand across it. 'It goes frizzy just at the sight of water.'

'It looked lovely when you came in. You've got nice hair. Nice and thick. Not like my thin, stringy strands.' Jessie said.

'I'd rather that than a frizz.'

'I wouldn't worry now,' Meg said. 'It's plastered to your head. That's what happens to you in the laundry. You end up looking like a wrung-out tea towel.'

'I certainly feel like one.'

'Then you can get to work on the wringer and see for yourself.' Lizzie's job now, Jessie told her, was to operate one of two mangles beside the rinsing tub. Anahira, the next most recent arrival, was on the other one.

The mangle wasn't quite as bad as stoking the fires, but it had frequent moments of terror when, turning the handle to feed the sheets and towels through, she almost got her fingers caught between the two fearsome rollers.

In her head, as she fed and turned, fed and turned, she wrote a letter to her mother telling her how it was, every awful detail of the laundry. But she knew she'd never send it. There was no point. What would her mother say? 'Sorry, all is forgiven, come home now?' Not a chance. She was stuck here at Bleak House for the next five months and there was no other alternative – she had nowhere else to go.

Chapter 5.

Christchurch. Christmas Eve, 1950.

The smoggy, misty Christchurch dawn cast a grey pall over the windows outside Bleak House, sending a lingering chill through the dormitories and shower blocks inside. But Lizzie scarcely noticed the cold – she'd become so used to it at this hour it was hardly worth a mention. In a few hours, the place would be hot and stuffy in the summer heat and she'd be looking forward to the cooler evening.

She raced with the others to the shower – the quicker you got there, the less you felt the cold – set down her spongebag, threw off her nightdress, turned on the taps and waited until the temperature was just right before jumping in.

'Your nipples have gone all brown, Lizzie.' Meg said across the chest-height dividing wall between the showers. 'Mine haven't yet.'

Lizzie unselfconsciously looked down at hers and, sure enough, the areola was a smooth chocolaty brown while each nipple seemed to be larger than before and almost hard.

'So they have.' she said. 'Pearl's and Anahira's went like that ages ago.'

'Isn't it funny how they seem to get so much bigger?'

'What, your nipples?'

'Yes. They never warn you it's going to happen.'

'That's what's so good about being in this together,' Lizzie said. 'You get to know what to look for.'

'And it saves you getting in a stitch about it. You just ask each other.'

'And if we don't know, you can ask the lot ahead of us.'

Jessie stuck her head over the wall on the other side of Lizzie. 'Like when Pearl's tummy button started to stick out,' she said.

The three of them laughed at this.

'You could see it through her dress at the dinner table, like she had a little bumpy knot on top of her belly,' Meg said. 'Pass me the shampoo please, Lizzie, I've run out.'

'It'll happen to all of us soon,' Anahira called from the next cubicle.

Lizzie squirted out a dab of shampoo and passed the bottle to Meg. 'Thanks.' She lathered her hair.

'Isn't it funny how we can talk so easily about such things?' Meg said, passing the bottle back.

'I'd never have believed it a couple of months ago,' Lizzie said. 'I'd never have dreamed of showing my breasts to anyone.'

'Not even to your boyfriend?' Jessie popped her head out from under the flow of water to speak then popped it back again to rinse her hair.

'Especially not to him.'

'Me neither.' Meg was still lathering. 'What about you Pearl?'

'I don't have a boyfriend,' Pearl snapped. 'I've told you before.'

'Oops, sorry. I'd forgotten how tetchy you were about him.'

'He's not my boyfriend.' Pearl shut off her shower taps, picked up her soap and stalked over to the bench where her clothes were waiting in a neat pile. Of all of them, Pearl was the tidiest and the most reserved, preferring to hide in the corner when getting dressed.

'Well there must have been a boy somewhere in the picture, or you wouldn't be here,' Jessie called after her.

Pearl plucked her towel off its hook and wrapped it tightly around herself before turning back to Jessie and giving her a withering look. 'It's none of your business.' She took a few steps towards the showers. 'That goes for all of you. Just leave me alone.' She was shouting now, her eyes narrowed in anger. 'If my father was here, he'd put an end to your prying questions.'

'Your father?' Jessie snorted as she lathered her arms with soap. 'The way you talk about him, you'd think *he* was your boyfriend.'

'How dare you!' Pearl screamed. Clutching her towel with one hand and grabbing her pile of clothes with the other, she stormed out, dropping her soap without stopping to pick it up.

'Now you've upset her,' Lizzie called to Jessie.

'Must have touched a sensitive nerve,' Meg said.

'Maybe it was her father who …' Jessie stopped soaping herself and put her hand to her mouth, not finishing the sentence.

'Jessie! That's a terrible thing to say.' Meg turned off her taps and stepped out of the shower, away from Jessie and the others.

'No, that's not possible.' Lizzie thought they were being ridiculous. 'Fathers don't do that with their daughters.'

'Don't they?' Jessie looked incredulously at Lizzie for a moment then suddenly changed her expression to one of conciliation. 'No, of course they don't.'

Lizzie shut of her taps with a determined twist, stepped out of the shower onto the wet duckboard and started to towel herself dry. How could Jessie suggest such a thing? She was sure Pearl had done it with one of the boys on the farm. She'd as good as said so and Pearl wouldn't lie to her. There were no secrets among any of them.

They were in this together, 'the bad girls', the girls who'd got caught, the girls who wore their disgrace out front, right where everyone could see it, so that the monthly trips to town to go to the library became a lesson in public humiliation.

Passers-by sniggered openly as the girls walked by, two-by-two, an ungainly crocodile weaving along Worcester Street and through the doors of the solemn brick central library building.

'It's so embarrassing,' Lizzie had said the first time it happened. She felt like cringing. This was quite different to the last time she'd walked in a crocodile with the girls at Marsden on an outing to the zoo. She was used to overhearing comments of admiration at their neat formation, their tidy uniforms, their obedient demeanour, not sentiments of disgust. She wished she could be invisible.

But Jessie was striding along beside her, swinging her arms nonchalantly. 'No it's not,' Jessie said. 'Why would it be embarrassing? We don't know a single one of those people.'

'And even if we did, I wouldn't care.' Meg, in front of Lizzie, waved an arm dismissively.

'But imagine what they're saying to each other,' Lizzie said. 'Imagine what they're thinking.'

'They're judging us,' Pearl said.

Lizzie turned back to see her shrinking from the stares.

'I hate it,' Pearl continued. 'They should mind their own business.'

'What does it matter what they're thinking?' Jessie shrugged. 'You worry too much, you two, what other people are thinking of you. All that matters is what you think of yourself.'

'And what your friends think,' Christine added, catching them up.

'Yes, the people that really know you.' Anahira was ahead of Lizzie, walking next to Meg.

'Not horrible busybodies like them.' Suddenly Lizzie felt hot with anger at the women across the street who were staring; she poked out her tongue at them.

'Lizzie!' Meg giggled.

The women looked horrified, turned their backs and walked away.

'That'll show them not to judge us.' Jessie grinned at her.

'You shouldn't have done that, Lizzie.' Pearl was looking away from the women. 'You shouldn't draw attention to us.'

'You should try it sometime, Pearl. It makes you feel a lot better,' Lizzie said.

Pearl looked at her resentfully.

They passed an old lady hesitating at the exit of a shop doorway, who had held up her hand to shade her eyes from the awful prospect of the obviously pregnant 'wayward girls'.

'I dare you.' She nudged Anahira and Meg then turned to Pearl and Christine behind.

All of them except Pearl stuck their tongues out at the old lady as they waddled by. Despite the blocking hand, the woman obviously saw, because she drew up her shoulders, pursed her lips and returned inside the shop.

The girls burst out laughing – all except Pearl.

'You shouldn't have done that,' she hissed. 'You'll get us all into trouble.'

Jessie stopped laughing and turned back to Pearl. 'Nonsense.' Then she looked across at Lizzie. 'It felt good, didn't it?'

Lizzie couldn't answer for a moment, she was laughing so much.

'Girls, pull yourselves together back there,' Miss Mayhew called from the front of the crocodile. 'You're making a public exhibition of us all.'

At that moment, they arrived at the library where they had free reign to select the books of their choice. For Jessie, predictably, books about medical complaints and human biology; for Christine, magazines like *The Weekly News* and books about child care, even though she knew she wouldn't be allowed to keep the baby; for Meg and Lizzie, any of the classics or the latest novels they could get their hands on, starting with the authors she knew, like Noel Streatfeild, enjoying again the perils of Pauline, Petrova and Posy Fossil, the three adopted children in *Ballet Shoes;* reliving the Waterbury children's train-watching spy story in Edith Nesbit's *The Railway Children;* before moving on at Meg's suggestion to Lizzie Sutcliffe's new book *The Queen Elizabeth Story.* Her reading had moved up a level when she borrowed Jessie's copy of George Orwell's *Animal Farm* and her most recent discovery, her first real adult fiction, had been Nevil Shute's *A Town Like Alice.*

Library visits represented the highlight of each month. Every day she painstakingly marked another cross on her home-made calendar – topped by a rose-tinted painting of her home – counting off the days to the birth and the day she could at last return home. Library day, marked in heavily scored HB pencil, was a welcome milestone in the horrendously long path of gestation, as were the weekly letters from her mother. Kindly but never emotional, filled with news from home – Penny's achievements at school and at her new ballet classes; Jerry's scores on the rugby field – there was no mention about how she, Helena Hamilton, was feeling about having her daughter so far from home in such an alien environment. Not that Lizzie told her the whole truth about just how drear her existence had become. Her mother would never believe it. She seemed to think her daughter was at a private school boarding house with the sort of jolly japes and iced lemonade serialised in those British girls' annuals her mother used to buy.

Lizzie could remember the way they spoke: 'Well played, Pip! Jolly well played!' for the heroine, while the bad girls were 'beastly', 'rotten' and 'mean'. The worst they got up to was 'ragging' a girl's study or pulling a girl's hair. Pregnant teenage girls were unheard of.

Her mother had sent her one of those thick story books, *Popular Stories for Girls*, last month in a parcel with one of her famous fruit cakes (they'd eaten it all within the week), some warm socks, and a painting of the family (or at least that's what her mother said it was of) by Penny. Penny had stuck a note on the back of the painting – her big-print notes were often included with her mother's – saying 'I miss you Lizzie,' which she'd had to put out of sight very quickly until her eyes stopped prickling.

She'd opened up the *Popular Stories for Girls* eagerly, hungry for something new to read, but had soon realised it was intended for girls much younger than her. Why couldn't her mother see she was a young adult now? An adult, in fact. Carrying a baby surely qualified her for something more grown-up to read than a schoolgirls' breathless story book. She'd put it away in the bottom of her cupboard, not wanting the other girls to see.

Library books remained her salvation. Although getting there was a mission, involving catching a bus into town then walking from Cathedral Square down the main street and across the river to the big red-brick library building.

She'd learnt to shrug off the stares but each month it became a little more difficult; the more advanced their pregnancy, the slower their steps. Her pelvis ached, the bones at the top of her legs felt sometimes as if they were splitting apart, as if the baby were preparing to pop out any minute. At the same time, burning liquid kept bubbling up in her throat and her stomach felt as if it had been squashed to one side of her body. Every time she ate anything but the blandest of food, it churned round inside. There seemed to be no respite. And she always felt so tired. The only relief had been promotion out of the laundry into the garden.

And now it was nearly Christmas Day.

After just a little over two months in residence, Lizzie was familiar enough with the place to know that Christmas at Bleak House wouldn't be a joyous celebration.

At home, her mother would getting out the Christmas decorations – the sparkly Kewpie doll masquerading as a fairy for the top of the tree, the many-coloured shiny balls and bells, the tinsel garlands, and her own cut-out silvery-painted stars hung at the back where the N.C.W. ladies wouldn't see; the baby Jesus in his manger tableau that went above the fireplace, the fir wreath at the front door – all much admired at Christmas parties, when she and Penny would hide at the top of the stairs and watch the guests arrive in their fur stoles and high heels. Later in the evening, the sisters crept out again to their hidden perch and giggled as the guests departed, tiddly from the sherry and whisky Daddy put out in his crystal decanters.

What she would give now to be helping with the devils on horseback hors d'oeuvres and the fiddly little curried egg sandwiches, to be taken to Kirks to buy a new pair of patent leather shoes, to be counting her pocket money to see if she could afford Penny's ballet book or Jerry's rugby socks.

They'd been warned by Matron that there would be the usual drudgery tomorrow to keep Fitzgibbon House and its neighbouring maternity hospital in vegetables and clean linen. Christmas Day would be like any other day.

'We all still have to eat, girls, and there will still be nappies to wash, sheets to launder and fruit and vegetables to be gleaned. So don't think you'll be having a lie-in on Christmas Day.'

It was to be like any Sunday, she'd added. Up at six as usual, chapel before breakfast, followed by domestic duties, walking to church, a light lunch then a short rest before preparation of Christmas dinner.

'You'd think we'd get one day off in the year,' Meg grumbled as she dug out new potatoes on Christmas Eve. Lizzie was surprised to find she quite enjoyed gardening during the warm summer days. Being outside in the fresh air was certainly better than stoking fires and scalding herself pulling sheets out of the boiling scummy water. Her hands, still dry and cracked from the laundry, were now deeply lined with rich brown soil.

'What would you expect at Bleak House?' Lizzie said, scooping up the earthy potatoes, rubbing as much soil off them as she could before dropping them in the heavy sack. 'Why pay for someone else to do it when they've got a ready source of slave labour for free?'

'It's inhumane,' Jessie said.

'It's good preparation for being a doctor,' Christine called from behind the runner bean stands. 'You won't get Christmas Day off when you're on the wards.'

'If I make it as an obstetrician, I'll be delivering babies with any luck.'

'I wish you could deliver my baby right now,' Christine said, cradling her bump. 'It's kicking like mad.'

'You're lucky, I haven't felt any little kicks yet.' Lizzie was getting worried about the lack of movement, but Jessie said it could happen any time, even after five months, and she wasn't quite there yet. Mind you, she wasn't sure just how much Jessie really knew and how much was bluster, pretending she had a lot more medical know-how than she'd ever had time to acquire.

Meg stopped digging and stretched her back, hands on her hips. 'I feel like an old woman,' she groaned. 'Its so hot today.'

'Imagine what it's going to be like in two or three months,' Lizzie said.

'I won't be able to bend over a spade, that's for sure.'

'Look over there – the southerly's arriving.' Anahira was approaching along the row of silver beet and pointing towards a bank of threatening grey clouds creeping over the Port Hills and piling up in the southern sky. 'We're in for a cold night.'

'It'll be a relief after this heat,' Meg said.

'Lucky we're not here through the winter,' Lizzie said. 'Imagine how cold that would be.'

'I've heard they get icicles *inside* the windows in the dorms when there's a big frost,' Anahira said.

'Well I'm glad I missed that. I'm planning to be well out of here long before the frosts start,' Lizzie said. 'It might get cold in Wellington, but it doesn't get *that* cold.'

'We'd better pack up, the rain is going to start soon,' Anahira said. 'I'm blowed if I'm going to wait until they tell us to come in.'

'They won't notice if we're out in the rain,' Christine said. 'I'm packing up.'

'Hadn't we better wait, though? We'll get told off if we go in now,' Lizzie said.

'Yes, and we don't want to lose any privileges on Christmas Eve,' Anahira said. 'I've spent all week making up for my last crime.'

'I know, I had to go to the shops for you,' Jessie said.

'It was so unfair being grounded for something as minor as being late for chapel. I reckon Miss Mayhew picks on me because she doesn't like Maoris.'

'She doesn't like me, either,' Christine said. 'She's always finding something wrong with the way I do things.'

'Let's face it, Miss Mayhew doesn't like any of us,' Jessie said. 'She thinks we're all evil sinners.' She looked up at the approaching bank of clouds. 'The storm's getting closer. I'm going to go in. Has anybody seen Pearl?'

'No, she went to the sick room during afternoon tea,' Christine said. 'She was looking awfully pale.'

'I noticed that, too,' Jessie said. 'We can go and see how she is when we go in.'

'We've got enough potatoes for one day, anyway,' Lizzie said. 'I'm coming with you Jessie.'

Pearl wasn't in the sick room when they went in. She wasn't in the dormitory either, or in the bathroom or toilets.

It wasn't until after they'd scrubbed the soil off their hands and changed into their ordinary clothes that they had a chance to look for her again.

'I don't know where she's gone,' Lizzie said after searching through the corridors and meeting the others as arranged in the girls' large sitting room.

'Well, she's not in here,' Jessie said. 'I wish she wouldn't do this. She's always going off on her own.'

'You'd think she doesn't like our company,' Lizzie said.

'We all need to have time to ourselves,' Christine said, 'but the rest of us don't disappear for hours at a time.'

'And make ourselves so hard to find.' Meg folded her arms and looked annoyed.

'There aren't many other places she could be,' Anahira said. 'I've looked in the showers and toilets. That's where she was last time.'

'She must have found somewhere new.' Jessie scanned the room, as if she might be hiding behind the curtains or under the window seat.

'Well, she can't be outside, look at it.' Christine pointed at the window.

The back lawn was being swept by squalls of wind-blown rain; the empty washing lines swayed, caught by the fierce gale, and the rain pounded down, bouncing off the concrete paths and covering the grass with puddles. In the distance, the oaks bent with the wind.

'D'you think we'd better tell Miss Mayhew?' Meg said.

They looked at each other, dismayed. To tell Miss Mayhew anything was a kind of defeat.

'It's nearly tea time,' Jessie said. 'We'd better tell Matron.'

'I think we should have one last look before tea,' Anahira said. 'You know what Matron can be like. She hates being disturbed after five o'clock.'

'That's because she's got the gin bottle open,' Jessie said. 'She tries to hide it, but she doesn't fool me.'

'Well I'm not going to be the one to go to her,' Meg said.

'Me neither,' said Lizzie. 'I think Anahira's right. We should look again.'

'All right.' Jessie looked at the wall clock above the door of the big sitting room. 'There's still twenty minutes before tea.' She turned back to them. 'Anahira, it was your idea to have another look. You go around the back, and make sure you check the garden sheds.'

'But it's pouring with rain. And anyway, we were in there putting the tools away before we came in.'

'Doesn't matter. Get a raincoat and look again.'

'Oh, all right.' Anahira pulled a face.

'Meg, you go round the front as far as the gates – and have a look up and down the street if you can get out there without Miss Mayhew having a fit.'

'Yes, Jessie.'

'Christine and I will do the south end of the building,' Lizzie offered.

'Good. I'll check the dormitories, all of them. And the bathrooms. I know we've all been in there since we came in, but I'll look again.'

They spread out, Lizzie and Christine checking all the doors along the corridor and looking behind the two that opened – the storeroom, stuffed with cleaning equipment, stacks of linen, toilet rolls, flour, sugar and other dried goods, but no Pearl; and the examination room, where Lizzie endured the cold hands of the maternity nurse during her monthly check-up. Pearl wasn't in there either, nor behind the curtain where the nurse kept her instruments.

That left the laundry.

'She can't be in there,' Christine said. 'Nobody goes there in the afternoons, it's out of bounds.'

'It's probably locked anyway,' Lizzie said. 'I'll see if it is.' She tried the handle and the door opened. Without the electric light, it was hard to see anything; the high window slits only cast a dim light from the overcast sky. She flicked on the light switch and froze.

'No!' It came out as a scream.

'What is it? What's the matter?' Christine pushed past her through the door and, at the sight that confronted them both, she too let out a piercing wail.

Not five yards away, Pearl was lying in the corner against the wall, a small pool of blood trickling from between her legs. Her eyes flickered recognition and she held her hand out towards them.

'Pearl, are you all right?' Lizzie could see that she wasn't but didn't know what else to say.

'I'll get Matron.' Christine fled.

Lizzie ran over to her friend and tucked herself in to kneel behind her, cradling her tiny body close. She didn't know what else to do so kept on saying 'It's going to be all right, Pearl. Matron's coming. It's going to be all right …'

After a few minutes, her knees hurt from the weight of Pearl pressing on her thighs and she sat on the cold floor, her legs out to one side. They brushed against something sharp. Gripping Pearl with one arm, she bent over to remove the sharp object and found Pearl's pink plastic number ten knitting needles beside her, covered in blood. What were they doing there? Then she realised and had to take in several gulps of air, her heart racing, her ears ringing. She heard footsteps. Quickly, she pushed the knitting needles away out of sight.

'Whatever's going on here?' Matron had arrived. Christine was close behind.

'Run quickly and get the stretcher out of the sick bay, Christine. Get one of the other girls to help you.'

She turned to Pearl. 'I've called the doctor for you. He'll be here in a few minutes.' Then she turned to Lizzie. 'You've done a good job, sitting with her. But you can go. I'll take charge now.'

'But is she going to be all right?'

'Yes, I expect so.'

'And the baby?'

'No. It's too late for the baby. Now run along. This is no place for you. It's tea time. You don't want to miss out.' This was said firmly, brooking no argument.

Lizzie 'ran along' as she was told, all the way to the dormitory where she flung herself on the bed, dry-eyed, drained of feeling, exhausted, shattered.

In the still of that moment she felt a fluttering in her belly; the baby had started to kick.

Chapter 6.

Christchurch, March 1951

In her thirty-eighth week, Lizzie changed her mind and sought an audience with Matron. Jessie told her she was mad. Christine and Anahira said it was worth a try and they wished they had as much courage.

'I'm sorry to trouble you, Matron.' She sat, as instructed, in the hard-backed wooden chair in front of Matron's desk, trying to hold back the fear that was threatening to make her voice quaver. 'But I've decided I'd like to keep my baby when it's born.'

'Have you, now?' Matron's normally stern expression turned even sterner.

'Yes. I'm old enough to look after a baby and I plan to do so.'

'And have you consulted your parents about this?'

Lizzie had prepared for this. 'No. I'm of legal age now. I'm eighteen. I don't have to consult them.'

'Indeed. That may be your opinion, but I'm afraid it doesn't hold in this instance. You see, you signed a form saying you were giving your baby for adoption, and that's what will happen.'

'But . . .'

'There is no but. It's quite simple. Do you want me to show you the document you signed?'

'No. Er . . .. yes.' Lizzie thought she was going to be sick. She hadn't signed anything about giving up her baby. How could Matron say such a thing? Was she trying to deceive her?

Matron sighed and went to a tall wooden filing cabinet in the corner behind her desk. After a few moments rifling through the top drawer she produced a sheet of paper and thrust it at Lizzie.

Lizzie scanned the page. Beside the typewritten questions was a series of handwritten answers, each one in her mother's neat hand. At the bottom of the page was her signature. Just above it was a paragraph that stated quite clearly that she,

Elizabeth Cecily Hamilton, was giving up all rights to the baby after it was born. She gasped.

'But that's not fair!' Her stomach was lurching. For a moment, she thought she might pass out; she gripped the wooden arm of the chair.

'What do you mean?'

She didn't know what to say. She recalled the moment with absolute clarity now. Her father had produced the form, already filled in with her name and address, and told her it was her application for admission to Fitzgibbon House; she'd signed without bothering to read it. What a fool!

'I . . . I didn't realise. . .'

'No? Are you saying that's not your signature?'

'Yes, it's my signature.'

She handed the piece of paper back to Matron and stood to go.

'I think you'll find you've made the right decision,' Matron said, indicating Lizzie's signature under the agreement to give her baby up. 'It always works out for the best this way.' She looked up at Lizzie over her glasses. 'You might not feel that way now, but you'll be glad in the end. You'll see.'

Lizzie fled without looking back, her cheeks burning with embarrassment. How could she have been so stupid? She was furious with herself. How could she give in so easily? You always do that, she scolded herself. You come up with all these clever ideas but as soon as someone pours cold water on them, you capitulate and give in. You're just spineless and a pushover. Like with Peter. Putty in his hands. A pushover.

'You poor thing,' Christine said, holding out her arms for Lizzie as she burst through the door. 'They always win.'

'I went in there absolutely determined, but somehow she took all the fight out of me.' She let Christine put her arms round her, hardly feeling her touch.

'It's like the stakes are loaded against you the minute you walk in the door of Bleak House.'

'They were certainly loaded against Pearl,' Lizzie said grimly.

They both looked across at the empty bed. It had remained empty since Pearl's miscarriage just over two months ago. Lizzie had retrieved the knitting needles from the laundry the following day and buried them in the big rubbish drum out the back; she hadn't told anyone about them, not even Jessie, though she seemed to have guessed anyway.

No one had arrived at the maternity home of a similar gestation to replace Pearl. This had been a relief – it would have been impossible to admit anyone else to their tight-knit dormitory group, no matter how accommodating they were.

Lizzie went over to Pearl's bed and picked up the pillow, stripped of its cover, bared to its ticking, and thought back to that awful afternoon when Pearl had hidden herself away in the warmth of the laundry.

She'd never forget the look on Pearl's face. She'd expected despair at the loss of her baby, but instead, mixed with the obvious pain and exhaustion, there was something approaching relief, as if she were glad it was over. Pearl had been trying to say something, but Lizzie hadn't been able to decipher it.

Christine had told them how she'd helped carry Pearl across to the hospital, and how nice Matron had been to her afterwards, kindly even, offering her a hot chocolate with as much sugar as she wanted and explaining that Pearl would go home in a few days to her family up north.

'Her father is coming down to get her. So good of him to look after his daughter like that,' Matron had said to Christine.

'Yes, I bet,' Jessie snorted when Christine relayed this.

Lizzie didn't say anything; she knew exactly what Jessie meant, had eventually worked it out for herself. She was doing her best to block it from her mind.

Matron's kindness had evaporated by Christmas morning: she insisted they get up at dawn as usual and herded them off to chapel. It was cold and bleak.

At home, there had always been a little tableau near the altar of the baby Jesus in his crib with Mary and Joseph behind him and fluffy white sheep nearby in the straw. She'd always taken it for granted, thought it was a bit babyish even. Now she missed it.

When her mother rang later on Christmas Day, she didn't say a word about Pearl's miscarriage: her parents wouldn't want to know.

And she certainly hadn't told her mother in her weekly phone call that she'd tried to persuade Matron to let her keep the baby.

Lizzie picked up the pillow on Pearl's empty bed. 'I probably would have been a lousy mother anyway,' she said resignedly.

'One day, you'll make a wonderful mother,' Meg said.

'One day, maybe,' she agreed. 'I don't want to go through this again for a long time.'

'I'm going to find a husband and have another baby as soon as I can,' Christine said. 'I've loved being pregnant and I know I'd be a good mother. I feel as if I'm cut out for it.'

'You wait 'til you have it. You might not be so keen after you've been through the birth.'

'You always say that, Jessie. I don't think it will be nearly as bad as you make out.'

'You wait and see.'

'What are you going to do, Lizzie? You've never said.'

Lizzie thought for a moment. She pictured going back home, the awful boat journey, her mother meeting her off the ferry. Would her father be there? Would Penny? Perhaps it would be a joyous reunion. She could live at home, help around the house for a bit, but then what? She couldn't go back to school – all the girls would have left and gone onto Teachers' College and Secretarial College, some even to the university. She would be too late for this year's intake.

What *could* she do? Not much. She'd wanted to be an architect, but without finishing her final year at school that would be out of the question. Her mother had suggested working in an architect's office, learning the ropes, perhaps being a draughtswoman one day. A bit of a come-down from her hopes and dreams of creating the most beautiful homes the town had ever seen, homes on stilts, homes that blended into their natural surroundings like the ones she'd seen in a library book about Frank Lloyd Wright, or designing offices and government buildings that people would be proud to work in.

'I don't know,' she said. 'Work in an office I suppose.'

'You should go back to school and finish your exams.' Jessie came round her side of the bed and stood facing her squarely, her arms folded. 'You could get a degree if you were prepared to start over.'

'I don't think I've the courage to go back to school. I'd be a year older than everyone else. They'd all know why, for sure.'

'Go to a different school then. You don't have to go to a posh school, you know, to get a good education.' Anahira grinned at her. She'd teased her many times about going to a private school, having been sent to board at one herself for a year. At the end of that year, she'd refused to return.

'I hadn't thought of that.' She managed a weak smile.

She couldn't wait to get out of this place and start her life again, she would rather be anywhere else than here, but she'd never had such close friends. Julia didn't know half as much about her as these girls. Yet after she'd had her baby, she'd never see them again.

'You've been so good to me. I'm going to miss you when this is over.'

'We can keep in touch.' Jessie sat on the end of the bed.

'We can write,' Meg said. 'I'm good at letters. There's not much else to do in the backblocks of Geraldine.'

'There's not much to do here in the evenings either,' Jessie said.

'It's like our lives have been put on hold for five months, like time has stood still while back home, our families have been carrying on as usual without us.' Lizzie picked up her photo frame and studied her family. Penny would be seven by the time she got home, Jerry would be in the upper sixth, his last year at school, and her mother would be the same as ever, busy with her meetings, busy in the kitchen. Life had gone on without her. What if they'd stopped noticing she wasn't around? Would they care if she never came home again?

'We *must* write. I will if you will.'

They promised. They swapped addresses.

As Lizzie wrote down hers, it occurred to her that her father might not want her staying at home, at least not for long. Where would she go then?

Christine was the first of the five of them to be due, but she was not the first to be delivered. Anahira was, her waters breaking just as she was getting out of the communal shower.

Her squeals were soon echoed by the others.

'You lucky thing.' Lizzie was standing in the next shower and paid close attention to the water as it flowed towards the drain, expecting it to be different. But the puddles of water all looked the same – clear, with a slight soap scum. 'How can you tell your waters have broken? Where have they gone?'

'You'll know when it happens.' Anahira pulled a face. 'It's like going to the toilet standing up.'

Lizzie winced at the thought. 'Eew.'

'I'd give anything for it to happen to me,' Christine said. 'I was supposed to be first.'

'Good timing, Anahira,' Meg joked. 'It's a lot easier to clean up in the shower– and a lot more private.'

'I'm glad it didn't happen in the dining hall. It would be so embarrassing.'

'Or in chapel. Imagine what Miss Mayhew would say!' Lizzie added.

'I suppose I'd better go and tell her,' Anahira said.

'Yes, you'd better. But you haven't had any contractions yet, so I wouldn't hurry,' Jessie said.

'Do they start soon?'

'They should. But there's no guarantee,' Christine said. 'The books were a bit vague about that.'

'She's right,' Jessie said. 'That's the thing about babies - you never can be sure when they're coming.'

Anahira's contractions started at breakfast, but with the rush to clear up the kitchen and prepare the midday meal, they didn't notice she wasn't there any more. She just slipped away to have her baby without telling them.

Lizzie didn't see Anahira again until she came up to the dormitory to collect her things. For five days, the girls had spoken of little else and they besieged her with questions as soon as she came through the door. But Anahira didn't want to talk about it.

'It's awful,' was all she'd say.

Lizzie felt a flutter in her stomach, like she imagined a contraction might be – a gripping, sickening feeling. But it wasn't a contraction. She recognised it as fear.

'Did they let you see the baby?'

'Yes. I saw him.' There was no life behind her eyes; her expression was unreadable. She turned away and started to pack.

Lizzie started to say something; she wanted to ask what it was like, seeing your own baby after all this time waiting. Was he beautiful? What colour was his hair? And what was it like giving birth? Was it as painful as Jessie made out? But the constriction in the pit of her stomach warned her not to speak. Anahira was struggling not to show any emotion but Lizzie could see she was close to tears; she couldn't bear looking at her any longer and turned away towards the others. They were pretending to be occupied with something else: Jessie started to pull hairs out of her brush; Christine returned to the book she'd been reading; Jessie fiddled with her nightgown; Meg crossed to the window and pulled at the blind tassel. Defeated, Lizzie sat on her bed and picked up the photograph of her family, staring unseeingly at the figures inside the frame.

The girls had been warned long ago by the others in the home that it would be like this. They'd never quite believed it; now they knew.

Anahira threw her few belongings in an old leather bag. There was a sharp click as she closed the catch at the top.

'It's goodbye, then,' she said, standing at the end of her bed.

They all said their farewells.

Lizzie hugged her tightly; the thin frame was limp and unresponsive. She wanted to say something comforting.

'Don't forget to write,' was all she could think of. It sounded hollow.

Anahira didn't answer.

'I wonder who'll be next?' Jessie said as the door closed behind her.

It was Christine. The girls knew nothing about it until they awoke one morning to find her bed empty. Lizzie immediately thought the worst, imagining a repeat of what had happened to Pearl, but Miss Mayhew told her Christine was over in the hospital having her baby.

They started to worry again that evening when she still hadn't returned, but Miss Mayhew assured them Christine was all right, it was a long labour, that was all. She deflected their questions with the same response until the following morning when one of the girls on laundry duty told Jessie at morning tea that Christine had disappeared.

'She's run off with the baby,' Jessie reported back.

'What!' None of them could believe it.

'Jenny said she and Freda had to go over to collect the laundry trolley this morning and they overheard one of the nurses talking about it. Apparently Christine crept into the nursery last night and stole back her baby when the nurse was out of sight. She hasn't been seen since.'

There was a chorus of cries: 'But where would she go?' 'Good on her!' 'I don't believe it.'

'She always said she was going to keep her baby.' Jessie said. 'And she did.'

'There's hope for me yet,' Lizzie said.

'I wouldn't count on it.' Jessie put down her cup with a clatter. 'They'll put a double watch on the nursery now in case any of us get the same idea.'

'There'll be all hell to pay,' Meg said. 'Matron will be furious.'

'Serve her right, the old bag,' Jessie said.

'Christine deserves a medal.' Lizzie stood and collected the others' cups to take to the servery.

Elation for their friend was short-lived. Two days later, Sally reported that Christine had been brought back and the baby returned to the nursery – without her. Sally didn't know what had become of Christine and Miss Mayhew and Matron and anyone else in authority they asked refused to say.

Christine's belongings disappeared when they were at work; they never saw her again.

What would happen to her? One day, they were all best friends, sharing everything, studying each other's bodies, knowing more and sharing more about each other than they had with anybody. The next day, one of them would be gone, never to be seen again. And all she had was an address, somewhere in Nelson. She would write, but would she ever hear back? Somehow, it seemed unlikely. It was so sudden, this loss of friendship. Who would be the next to go?

'That's two deliveries now. I bags be next,' Meg said. 'I'm due before you two anyway.'

Lizzie wasn't due for nearly another week when the first contraction came. They were in the kitchen cleaning up after lunch.

'I'll see how far they're apart,' Jessie said, putting down the tea towel and looking at her watch. She sent Lizzie over to the chair beside the servery. But she couldn't sit still. She started clearing away cups. It seemed like an eternity before the next sharp pain shot through her.

'Twenty minutes,' Jessie called out, looking at her watch. 'You've got ages yet.'

'But shouldn't I go see the nurse?' Lizzie was terrified. This was the moment she'd been dreading – and also the moment she'd been looking forward to, because soon she would be free of this tremendous burden she'd been carrying around for so long through the hot summer days, restless in her bed, impossible to sleep at night. But before she could be free, she somehow had to get the baby out.

'If you like. But she'll just put you in that claustrophobic windowless room and make you lie on that uncomfortable high bed while she sticks cold stainless steel instruments up your fanny.'

'Jessie!'

'Well it's true. And that's just the beginning of the nightmare.'

'I suppose if we got to have an adorable little baby at the end of the nightmare it would be bearable.'

Jessie folded her arms and looked at Lizzie as if she were mad. 'But we don't, do we? Not even Christine managed to pull it off.'

'We should have seen it coming. She was absolutely nuts about babies, right from the start.'

'And she never changed her mind.' Meg came up behind Lizzie waving a spare tea towel at her.

'Maybe she thought she deserved a reward at the end of all that pain,' Lizzie said, ignoring the waiting dishes.

'The only reward we'll have is an *end* to the pain,' Meg said.

'Don't count on it. If you get stitches, you'll be in pain for some time to come.' Jessie grinned mischievously.

'Stitches? Nobody said anything about stitches before.' Lizzie nearly dropped the cups she was stacking.

'You can't have been listening,' Meg said. 'One of the girls two groups ahead of us went into all the gory details when we were in the garden one Sunday afternoon.'

'I never heard that. Where do you have them?'

'Where do you think?' Jessie pointed to the area at the top of her legs. 'Where the baby comes out, silly.'

Lizzie swallowed hard and bit back a cry.

'She said it happens to a lot of girls at the hospital,' Meg continued.

'That's because they don't care about us,' Jessie said. 'They only care about keeping the doctor's bill down, so they try to avoid calling him. And the result? A lot of us get torn apart and have to get stitched up afterwards.'

'Oh God, I hope it doesn't happen to me.' Lizzie's voice started to quiver.

'Oh, Lizzie, I'm sorry, I didn't mean to upset you.'

'No, it's all right, I've got to know. Christine used to tell us everything she knew from those books, but she never told us about stitches.'

'The nice books she reads wouldn't go into that sort of unpleasant detail.'

Lizzie felt another stabbing pain in her abdomen and yelled in pain.

'You've still got a long way to go,' Jessie said, looking at her watch.

'You make it sound so matter-of-fact, so clinical.'

'That's what doctors are supposed to do.'

'Well I hope you're not like any of the doctors I've met so far. They've all been awful.'

'I'm going to be brilliant.' Jessie grinned. 'Though I've a long way to go.'

'Anyway, I hope I don't need a doctor. I want a nice easy birth . . . like I was.'

But lying on the high narrow bed with its stiff, plastic-covered mattress, Lizzie soon realised she wasn't in for an easy birth. She was stripped down, her clothes taken away – she never thought she'd be sorry to have the ghastly grey smock disappear – and made to wash in front of the nurse, 'even down there'. Then the added humiliation of having her pubic hair shaved. Now that it was gone, she felt totally and utterly exposed.

All that covered her was a worn old hospital gown the nurse had to tie at the back. Her bare bottom was visible; her underpants were nowhere to be seen.

The nurse approached with a long rubber tube, a stainless steel dish, and a grim smile. 'You have to have an enema,' she said.

'An enema – what's that?' It sounded like a banana. Would she have to eat it? And what were the rubber tubes for?

She soon found out. And she hoped she would never in her life have to go through that again.

Once in the delivery room, the nurse kept telling her off, that she should be more dilated by now, while the contractions kept coming so far apart she found herself almost dozing off in her quiet isolation – until the sharp stab in her abdomen brought her back to reality.

After enduring the agonising contractions for five hours Lizzie asked if she could have something to make it less painful. She was given a couple of pills to take, but they didn't seem to make any difference.

'I can't give you anything stronger than that. You'll have to wait until the doctor comes.' The nurse, to her credit, looked sympathetic; Lizzie soon came to the conclusion she was the only member of staff in the whole hospital with any feelings.

The nurse departed and Lizzie dozed off again, alone – terribly alone – in the sterile white room, bare of any adornments and smelling strongly of antiseptic.

She awoke to another gripping pain, but this time it felt different, lower down somehow. It was followed quite soon by another. She felt an urgent desire to go to the toilet and staggered down off the high bed, padding off in her bare feet to the door.

'Where are you going?' The nurse was in the corridor, her voice urgent, almost fearful. 'I told you to stay on the bed.'

'But I have to go to the toilet, right now!'

'I'll get you a bed pan.'

Lizzie wailed as another sharp jolt went through her. 'I'm sure my contractions are a lot closer together.'

After being told off so severely for not being sufficiently dilated, Lizzie felt she deserved praise for this, but the nurse said nothing, just helped her up on the bed then fetched a bed pan from behind the curtain. But Lizzie couldn't produce anything in it. By now the contractions were coming so close together she hardly had time to get her breath back.

The nurse disappeared behind the curtain then produced an unsightly contraption with what looked like horse stirrups dangling down from a bar and insisted Lizzie put her feet through them. Protesting made no difference. The nurse was firm: this was the way it had to be; all the girls had their babies like this, she insisted. Weakened by the constant pain, Lizzie did as she was told, lay back on the uncomfortable hard bed with its clingy plastic cover and held her legs in the air. Was there no end to this public humiliation? First the enema and now this. She'd never been so exposed in her life, especially when the nurse started peering between her legs.

'Looks like the baby is ready,' the nurse smiled at last. 'I was beginning to wonder if you were going to get there.'

The momentary relief Lizzie felt at this news was quickly dissipated by another contraction, awful in its intensity.

'I think I'd better ask Matron to get the doctor,' the nurse said. 'I'll be back in a minute.'

'Don't leave me,' Lizzie implored as the young woman left the room.

It seemed an eternity before she returned, bringing Miss Mayhew with her.

'Matron's gone for the evening. I've made the decision to call the doctor. He should be here soon,' she said, only looking at her momentarily before departing again.

Lizzie screamed in pain as another contraction tore through her.

'I need the bedpan again,' she cried out.

'Oh my goodness, the baby's coming. I wish the doctor would hurry.' The nurse looked up from her position at the end of the bed. 'You need to push now. As if you're going to the toilet.'

Lizzie thought her pelvis was going to give way, such was the pressure on it, it was as if her fanny, as Jessie called it, was on fire. She screamed again. She'd never felt such intense, burning pain, not even during the strongest contractions.

'There, you're doing so well. Keep pushing.'

She thought she was going to explode. She pushed as hard as she could, gripping the sides of the bed as if it might run away.

And through the mist of pain and terror, she heard a baby's cry.

She wept.

It was done.

'A baby girl!'

'Can I see her?'

'Not yet. There's a lot of blood.'

The door opened and a young man appeared.

'Oh, Doctor Gardiner, thank goodness you're here. She's going to need stitches.'

That was the last thing Lizzie remembered hearing as she passed out.

When she came too, she was in a small hospital room and was quite alone. She tried to get out of bed but was so woozy she couldn't make her limbs move.

'Help!' she cried out. Or thought she did, but it sounded nothing like it and her voice was croaky and weak. 'Help,' she tried again.

A different nurse came in. 'Oh, you're awake.' She approached the bed, shook a thermometer and put it up to Lizzie's mouth; she obediently sucked on it.

'Can I see my baby?' Lizzie asked, twisting her mouth round the tiny glass tube.

'No, I'm afraid not. She's asleep now.'

'But I want to see her. I want to hold her.'

'You'll have to ask Matron.'

'Is she . . . is she all right?'

'Of course she's all right. She's been bathed and dressed and given a bottle, and now she's asleep.' The nurse took the thermometer and wrote something on Lizzie's chart.

'But she's my baby.'

'I'm sorry, dear.' The nurse softened. 'But you know the rules.'

The rules. She'd signed the papers; she'd agreed to give her baby up and now it was happening.

'But can't I just see her, just the once? Can't I hold her?'

'I'm sorry, dear.' The nurse gathered the thermometer and its kidney-shaped bowl, the chart and an empty water jug and bustled out.

Lizzie turned her face into the pillow and screamed 'I want my baby!' But it was muffled, lost inside the kapok. She couldn't even get out of bed, she couldn't walk. Her bottom hurt. A lot. She desperately wanted to find the nursery and see her baby girl, just one look, that wasn't much to ask. Her arms ached from the emptiness. She wished she could die.

Chapter 7.

Wellington, 1952

Lizzie put down the protractor and rubbed her eyes, sore after hours of close, detailed tracing work. She looked at her watch, a present from her mother when she'd been hired by Paterson and Paynter Architects just over a year ago and the most beautiful piece of jewellery she'd ever owned. Delicate traceries of silver filigree surrounded the small oval face; the fine silver hands showed it was five to four. In half an hour, she could start packing up her desk and get ready for the journey home.

She looked across the big open-plan drafting room, past all the other tables where men and women bent in concentration on their drawings, through the windows beyond and the view across the harbour all the way to Eastbourne. Being the most junior on staff, her post was furthest from the view and closest to the draughty door and neighbouring tea-room, where she was expected to make both morning and afternoon tea for the entire team of draughtsmen and women. The architects had their own tea-lady presiding over their separate tea-room on the floor above.

She didn't mind making tea; she'd dreamed of all this – the drafting office, the clever men and women who knew how to get the angles and trajectories just right, how to turn the architects' visions into practical detailed drawings – but she never dared hope in all that time down south it might actually happen. Only last week, Mr Simes, the head of drafting, had asked her if she'd like to take an evening course at the Technical Institute next year to help her qualify as a draughtswoman. Straight off, she'd written away for a prospectus. She could just see herself, a student, like the other girls in her class who'd gone on to teachers' college, secretarial college, even to university. Julia had told her about them when she'd seen her at netball over the winter – Lizzie playing for the Karori team, Julia for the Kelburn club.

Julia had seemed a bit stand-offish when they'd spoken after the game. But Lizzie hadn't made many friends since returning home – she hadn't even had a single letter from the girls at Bleak House, but then, she hadn't written to any of them either – and hoped to see Julia again. They'd agreed to have lunch in town one weekday.

With just half an hour for lunch, by the time they walked to the tearooms – Julia was attending secretarial college a few blocks away from the architects' offices – they would be lucky to have twenty minutes. Which suited Lizzie perfectly. No time to go into too may details; no time to talk about the past.

But she was wrong.

As soon as they sat down, Julia said 'It's been so long since we were able to talk, just the two of us. Where were you all that time? I mean really?'

'I was sick. I had glandular fever. I thought they would have told you.'

'Come on Lizzie, don't try to pull the wool. How well do we know each other?'

'Pretty well, I guess.'

'I know what happened. I know about the baby.'

'You do?'

Lizzie felt sick. But there was clearly no point in denying it. The last person she wanted a row with was Julia. Lizzie put down her knife and fork, the chicken pie no longer having any appeal. 'How do you know?'

'One of the girls at school . . .

'You mean everyone at school knows?'

'No, not everyone. In fact, hardly anyone. Just a few of us in our class. You know how it is.' Julia was looking uncomfortable.

'No.' She waited for Julia to finish.

'Well, there was me and Sylvia and three or four others. Sylvia was the one who seemed to know in the first place. But we swore we wouldn't tell anyone else.'

So that was six girls who knew. And how many others had they told, despite promising to keep it a secret? And how many had told their parents? There seemed to be no end to the suffering for that one irrational night in the Karori

Pavilion, paying again and again, facing one consequence after another. When would it be over?

'Lizzie?'

She swivelled round on her chair. Her supervisor Pauline was standing behind her carrying a set of plans.

'You were miles away.'

'Oh, sorry.' She rubbed her eyes. 'I just looked up for a moment.'

Pauline smiled. 'It's all right, don't worry, I'm not complaining. I know how hard on the eyes all that tracing work can be. You need to take a short break every now and then.'

'Thanks.' She gave Pauline a grateful smile.

'Here, I've got another project for you to work on. You can leave it 'til tomorrow, though.' She put down the big sheets of paper at the end of Lizzie's desk. 'They should be quite straightforward, but come and see me if you need anything more.'

'I will.' Lizzie smiled again. She liked Pauline. Although she wasn't much older, she'd become a role model, working her way up from the same job Lizzie was doing now to become a top draughtswoman, in charge of seven underlings, with Lizzie on the bottom rung. Every time she looked at Pauline, she felt inspired to produce perfect plans, even though they were mere tracings of other craftsmen's fine line drawings. If Pauline could make it, so could she. She knew there was a long way to go to climb up the career ladder, especially without any qualifications. But she had plenty of time. There was nothing else in her life. She hadn't even any letters to write.

Returning to her task, she completed tracing the set of plans in front of her and signed herself out of the book to go home, walking companionably with the others along the road to Lambton Quay, where they split off to their various tram stops.

Moments later, the Karori tram arrived and she clambered up the steep high steps, found a seat and fumbled in her purse for the fare home. She looked up to see if the conductor was on his way. She could see him down the other end, collecting fares. He looked vaguely familiar, that sandy hair, that tall, narrow back, the way he joked with the passengers. It was Peter.

She hadn't seen him since that humiliating trip to the tram depot before she'd gone down to Christchurch. She'd wondered if he might appear one day down the aisle of a tram calling 'Tickets, please,' smirking, making smart remarks. But for over a year now she'd caught the tram to work and home again every day and hadn't seen him once. She'd assumed he'd moved on, maybe gone up the east coast like he'd mentioned, not that there were trams up that way. 'I don't want to be a tram conductor all my life,' he'd said.

But here he was, nearly two years on. And on her route.

She looked away from him, out the window. The tram had only just commenced its steep climb out of the city. Perhaps she could sidle down the back and jump off at the next stop before he spotted her. But then how would she get home? It was too far to walk and she could hardly ask her father to come and get her in the car; he'd only want to know why she hadn't stayed on the tram; besides it was Thursday so he'd probably still be at his club.

Perhaps if she kept her head down, she could avoid paying? But Peter prided himself on never missing a fare. 'I remember them all,' he used to tell her. 'I know exactly who's paid and who hasn't.' Still, that was her only option. Perhaps he wouldn't recognise her. She'd worn her new beret today and it would at least keep her hair hidden.

She heard him approaching down the aisle. 'Tickets, please,' he called above the rattle and click of the rails. His voice was getting closer. 'All fares.'

The tram stopped to let people on and off and, with all seats taken there was a crush in the aisle. She knew she should be offering her seat to the elderly, but she didn't dare look up. If there was a little old lady who needed a seat, too bad: she'd have to find one elsewhere. Lizzie kept her head down and made a fine study of her purse, the soft pigskin one her mother had given her. She followed the swirls in the leather with her finger.

'Ticket please, miss.' That voice.

It was right beside her. It still caused a ripple of excitement, even after all he'd done. She held out her coins without looking up.

'Karori, please.' She waited for the ticket to be handed back. She heard him drop the money in his bag and the snap of the clicker making a hole in the ticket. She could picture it, a jagged-edged gap right in the little square that said 'Journey Out' and '3' to mark the number of sections she was travelling. But there was no ticket. She waited.

'Your ticket, Miss.' She raised her eyes slightly and there was her ticket, hanging down between his thumb and forefinger, waiting for her to take it. She reached up. The ticket jerked away higher. Her eyes followed it to find the owner of the thumb and finger grinning at her, clearly aware of her identity and not a single qualm about seeing her again.

Suddenly the fear and mortification left her. That taunting grin, the grin that had got her into all that trouble in the first place, the grin that had turned into a sneer when she'd told him about the baby, how dare he look at her like that?

She narrowed her eyes and gave him a furious stare, snatching the ticket from his hand then turning away and looking out the window.

'I say, what side of bed did you get out of this morning?' she heard him say sarcastically under his breath.

Not your side, thank goodness, she wanted to say, but didn't, and continued to stare out the window, ignoring him completely for the rest of the journey.

But she couldn't stop thinking about him and the baby – his baby; her baby; the baby she'd never hold.

Leaving Bleak House was a wrench, but also a relief. She was sad to say farewell to her friends, the closest friends she'd ever had. She'd made a point of returning from the hospital across to Fitzgibbon House at a time when she knew they'd be gathered in the lounge – the two that were left from their group and the other girls she come to know. Jessie was there, and Meg, and that was it. They'd just had time for a hug and Miss Mayhew appeared to hustle her out the door.

But at the same time, she was overjoyed to be at last going home. She couldn't wait to see the gates disappear out the back window of Miss Mayhew's car, to get on the boat train then the ferry, wave that bright red Lane's Emulsion sign goodbye and sail out of Lyttelton Harbour never to return.

The whole family was at the Wellington dock to meet the ferry. Her mother ran forward up the gangplank to meet her and took her suitcase.

'Welcome home, Lizzie.'

'Mummy!' She flung into her arms and breathed in the familiar Shalimar perfume, willing herself not to cry, not in such a public place with hundreds of people milling around staring. He mother looked beautiful, in a dove grey tailored woollen suit, a jaunty grey hat and matching court shoes – the immaculate style that Lizzie realised, to her surprise, she'd missed so much.

'You're looking well,' her father said, waiting his turn.

'I am, now,' she said, giving her father a more subdued hug, feeling the reticence behind his embrace.

Jerry, under the false impression that she'd been to a posh finishing school in the South Island, teased her about being above them all now; Penny, not quite understanding what a finishing school was, asked if she'd brought her a present because it was her birthday next month.

Penny had chattered all the way home, asking interminable questions about her schoolfriends – if only she knew! – and what the girls did all day. Lizzie had made up stories about walking up and down the room with an encyclopaedia on her head for deportment lessons, and practising her vowels to imitate the King's English. Penny seemed satisfied. Her father's face remained unreadable.

Later that night, when Penny was in bed and Jerry was in his room pretending to do his homework, Lizzie summoned the courage to talk to her mother alone. She was in the living room reading through committee papers. She waited until her mother looked up then asked if she had a moment to talk.

'Of course,' she said. 'What is it?'

'Did the Matron tell you anything about what happened?'

Her mother looked surprised. 'Why? What happened?'

'Did they tell you it was a baby girl?'

'No.' Her mother shifted uncomfortably. 'Don't . . .'

'I wasn't allowed to hold her.'

Her mother put her hand up to her mouth and gave a stifled cry. 'I'm so sorry . . .' She tailed off.

There was a moment's silence while Lizzie waited for her to continue. But she looked away, blinking quickly. After a while Lizzie said, 'She went home to her new family with the layette I knitted her.'

'Yes, you told me you'd knitted something.' Her mother looked back at her and forced a smile. 'I was very impressed.'

'I got quite good at it.'

'It will stand you in good stead for the future.' The smile became more natural, more relaxed. 'I could never quite grasp how to do it, all that plain one, pearl one. It just didn't make sense to me.'

'Maybe I could show you.'

'Maybe you could.' Her mother patted the seat next to her on the sofa.

Lizzie sat beside her. 'The nurse said she was a very good baby. She didn't cry a lot, took her bottle first thing. She had thick dark brown hair, all in curls. And a rosebud mouth.'

Her mother slipped an arm around her and gave her a gentle squeeze. 'I expect she would be beautiful, being a Hamilton.'

'Matron said she went to a good family. A nice couple who hadn't been able to have a baby, who had plenty of money and lived in a nice suburb. She said they were going to call her Katharine.' She pulled a face. 'That's not what I wanted for her name. I decided to call her . . .'

Her mother leant forward and held up a finger to Lizzie's lips, stopping her saying the name. 'Don't tell me. I'd rather not know.' With her other hand, she squeezed Lizzie's shoulders again.

'But Mummy, I want to tell you. I haven't been able to tell anyone else.'

'Look, dear, I know you've been through a very difficult time.' She dropped her arm, faced her daughter and took both her hands in hers. 'But it's over now. You have to put it all behind you and move on. And the best way to do that is to forget all about it . . .'

'But how can I? I can't just forget . . .'

'Yes you can, and you must. You must never speak of her again, not even to me or to Daddy. Do you understand?' She dropped Lizzie's hands and looked pleadingly at her daughter.

Lizzie shook her head, no, she didn't understand. Not for one moment.

'These things are best left unsaid. Otherwise you'll find yourself dwelling on it, and you won't be able to get on with your life. And that's the most important thing, don't you agree?'

Lizzie nodded, yes.

'Good. You've your whole future to plan now. We've got to find you a job, something you'd enjoy doing, something that will take your mind off it all.'

'But what if I . . ?'

'You'll be fine. Positive thinking, that's what you must do. Think only of the future, not the past. You wrote in your letters about wanting to be a draughtswoman.'

'Yes.'

'Well, I think that's a splendid idea. Your father has been talking to a friend of his who owns an architectural practice and he thinks he might have an opening.'

The opening had been for the most junior of dogsbodies, but at least it was a start. And it got her out of the house every day.

'Next stop, Karori shops!' Peter's voice seemed right in her ear. She looked away from the window and into the aisle, being careful to keep her head down.

He was right next to her. The tram started to slow with a squeal of brakes on the rails. There was nothing for it but to stand and edge past him to the back door.

For a moment, as she brushed past, she couldn't avoid looking at him. His expression was mocking and hard. Why hadn't she seen that before?

She said nothing and walked as fast as she could to the back, waiting for the tram to stop. It was still moving slightly when she jumped down onto the street, careless of the drop to the asphalt below, and hurried away. She did not look back, not even after she'd rounded the corner for the long climb homeward.

She'd show him. She wasn't going to let someone as mean and vain as Peter get her down. She'd make sure she caught the Karori tram with her boyfriend Steven as often as she could so Peter could see them together and how happy she was.

Steven Davidson was everything that Peter wasn't – he was kind and he genuinely cared. And he was clever too, and was going places. Not like Peter. The only place Peter was going was up and down the wooden-slatted aisle of the Karori tram. She believed Steven would go far – and that her father would see the potential in him too. A junior in the government survey office, Steven had got top marks in his exam at the end of last year. He'd told her, so proud, on their first date. Well, it wasn't exactly their first date, if you counted the time they'd walked outside the ski lodge on that trip with Julia two years ago. She could tell then that he'd liked her from the way he kept singling her out, teasing her about little things like her thick hockey socks, her freckles, her short legs. He hadn't said much, but over the course of an evening around the big stone fireplace and its crackling log fire, it had added up to more attention than she'd had before from a boy her age.

But after the ski race, after he'd fallen against her and they'd gone outside – nothing.

Of course she'd been out of town for nearly six months and hadn't seen anyone from that old life until she'd spoken to him on the beach last summer when she and her family were staying at Waikanae.

She'd never forget his tiny dinghy with its feeble outboard motor putting slowly over to Kapiti Island – just herself, Steven, his friend Mike and his girlfriend Selena. It had been okay on the way over, the sea calm, not a breath of wind. But on the way back, a stiff breeze threw the waves over the gunwales and their combined weight threatened to sink the flimsy craft as soon as they were out of the lee of the island. Mike had treated it as a huge joke but Steven had taken his responsibility very seriously and steered a steady course back to the welcome shallows of the Waikanae beach.

He was good like that, she'd come to realise – steady as she goes, solid, reliable, appearing older than his twenty years, his maturity boosted by his thinning hair and steel-rimmed glasses that he was always losing. Not the sort of chap to set the world on fire. But not as dull as he might at first seem either.

She remembered the excitement in his eyes that Sunday afternoon he'd taken her home and opened his drawer of photographic prints. Some of them had taken her breath away.

'They're beautiful,' she'd said, amazed. 'You have such a good eye for finding the right angle.'

His best photos were on the wall of his parents' lounge – black and white shots mostly of sunsets off the beach, ripples across the sand, the backlit wings of a seagull in flight, his father out fishing, reeling in a heavy line.

'One day I'd like to have my own darkroom,' he said. 'I develop all my own films but I can only print up the best.'

He used the darkroom at the Kapiti Camera Club and attended their meetings whenever he could.

In the last three months, as their friendship had firmed, he'd taken her on two of the camera club field trips, combining his love of the outdoors with photography, lugging his heavy camera and lenses wherever he went and pulling it out whenever something caught his eye.

Looking at the negatives on their return, she'd noticed a remarkable number of shots of her – shots she didn't recall being taken. She'd smiled, pleased, but hadn't said anything.

Tomorrow night he was meeting her in town after work and taking her to the movies to see Audrey Hepburn and

Gregory Peck in *Roman Holiday*. She would have to go through her wardrobe tonight – what there was of it – and find something decent to wear, something she hadn't worn already on a date with him, something that would make her hips slimmer and her chest smaller. Julia used to say she was lucky to be so well endowed; she'd give anything, she'd say, not to have to pack cotton wool inside her bra. But Lizzie wished she could get rid of some of her natural padding; it was an embarrassment. It was even more embarrassing since the baby, her breasts had been so big then and even now, over a year later, they were much bigger than other girls her age. It made buying dresses and blouses so difficult because most of the clothes in her size were only fit for old ladies. She hated being different; if only she could be like other nineteen-year-old girls, without such a shameful secret.

She puffed up the driveway and climbed the steps up to the front door, wishing as she always did at this point that she was a lot fitter. Having the baby certainly hadn't helped her physical condition; she'd put on weight, especially since coming home. It was as if she was eating to compensate for the loss – the loss that threatened to overwhelm her almost every day, the loss that still made her arms ache every time she remembered that moment after giving birth when the baby was taken away.

Standing on the front porch and looking across to the hills - misty and mauve as the sun tracked behind them, the houses beginning to light up as the twilight settled over the valley - Lizzie again felt the familiar ache. Where was she now, baby Katharine? Was she happy in her nice home with the nice couple? The man working away in a bank, the woman at home with the baby that should have been hers, were they looking after Katharine properly? Were they giving her all the love she would have given?

She felt the locket hanging at the end of a silver chain right above her breastbone, close to her heart. Inside was a tiny lock of her baby's hair, a snippet: dark, fine, slightly curled.

The nurse had brought it out to her after seeing Lizzie's distress. She'd thought the nurse had disappeared for good, had felt no sympathy, but she'd returned later, when the hospital was quiet and Matron had gone home for the night, producing the few wisps of hair.

'Don't you dare tell anyone I gave this to you,' the nurse said. 'It's more than my job's worth.'

She'd treasured it, keeping it inside her diary until she'd found the little locket at the bottom of her mother's jewellery box.

'Can I have this, Mummy?' she'd asked one night.

'That's your grandmother's,' her mother said, holding the fine silver and turning it over in her hand. 'I suppose she wouldn't mind if you had it.' Her mother undid the clasp and clipped it around Lizzie's neck. 'There, it suits you.'

'Thank you. I promise to look after it.'

'What are you going to put inside it? A photo? Your brother and sister perhaps?'

'You're joking!'

Her mother was grinning. She was joking.

'I don't know. Nothing yet.'

She'd never told her mother what was inside. She'd never tell anyone. Except perhaps Steven. But even then, not for a long, long time.

Lizzie loved Audrey Hepburn in *Roman Holiday* playing the part of an escaped princess who fell in love with a commoner. Coming out of the theatre, Steven seemed surprisingly romantic, taking her arm and holding her close. He said he'd like to take her somewhere for a coffee or a meal.

'I know just the place,' he said, leading her across the road and into a narrow, dimly lit dining room with a high counter on one side and a series of small tables lining the other. Each bore a candle burning on top of an empty sherry bottle, the wax dripping down in thick teardrop cascades towards the crisp white linen-covered table-top with its array of silver cutlery. She felt very grown up. Steven had taken her to milk bars, he'd taken her home to have dinner with his parents, but he'd never taken her anywhere as sophisticated as this.

They sat down on the dark wooden ladder-back chairs and a waitress in a long black satin skirt and a frilly white high-necked blouse brought over a menu.

'What would you like, Lizzie?' Steven said. 'Coffee? Something to eat? I'm feeling a bit peckish, myself. You can have anything you like. My treat.'

She smiled at him then opened the plush red velvety, gold-embossed cover of the menu. What would a young sophisticate choose? She didn't want to look as if she was out of her depth. Her parents had taken her out to dine before, but they'd been large brightly lit rooms in hotels and her mother had been quick to tell her what to do, what to order, how to choose the right knife and fork. Here, it was completely different.

'What do you suggest?'

'I think we should start with a coffee – or would you prefer a glass of sherry?'

'Oh, no, thank you.' Lizzie shook her head then wondered if perhaps she should have said yes. That's what a sophisticated young lady would have done. Trouble was she hated sherry. It burned her throat and made her gag.

'Righto, then. We'll have coffee then perhaps something to eat. Would you like to start with the soup, cream of chicken? No? Then how about the sole meuniere? Filet mignon, perhaps, or beef tournedos?'

Lizzie was annoyed with herself. She never had any trouble ordering when her mother was there. Why was she so tongue-tied now? She was fast losing her appetite. She ran her finger down the printed words, trying to pick out a French name that was familiar, wishing they'd put the prices next to each dish so she didn't choose the most expensive. Steven wouldn't be able to afford lobster thermidor on his wages, she knew that much and kept looking.

'I'll have the soup, I think,' she said at last.

'Just the soup, nothing else?'

'No, I'm not very hungry.'

'Maybe some dessert later then?'

'Maybe.' She flashed Steven a grateful smile. He was being so sweet.

He ordered for them both and the waitress brought their coffees over almost instantly.

Unusually nervous, Lizzie took a sip. It was too hot. She swallowed it quietly, holding back a cry of pain. She could feel it burning her tongue and the back of her throat as it slid down. Why was she so on edge? It wasn't as if she hadn't been to a restaurant before. Was it because this was such a special place, small and intimate and so sophisticated? Or was it because she was with Steven and it was the first time he'd taken her anywhere as elegant?

'You're very quiet, Lizzie. That's not like you,' he said, interrupting her thoughts.

'Am I?' She should say something, but what? Words, usually slipping so easily off her tongue, were failing her. He was looking at her expectantly. She swallowed. Seeking inspiration, she looked around. 'This is such a lovely place,' she said lamely.

'Yes, one of the chaps at the office recommended it. I wanted to take you somewhere special.' He paused and looked closely at her. Was there some singular meaning to this? 'You see, Lizzie, we've known each other a while now and I think we get on pretty well.' He was looking at her that way again. She wondered if she was expected to say something. He cleared his throat and shifted awkwardly on his seat. 'I was thinking perhaps we could get married, you and I.'

'Heavens,' was all she could think of to say. Was he proposing? Then why wasn't he down on his knees? That's what the men did in all those romantic novels she'd read.

Suddenly, as if he'd read her thoughts, he pushed back his chair and knelt beside her, taking her hand. 'Lizzie Hamilton, will you marry me?' Then he let go of her hand, fumbled in his jacket pocket, pulled out a blue velvet-covered box and flipped it open. Inside, nestled on white satin, was a solitaire diamond ring.

Everything went quiet and very still. Out of the corner of her eye, she could see the waitress stop in her tracks on her way to one of the tables behind them.

What was she waiting for? Of course she should marry him. She liked him, didn't she? He was right, they did get on well. And she couldn't be too picky. She was damaged goods, wasn't she?

'Oh, God!' It slipped out, just like that. She'd have to tell him. Now. She couldn't let this nice man take her down the aisle without knowing about her past. But she couldn't tell him here, not with all these people staring. 'I'd really like to marry you, Steven,' she said hesitantly. 'But there's something you need to know. Something I haven't told you about me.'

Steven closed the lid on the little blue box and stood, clearly taken aback, then sat down hard in his chair where he continued to stare at her, wide-eyed. The box containing the diamond ring sat tantalisingly on the table between them.

The waitress passed by, giving her a rueful look.

'What is it?' he said after a moment.

'I can't tell you here, not in front of all these people.'

'When can you tell me?'

She thought for a moment. 'Tomorrow. I'll tell you tomorrow. After netball. We're going up the coast, remember, to take photos?'

He sat back in his chair, his hands falling into his lap.

'We can talk then,' she said. 'There'll be nobody around.'

The walk along the coast and around the estuary was unaccountably busy on Saturday morning; the whole way Steven was unusually tense, on edge, glancing at her nervously whenever it seemed nobody was around then looking equally irritated when someone appeared around a corner, or voices could be heard approaching from far off. He cursed several times when he missed a shot he would normally have caught easily – a bird that took off as he fumbled the focus, a seagull arching its back and ruffling its feathers to defend its split shellfish. By the time he unclipped the lens cover, its opponent had backed off.

'I can't seem to get anything right this morning,' he said.

Lizzie was waiting for him to say something, to blame her. But he simply clipped the cover on again, wiped his brow with the back of his hand, and kept walking.

She was just as apprehensive, waiting for the right moment to broach the subject she'd hoped never to mention again.

As she walked she planned what she would say, but every time she came to the most difficult bit, her mind went blank. Did she want to marry Steven? Did she love him? She liked him; she knew that much. But she wasn't sure if she loved him. Julia used to talk about chemistry, about the sparks that were supposed to fly between a couple in love. There were no sparks with Steven, but perhaps they would come. Perhaps once she got this awful secret out in the open, she could relax more with him, be herself again. Maybe she would come to love him.

They stopped to eat their sandwiches under the shade of a macrocarpa tree. At the water's edge, estuarine crabs were scuttling in and out of their holes. Steven pulled his camera strap over his head, set the camera gently on the grass and plumped himself down beside it. He wiped his glasses on his handkerchief before putting them on again then looked up at her expectantly.

'I won't keep you waiting any longer.' Lizzie sat next to him.

'I was beginning to wonder if you'd been pulling my leg,' he said. 'If you really did have something to tell me. Or if you were just looking for an excuse to put me off.'

'Oh no, it's not that. I wouldn't do that.'

'So what is it then?'

This was the moment she'd been dreading. She knew she'd been looking for excuses, to put this moment on hold. The people on the track hadn't been so numerous that she couldn't have found the opportunity to say something. But each time they'd had the track to themselves, she'd found a distraction –

a bird he could photograph, an unusually shaped piece of driftwood, a striking land formation.

'Lizzie, you're exasperating. What is it you don't want to tell me? Have you had another boyfriend?'

'No, I … That is, yes.' There, she'd said it. Well, half of it – the easy half.

'Do I know him?'

She took heart from the fact that he didn't seem angry. 'No. You wouldn't know him.'

'So how long ago did you go out with him? Is it over now?'

'Yes. It's over. It was a while ago. Over a year ago, maybe two.'

'Well, that's all right, I suppose. As long as it's over. I don't see…'

'That's not the … I'm not doing this very well.' She fiddled with the zip on the backpack then faced him front on. 'You see, I did it with him and I got pregnant and I had the baby down in Christchurch and I gave it away and came back here and …'

'You had a baby?' Steven's eyes were bulging and his adam's apple was bobbing up and down furiously.

'Yes.' It came out as a whisper.

'Christ!' he shouted.

Lizzie winced.

He jumped up, strode over to the macrocarpa tree, kicked at its exposed roots and stood there, his hands braced against the trunk, his back to her.

A crab popped out from a hole close to her feet making her start; she watched it scuttle sideways across the mud until it reached the water and disappeared down another hole. Another crab surfaced; then another. She blinked. She was not going to cry.

Steven was just standing there, silent.

She didn't know whether to get up and go to him, put her arm around him, say she was sorry; or leave him be, wait for him to recover.

If only Jessie were here, she'd know what to do. Of all the girls in the dormitory, Jessie was the one she admired the most, would like to have remained friends with. Not long after she'd come home from Christchurch, she'd started a letter to Jessie, asking her advice about period pains and why her stomach wouldn't go flat again the way it used to be. But each attempt at the letter ended up torn into shreds and she'd never sent it. She regretted that, regretted not writing to any of the girls.

There wasn't a crab in sight now. The water lapped towards her, the sand was empty of life.

Suddenly, Steven was sitting beside her. He unzipped the backpack and extracted the packet of luncheon sausage and pickle sandwiches she'd made, unwrapped the greaseproof paper, pulled out a sandwich and started munching on it, his jaw clicking softly as he chewed.

She waited a moment, hoping he would say something.

'I'm sorry, Steven,' she said at last.

'Let's not speak of it again, shall we?' He sounded tight, constricted, as if he were fighting to contain himself, not let his feelings show.

It was for the best, she decided. It would be easier for her, too, to keep quiet about it, to keep it a secret. Maybe that way Katharine would be more easily forgotten.

Lizzie thought her parents would be overjoyed to have her off their hands, especially so soon after disappointing them so badly. She wondered herself if she might be rushing into the union for that very reason, but brushed it aside. Steven was right for her: strong, sporty, always doing something at weekends – if he wasn't taking photographs he would be playing rugby for Old Boys', crewing on friends' yachts on Wellington Harbour. And he was a hard worker.

'I'm not sure you've given it long enough,' her mother said. 'You know he's not the same as us, don't you? His parents have …'

'Oh, Mummy, don't be such a snob.'

'Elizabeth, how can you say such a thing? I'm not a snob.'

She suppressed a smile. 'It doesn't matter about his social status, or his parents'. Besides, he's got very good prospects in his job.'

'Does he know about what happened? Did you tell him about that?'

'Yes.'

'And what did he say?'

'He didn't mind.' At her mother's raised eyebrow, she added, 'Like you, he thinks it best if we don't mention it again.'

Her father's first question was about Steven's prospects. But then he surprised Lizzie by asking about her own career.

'What about your job at the architects' office? I went to a lot of trouble to get you that job.'

'I know, Daddy. I'm sorry, but …'

'And Joe Simes was encouraging you to do that course at the Technical Institute. He must have seen something in you. Surely you wouldn't throw that all away so soon.'

'But Daddy, Steven wants me to marry him. I can't keep on working after I'm married.'

Her father sighed. 'I suppose not.'

On Sunday afternoon, when Steven came round to formally ask her father for her hand in marriage, affecting a confidence she knew he didn't entirely have, her father said yes. Eventually.

Steven told her later there'd been a lot of discussion, though he never told her what about, and that her father had a bit of a heart-to heart with him, 'as a future son-in-law' he'd said, but the end result was what she wanted.

‘So that means it’s a yes?’ Steven said when they were alone on the front porch. ‘You will marry me?’

‘Yes.’

He slipped the ring on her finger.

The wedding preparations absorbed her mother from that moment on. Lizzie could tell she was determined to see her daughter return to some sort of social standing, as if the past had never happened. The wedding was to be done properly: St Mary’s Anglican Church in Karori Road, with the vicar presiding; a traditional long white dress, flowing silk, pearl buttons, with guipure lace bodice and sleeves, her mother’s triple string of pearls – because her mother wanted to keep up appearances, even though she knew virginal white was not quite telling the truth; Julia, her only bridesmaid, and Penny, the flowergirl, in pale aqua satin, three-quarter length frocks with scalloped hems; and the venue for the reception? Despite all her objections, her father insisted on hiring his cricket club rooms: the Karori Pavilion.

Chapter 8.

London, Late 1986.

The Harrods saleslady, immaculate in black, not a hair out of place, took the Bunnykins mug and bowl from Liz and started to wrap them in tissue.

'Thanks, Mum,' Jessie said, nudging against her affectionately, a touch of intimacy in the midst of crowded commercial excess.

Behind them in the queue for the sales counter was a crush of people from seemingly every country in the world. Liz had never seen so many different coloured faces, never heard so many foreign languages, never imagined so many people could be so wealthy. Some of the big spenders were women, covered from head to toe in a black sheet, anonymous, a bit scary; all you could see of them through the post-box opening in the shroud were their heavily made up eyes, beautiful eyes. But these strangely dressed women were just as attached to the Bunnykins china as she was.

'Bunnykins is traditional,' she said, studying the brown bunnies leaping across the grassy rim of the plate. 'You had one when you were a baby, and so did I. I want your little girl to have one too when she's born.'

'Hopefully that's not going to be too far away,' Jessie said, cupping a hand under her full-term belly.

'Well I hope it's not today,' Liz said as she handed over her credit card to pay. 'I don't know how you manage it, on your feet all afternoon pushing though these crowds of people – you'll be worn out.'

'I'm fine, Mum, really. Pregnant women don't stay locked up at home these days, you know.'

'No, maybe not, but at nine months, Jessie, you ought to take it easier.' She took the chit from the saleswoman and signed: Liz Davidson. She'd practiced that signature so many times before marrying Steven. Lizzie had sounded too juvenile for a married woman; Elizabeth Davidson was such a mouthful; she'd settled on Liz. She handed the Harrods receipt back to the woman, thanked her and turned back to her daughter.

Jessie rolled her eyes. 'I'm fine. I'm a big girl now. Very big.'

Liz took the Harrods bag with its present for Jessie's baby.

'Why don't we go to the tearooms upstairs,' Jessie added. 'I wouldn't mind a bit of a sit-down.'

There was another queue to get in, but at last they were seated and a waitress arrived to take their order.

'My shout,' Liz had said when ordering tea and scones. 'You need building up.'

'I've put on quite enough as it is,' Jessie said.

'You'll be losing most of it soon.' Lizzie looked around at the veritable United Nations collected in the café. 'I can't believe I'm really here, you know. I never thought I'd get to Harrods, ever.'

'You should have come over ages ago, Mum.'

Liz had been thinking about it for the four years her daughter had been in England, but hadn't been able to persuade Steven. He always said he hadn't been out of New Zealand all his life and wasn't about to start now. 'I know, but your father…'

'He's so insular. Always has been.'

'I wouldn't miss this for the world.' Liz smiled, indicated the bustling tearoom, and patted her daughter's hand.

'It's good to see you smile, Mum.' Jessie put her hand over her mother's and looked concerned. 'You don't seem to have been very happy since you arrived.'

'Me? I'm fine. I'm perfectly happy.'

'Is something wrong?'

Liz took her hand away and fiddled with the sugar bowl. 'Of course not.'

'Mu-uum.'

She didn't dare look at Jessie. Her eyes might give her away. Of course she wanted to see her new granddaughter when she was born. Of course she wanted to be with her daughter at this precious time. But she hadn't told Jessie the real reason she'd come to London. Jessie would never know. Nor would their son Richard. Now both her parents were dead, Steven was the only one in the family who knew. She planned to keep it that way.

She could feel Jessie's eyes piercing into her. She needed some sort of excuse for her behaviour. What could she say?

'It's just being in such a different place, I suppose,' she said at last. 'It's so vast, and there are so many people.'

'I don't believe you. You seemed fine when we were driving around yesterday.'

'I like being driven by you, Jessie. I loved watching you negotiate your way through the traffic, so confident, you seem right at home here. I had a lovely day yesterday, driving past all those places I'd only heard the names of before – St Paul's where Diana was married, and Kensington Palace where she lives. The bus went all over the city, but those were the two places I really wanted to see.'

'But when we got home, you just went up to your room.' Jessie rolled her eyes. 'You were up there for ages.'

Liz felt cornered; she didn't like talking about herself. She tapped the side of the sugar bowl, wishing their tea would arrive so she could talk about something else. 'I wanted to get a letter off to Steven. And I started one to Richard.'

'Mum, you're changing the subject again. Something's really wrong, isn't it? You seem depressed.'

'Heavens, I'm not depressed. Just a bit homesick, that's all. And I worry about your dad on his own.' She looked around the tearooms. Every table was full; people were crowded in. But there was no sign of a waitress. Where was their tea?

'Dad is perfectly capable of looking after himself.'

'I wouldn't be so sure. He can't even boil an egg. I've always been there to look after him. And Richard promised to keep an eye on him.'

'Richard? He can hardly boil an egg himself. Besides, he and Dad don't always get on.'

'I think they get on a lot better when I'm not around. They can talk about men things, like fishing and cars.'

'Richard doesn't know the first thing about cars. Besides, he's working three jobs. I can't see him having time to even go and see Dad let alone cook for him.'

'He won't need to cook for him. I left Dad a meal for every day in the freezer.'

'I still can't see why he didn't come with you.'

'He'd hate it here. All these women in black hoods …'

'Burkas.'

'… yes, all them, and all the crowds, and the underground. He'd hate it. You know Dad. He likes to be in the outdoors, not cooped up in a tube train rushing through smelly, sooty tunnels where you get black stuff up your nose.'

Jessie laughed. 'You're an expert at changing the subject, Mum. You always were good at tricking me and Richard into thinking about something else when we wanted lollies.'

'Really, I'm fine. Just give me time to get used to it here.' Liz recalled the disbelief of her friends that she hadn't travelled abroad before. But she'd never wanted to. There'd always been so much to do at home, with holidays camping by the sea in their caravan. But the time had come to get further away, to get out of New Zealand, to escape.

Jessie put her hand below her pregnant belly. 'I'm going to have to find the Ladies again.' She winced. 'It's such a pain.'

'I think I saw one just before the tearooms.'

'Good. I shan't be long. Hopefully the tea will have arrived by the time I'm back.'

'I expect there's a wait with all these people.' Liz looked around at the crowded tearoom again: still no sign of their tea.

'Try and cheer up a bit while I'm away. You've such a long face.' Jessie was gone before Liz had time to reply.

Cheer up? Impossible, under the circumstances.

It was unfair, she knew, to burden Jessie with her in such a mood. But she would have been worse if she'd stayed at home. Steven just didn't understand.

'What does it matter?' he'd say. 'No one's going to care.'

'But I care. It would be terrible if Richard or Jessie found out.'

For thirty-six years, the secret had remained in its closet. With time, it had faded in its intensity; eventually she had been able to get through days at a time without thinking about it. For years now she'd been fine, had focused on her family, on ensuring they had a good upbringing, had filled the tins with baking, knitted sweaters, supervised homework and music practice. And when the children had grown up and left home, she'd kept the tins full for Steven, helped him with his photography, sewn for his operatic society productions, got a part-time job in the local bookstore. She'd kept herself busy and had almost forgotten about Katharine. Almost.

Occasionally she'd look at Jessie and wonder if she would look like her. Sometimes at home she wondered if she might pass her in the street, if she would recognise her, if she would look familiar, or would she just keep walking by without realising?

Did she have a good life? Would she have had a better life if Liz had been allowed to keep her?

And now, would Katharine try to track her down, now that the law was about to change?

She was adamant that the secret remain locked away forever; she couldn't bear to relive the shame.

But how could she be sure? Her past could come knocking at the door. Everything could change in the stroke of a parliamentarian's pen.

She still had the newspaper clipping in her wallet, but she didn't need to read it to see what it said; she knew it by heart.

'ADOPTION LAW REFORM' the heading said.

'A Bill before Parliament proposes a change to New Zealand's adoption laws,' it went on to say. 'If passed, the new law would give adopted children the right to trace their birth parents, and parents to find their children. The Bill is expected to go before Parliament before the end of the year.'

The newspaper article went on to quote various politicians about whether the law change was a good idea, and the effect it would have on adopted children and the women who had given them up for adoption twenty or more years ago.

But it was the comment from one of the Adoption Law Reform spokeswomen that was closest to the bone. She pulled the well-thumbed clipping out from the back pouch in her wallet and read it again: 'At last, adoptees like us will be able to find out where we come from. The question 'Who am I?' we have been asking all our lives will at last be answered'.

Liz rubbed her forehead distractedly. A law change was the last thing she wanted. What if her daughter decided she wanted to make contact? What if she turned up unannounced on the doorstep one day? It would be a disaster; it would bring it all back again, that terrible time after the baby had been stolen away, with only a lock of hair to remind her. Unconsciously, she touched the silver locket around her neck. She had worn it for thirty-six years, only taking it off to go swimming for fear of losing it in the sea. She'd never told anyone what was in it, or even that it had a clasp; it remained the only tangible reminder of the past and she wanted it to stay that way.

She knew she'd been different since she'd read that newspaper article, but she couldn't help herself. She was terrified. She found it hard to talk to people, even to Steven; she found it hard to get up in the morning. Fleeing to London had been the only way to escape the consequences of the law-change.

'Here you are, madam, your tea.' The waitress delivered a silver tray with silver teapot and hot water jug, china cups and saucers, scones, cream and jam, all on china plates covered in lush red painted roses.

Liz slipped the newspaper clipping back in her wallet and dropped it in her bag before Jessie came back then turned her attention to afternoon tea. How grand! She could pretend, for a few moments anyway, to be a real lady, taking tea in Harrods.

Jessie insisted on paying for the taxi home. 'We earn plenty, Mum, you don't have to worry. Besides, the New Zealand dollar is only about a third of the pound. Save your money for a sightseeing trip.'

The cab delivered them outside Jessie's compact flat, located at the top of a three-storey brick row in St John's Wood, with Liz carrying a green and gold Harrods Food Hall bag bearing the ingredients for a special dinner – fresh pasta, which she'd never seen before, mushrooms, bacon, spring onions and a ready-made sauce. If she hadn't had Jessie to take her by the arm, she'd probably still be there, such was the magnificence and bounty all around her - so many different meats, row upon row of whole fish, prawns, shellfish, vegetables and fruit, many of them unknown at home. She'd had no idea so many cheeses existed; at home, she and Steven had only recently ventured from colby to edam but here there had been hundreds of varieties, some soft and runny, some with mould, some with big red and yellow rinds. Jessie had bought a selection for after dinner.

There was very little preparation needed for the dinner so Liz accepted a glass of chablis from Michael, who was home from his commute to the new Docklands development where his computer firm was based.

Liz didn't understand computers but Michael said they were the future. He'd tried to explain it to her last night on the heavy little flat box he had at home, but try as she might, it was beyond her, all those code words and blinking white 'curses', as he called them, on the screen. She couldn't see the point.

'And for you, Jessie, a ginger ale again?'

Jessie nodded, yes. 'They seem to help my digestion.'

Liz sipped the chablis and tried not to pull a face. It was much drier than the sweeter wines like Blenheimer she'd been used to at home. She nursed the glass and hoped he wouldn't notice her not drinking much of it. She felt his opinion of her was already low enough. Perhaps he thought her a bit dull?

She had to admit she wasn't her usual lively self, even though she'd tried to pass it off to Jessie in the tearooms as a bit of homesickness.

Her son-in-law was an unusual fellow she thought as she watched him holding up the wine bottle, reading the label, twisting and turning it against the light bulb before recorking it painstakingly. She wouldn't have been surprised to see him stroking it. A bit of a fusspot, Michael Pearson, and a bit up himself, really, no doubt due to his excessive Englishness – he came from a family somewhere north of St John's Wood who were extremely well off and had sent him to one of those plummy public schools where he'd learned how to speak like the Queen and affect a reticence that must surely drive her daughter crazy. Although, to be fair, Jessie was so gregarious, she'd fill any conversation gaps without anyone noticing his silence.

They were dead opposites, the two of them. She was tiny, dark, vivacious, colourful, eccentric at times, especially the way she dressed. He was tall, fair, almost pasty, and more than a little pudgy from sitting at a computer all day and being too fond of his food. His receding chin was covered by a beard that was blond but verging on light auburn and he peered at everyone through glasses so thick they could have come from the bottom of a lemonade bottle.

'Mum, you're not listening.'

'Sorry, dear. I was miles away.'

'We were talking about naming the baby.'

'Oh. Have you got a name already?'

'We're not settled on one yet. We've got several we like though.'

'I can't understand how you already know it's a girl.'

'We were thinking of Katherine. Or Katie.'

Liz's heart missed a beat. Did Jessie know?

'But we also like Madeline, Alice and Emily.'

'They're all nice dear,' she said.

Choosing Jessie's name had been easy. There'd never been any doubt in her mind and Steven had been quite happy with Jessica, which had immediately been shortened to Jessie and sometimes Jess. She'd often wanted to tell her about her namesake, the nineteen-year-old doctor-in-training who'd had to take enforced time out at Fitzgibbon House. Jessie had done just what she said she'd do – be a doctor. Not like herself, who'd thrown away her chances after just a short time in the draughtsman's office. She'd handed in her notice before she'd married Steven. Without a career of her own, Liz had always felt as if she had a share in Jessie's success when she went on to be a paediatrician. Even though they hadn't kept in touch as promised, she'd seen Jessie on the television at home a lot lately for her work preventing cot death. She often thought her daughter would be quite proud to be associated with Jessie the paediatrician, but she'd never be able to tell her.

The next day, Jessie squeezed behind the wheel and drove to the Kensington High Street art gallery she managed, Liz coming along reluctantly for the ride.

'I won't know a soul,' she'd protested when Jessie insisted she find something to wear.

'I'll look after you. Besides, I need you near me in case something happens.'

'What? You're not …'

'Only joking. I'm fine. There's over a week to go yet. I reckon this baby's determined to hang in there right to the end.'

So Liz had pulled out her black pants, black top and checked jacket, doing her best to emulate her fashion-conscious daughter and knowing she'd failed miserably. Even adding Jessie's red and black jet beads didn't make her feel anything better than dowdy.

Jessie emerged from her room a fully fledged arty type in flowing black pants, a floaty black top that draped nicely over her bump, and a loose peacock blue jacket covered in brightly coloured patterns of tiny flowers and flying birds. The striking ensemble was completed with a little black beret jammed down over her hair, which was dyed a conspicuous bright red and permed. She'd said it was the start of a new trend, but Liz couldn't understand it. Jessie had spent her teenage years trying to straighten her lovely, thick, curly brown hair and now she'd paid a lot of money to have it ten times as curly. At least she'd stopped wearing the high-heeled black boots Liz had seen poking out of her wardrobe.

Liz had her bag under her arm, ready to go.

Jessie looked her up and down. 'You can't go like that, Mum. What's come over you? You always used to look so smart.'

'I didn't bring my going-out clothes. I didn't think I'd be going to parties.'

'Come into my room. I'll find you something.' Jessie beckoned her to follow her into the bedroom where she started to rummage in her drawers, pulling out bangles and beads then in her wardrobe, holding out hanger after hanger of tops and jackets until she found something that appealed.

'Here, try these on.' She thrust the hanger and jewellery at Liz. 'They should look good on you.'

Liz did as she was told, reluctantly slipped off her jacket and pulled the heavily patterned multi-coloured tunic over her fitted black polo-neck.

'No, don't look in the mirror yet.' Jessie took her mother by the arms and guided her away from the dressing table then proceeded to drape necklaces around her. 'Now, put these on.' She handed Liz several brightly coloured bangles. 'You need lipstick to match.' Jessie picked a silver tube off the dresser and painted her mother's lips. 'Now, your hair. Hmm.' She grabbed a red velvet pillbox hat, thrust it on Liz's head and stood back, smiling. 'That's better. Now you can look in the mirror.'

Liz didn't recognise herself. Staring back at her was an unfamiliar creature almost as exotic as her daughter, with bright red lips and the Bohemian appearance of some of the women who performed in Steven's operatic productions. She could feel her shoulders lift, her depression fall away.

'That's better. More like the old Mum.'

'But Jessie, I've never dressed like this.'

'Never too late to start Mum. You look just the part.'

Liz did feel like she was playing a part. In Jessie's car, she pretended she was sitting in a Rolls Royce on the way to a premiere, not cooped up in a Mini.

'Damn, it's all double yellow lines in this street,' Jessie said as she drove round the block somewhere in the West End.

'You'd think there'd be a park somewhere this late in the afternoon. People should be starting to go home.'

The car swerved suddenly to the left. 'Thank God, a park at last,' she said, manoeuvring the Mini into the tiny space. 'If this car was any bigger, I wouldn't have fitted.'

'You'll have to think about a bigger one when the baby's here,' Liz said.

They made their way along back streets to Kensington High Street and through the open doors of the brightly lit Beaufort Gallery.

'Goodness, Jessie, all these stairs,' Liz said as they climbed to the second floor, trying to balance a glass of wine in one hand while clutching the staircase with the other. 'How on earth did you get up these every day at eight months?'

'The exercise was good for me.' She laughed.

'And those huge canvases. I hope you weren't expected to heave them around.'

The art on the walls looked very drab, as if someone had dragged a line of white canvases through a mud puddle and swirled the mud and dirt around in stripes and circles. The people inspecting the art were incredibly thin, excessively beautiful and expensively dressed. Almost everyone wore black, affected big, horn-rimmed spectacles and wafted aromas so powerful it smelt like the Harrods perfume counter. The women wore so much make-up she felt naked, even with Jessie's bright red score on her lips. These women had lipstick in deep shades of red bordering on black, with perfectly manicured nails to match. Every time they met someone new, there was endless air-kissing and cries of 'Darling!'

In Jessie's trail, Liz was introduced to one arty type after another. She was glad Jessie had dressed her; at least she didn't feel too out of place. She played the part for as long as she could, air-kissing people she didn't know, laughing, pretending to understand the art while being careful not to comment on it, making up stories about why she'd come to England, what she did at home.

'You seem to be having a good time, Mum,' Jessie said during a brief gap when there was no one to schmooze.

'I'm glad I came. I haven't had so much fun in a long time.' Surprised at herself, she realised she was having fun. For over an hour now, she'd been able to forget the real reason she'd come to London and it felt good. But making stuff up was getting exhausting. She was beginning to forget what story she'd told to whom. She was in danger of being found out.

'They're going to have the speeches now. But they won't last long – I hope.' Jessie pulled a face. 'Some artists find it hard to string two words together. Others start talking about themselves and can't stop.'

'My feet are getting sore. I wouldn't mind sitting down for a minute. Why don't I go over there?' Liz pointed at a black leather sofa in one corner.

'Good idea. I'll come and get you after the speeches. Then we can go home.'

Liz took her glass of wine off and sank into the soft reaches of the vast sofa, crossing her legs as elegantly as she could and affecting to study the nearest artwork. After a few moments, a young woman approached. Much younger than Jessie, she had an alarming arrangement resembling two knitting needles sticking out of a tightly coiled knot of hair at the nape of her neck. Tall, sleek, in black, of course, she had the leggy grace of a ballerina.

'Are you all right on your own there, sweetie?'

'Yes, perfectly, thank you.' Liz summoned up as much hauteur as she could muster. 'I thought I'd sit out the speeches.

'Good idea,' the woman said and glissanded away.

The speeches started. It seemed the artist was fond of the sound of his own voice. Liz put her glass down on the floor, rummaged in her bag and pulled out the letter from Steven she'd received that morning to fill in the time. She'd been surprised to receive it, not expecting him to write – he never wrote to Jessie; she always did that for him. The letter hadn't contained much news. Richard had a new play coming up at Downstage, a breakthrough at last. Steven had been out fishing with a friend from work and caught four kawahai and a snapper which he'd cooked for his tea; he'd smoked the other fish for her to enjoy when she got home. She could taste it now, the firm brown smoky flesh, and it made her wish she was home rather than in this strange place where she knew she was a bit like a fish out of water. She smiled at her own pun.

'Mum, I think we'll have to go.'

'Now?'

'Yes. We have to go!'

The urgency in her daughter's voice was telling. 'You're having contractions.'

Jessie winced. 'Yes. I've had two so far. Quite a bit of time between them, so we don't need to panic. But we do need to go.'

'Will you be all right to drive?'

'I think so. It's only about ten minutes away.'

'Have you told Michael?'

'Yes, I got the gallery to phone him at work. With a bit of luck he won't have left yet and he can go straight to the hospital. He'll catch the underground.'

'Lucky you've got your overnight bag in the car.'

'Mum, give me a break. It's not luck. I take it everywhere.'

Queen Charlotte's Hospital was more than ten minutes away, as it turned out, because the traffic was terrible.

'Just my luck to go into labour during evening rush hour,' Jessie wailed after another contraction hit her. 'We'll never get there.'

Liz was relieved when the fraught journey was over. Jessie was an impatient driver under normal circumstances; having contractions made her much worse, berating other drivers for crawling along at a snail's pace, waving her fist at another for cutting in on her, flicking her lights and pulling up so close behind she thought they'd bang into them. 'What are you waiting for? A Papal dispensation?' she shouted ineffectually at a driver who hadn't noticed the lights had turned green. But arrival at the hospital brought a terror of a different sort.

'You'll have to take the car through there to the parking area, Mum.'

'But I can't drive.'

'Don't be ridiculous, of course you can.'

'No, I never got my licence, remember?'

'Christ, don't tell me you never finished those driving lessons with Dad?'

'No, never. He got so cross with me I gave up on them.'

'Oh, God, that's all I need.' Jessie put her head down on her hands, which were resting on the steering wheel. 'I can't leave it here. They don't have valet parking at public hospitals, you know.'

Liz was furious with herself for not persevering with the lessons. If only Steven hadn't been so rude whenever she made a mistake. It wasn't her fault she'd broken the axle. Jessie had to get into the hospital, and that meant doing something with the damn car.

'I suppose I could get the car as far as the car-park if I tried. It's been a while since I drove, but it can't be that hard to remember.'

'Oh, Mum, would you?' Jessie looked up, relieved.

'I'll give it a try. We can't leave it here.'

'Thanks Mum.' Jessie was out of the car before Liz could change her mind, grabbed her overnight bag out of the back seat and took off, disappearing moments later through the main door of the hospital.

Liz got out, walked round to the driver's door and sat in the seat, terrified. What did you do? There was no clutch. Just a gear stick running in a straight line. She knew how they worked, she'd watched others often enough, but they'd never had an automatic at home. Steven preferred the manual; it gave you more control, he said.

Putting her foot on the brake, she slid the lever forward to the 'D' and slowly let go on the brake, like she'd seen Jessie do. The car jolted forward and stopped. Now she'd messed it up. She'd be stuck here forever.

She took it out of drive, turned the key in the ignition and tried again, a little more gently this time. Miraculously, the car edged forward, nice and slowly, and she steered towards the back of the building, round the corner to where the Parking sign pointed. It was all starting to come back to her, and it so was much easier without having to mess around with the clutch and gear stick all the time. The parking area was quite some way back but luckily you could just drive straight into the park. She'd never been able to master parallel parking on the street, especially not with Steven telling her she was doing it wrong all the time.

She even remembered to turn the headlights off.

Feeling extremely pleased with herself, she picked up her bag, locked the car and almost danced her way to the hospital entrance. Steven would never believe she'd done it. Nobody would. She could hardly believe it herself.

Her new-found confidence deserted her soon afterwards when Jessie asked if she'd like to watch the birth.

That was the last thing she wanted. 'I'm sure Michael will be here any minute, dear. I'm happy to hold your hand 'til then.'

'It could be a while, Mum. My waters haven't even broken yet.'

Jessie was sitting on the bed in a homely little room on the first floor. The pale lemon walls were hung with colourful framed botanical prints and the pale green curtains, drawn against the dark, had similarly flower-themed patterns. It was all very tasteful and bland.

'Maternity hospitals have changed a lot since my day,' she said, opening a side door and inspecting the ensuite. 'You had to walk down a corridor to the bathroom and there was no privacy like this.' It had been basic enough in Wellington; but it had been ten times worse in the Christchurch maternity hospital, where she'd been treated as some sort of pariah, one of the naughty girls having a baby out of wedlock. The naughty girls were kept away from the real mothers, the ones with husbands who waited nervously in the corridor outside, chain-smoking.

The door opened and Michael burst in, his jacket and tie askew. 'It was packed on the tube, I only just got on,' he said as he made a beeline for his wife and gave her a kiss. 'How are you? Does it hurt much?'

'Yes. But only every eight minutes. I've got a way to go yet.'

'Where's the midwife? The doctor?'

'She's on her way. A nurse checked me as soon as I came in and said they'll let my doctor know I'm in labour. Don't worry, Michael, everything's fine. It's all going to plan, so far.'

The plan went slightly awry when the baby still hadn't come by midnight, but soon after one, the contractions speeded up and Jessie was wheeled into the birthing room. Liz stayed behind.

'I'd rather stay here,' she insisted. 'This time is for you and Michael to share.'

She made herself a cup of tea and helped herself to a biscuit from the kitchen along the corridor then settled down in Jessie's room to wait in the big comfy chair next to the bed. The next thing she knew, she was being gently shaken awake by Michael.

'She's here,' he said.

'Who, Jessie?'

'Yes, Jessie, and …' He stood back so Liz could see the bed. '… Your granddaughter. Meet Emily Elizabeth Pearson.'

'Emily Elizabeth?'

'Yes, we wanted her to have your name too,' Jessie said, smiling beatifically from the pillows.

'Six pounds eight ounces,' Michael said proudly.

Liz stumbled to her feet, still half asleep, and approached the bed, narrowing her focus from Jessie to the tiny bundle in her arms. Wrapped tightly in a white cotton blanket, little Emily was wide awake, her blue eyes fixed on her mother. All she could see of her was her round little face and a tuft of fine dark curly hair – just like all her babies.

'She's got your eyes, Jessie. And your hair. You looked just like that when you were born.'

And so did Katharine. At birth, both girls had weighed exactly six pounds and eight ounces.

'Well done, Jessie. She's beautiful.' She felt a tug in her throat, as if she might choke. She swallowed quickly and stood back a little to achieve some distance from both mother and daughter.

'Your first grandchild.' Jessie was beaming.

'How was the birth?' Liz made herself sound business-like, determinedly unemotional. 'Was there much pain?'

'I'm afraid I said yes to pain relief. I didn't mean to, but it was so intense. Just at the end.'

'But it was only gas,' Michael added. 'You did so well.'

'And Michael rubbed my back when it hurt and held my hand when I screamed.' She smiled across at him; he was standing behind his wife, looking down on his family with such love Liz felt she could like him after all.

Suddenly she had a powerful urge to sit down. She couldn't hold back a low cry as she flopped down in the chair.

'Are you alright, Mum?'

'Yes, I'm fine. Just happy, that's all' She mustered a smile, though she didn't feel happy at all. Seeing Jessie holding her baby so tenderly, so close; it hurt. A lot.

She'd never felt that way with her babies. When Jessie was born, they handed her over and she'd looked at her as if she were a stranger. She was supposed to bond with her daughter, but she hadn't felt a thing; the baby didn't feel like she belonged to her, that she might be taken away at any moment, that she would never be truly hers.

If she loved Jessie, even for a moment, she risked the tremendous pain of losing her, of never holding her again. So there had been no love; no real love. She had filled her days with busyness – the nappies, the bottles, the washing, ironing, cleaning, baking and cooking dinners that Julia Childs would have approved of. The busyness had made up for the distance she had deliberately wedged between herself and Jessie, and then again with Richard two years later.

Watching Jessie with little Emily brought it all back, the unforgettable aroma of Johnsons baby shampoo and talcum when they nuzzled into you, the warmth and the deep, enduring trust.

'Would you like to hold her, Mum?' Jessie held the baby out towards her mother.

Would she? Could she? Perhaps it was time to make up for all those years of holding back? Perhaps now she could allow herself to love?

Jessie was looking expectantly at her. Grandmothers were supposed to cluck over newborns, to swoop them up in their arms and coo and gurgle like they'd lost their grasp of language. Come on, Lizzie, you can do it.

She took the baby from her daughter and held onto her, hesitantly at first, forgetting what it was like to hold something so fragile, so precious, so alive.

Emily started to wail.

'Don't you like your grandmother? Goodness, that's no good.' She held the baby away from her, distanced, unattached. Emily continued to wail, building up to a crescendo, her little face turning bright red. 'Here, you'd better have her back.' She handed her over, secretly relieved. 'She's not ready for me yet.'

'Oh, Mum, you've got to give her a chance.' Jessie took her baby and held her close. 'Perhaps she wants a feed. Do you want something to drink, little Emily?'

The baby's cries were piercing.

Jessie started to undo the buttons down the front of her nightgown and steered Emily in the direction of her breast. 'Here, that should help quieten you.'

Liz wasn't sure she was ready for this. She'd never breastfed her babies. It wasn't possible with Katharine, of course, then with the other two, the hospital had insisted on bottles and she'd been more than happy to go along with it. That was what almost all the other mothers were doing then too.

Watching her daughter and the ease with which she pulled aside her nightie and undid the front of her bra, it seemed the most natural thing in the world and so easy.

Jessie's smile turned to a wince. 'Ouch! I can see why you've got to be careful in these first few days. She latches on like a leech.'

Liz decided she'd seen enough.

'I think I'll pop out for a cup of tea. Would you like me to bring you one back?'

But the new mother and father were too absorbed to hear.

She escaped into the corridor and headed for the patients' kitchen, wishing she could keep on walking out the hospital door and go home. She longed to be back at Jessie's place, where she could climb into bed and escape for a while from babies, from memories. Suddenly, she felt very tired.

It seemed forever before she finally got to bed and the next day, she found it hard to get out of it again, dragging herself out only just before Michael came home.

She just couldn't face the trial of getting up, becoming part of a world that didn't seem to be her world, that was foreign; a world where mothers breastfed and bonded with their babies. So she hid under the covers, making patterns out of the flowers on the darkened wallpaper, watching the sunlight dimly trace its way through the blinds from one side of the room to the other.

The following day was the same. She stayed in bed, blinds drawn, only getting up at the time when Michael said he was bringing Jessie home from hospital.

He made several trips up and down the stairs, bringing in all Emily's and Jessie's paraphernalia then set about making them a cup of tea while Liz sat with her daughter on either side of the carrycot, watching over Emily.

'How are you getting on?' Liz asked.

'She's fine. My milk's started to come in and she's much more settled now. They said I'd be fine at home with her.'

'That's good. She looks very contented.'

'She is.' Jessie turned her attention away from the baby and looked across at her mother. 'It's you I'm worried about, Mum. Michael says you've been locked away in your room every day, not even getting out of bed. What's the matter with you?'

Liz was taken by surprise. 'Nothing. I'm okay. Just a bit tired, that's all. I think it must be the jet lag.'

'Jet lag? Don't be silly, Mum, you've been here nearly two weeks. There's something wrong, isn't there?'

'No. Nothing's wrong.'

'Is it something to do with Emily? Are you upset about being a grandmother? Does it make you feel old or something?'

'Heavens no. I'm thrilled to be a grandmother.'

'Then what is it? What's wrong?'

Liz looked away out the sash window at the leafy branches of the oaks lining the street. 'I don't know. I've been out of sorts for some reason. I'm sorry to be such a burden …'

'You're not a burden.'

'I am. This is such a happy time for you both. I'm just dragging you down. I'll get a flight home as soon as I can and get out of your hair.'

'Mum, you don't have to do that. You're welcome …'

'No, I should go. I think I'll come right when I get back home to Steven. He says it's much warmer now and he's been out weeding the vegetable garden nearly every day. I'll ring up the airline and book my flight tomorrow.'

Jessie tried to persuade her to stay but she was adamant: she'd be fine at home. It was time to go.

~ ~ ~

The plane took off from Heathrow on the first sunny day that week, climbing over the green hills and dales of Surrey before rising through the clouds to the eternal sunshine of thirty-three thousand feet. Her hands still smelt faintly of the 4711 eau-de-cologne lingering in the wet hand-towel the stewardess had handed her.

Liz pressed her nose against the plane's small oval window and peered down on the patchwork of grey roofs packed between roads jammed with traffic. They seemed much too close. Was the plane about to crash into the ground? She'd felt the same leaving Auckland, then Sydney and Singapore, Cairo and Rome, and it was even worse landing; she'd been terrified as the ground rushed up to meet the plane. But now, on the return journey, she was a seasoned traveller of some twelve-thousand miles, with another twelve-thousand ahead over the next two days.

The high-altitude sun warmed the side of her face, reminding her of the summer she was flying home to. She basked in it for a moment, eyes shut, trying to empty her mind from the disturbing, jumbling thoughts of London, as crowded and intrusive as the Bakerloo line at rush hour, while keeping at bay further disturbing thoughts of the new Adoption Bill.

The stewardess offered passengers in her row a drink. She asked for a gin and tonic so she could make it last for two drinks; she felt like drinking a whole bottle. Quickly, while she was fiddling with the miniatures and finding the tonic, Elizabeth reached down and pulled the last letter she'd written to Steve – and never sent - out of the black handbag Jessie had persuaded her to buy, releasing an aroma of new leather.

'Thank you,' she said, accepting the drink and juggled the plastic cup, the tonic bottle and the letter so they all managed to squeeze onto the tray table. She sipped the drink and nearly spat it out again it was so strong. After adding a little more tonic she opened the letter and started to read.

She'd said far too much, that was immediately obvious. All that stuff about Katharine; she must have been half way to the loony bin putting it down on paper. What was wrong with her? She had definitely not been herself in London. Jessie had noticed, had even asked her if she'd like to see the doctor. Was that why she'd written so freely about her babies – all three babies including Katharine? Or was it seeing Jessie with her new baby, the way she bonded so quickly, the unconditional love that shone through so clearly? Was she jealous of her daughter?

She sighed. Only three sips of gin and already she was feeling maudlin.

She turned the page.

She should throw it away, she knew that. But there was a strange attraction to the words on the page, words she'd never written before and certainly never spoken. Would it help her feel better, keeping those words, reading them again? She could lock the letter away in the secret compartment in her mother's mahogany escritoire. Or she could rip it up and throw the pieces in one of the rubbish bins at the stopover in Rome.

She took another swig of gin.

March 22, 1987

Mrs Elizabeth Davidson
109 Marine Parade
Eastbourne
Wellington.

Dear Mrs Davidson

I am researching my family tree and your name came up while sifting through some old Hamilton family papers. I am writing to you therefore to see if you can supply information about your branch of the family.

The name on my original birth certificate is Felicity Francis Hamilton. I was born in Christchurch on March 17, 1951. I am now 36 and will soon give birth to my second child. I would be most grateful if you could let me know about your line of the family and your children.

Yours sincerely

Katharine Stewart

Part 2: Rose

Chapter 1.

Christchurch, March 1951

There was a policeman in the nursery. Over six feet tall in sombre black serge and shiny silver buttons, he made a stark contrast with the wall frieze of brown baby rabbits romping across pastel meadows. Ducking his head under the low ceiling, he shifted uncomfortably from foot to foot, his outsized black boots marking an awkward dance pattern on the cream, rose-patterned rug.

So far, he'd been a man of few words, clutching his black round-topped helmet tightly to his chest as he'd followed the inspection party from room to room. It was as if he knew his presence was barely tolerated.

Rose couldn't see why his presence was necessary at all. Even though she'd been warned a policeman would be present, she still couldn't understand what a member of the local constabulary could add to the picture the Social Security Department was supposed to be building up on their suitability for adoption.

The Lady Inspector, hunched beneath the sloping ceiling, looked around disapprovingly. 'This room is very small for baby.' Her mouth remained a rictus of disapproval. 'And the roof comes down very low.'

'It's the only other bedroom apart from ours,' Rose said. 'George has worked hard to make it ready.' For weeks, he'd spent his evenings sanding and oiling the doors and skirtings, his fussiness and slowness driving her to distraction. She recalled the row over the frames round the dormer windows when he'd chipped away the wood by mistake and given up on the whole project.

'You can't stop now, for heaven's sake,' she'd cried the night he'd refused to get out his old clothes and return to the tiny box room, which remained a jumble of sandpaper, oil, brushes and paint tins on a stained and scarred wooden floor. She despaired of it ever becoming a nursery. But George stubbornly harboured a grudge against the window frame for almost a week before he conceded he might be able to fill the gouge and allow Rose's curtains to cover it.

The policeman remained just inside the door, the roof too low for him to come any further. George hovered behind, his expression one of suppressed irritation.

The Lady Inspector, Mrs Lowe – whom Rose had dubbed the Grey Invader ever since she announced herself at the front door half an hour ago dressed from head to toe in light grey – was making it clear, she was not going to be fooled, not for one minute. She plucked at each finger of her grey felt glove and pulled it off, giving the glove a fierce flick as she did so. Then holding out her index finger at an awkward angle, she ran it along the windowsill in the nursery, sniffing contemptuously at the few motes of dust she managed to dislodge.

Lips tightly pursed, she then proceeded to open all the drawers in the dresser.

'Hmm, towels, facecloths, nappies, feeders, muslin cloths.' She shut one drawer and opened another. 'Nightgowns, cardigans, hats, mittens, booties, woollen pants. Did you make these yourself?'

'Yes,' Rose answered. 'All of them.'

'Hmmm.'

Was this faint praise or faint disapproval?

'Baby may come with a layette from the mother, but you don't have to bother with that if you don't want to.'

'Oh, I'm sure it will be very fine and knitted with a lot of love.'

'Hmmm.' The Grey Invader's lips remained pursed as the bent over the bassinet, lifting the bedding piece by piece.

Rose had known this visit was imminent; she'd had a letter from the Department saying one of their lady inspectors would be coming to check the premises and the baby's things; but she'd had no idea exactly when the visit would be. Her friend Joan, who'd had the same experience when trying to adopt, had warned the inspection would be extremely thorough but not that it would be demeaning.

They passed from the baby's room to the bathroom, where the Grey Invader swooped on the claw-footed bath. 'This is far too large for bathing baby,' she said.

'I know,' Rose said. 'The baby bath is downstairs in the washhouse.'

'In the washhouse? You're surely not proposing to bath baby there?'

'No, of course not. I was planning to bath the baby in the kitchen. We have a new tin baby bath.'

Mrs Lowe craned her neck over the toilet bowl, which Rose knew was whiter than the new nursery sheets, then inspected the basin, turning on the tap and waiting for it to run hot. 'Yes, I suppose that will do,' she said, turning off the tap before removing the other glove and tucking them both into her small grey leather purse, which she clicked shut again with a loud snap. She made more notes on the official form. Attached to a cardboard-backed pad, the form had two long sheets of carbon paper so everything could be recorded in triplicate.

The whole time she was writing, the water pipes clanged and juddered – as they always did when the hot tap was turned off.

'That sounds like you've got a water hammer problem,' the policeman said, turning the tap on and off.

The pipes clanged again.

Rose winced.

'You've lost the air out of the pipes. I know just how to fix it – my brother's a plumber.' The policeman brightened at the prospect of making himself useful. He turned to George, who was standing in the doorway looking as though he'd like to escape. 'You need to shut off the water, Sir, then drain the pipes to refill the air chambers.'

'Is that right?' George looked even more uncomfortable. Rose knew fixing up the nursery, with its many frustrations and mistakes, was likely to be the full extent of his home improvements for some time.

The pipes had been making that racket since Rose's parents had built the house in a cow paddock on the outskirts of the city ten years ago. Her parents' two-storeyed house, with the flat she and George occupied attached to the side, was one of the first to be built in the area and had soon been accompanied by a row of big weatherboard homes, surrounded more recently by fledgling oaks and sycamores in the grounds of the neighbouring girls' school – the school where Rose hoped her baby girl, if it were to be a girl, might one day be a pupil.

Her mother and father had been waiting ten years for their only daughter to produce a grandchild. Rose was relieved to be living under the same roof as her mother. Her parents, and her father in particular, had become much frailer in the last year.

The Grey Invader asked to see Rose and George's bedroom.

Surprised, Rose stepped back. She hadn't expected that sort of inquisition again; surely the prying questions in Te Kuiti had been sufficient to convince the Department that they were unable to conceive. Steeling herself, she led the way through.

'I hope you won't be bringing baby in here with you.' Mrs Lowe peered at the pink puffy eiderdown covering the double bed.

'I wasn't thinking …'

'Good. It's not right for baby to sleep with the mother at night. Baby has to learn to be independent and look after himself. I'm pleased to see that new-fangled Dr Spock agrees.' She approached the bed and fingered the eiderdown. 'Do you and George sleep here?'

Rose looked at her husband.

George cleared his throat noisily. 'Yes, of course we do,' he said.

'And you always sleep together?'

Now it was the turn of the policeman to clear his throat. He then commenced a close inspection of the clothes brush on top of George's tallboy.

'Of course.' George sounded very measured.

'But you haven't been able to have a baby in, let me see, how many years is it?'

'Ten years,' Rose said quickly. She turned to her husband. 'Oh, George, I forgot to put the kettle on the hob for our tea. I'm sure Mrs Lowe and Constable Jennings would like a cup of tea soon?'

The constable nodded, clearly relieved to have an escape plan. 'Yes, that would be much appreciated.'

Mrs Lowe looked at her watch. 'Very well, then. Thank you.'

George excused himself and departed down the stairs; the constable put on a remarkable turn of speed and followed him. Rose could hear laughter as the sitting room door closed behind them.

She continued to show the Grey Invader through the rest of the house, each room an agony of niggardly criticism. The kitchen, which she proclaimed 'too small to swing a cat in', received close inspection and she asked a lot of questions about bottle sterilisation and formula preparation. Rose showed her the pantry.

'Goodness, I don't think I've ever seen quite so many preserves and jams laid aside since I came to town from the countryside four years ago. Very satisfactory.'

Rose quickly plucked a jar of blackboy peach chutney from the shelf and offered it to Mrs Lowe. 'This is from the tree in our back garden at Te Kuiti,' she said. 'It's for you.'

Mrs Lowe's tight-lipped expression relaxed momentarily into something approaching a smile. 'Very kind of you, Mrs Stewart, very kind indeed. But I'm afraid we're not allowed to accept gifts.' The semblance of a smile faded.

At last Mrs Lowe agreed she was done and was ready for a cup of tea. Rose took her through to the drawing room where Constable Jennings was standing in front of the picture window gazing out across the lawn. He smiled nervously at Mrs Lowe and more warmly at Rose.

'We share this room with my parents.' It was an easy arrangement, since her mother was now too unwell to entertain. Rose looked nervously at the door leading to her parents' side of the house. It wouldn't be a good time for her mother to pop in, although she was usually discreet when she heard Rose was entertaining.

As she entered, even the Grey Invader looked impressed. 'This *is* a nice room. Do you play the piano?' she asked as she ran her finger across the top of the keys.

'Yes. A little.'

'That's good. Baby needs to be stimulated. Some Mozart perhaps? Brahms? Schubert?'

Rose nodded. 'Yes.' It was true, she could play the classics; she didn't dare tell Mrs Lowe her favourite tunes came from the shows and the radio. 'And George has a fine tenor voice.'

'Ah.' Mrs Lowe's frosty demeanour was warming a little. 'A little lieder in the evenings perhaps? That will be good for baby.'

'Baby' was more likely to be hearing *Me and My Gal* than *Death and the Maiden* but Rose knew better than to say so.

'May I take your coat and hat?' Rose held out her hands. 'You might like to take a seat while I get the tea.'

Mrs Lowe slowly removed her coat, revealing a grey dress swirled across with washed-out green and mauve flowers and a grey cardigan. Nobody could say she hadn't spent a lot of effort ensuring her wardrobe was perfectly matched. Her stockings and shoes were grey, even her complexion was wan.

'Let me take that. Please, do sit down. You too, Constable Jennings. I'll only be a moment.'

The policeman shifted uncomfortably, looking around the room as if searching for a plain wooden chair to sit on rather than the deeply cushioned armchairs and sofas with their pink peonies and blue fleur-de-lis.

She hurried back into the tiny kitchen to take over from George, who had coaxed the kettle to boil on top of the range, sending him off to make polite conversation in the next room. By the time she'd made the tea, laid out the best cups, saucers, plates and cake forks, and retrieved the sponge from the cool safe just outside the back door, George and the constable were getting on very well: she could hear the laughter as she stood in the hall.

'Constable Jennings has two little ones, Rose,' George said when she entered with the tea tray – her mother's new silver one, laid with her own appliqued tray cloth. 'He was telling me about the mischief his two-year-old gets up to, teasing the cat and pulling its tail.'

'Perhaps we should get a kitten?' Rose had always fancied having a cat for her child to play with.

'Cat hairs are known to cause allergies,' Mrs Lowe said dismissively.

'Perhaps not then.'

Rose set about pouring the tea, cutting the cake, offering slices. Mrs Lowe declined; the policeman started to devour his piece immediately, the tiny silver cake fork dwarfed in his big sinewy hand.

'Delicious,' he said. 'I always thought my wife made a superb sponge, but I can see she could learn a thing or two from you, Mrs Stewart.'

'The farmers' wives in the King Country set the standard very high. We used to live there until we came to Christchurch just a month ago.'

George put the cake fork on his plate. 'Yes, the bank gave me a transfer. It's much easier for Rose now to be near her parents.' He fixed the policeman with a hard stare.

Rose felt a tremor of anxiety; George had that stubborn look on his face.

'Tell me, Constable Jennings, why is it that a policeman has to come on these visits? It seems a bit excessive to me – I mean, it's not as if we're common criminals.'

The policeman lowered his cake fork and swallowed, making his adam's apple bob up and down. 'It's certainly hard to fathom. I'm afraid I haven't a clue. They never tell us the whys and wherefores; they just tell us what we have to do.'

George turned to the Grey Invader. 'Do you know, Mrs Lowe?'

The Lady Inspector put down her cup and wiped her top lip on the dainty napkin Rose had embroidered for her trousseau. 'Adoptions have to be taken very seriously indeed,' she said. 'We can't have our babies going to just anybody. We have to make sure the families are thoroughly checked out and there are some things only the police can do.'

'And what are those things?' George asked.

Rose held her breath. There was an awkward moment's silence.

Even Mrs Lowe had the grace to look slightly uncomfortable. 'Well, for example, in case I needed protection,' she said, 'or in case the environment was, well, shall we say, unsuitable.'

Rose could see in an instant that George was intending to pursue this line of questioning and that it could all too easily end in disaster. 'More tea, Mrs Lowe?' she said quickly.

'No, thank you.'

'Constable Jennings?'

'Don't mind if I do.'

'And another piece of cake?'

'Yes please.'

As she turned away to cut another piece of sponge she gave George what she hoped was a warning look and held her fingers up to her lips. After handing the policeman his second helping she approached the Lady Inspector.

'Tell me, Mrs Lowe, is everything to your satisfaction? Do you think we will be approved again now we are in Christchurch?'

'I'm not allowed to say at this stage, I'm afraid. I have to make my report and the Department will let you know in due course.'

'But surely…'

Mrs Lowe held up her hand. 'I can't say.'

Rose sensed the atmosphere becoming tense.

'Let me show you the garden, Mrs Lowe. George, perhaps you and Constable Jennings would like to help yourselves to more tea and cake?' She led the way out the veranda door to her parents' big garden.

'This is good. There is plenty of room here for putting the perambulator outside in the afternoons.' Mrs Lowe turned to Rose. 'I hope that is what you are planning to do? Baby needs lots of fresh air. No matter what the weather, baby should have at least one nap every day in the fresh air.'

'Yes.' Rose wasn't so sure she'd be putting her baby out in the rain, hail and frost, but didn't raise it.

Glancing across at her parents' side of the house, she glimpsed her mother standing back from the sunroom door, clearly trying to be invisible. She waited until the Grey Invader was ahead of her then turned back and waved.

'Well I dare say that will do for today,' Mrs Lowe said when they returned to the veranda. I'll see if I can drag Constable Jennings away from the sponge cake.'

Rose thought she could detect a trace of a smile on Mrs Lowe's lips.

'I'm glad he liked it. Are you sure I can't tempt you…?'

'No thank you. If I accepted all offers of cake and scones, I'd never fit into babies' rooms as tiny as yours.'

Rose could have sworn that was another smile. 'No,' she said, smiling in return.

'You'll find that, once baby arrives, there will be another unannounced inspection, rather like this one. After that, the Department tends to leave it up to the Plunket nurse to report anything untoward.'

'Thank you.' Rose could hardly contain her excitement. Mrs Lowe had said 'Once baby arrives,' not 'If baby arrives'. That must surely be a good sign.

~ ~ ~

George was sitting in the passenger seat of her father's car looking miserable. Suddenly, he sneezed. 'I'm sorry, Rose.'

She drove the car through the gates of Essex Maternity Hospital. Backing onto the maternity home known around the town as a refuge for fallen women, it was located just a short drive from home in Essex Street in a long, white weatherboard building that had seen better days.

The hospital administrator rang for a nurse, who showed them to a waiting area in a corridor.

Rose smiled at the familiarity of the uniform, the crisp white pinafore nipped in at the waist, the starched white cap. It seemed such a long time since she'd worn it, when she'd just graduated as a fully registered nurse, imagining in her naivety that she'd wear it forever.

'The nursery is in there,' the nurse told them. 'Sister will be out shortly to take you in.'

George sneezed again.

'Oh dear, I'm afraid you won't be able to go in there with a cold like that,' the nurse said.

'But we're supposed to be taking her home today,' Rose said.

'I don't think Sister would approve. I'll see what she says.' The nurse disappeared into the nursery leaving Rose and George waiting anxiously outside.

After a few moments, another nurse came out.

'I'm Sister Marks,' she said to Rose, shaking her hand formally. She then looked suspiciously at George. 'Nurse has told me you have a nasty cold, Mr Stewart.'

'Yes, I fear so.' George put his hand to his mouth, trying to suppress a cough.

'Then I'm sorry but it would be wrong for you to take the baby home with you today.'

'Oh, but …' Rose felt crushed; she should have known better.

'I'm sorry, but it's not fair to expose a newborn to germs in her first few days. I can't let you take her until Mr Stewart's cold is better.'

'I'm sorry Rose.' George looked abject. He knew how much this meant to her – to both of them.

'Can we at least see her, then?'

'*You* can come in, Mrs Stewart, of course. You can hold her if you like.'

'Yes, please.' Rose looked across at George, who was staring at the floor, then followed Sister Marks into the nursery, tip-toing past a row of little cots to one in the far corner with a pink blanket tucked neatly into the sides. Lying there on her back, big blue eyes gazing about her, was the dearest little girl with curly dark brown hair and a chubby face covered with tiny spots and blotches.

'Her complexion will soon clear,' the nurse said when Rose approached the cot. 'She's also got a small pressure mark on her forehead – it's hidden by her wee bonnet - but that will go quick enough.'

'Is the pressure mark from …?' Rose hesitated. She wasn't sure how to put it. 'Was it a difficult birth?'

The nurse shook her head. 'I don't know.'

'I mean, the young mother, is she all right now?' As soon as she said it, Rose realised it was a stupid question. Of course the mother wasn't all right. How could she be all right when she'd just given her baby away to another woman, the baby she'd carried for nine months and delivered after a hard labour? Rose had seen women giving birth when she was a nurse; she knew how painful it could be. And she knew how emotional the mother became after delivery.

'I'm sorry, Mrs Stewart, we're not allowed to say anything of the mothers.'

'Of course, I should have remembered that.'

'Would you like to hold her now?' The nurse unwrapped the blanket and sheet and picked up the baby, covered her with a shawl and handed her to Rose.

The second the nurse lifted the baby up, she started to cry, but as soon as Rose held her in front of her face and made contact with those big staring eyes, the baby stopped crying and gazed at her.

'Hello Katharine,' she said, ignoring the red spots and the bright red birthmark. 'You're beautiful to me.' Rose held the tiny form, careful to cradle her head in the crook of her hand as she'd been taught.

Unexpectedly, she felt a warm rush, as if her blood, her entire being, was surging towards this tiny baby, wanting to make it her own. It was such a strong, overpowering, uncontrollable urge she was frightened. It felt as if she might drop Katharine any minute.

'Are you all right?' The nurse must have noticed her hesitancy.

She pulled the baby closer to her and held tight, lifting Katharine's head up so she was looking straight into her unfocused, unblinking, trusting blue eyes. Rose took a deep breath. There was the most wonderful smell of new linen and baby soap. 'I wish George could hold her.'

'I'm afraid not. Not yet.'

'We've waited so long for this day.'

The nurse visibly softened. 'Tell you what, I've just the thing.'

She hurried over to a set of drawers at the far end of the room, rustled around for a few moments, disappeared out into the corridor then reappeared with a bewildered-looking George in tow. Ushering him over to a spot beside the door, she handed him a pair of field glasses.

'There. You can see your new baby girl close up now,' she said, smiling. 'Just don't come any closer.'

George accepted the binoculars and held them to his eyes.

Rose held the baby out towards him.

'Look, Katharine, there's your new Daddy.'

George took a moment focusing the glasses. 'I say, Rose, she's lovely.'

Katharine started to cry.

'It's getting near time for her four-hourly feed,' the nurse said. 'I'd invite you to stay and feed her, but with your husband …'

'It's all right, I understand.'

~ ~ ~

Rose drove George back to the bank then took herself home. She'd learnt to drive as soon as they'd arrived back in Christchurch; she didn't trust George's driving skills any more after a frightening incident up north where he'd nearly driven off the road.

Driving lessons with her father had required infinite restraint. Fastidious, far from patient, Jim Stewart was known for his meticulous attention to detail. Even after his retirement nearly twenty years ago, he'd remained finicky, criticising her mother's housekeeping if it didn't meet his strict criteria and complaining over the newspaper about the way the Mayor was running the city. He'd become an inveterate writer of letters to the editor, exclaiming with displeasure whenever another letter-writer disagreed with his point of view and hurrying to his study to pen a reply.

Doubling the clutch was the hardest task to grasp. Rose didn't think she would ever get it right and her father's brusque impatience didn't help. Every time she crunched the gears, he'd grunt and throw his hands in the air, which only made her more nervous and crunch the gears again.

'I'll never get to my club at this rate.' He blocked his ears at the terrible grating noises under the floor.

Rose pursed her lips. She'd had enough. 'I can fix that for you, Father,' she said after a moment. 'I'll drop you off at the club and drive myself home.'

'But you can't drive.' He was spluttering now.

'I'll be fine.' What she meant was, she'd be fine without him, but she didn't say so.

He looked across at her, scratched his head, opened his mouth to say something, thought better of it, scratched his head again and said, 'All right then. But if you crash the car…'

'I'm not going to crash the car. And if you telephone home when you're finished at the club, I'll come and get you.' She spoke firmly, brooking no argument.

Still looking perplexed, he agreed then sat in silence as she drove him along Park Terrace, turned left by the Museum and dropped him at his club overlooking the Avon River. He didn't even comment at the noise when she changed down to turn the corner in front of the Museum and only winced when she did it again outside his club.

Shaking his head and muttering 'We'll see, we'll see,' he climbed down from the car, gathered his hat from the back seat, put it on and walked the short path up to the imposing oak and glass doors with their gold-embossed 'Members Only' lettering.

Rose watched him enter then, with a determined expression, put the car into first and slowly let go the clutch. At the corner, she managed the complicated double compression of the pedal without any problems and from there it was easy.

She smiled to herself as she drove back down Park Terrace and followed the Avon home.

Back inside the flat, empty-handed, with George at work, Rose spent the rest of the afternoon trailing disconsolately around the house, returning again and again to the tiny nursery, trying to find something to do. She had arranged everything so she could be completely free to enjoy their new baby for the afternoon.

Her mother, who had planned an afternoon tea party with her two sisters to show off the new baby, put the aunts off 'until further notice' and tried to console Rose with a gift of the tin filled with queen cakes, intended for the party.

'I'll make something else for the homecoming,' her mother said. 'Queen cakes must have been unlucky.'

But Rose didn't want to eat. She didn't want to do anything.

~ ~ ~

It was three days before George got rid of his cold.

'Welcome to your new home, Katharine,' Rose's mother said as she carried her new baby up the steps to the front porch. 'And welcome to the new parents,' she added as George came up behind Rose, carrying the tiny bag of the baby's belongings from the hospital.

Rose thought she could detect a slight mist on her mother's steel-rimmed spectacles, a trace of a tear in her eye, but didn't say anything. Her mother had been asking for a grandchild ever since she and George had married, but with decreasing frequency as the years had passed. It had only been since her return to Christchurch – and the visit of the Grey Invader – that Rose had sensed a renewal of hope. After months of holding back on any mention of babies, her mother had hesitantly broached the subject, a bit like Mrs Lowe: 'When the baby arrives', rather than 'if'. And when Rose had suggested a shopping trip to Ballantynes baby department, it had been impossible for her mother to contain her excitement.

Neat, petite, always buttoned up to the neck in high collars and demure down to the floor in long, tailored skirts, her unruly, wavy hair pulled back in a tight, disciplined bun, Mother had always been her role model and guide in everything domestic and in understanding and perpetuating the social graces. There had never been any question about it: Rose had always done what her mother decreed. Even when she had desperately wanted to enrol to be a nurse, her mother had said she was too young and, obedient as ever, Rose had trained to be a secretary instead, only taking up nursing after she'd turned twenty-one.

As she stood on the front porch holding her new baby out to her mother for approval, Rose was overwhelmed with happiness; all she could do was smile.

Her mother stroked the baby's cheek with her little finger. 'She is adorable.'

'I know,' was all Rose could say.

'Well, don't just stand there, Rose. Come in. Come in.' Mother hurried her through the door. 'Doris has just made the tea. And I've made louise cake for the party.' She turned to Katharine. 'Yes, it's your first afternoon tea party, you beautiful little girl.'

In a daze, Rose was ushered into the drawing room she shared with her mother and served tea and slices of cake after Katharine was lifted from her arms and handed to her grandmother and then grandfather. Rose gave her up without protest; she felt as if she were in a dream and she would wake up any moment to see the Grey Invader back again.

'Rose, dear?' Her mother drew her aside. 'You've forgotten to thank your aunts for their gifts.'

Returning to her senses, she returned to the party at once to make amends, perching on the arm of Aunt Doris's chair. 'Thank you for your beautiful matinee jacket,' Rose said. 'Your knitting is so fine. Not like mine. I seem to drop stitches without even noticing.'

'Thank you, dear,' Doris said absent-mindedly. She was absorbed in her new great-niece, all of fifty years younger, who was fulfilling everyone's very high expectations by gurgling contentedly in her great-aunt's arms.

When they'd picked Katharine up from Essex Maternity Hospital, she'd been crying but the journey in the car had pacified her and she'd seemed contented ever since. It was as if Katharine knew how important it was to impress her grandmother Amelia and two aunts, Doris and Lottie. If she kept this up, she'd never be short of babysitters or of a ready supply of crocheted, knitted and hand-sewn garments.

It was even better that she was behaving so well for Aunt Doris. The maiden aunt could be more than a little prickly at times, but once you'd won her over, she was a staunch ally. Rose was never quite sure whether Doris was her ally or adversary, but she seemed fully engaged with Katharine. She waited until Aunt Doris's interest was waning.

'It's Aunt Lottie's turn now,' she said, taking her daughter from one aunt and handing her to the other. She was beginning to wonder if she would have any time herself with her baby.

While Aunt Lottie cradled the baby in her arms, Rose dutifully passed the tea and cake, helped her mother refill the shining silver teapot from the tall silver jug – all the best tea things had been polished for the occasion – and reassured

George, who was worried about establishing Katharine's routine in her new home.

'It's only twenty past three,' she said. 'She's not supposed to have her next feed until four and she's wide awake. She's fine.'

'Of course she's wide awake. She's being passed from pillar to post,' George said, looking quite pleased, nevertheless, that his daughter was the centre of so much attention. 'But shouldn't she be having her afternoon sleep?'

'I don't think so,' Rose said, feigning authority. She really didn't have the faintest idea. She'd read the Truby King book from cover to cover, but there was no chapter on the etiquette for the first day you brought your baby home from the hospital, especially when it was the first time you'd fully met her.

Aunt Lottie was signalling her over. 'Can you please take her now, dear? I'm not as young as I was.' Lottie, as tall and thin as Doris was short and plump, had never been overly fond of children, had never had any of her own although she and her sea-faring husband Donald had been married forever, whereas the maiden Aunt Doris was positively besotted with babies.

Rose took Katharine back and snuggled her into her shoulder, breathing in the newness of her, the scent of Pears soap and talcum powder, rubbing her cheek against the soft two-ply baby wool of her tiny knitted bonnet. Her daughter wriggled in her arms and straightened her tiny body, cried out a few times then relaxed back in her mother's arms.

Suddenly, Rose was aware of an overpowering odour.

'Oh dear, I'm going to have to change her,' she said.

'There you are Em, there's your first job as a grandmother.' Aunt Doris grinned at Rose's mother Amelia – whom she and Lottie always called Em – with what Rose suspected was a touch of malevolence.

'Goodness, it's a long time since I've had to deal with one of those. I think I'll pass,' her mother said. 'Good luck, Rose!'

Rose took her upstairs to the nursery. The towelling changing cloth was laid out on a small table, ready for its first use. She'd practiced often enough on a stiff-limbed doll; could she manage it with a real baby?

Terrified of hurting her, she settled Katharine on the soft cream towel, whereupon she started to cry.

'Shhh, little one. It's all right.'

The baby cried louder.

She undid the two nappy pins on either side so the nappy was laid flat, ready for removal. But unlike the doll, the baby wriggled constantly, kicking her legs at just the moment Rose was going to remove the dirty nappy.

The smell was revolting. Rose thought for a moment she was going to be sick. What sort of a mother was she, if she couldn't cope with a little baby poo? She wiped the wet flannel across the baby's chubby white bottom, whereupon the crying reached a crescendo and Katharine stomped her tiny, bootie-clad foot down in the mess, covering the new white wool in sticky yellow-brown poo.

'Oh, no!' She was so stupid; she should have seen that coming. Any mother would have known to watch out for it. Quickly, she plucked off the bootie, dropped it in the bucket to deal with later and reapplied the cloth to the wee bottom several times until she'd cleaned every last ounce of the mess. The flannel joined the bootie in the bucket then she folded up and whipped out the dirty nappy with one hand while holding the baby's legs with the other, dropped the dirty nappy in the bucket, and plucked a clean nappy from the pile. At that same instant, Katharine gave another mighty kick and dislodged the baby powder and nappy pins off the side of the table onto the floor.

'Oh dear, this isn't going too well. How am I supposed to pick them up while holding on to you? I don't think I can.'

After pausing for a moment, trying to work out how to manage this seemingly insoluble problem, she figured she'd have to let the baby go, dive down to pick up the things off the floor and bob up again, hopefully before Katharine plunged off the side of the table. She was terrified. She'd only been a mother for two short hours and already she was incompetent. Luckily, her plan worked.

'There you are, my sweet. All done.' The talcum was applied, the clean nappy was pulled up just the way she'd practiced, all she had to do was fix the jolly pins into the cloth – a task that was apparently impossible, as the layers of thick white towelling puckered up into an impenetrable mass that the pin simply refused to pass through.

It hadn't been this difficult practicing with the doll. But then the doll didn't wriggle and cry the whole time.

'Ouch!' She didn't know nappy pins could hurt so much. Twice. She could feel tears of frustration pricking against her eyes. Meanwhile Katharine kicked and cried, her little face turning quite red with the effort, making the small oval birth mark on her temple and all the tiny milk spots blend into the background. She looked quite fearsome. Kate was terrified.

After much manoeuvring, Rose finally snapped the second pin into place, pulled on the woollen pants and picked up this wee stranger who was by now bellowing so loudly she thought she'd go deaf.

'Let's find you another little bootie to wear. We can't let your foot get cold.' She fetched another one from the drawer, put Katharine back down on the table, tied on the bootie, and carried her downstairs to the kitchen, where she found her mother busily heating a bottle in a double boiler. The baby continued to cry lustily; quite different from the sweetly compliant baby at the tea party.

Rose's mother held out the warmed bottle. Katharine seemed to sense it because the crying reduced to an occasional whimper. 'Here you are, dear. All ready for Katharine's first feed.' Then she turned to her new granddaughter and smiled, with a wistful, far-away look. 'She's so beautiful Rose, even when she's been crying. She looks just like you did when you were a baby.'

'You can't mean that?' Rose thought her mother must be trying to make her feel Katharine was really hers. But Katharine would never look like her, would never be her flesh and blood. Rose faced a lifetime of never knowing what her daughter's mother was like, or whether Katharine would follow any of her birth mother's traits and characteristics.

She wondered how it must feel to have to give your baby away to strangers and never know how she would fare. She'd asked again at the hospital, trying once more to find out whatever she could about the mother. But they'd refused to tell her a thing. And the Department was just as tight-lipped. All she could discover was that the mother was about eighteen, was from Wellington, and had returned without seeing her baby. It made her shiver with fear – and guilt – just to think about it. Blocking it from her mind, she clutched Katharine closer and made a quick, silent promise that she would never let her down.

'It's true,' Mother said. 'I wouldn't tell you wrong.'

'But she's not my …'

'Hush. She is.' Her mother looked so certain, so joyfully certain, that Rose thought she could almost believe it.

She took the bottle gratefully and turned to go back upstairs, then hesitated. 'Do you think I should take her back in the sitting room with the aunts and feed her there? Or should I take her upstairs again to the living room?'

'Whatever you think is right, dear.'

'Well, they said I should establish a routine right from the start.' Rose took the bottle and held it up to her daughter. 'Is this what you want?' Katharine started to wriggle and cry again. 'I'm not supposed to feed her for another fifteen minutes yet.'

'Heavens, dear, I wouldn't worry about a few minutes either way. Surely it's not as regimented as that?'

'The Matron at the hospital said that routine was important. She said "Baby must not dictate to you. You must remain in charge." I don't like to disobey at the very first feed.'

'I'm sure you'll find by the time you get settled with her in a chair, your fifteen minutes will nearly be up.'

A burst of laughter drifted through from the sitting room.

'I don't like to leave them on their own,' Rose said. 'Perhaps I'd better feed her in there, so they can see her?'

'Don't worry about them. They can keep themselves amused.'

Rose took the baby upstairs, which was just as well. Katharine proved as difficult feeding as she was having her bottom cleaned. She refused to settle and rejected the rubber teat every time she held it in front of her, turning her head away and crying all the more fiercely.

Rose felt close to tears. 'I'm a hopeless mother,' she said to her daughter. 'You'd have been better off with someone else. I've got no idea how to do this.'

Katharine kept crying.

Rose shook a little bit of milk on her finger. It felt just the right temperature, just as it had after she'd practiced these past weeks to get it right. She tried again. Still the baby turned her mouth away.

'I'm sorry, Katharine. Perhaps I should have called you by the name your birth mother wanted for you. Perhaps I shouldn't have changed you out of her layette. Perhaps I shouldn't have bought the perambulator before you were born, like Aunt Doris said. She said it was bad luck to do that. She said I should have waited. Oh dear, I don't know what to do.'

Suddenly Katharine stopped squirming and was calm and still. Her lips nuzzled the teat and sucked it into her mouth. The crying ceased. The only sound was that of the baby sucking at the teat, swallowing the milk. The sound of contentment.

Perhaps she wasn't going to be such a bad mother after all.

Chapter 2.

Te Kuiti, January 1951

Rose nearly missed the letter announcing she and George had been approved for adoption. If she hadn't found it by chance, days after its delivery, they might never have been able to adopt, passed over by the Department in favour of a couple capable of responding by the due date.

The envelope was lying hidden in the agapanthus beneath the letter box. She was in the garden cutting flowers for a table arrangement when she'd spotted it under the leaves, down where the snails had chewed their way across the neat cream square, cutting a trail of tiny holes through the handwritten address, leaving a winding line of silvery slime.

She'd asked George to fix the catch on the letter box some months ago. But George was a dreamer, she'd realised that long ago, long before their pared-down wartime wedding. Ask him the minutest detail about the Battle of Hastings or who issued the first banknote, he could tell you without a moment's hesitation. But fix a letter box? Not a chance.

She bent down to pick it up. Sure enough, the postmark was nearly two weeks old; the envelope had been feeding the snails for at least a week. It was addressed to Mr and Mrs George Stewart, Ward Street, Te Kuiti, in neat handwriting and bore an official government stamp.

A government stamp!

She let go her basket, heedlessly scattering the flowers and secateurs across the path, and slid open the back flap carefully. She had a feeling this would be a letter to keep.

'Dear Mr and Mrs Stewart,' she read. 'It is my pleasure to inform you that you have been selected to adopt a baby. At this stage, the baby we have selected for you is due to be born in two months' time. . .'

She could read no further. Ignoring the strewn roses and secateurs, she ran up the path, plumped herself down on the front doorstep and absent-mindedly pulled her handkerchief out of her pocket before holding the letter up, turning it over, waiting for it to vaporise into the mirage she feared it might be. But it remained very real. She read it again, expecting at any moment there would be a catch, that this precious gift could be taken away with a 'but' or a 'maybe'. But there were no conditions, no qualifying clauses. The baby was to be theirs, providing they responded to the Department within ten working days.

She gasped. That was today!

Without stopping to think, without even powdering her nose or checking her lipstick, she pocketed the letter, ran inside and grabbed her purse then ran out the door, dashed down the path, along the street, over the railway line and all the way down the main road until she reached the Union Bank, totally breathless but not caring. She pushed her way through the big, heavy wooden doors and searched around for her husband. He wasn't at his usual teller window. Where was he? Was he at lunch perhaps? More likely, he'd be talking banknotes with his friend Charlie Bates, forgetting about his lunch entirely.

The hands on the bank's enormous Roman numeral clock read twenty-five to one. He should still be here.

'Hello, Mrs Stewart. Are you looking for George?' It was Mr Smythe, the manager. Her heart sank as she realised she was breaking the rules. It was not the done thing for a bank wife to turn up at the banking chamber and harass her husband during banking hours.

Well, too bad. She had important news. She steeled herself. 'Yes, Mr Smythe. I'm sorry to trouble you, but I'm afraid I have some urgent news. Would it be possible to see George for just a minute please?'

Mr Smythe's thick black moustache quivered with irritation and his brow furrowed as he swept past the long counter, pulled his key chain from his pocket and unlocked the distant door to reach the offices beyond.

All the bank tellers seemed to be looking at her; in the aftermath of her outburst to Mr Smythe, she felt silly and a little embarrassed. Her news seemed insignificant compared to the important financial transactions occurring all around her. She slunk over to one of the writing counters fixed to a rear pillar and tried to appear invisible. Time passed. She was just about to leave, feeling really intrusive by now, suspecting that Mr Smythe had deliberately forgotten all about her, when George came through the far door and hurried over to her, looking perplexed.

'Whatever are you doing here, Rose?' he said, taking her by the elbow and steering her towards the exit. 'You know Mr Smythe doesn't like it.'

'I know, George, but I've got some good news.' By this time he'd pushed open the door to the street and was ushering her through it. She waited until they were on the pavement, turned to him and seized both his hands. 'We're going to be given a baby. We've been selected for adoption.'

'We have? Really?'

Rose nodded.

'How do you know?'

She produced the envelope out of her pocket. 'This arrived in the mail. Look.' She handed it over to him and watched while he read, smiling as he smiled, nodding as he shook his head in apparent disbelief.

'It's wonderful news for you, Rose. After all this time, you've finally got there. You've made it to the top of the queue.'

'Not just me, George. You too. This is addressed to both of us.'

A look of concern crossed his face. 'But it's mostly been you that wanted it.'

'But you do too, don't you?'

'Well, yes, but…' George looked away up the street, seemingly avoiding her gaze.

'But what? Don't say you've changed your mind after all this time?'

'No, I haven't changed my mind. It's just a bit sudden, that's all.'

'Sudden? We've been married for ten years this month. This isn't sudden.' She held up the letter again, waving it, demanding his attention again. 'What is it George, what's troubling you?'

He shrugged. 'I don't know. It's just a big responsibility, taking on somebody else's baby.'

'Isn't that what you wanted? What *we* wanted?'

He turned back to her, wiped his brow and smiled. 'Yes, of course. It's just now that it looks as if it's really going to happen, I hope we're up to it, that's all.'

She took his hands and placed them on her shoulders, pushing herself into his arms.

'Of course we can do it,' she said quietly. 'I'll make sure everything's fine. You won't have to worry about a thing.' She decided not to tell him about the deadline. She could phone the department herself, as soon as she got home.

He gave her a comforting squeeze then looked at his watch and said, 'I'd better be getting back to work or Mr Smythe will dock my pay.' So Rose slipped the letter in its envelope, stuffed it back in her pocket, kissed her husband goodbye and walked on air all the way back home to find the path strewn with roses, the front door still wide open and her neighbour Mrs Abercrombie's cat up on her bench sniffing around the butcher's parcel from the morning's shopping.

She didn't care. Normally, she would have shooed it outside straight away. Today, she undid the paper parcel and cut a small portion off for the cat, smiling as she fed it to him.

'George won't miss that tonight,' she said. 'He'll have a lot more important things to think about.'

After she'd phoned the department – worrying about how much the phone bill would be for spending so long waiting for the woman who'd written the letter to come on the line – she turned on the radio and set about preparing dinner. Frank Sinatra was singing *Some Enchanted Evening;* she turned up the volume and sang along.

Rose had enjoyed their six years under the wide-open skies and warm summers of the King Country. For the first time since the nurses' hostel, where she'd been surrounded by dozens of trainee nurses and formed close friendships among those in her group, she'd found the women from both town and country welcoming and easy to get on with. In particular, she'd become close friends with the other bank wives, Bea and Sally.

Not that she had much time for socialising. She'd persuaded George to let her take on two private nursing patients – a young woman confined to a wheelchair and an elderly lady who needed help with showering three mornings a week – just a few hours each, but enough to keep her hand in.

Old Mrs Rutherford was always trying to get Rose to stay longer, do more than just shower her and Rose would try to be as accommodating as she could. But if she delayed her much after ten-thirty, Rose knew the cuts of meat she wanted and the freshest vegetables for George's dinner would be sold out before she walked back into town. She'd tried to fit in the old dear's demands by arriving early, but she only added more tasks to her list of chores. Just yesterday morning, Rose had taken a firmer line.

'How would it be if I arrived after ten in the morning, Mrs Rutherford?' she'd said. 'Then I'd be able to get the shopping done on the way here. I could get yours too if you like. But coming here first and spending all the extra time with you, I miss out.'

She could see the old dear weighing up her options: having her shopping done three mornings a week or having to wait until after ten before she could be assisted out of bed and showered.

'It's all right, Nurse. Don't you worry about me.' Mrs Rutherford took on the martyred air she was so adept at. 'I wouldn't want to put you out. You come at half-past-eight as usual. I won't keep you past ten.'

Rose would find out tomorrow if her ploy would work.

She enjoyed the long walk to Mrs Rutherford's cottage at the roadside entrance to her son's big farm. A widow, with no daughter-in-law to help her, Mrs Rutherford was lonely and in need of both social and physical aid. Rose didn't mind listening then dismissed the chatter and let her mind wander freely on the walk home.

Her new-found pleasure in walking for miles exploring the surrounding countryside had unleashed her creativity: she'd started writing poetry - bad poetry, she suspected, but poetry nevertheless.

'The Mangakino softly slips between the silent stones …' She whispered it to herself, emphasising the sibilants, smiling at the memory of the picnic she and George had at the stream surrounded by bush and birdsong.

She was under no illusion about her poems. But there was something about the endless space after the city, the unbelievable greenness of the bush, the hills and pastures after living through dry summers on the Canterbury Plains and negotiating the narrow windy streets of Wellington. She didn't remember ever being so contented since she'd passed her exams and become a fully qualified, fully employed registered nurse.

Her marriage to George – a quiet affair at her family church St Mary's, Merivale, with no bridal finery and no attendants because of wartime austerities – had meant an end to nursing, a decision that she embraced without question, while harbouring an unspoken desire to return.

She had made no secret of her ambitions when she'd been going through her three-year training at Christchurch Public. All the other nurses were in awe of Matron but not Rose.

'You're too bold,' her friend Joan told her. 'You shouldn't have buttonholed Matron like that in the corridor. You didn't even have you hands behind your back.'

'She's not God, you know.'

'She is around here!' Joan tittered nervously.

'Well somebody had to ask her. I'm not going to let injustice lie.'

'She doesn't even know who we are.'

'She will one day.' Rose folded her arms. 'I'm going to work my way up the rungs on the nursing career ladder until I get to the top. One day, I'll be Matron, you wait and see.'

'I don't believe you!' Joan put her arm around Rose's shoulder. 'I thought you wanted to get married and have babies. You can't do both.'

'I'll think of a way.'

When George had finally been sent to New Caledonia with the 2nd New Zealand Expeditionary Force to man the heavy artillery – his early enlistment long delayed after he was run over by a taxi on Lambton Quay, his broken leg refusing to mend for months – she'd been manpowered, first as the secretary to the Director of Maternal Welfare and then in charge of a ward in the Clearing Hospital on Aotea Quay. Once again, she could put on the uniform she loved: the uniform of a nurse. Once again, she could wear her hard-won red, white and blue Registered Nurse pin and perform the well-practiced tasks involved with caring for the sick and maimed. It had only been a few months since her marriage, a few short months of married life before George had been called up, meaning she'd hardly lost any time out of the nursing service; returning to it was like slipping on her soft pigskin gloves: comfortably familiar.

For four years during the War, Rose had been seconded to various posts around Wellington, nursing both soldiers and civilians, who didn't stop getting sick and injured just because there was a war on. But it was the Clearing Centre she never forgot. It was there that the soldiers were brought straight off the troop ships after suffering, sometimes for weeks at sea with only temporary relief and often indifferent treatment.

The Clearing Centre was set up in a large, long white tent next to an empty warehouse on the quayside. Each time a ship docked, Rose and the other nurses would line up behind the medical officers and wait, suture trays and bandages at the ready, for the wounded to disembark. On crutches, on stretchers, sometimes walking unaided, they would arrive, overwhelming the hospital facilities, so that the gurneys would line up at the entrance, each containing a man who had once been whole, healthy, unencumbered by dressings, unbloodied by war and untroubled by the demons that seemed to haunt them night and day.

After several months, Rose lost count of the number of ships docking, the men blurring into one another, their injuries and nightmares merging into an overriding, all-encompassing horror that she survived only by committing it to prayer nightly, waking up the next morning to face it all again.

There was one soldier, however, who was harder to forget.

Towards the end of a line of new arrivals, Rose pulled back the calico curtains around a cot and recoiled in shock.

It wasn't the extent of the man's injuries – she'd seen much worse before. His eye had been blown out and shrapnel had embedded in his chest and upper arm. He'd been treated at a field hospital and made comfortable for the long voyage, but his dressings were badly overdue for replacement. She was busy assessing the bandages she would need to fetch for the doctor when she realised she knew him.

'It's Joe Doyle!' She covered her mouth with her hand. It had just slipped out.

Joe was her friend from school, from primer four. She and Joe used to play in the sandpit together, used to dig holes to Ireland and build igloos to hide from polar bears.

The man opened his remaining eye and tried to pull his bruised mouth into a smile. 'Rosie,' he said in a whisper.

Rose had been dreading this moment, of finding a familiar face in the next cot. But Joe's face was barely familiar. It was so disfigured, he was hardly recognisable. If it hadn't been for his bright red hair and stand-out freckles, she could easily have missed him, regarded him as just another soldier.

He'd not stayed in the Clearing Centre long, only a few days, but while he was there, Rose spent as much time with him as she could, listening to his dreams of getting home to his mother and father in Christchurch, telling him he would be there soon. Of his war experiences, of how he came to be injured, he said nothing.

Most of the injured troops had been shipped home from the front in North Africa where many had been since the start of the War. Few came from the Pacific, where George had been posted, which gave Rose comfort.

Letters came from him sporadically – sometimes there would be several in a month, sometimes none. She had no idea exactly where he was when he wrote – all that information was top secret until the War was over and it was only after he returned she learned he'd been in New Caledonia. He came home once on leave – a tense and terrible time, knowing he had to return so soon – and it was another year before she saw him again, when he was invalided home in 1944.

The War years were the only part of George's life hidden from her. He refused to speak of it. He'd kept nothing from those years except a fine pencil drawing one of the men in his battalion had done of him – a remarkable likeness – and an official publication about the 2nd Expeditionary Force the army had sent him last year. Rose had never seen him open it and she didn't like to read it without his permission.

George refused to tell her what he was supposed to be recuperating from. He seemed perfectly fine, if a little quieter than before. The only indication there was anything wrong with him was his left leg, which was at least an inch shorter than his right one, a result of the complex fracture that had refused to heal for so long.

She would never forget the evening, not long after the War had started, when Matron summonsed her to her office to tell her the news.

'You'd better sit down, Nurse.' Miss Widdowson looked her usual daunting self, unsmiling, unfailingly severe.

Rose sat, wondering what it was she had done wrong.

'I received a telephone call just now from the Matron of Wellington Hospital.' She looked at Rose over the top of her glasses.

Rose was perplexed. What did Wellington Hospital have to do with her nursing career? Was she to be offered a position there?

'It seems that your fiancé, Mr George Stewart, has been admitted to hospital …'

Rose gasped, covering her mouth with her hand.

'… with a fractured tibia and fibula after an encounter with a taxi on Lambton Quay. Matron said he is likely to be in traction for some time.'

Rose could remember staring at the inkwell on Miss Widdowson's desk, with two fountain pens plunged into matching glass jars beside it, arranged in a neat triangle at the edge of a pristine leather-bound blotter. She didn't know what to say. If George was to be in hospital for some time, she would have to be with him. But she had only recently graduated; she wasn't due for any leave for almost another year.

But Matron astonished her, granted her leave of absence to go to Wellington and even asked her secretary to make a booking on the ferry for her.

'You've always struck me as a nurse who knows her own mind. I wouldn't want to hold you here against your will.'

Rose had tried to thank her, but Matron wouldn't hear of it.

'I know you'll make up for it when you come back.'

George's fractures had taken so long to heal she'd arranged for him to return home to Christchurch with her and board with her parents while she helped him learn to walk again. Then it seemed as soon as he was mobile, he was sent off in a troop ship to the Pacific.

Rose accepted his need to forget what had happened during the War and had instead made the most of the fact that, now he was home, their married life could at last truly begin.

The Government had given them two railway passes to travel by train around the North Island together before the Medical Board recommended to the bank that George be 'transferred to a country atmosphere' to help him recuperate and Te Kuiti was the chosen location – six years ago last autumn.

He'd seemed perfectly fine. That was, until the day when George was driving the bank manager's car to the weekly agency day at Piopio, fifteen miles out of Te Kuiti. She'd often go along for the ride, sitting at the back of the tiny office knitting or reading while George conducted the bank's business with the locals, many of them Maoris farming their own land in the surrounding district. George liked driving; she always felt safe when he was behind the wheel. But on this particular day, just as they were passing the turnoff to another highway, she noticed the car swerve suddenly towards the ditch. She looked across at George. His eyes were closed; he seemed to have fallen asleep. Quickly, she seized the steering wheel and turned the car back onto the road, jolting her husband awake again.

'What were you doing?' she exclaimed, frightened.

'I'm sorry, Rose, I don't know what happened. I seemed to just nod off.'

'While driving? In broad daylight? I don't understand it. You had plenty of sleep last night. Is there something wrong?'

'I don't know what came over me.'

She resolved to learn to drive, just in case it occurred again.

She'd blamed the War and subsequent dislocation on their inability to have a baby. But after they'd been settled in Te Kuiti for a few years, they both realised that something else must be wrong and had approached the Department seeking an adoption. The whole experience had been the ultimate test of their affection for each other. Rose still refused to give up hope of conceiving.

Only last month they'd had another row about it. She'd let slip that it was the middle of her cycle, that it might be a good time to try. George had hit the roof.

'By Christ, Rose,' he'd shouted – George who hardly ever shouted, hardly ever swore – 'how can you expect me to perform like a circus pony? When you say that, it just makes me go right off you.'

She'd been so wound up she'd cried hot, angry tears, which had only made it worse.

As a result, the time had eked away and another month was lost.

She felt everyone was talking about their inability to conceive. That morning, long before the post had arrived, she'd run into Bea in town and the subject had come up – again.

Like Rose, Bea was as yet childless, which gave them an added camaraderie, although Bea was several years younger and had not developed Rose's quiet desperation. Their friend Sally occupied the third bank cottage in town, had a two-year-old son William and was seven months pregnant. She was finding the hot summer days hard-going.

'I'm doing the shop for Sally today,' Bea said as she and Rose met by chance outside the general store – not that running into people in a town as small as Te Kuiti was unusual. 'She's looking so tired, I took pity on her, and it's no trouble.'

'That's kind of you. I should help too.' Rose shifted her heavy basket laden with groceries into her other hand.

'You do plenty, Rose. You've taken her so much baking. She told me she's lucky to have friends like us. I said we were making the most of it while we could, before we're burdened with babies too.'

Rose laughed without enthusiasm. 'That's true.'

'I certainly hope it doesn't happen too soon. Seeing Sally struggling like that, with William running rings around her and her too tired to stop him, I'm not looking forward to it.'

'I don't believe you. You know you'd love having children.'

'Well, maybe a little. I keep expecting it to happen. Maybe …' Bea stopped to let a noisy goods train trundle past on the Main Trunk Line across the main road. When the noise finally died down, she turned back to Rose and continued. 'Do you think you'll be in the family way soon?'

Rose wished she could escape on the goods train. Anything rather than face such a question. What could she say?

'I hope so.'

'You've been waiting such a long time. I hope so too, for your sake.'

Rose looked down at her low-heeled brogues and attempted a smile. 'Thank you.'

They walked along the pavement towards their homes, just a street apart.

'I know, let's treat ourselves,' Bea said, taking her arm as they waited for a farm truck to pass before they crossed Carroll Street. 'Let's go back to Paton's tea shop and share a piece of tea cake over a cuppa. I love going there.'

It was tempting. It was over a week since she'd had the chance to have a gossip with Bea. 'I'd love to, Bea. As long as you promise not to talk babies.'

Bea had been as good as her word. The subject wasn't mentioned once, not even when a large perambulator blocked the aisle in the tea shop while women gathered around to coo at the contents. But all the way home afterwards, Rose had been haunted by the sound of the baby's cries – somehow they'd remained in her head, taunting her, reminding her she wasn't like other women.

All through the beef stew, and then the strawberry tart with fresh farm cream for George, she talked about the baby – what he or she would look like, would they be lucky enough to be given a baby with blue eyes like them, would she be dark or fair, would she be healthy in every way? In the end, they agreed, nothing mattered as much as the simple fact of having a baby at last.

'What I really want is to be able to go out and buy what the baby will need,' Rose said. 'But everyone will start asking questions. They'll want to know who I'm buying baby things for, since I clearly don't need them for myself.'

'But we can tell people, surely?' George said.

'I don't think I can. People might laugh at me.'

'You sound like your mother, worrying about what other people think.'

'But it's important. I don't want to be gossiped about.'

'Surely not the people here? They're so kind.'

'To your face, yes. But they talk behind your back. I can just imagine what they will say.'

She recalled the time when Beatrice had suffered a miscarriage, how other women looked at her in the street, as if she had done it deliberately. Bea had been almost as distraught about that as she'd been about losing the baby. The next time it happened when Rose was with her, she'd poked out her tongue at the offending old bats that had been staring. The two of them had giggled all the way home about such unladylike behaviour and she knew it had helped Bea feel a lot better.

'Surely your friends Beatrice and Sally would stick up for you? They wouldn't let people say anything bad.'

'I just don't think I can, George.'

'But you can't put it off forever. What about when the baby comes? You'll have to have the baby's things ready by then.'

'I know. I don't know what to do.'

'I'll start by making the baby's room ready. The little room next to ours with the window over the back garden, that's where we always thought our baby would go.'

'Would you?' She smiled; it was starting to feel like it was really happening.

He nodded.

'I can choose a pretty wallpaper without everyone knowing, I suppose,' Rose said. 'And I can make some curtains. Trouble is I don't know whether to get pink or blue.'

'Then choose another colour.'

'And how will I buy cloth nappies and nappy pins? If I ask for them in the general store, everyone will start asking questions.'

'If only we were down in Christchurch, your mother would take you into Ballantynes and help you pick out everything you need.'

'If only. I'd like very much to have Mother here when the baby arrives.'

'Maybe we can persuade her to travel up and stay.'

'I'll try. But you know how much she hates the sea. She refuses to go anywhere near the Wellington ferry.'

'She could come up by aeroplane to Paraparaumu and catch the train.'

'She's scared enough of the ferry. I can't imagine her trying out something as new-fangled as an aeroplane.'

'If it means seeing her first grandchild, I'm sure she'll make the effort to at least try the ferry. You'd better write and tell her at once. She'll be thrilled to bits.'

'I have already. And I wrote to Joan too. She's the only other person I know who's been through this. I posted both letters this afternoon so they'll know in a week or so.' Joan had adopted a baby a couple of years ago. Her letters made it sound a breeze.

'You should treat yourself to a trunk call to your mother. And hang the expense!'

Rose felt momentary guilt at the call she'd made that afternoon to Wellington and confessed. George didn't mind.

'We might get a baby any day. Had you thought about that?'

She had. She would be ready.

He helped dry the dishes then settled into his chair with the paper – the bi-weekly King Country Chronicle. It was edited by their friend Dick Craig; his sister Ailsa covered all the local events.

'Has Ailsa reported on the Bank Wives' meeting?' Rose asked.

'Of course,' George beamed. 'It's on page three. And you'll never guess how she finishes…'

'Don't tell me, "A sumptuous supper was enjoyed by all".'

'A sumptuous supper was enjoyed by all,' George said in unison with Rose; they laughed. Ailsa wrote that at the end of all her reports.

'What's on at the pictures on Saturday night?'

George flicked over the page. '*National Velvet.* With Elizabeth Taylor.'

'Shall we go?' She knew he'd say yes. They almost always went to the pictures on Saturdays, no matter what was showing, sitting upstairs with their friends while the Maoris sat down below. Rose had never felt comfortable about this arrangement, but it wasn't her place to upset the order of things.

'Elizabeth Taylor? Let's go.'

'You fancy her.'

'Never. I'm only interested in the horse.'

~ ~ ~

Rose checked herself quickly in front of the bedroom mirror then, not happy with what she saw, sat on the cushioned stool to make amends. Across her face, paler than most in this farming community known for sun-browned and ruddy complexions, she brushed a trace of powder; on her lips, thinner than she would have liked, she dabbed lipstick the shade of ripe plums, then smiled half-heartedly at the result. Her hair was impossible. She pulled out the restraining pins but her curls, instead of remaining flat on her head, sprang up in joyful unison, untamed and frizzy, the exact opposite of what was in fashion. She sighed and fetched her hat from the box on top of the wardrobe. Thank heavens for hats, she thought as she jammed it down on the annoying curls, removing all but a few around her forehead from public view. Finally, she pulled her summer coat from its hanger in the wardrobe and slipped it on, covering her blue and cream iris-patterned dress. It was one of her favourites, that dress; she knew its hip-hugging skirt flattered her tiny waist without being too fancy for the country-folk she would be mixing with at the Te Kuiti Agricultural and Pastoral Show.

'The car's here,' George called.

She gave herself one final check in the mirror, adjusted her hat again, and picked up her bag from the bed. 'Coming,' she called back.

The four of them – George, Rose, her friend Bea and Bea's husband Maurice – drove across the bumpy pastureland of the show grounds car park with Rose and Bea carefully nursing the flowers and cream china vases.

George and Maurice paid for the tickets at the turnstiles and they entered the show grounds - a vast domain more familiar with hosting rugby and cricket matches but now filled with more than a dozen tents, large and small, hundreds of people and an array of sheep, cattle, pigs and horses of almost every known breed.

'I'm off to see the show-jumping,' Maurice said.

'You girls won't want us chaps hanging round.' George followed him. 'We'll meet you after the judging and we can have lunch at the tea tent.'

The grass floor of the exhibition tent was lined with neat rows of trestle tables covered in long white starched linen cloths, which were fast filling up with home-made produce as, all around, men and women continued to pour in bearing jars of jam, relish, preserves, baskets of cakes, sponges, scones and biscuits, along with newspaper parcels containing a sizeable portion of the district's vegetable gardens.

In the floral art corner, the bank manager's wife Mary Smythe and several other ladies were already snipping and arranging.

'Oh, there you are Rose. I didn't think you were entering this year.' Scary Mary, as Bea had nicknamed her, looked a bit put out. 'What have you got this time?' She examined the two arrangements Rose was taking carefully out of her large flat basket and sniffed. 'Pink and cream? Just two colours? That's unusual.' With one eyebrow raised, Mary Smythe turned back, evidently unthreatened, to her own arrangement; Rose took a peek, while pretending to be occupied with her own flowers.

It was a tall, sweeping affair, juxtaposing red gerbera and roses with almost all the colours of the rainbow, a bright crescent-shaped splash that shocked Rose with its boldness. She could see why Mrs Smythe wasn't worried about her own inferior pastel arrangement; not only was it pale by comparison, it was positively insipid.

Not that it mattered – it was fun creating it, Rose said to herself as she set about the finishing touches, fixing a few stray pieces that had dislodged in the car and setting the two creations together on the white cloth – the large one (representing the mother), reaching out through fronds and tendrils to embrace the more delicate bowl (the baby) – draping the gauze artfully between them. She placed the label, 'Mother and Baby' beside the pair, picked up her basket and quietly slipped away while Mrs Smythe was busy berating one of the organisers about the lack of space for her work of art.

Bea, who always spurned the baking and floral competitions, had completed her circuit of the tent while waiting for Rose and was standing outside the door. 'I saw that,' she said, grabbing Rose by the arm and leading her round the corner, laughing. 'The old biddy has taken over the whole section with her ghastly construction. I'm amazed you didn't laugh as soon as you saw it.'

'You never know, it might win. She won last year. And it's very striking.'

'It's so striking it jumps out and hits you right between the eyes.' Bea touched Rose lightly on the arm. 'You might be in with a chance, Rose. Yours is so pretty. What is it?'

'It's supposed to represent a mother and child,' Rose said softly, hoping Bea wouldn't hear.

'Mother and baby girl, by the look of it. There's so many pink roses, it's got to be a baby girl.' Bea looked more closely at her friend. 'Is there something you're trying to tell us all? Are you. . .?'

Rose couldn't help herself. She blushed.

'You're having a baby!'

'You have to promise you won't tell anyone, Bea. It's absolutely a secret.'

'A secret! This is the best news, the news you've been waiting for and you're not telling anyone?'

'I can't, Bea. I can't. It's not my baby.'

'Not your baby?'

'Shhh!' Rose held her hand up to Bea's lips.

'Then whose baby is it?'

'I don't know.' Rose had dreaded this moment, had hoped she could avoid it but, in her most lucid moments, had known she couldn't keep it from her best friend.

'You don't know? I don't understand.'

Rose looked around to make sure there wasn't anyone within earshot. 'George and I have been told there's a baby for us to adopt. We're expecting to have her – or him – in March.'

'In March? That's just a couple of months away! Rose, this is so wonderful.'

She could feel herself breathing again. 'You don't think there's anything wrong with that?'

'Why would there be anything wrong with it?'

'I don't know. I thought people here would think it was a terrible thing to do, take someone else's baby. Because no one else has ever done that here. I'd be the first. They'd think I was a baby thief.'

'Nonsense, Rose. That's absolute nonsense. Didn't you know the Smythes adopted Harry? They've done it. And I bet they're not the only ones around here. You won't be the first.'

'Mary Smythe adopted a baby? I don't believe it.' Rose felt ashamed of herself. All these years she'd regarded Mary Smythe as a bit of a joke.

'She did. Sally said she arrived home one day with a baby, nobody had a clue. She paraded him through town as if he were her own – and pretty soon that's how everyone took it. As if he *were* her own. And now look at him – a great strapping lad of seventeen off at university in Auckland.'

'You'd never know he was adopted. He looks like Mr Smythe.'

'In some ways. But when you look again, there are lots of differences. The thing is, though, nobody really cares. He's theirs. And your baby will be yours. Yours and George's. Nobody will care, Rose. Really.'

'You think so? I've been so worried. I didn't want anyone to know.'

'So what were you planning to do when you brought the baby home? Keep it locked away inside for the next few years?'

'I don't know.' Rose looked away in the distance, beyond the show grounds and all the people milling to and fro, beyond the show ring and the parading horses. What *was* she planning to do? She and George hadn't been able to agree.

Just that morning, they'd had a row. Rose wanted to keep the adoption a secret. She was terrified of telling anyone, terrified of what people might say. She'd seen the rumour mill at work in this town and she'd put so much effort into being just like every other woman to avoid being subjected to it. She didn't want that to change.

George wanted to tell everybody.

'I don't see what the problem is, dear,' he'd reasoned with her as he was leaving for work. 'People will be so pleased to see us starting a family at last they won't care a jot that you didn't give birth to the baby.'

'But they will. You know how they can talk here.'

'Rose!' George had stood with his arms folded, his face red, his lips pursed in anger.

She knew better than to argue. George didn't get angry very often.

He'd said she'd have to tell people sooner or later and had gone off to work without kissing her goodbye. He'd never done that before.

'Well then,' Bea said. 'You should start thinking about how you're going to do it, because there are a lot of people to tell.'

'I don't know. . .'

'I know. I'll throw a baby shower. That's what we'll do. A baby shower at my place next month and then everybody will know. And everybody who comes will have to bring a present for the baby.'

'Oh, Bea, I couldn't.'

'You don't have to do a thing except turn up. And you can't say no to me. I'm your best friend.'

'But what if we never get the baby? What if the Social Security Department changes its mind?'

'Have you ever heard of a government department changing its mind?' Bea countered. 'They don't have a mind to start with. They just follow the rules.'

Bea wouldn't hear any further objections. She insisted on planning the party. She would hand-write all the invitations with clever wording that made it clear Rose's baby was being adopted.

'That way, there won't be any silly questions about why you don't look pregnant,' she said firmly.

~ ~ ~

Rose won first prize for her floral arrangement, with Mrs Smythe's creation coming in only third.

'Well done, Rose.' Bea congratulated her then whispered, 'I'd stay away from Scary Mary for a while. She'll never forgive you.'

'Oh dear, I hope it doesn't spoil George's chances at the bank.' It dawned on her, as soon as she'd said it, that George wouldn't worry about his prospects for a moment. His lack of ambition was incomprehensible.

'Oh, excuse me.'

Rose looked around and realised she had bumped into Mary Smythe.

'Oh, no, I'm so sorry,' she said, blushing. Bea had grabbed her arm, too late to prevent the collision, and was now nudging her energetically.

'Well done, my dear,' Mary said. 'Your floral arrangement won high praise.'

'Oh, thank you,' Rose stammered. 'Yours was lovely too.'

'Well, we can't all win on the day,'

Rose fended off Bea and took a deep breath. 'Mary, I wondered if you and I might … er …if we could meet for a cup of tea at Paton's. Or if you would like to visit my house one afternoon for tea. There's something I'd like to talk to you about.'

There was a moment when Mary Smythe looked taken aback, as if this was the last thing she was expecting, but just a moment before she smiled graciously. 'Of course, Rose. I'd be happy to have afternoon tea with you. Would next Tuesday suit?'

'Yes, it does. That would be lovely. Please come to our place.'

They parted and Bea said, 'What came over you Rose? I didn't know she was your friend.'

'I've seen her in a different light …'

'You mean about the adoption?'

'Yes. Now I know about that, I think there's a lot she could help me with.'

Bea chuckled softly. 'I hope you're right. Or you could be in for a very awkward afternoon next Tuesday.'

Apart from her nursing friend Joan in Christchurch, who wasn't the greatest correspondent – her letters were always short and hurried – Rose hadn't anyone to confide in about adoption. She had a lot of questions she needed to ask.

~ ~ ~

The afternoon with Mary Smythe flew by as Rose confided her news about the baby. 'But I don't know what to say to people,' she concluded.

Mary smiled sympathetically. 'I decided right from the start to carry on as if it was nobody's business but my own,' she said. 'You should try to see it that way. If you always worry about what people think, you'll never go anywhere or do anything different.'

'But look what happened when I went home to Christchurch to look after my mother last year,' Rose said.

'What was that?'

'Some people here said I'd left George.' Rose put down her cup and dabbed at her face with her handkerchief to hide her embarrassment. 'It was awful. I couldn't look anyone in the eye for over a week.'

'People will talk, I know. But you must pay no heed. You know how it goes: "Sticks and stones may break my bones, but names will never hurt me".'

'The trouble is I should really go back to Mother. She's not well.'

'Is she elderly?'

'Yes, she's seventy. I worry about her, but I can't leave George again. Even if people didn't gossip, it wouldn't be right.'

'I wouldn't worry about it. You should tell the world you're having a baby and let the tongues wag.'

'But …'

'Besides, they've already come to terms with me adopting. One more and they'll begin to think it's the latest fashion.' Mary laughed at her own joke.

'It's such a big step to take.'

'You've got to tell them sooner or later. The worst source of ill-informed gossip is when you try to hide something. Get it all out in the open, I always say.'

Rose never found out the truth of it, but it looked very much as if Mary might have pulled some strings because, not long after that afternoon tea, in fact the same day Rose and Bea had written out the invitations to the baby shower, George came home from the bank with news: he'd been transferred down to Christchurch.

'You can be near to your mother. You won't have to worry how she and Jim are getting on,' he said.

'But what about the baby?' Rose was conflicted.

'It shouldn't matter what town we're living in. We should be all right.'

'It will probably mean another home inspection,' Rose said. It might be a terrible risk they were taking. The Department had granted her dearest wish, and now she was jeopardising it by moving to another town. What if the

Department said no? 'I'll write to them first thing in the morning.'

'I think you should telephone. You want to be certain.'

~ ~ ~

Later, over dinner, she asked George if the transfer would enhance his prospects at the bank.

He looked anxious, put down his knife and frowned. 'Getting a transfer to a big city like Christchurch is regarded by my colleagues as going up in the world,' he said.

'By your colleagues? Don't you think so too?'

'Well, dear,' George looked abashed, 'it's a bit of a challenge for someone like me. You know how I like to take a back seat.'

'But don't you want a promotion?'

'It's not really a promotion.' He toyed with the remains of his dinner, pushing it around with his fork. 'I'll still be doing the same job, but you get a bit more pay in a big bank like that. There'll be a lot more commercial customers, big companies coming in to make their transactions. And there'll be a lot more staff.'

Rose could see he was feeling anxious. She'd noticed how much happier he'd been since they came to Te Kuiti but had put it down to the people he worked with, the small-town camaraderie. But maybe it was the comparative lack of a hierarchy at the bank that he'd responded to. There was such a small staff, and none of these big companies to kowtow to like in Christchurch - the Beaths and Ballantynes, the Wardells, the rural giants like Pyne Gould Guinness. She could remember the famous southern names from hearing her parents talk about them. Soon she would be back there and this time it would be George repeating the familiar names.

Leaving him to think it over, she cleared the table and took the dishes through to the kitchen.

Rose didn't want to force George into a position he couldn't cope with, but just the same, she'd hoped he would rise in the bank – to be a manager one day perhaps. She knew such things took time, that George would have to slowly work his way up. But he didn't even seem to want to begin.

How unlike her he was. She would have liked nothing more than to work her way up the hospital ranks, to become Matron one day or, at the very least the Sister in charge of a ward, with all those tremulous 'pinkies' – the trainees wearing pink uniforms until they were qualified to wear white. A pinkie herself for three years, she'd overheard a doctor saying, 'The salmon are running', one day on his rounds when she and several others had passed by.

George would never have dared write to the Postmaster, as she had when a pinkie. She'd written the letter because her crystal set, the only way of hearing what was going on in the outside world, was to be subjected to a new license fee. On her salary of forty pounds a year she could never afford to pay such a fee and neither could any of her friends who relied on this primitive form of radio reception for their daily news during the long working hours of the six-and-a-half-day week.

Her year of secretarial training need not go to waste. She composed and neatly typed a letter to the Postmaster General. A fortnight later she'd been called up to the Lady Superintendent – the first time she or any of her friends had faced such an ordeal.

'Nurse, what have you done?'

'I don't know,' Rose had stammered.

'You have had the temerity to pen a letter to the Postmaster General. That is completely out of order for a mere pinkie.'

Rose was stunned. How did the Lady Superintendent know?

'If you had a complaint,' the Lady Superintendent continued, 'you should have told the Home Sister and she would have reported to the Sub-Matron, who would have told me. If I thought it necessary to go further, I would have told the Medical Superintendent who would have put it to the Board, and if they agreed, they would have instructed the Board Secretary to write the letter. Not you.'

'I'm sorry, Ma'am. I didn't mean to …'

'However, the Postmaster General has seen fit to grant your request. No individual licenses will be necessary. He has written that one licence will do for the whole home. You may go.'

She had to admit she'd been terrified facing up to Matron; one day she would be Matron then she could terrify the pinkies too.

She decided to ignore George's fears, his lack of ambition. She didn't want an argument; she might just have to go along with it – for a while, at least. Until they were settled in. She had plenty of other things to occupy her in the meantime. She had to tell her private nursing patients that she would be leaving and help them find a replacement; cancel the baby shower; tell the Department about their change of address; pack up the house and all their things – they seem to have accumulated so much since they'd settled in Te Kuiti; and say goodbye to all her friends. After six years, that would be hard.

She would have to focus on the end result: having a baby and being close to her mother. Friends were important, but family was everything.

She'd made peach crumble for dessert. She pulled it out of the oven and carried it through to the dining room, where plates and cutlery awaited.

'I can't wait to tell Mother about the transfer,' she said as she served George his plate. 'She will be over the moon. How soon will it happen?'

'In two weeks.'

'Two weeks! My goodness, there's so much to do. How will we ever manage it?'

She noticed a slight look of irritation on George's face.

He sighed. 'The bank will take care of our things.'

'But we'll have to pack everything …'

He smiled patiently. 'All you have to do is think about getting ready for the new baby. You can write yourself a big long list and buy everything when we get to Christchurch.' His smile warmed. 'I'd better warn Ballantynes' baby department that you and your mother are on the way.'

Chapter 3.

Christchurch, June 1951

Rose lay back in the deckchair on the veranda she shared with her parents, a clear line of sight to the perambulator nestled under the shiny green leaves of the tall magnolia tree, where her baby was receiving the requisite dose of fresh air the baby book said was compulsory. Her parents had made a point of retreating as soon as their granddaughter fell asleep, suggesting she make the most of this chance for a rest.

Rose closed her eyes and tried to empty her mind. But it was crowded with worry. At this moment, when she should be experiencing sublime maternal joy, or so the book told her, she could only feel guilt and shame – shame at her inability to satisfy a three-month-old baby, and guilt that she wasn't capable of fully loving her. But how could she? How could any sane human being provide unconditional love to a squawking, wriggling, red-faced picture of misery that was all sweetness and contentment during the day but turned into a determined little demon every night, refusing to settle, refusing to stop wailing, refusing to sleep.

Even her father's most resolute efforts had failed to make a difference.

'I'll see to her tonight,' her father had said, mounting the stairs to the nursery just the night before last.

As soon as he'd pushed open the nursery door and gone in, the wailing had stopped. Contented gurgles could be heard. Twenty minutes later, she'd heard him tiptoe back downstairs. But as soon as he reached the sitting room door, the wailing broke out again.

'The child's impossible,' her father had said, sinking into his fireside chair with a deep sigh.

George had also done his best. For several nights in a row, he'd put the carrycot in the back seat of the car and driven Katharine round and round the block until the crying stopped and she fell asleep. Sometimes, when he returned home and carefully lifted the carrycot out of the car, she'd stayed that way. More often than not, she'd woken up and started crying again.

'Once more around the block,' George would say philosophically, loading the carrycot back into the car.

But he was as tired as she was, catching the bus to work in the morning rubbing sleep out of his eyes and eating his toast at the bus stop just outside the front gate, only half awake.

She spent her days in fear of the new tyrant, worried that the Karitane nurse from Plunket or the Grey Invader would return unannounced and find her out. She had read Plunket founder Dr Truby King's book *Feeding and Care of Baby* several times but it didn't seem to make any difference. Her baby didn't appreciate the rules. Routine was everything, he wrote, a scientific approach was best. Baby should be fed every four hours, never in between.

Katharine didn't agree. She wanted to be fed just two hours later. Rose would have dearly liked to take Katharine along to see Truby King in those remaining two hours. 'What am I supposed to do with her?' she would have said. 'How can you expect me to listen to my baby screaming with hunger for two hours on end?'

There were to be no cuddles. And, according to the book, Katharine was supposed to poo on cue. But she didn't take any notice of that either.

Worst of all was at night, when Katharine refused to go to sleep at the appointed time. She wasn't interested in going to bed when the book said she should and when she finally went to sleep, every night, without fail, she would wake up around two. It was immaterial to her that she wasn't supposed to be fed at this hour. 'Baby has to learn to fit with your routine,' the book said, not the other way around. No feeds in between ten p.m. and six a.m. But at two a.m., Katharine made it clear this was blatantly unfair.

Night-time had consequently become a nightmare. She couldn't remember the last decent sleep she'd had, and it hadn't been much better for poor George. It would be helpful if she could take a nap in the afternoon, when Katharine slept for three hours straight, no problem. But it didn't seem right, somehow, nodding off like that when she should be catching up on the housework or preparing tonight's meal …

'Are you all right, dear?'

She sat bolt upright. It was George.

'What? Was I asleep?'

'Yes, dear. Completely out to it.'

'Heavens, you're home from work. What time is it?'

'Half past five.'

'Oh no! Where's Katharine? Is she all right?'

'She's asleep too.' George started to laugh. 'It seems the only member of this family to miss out is me!'

Despite the laugh, she could tell George was annoyed, as well he might be, going off to work every morning after another disturbed night. 'Oh, I'm sorry, George. I didn't …'

'Don't worry about it, Rose. Lord knows, you need it.' He touched his forehead with his fingers, brushing the irritation away, then rubbed his eyes, blinking into the lowering sun.

She leapt out of the deck chair, worried that Katharine might be fretting for her, worried that she wasn't crying, and ran across the lawn to the pram. Her daughter was sound asleep.

'I expect she's just as worn out as we are.' George had followed her and put his arm around her waist, bending to see under the pram hood.

'Do you think so?' She looked at her husband, at the shadow under his eyes, which seemed less blue, less clear than usual. Then she looked down at her sleeping daughter, her dark eyelashes a soft smudge against her pale closed eyelids, her almost black hair a curly corona under her white knitted bonnet. 'I wish she slept as well as this at night.'

'We seem to have it back to front.' George smiled wistfully and straightened, turning away towards the garden. 'I wonder what we should do to turn her sleeping patterns around.

'It's my fault.' Rose turned her body into his, wrapping one arm around him while resting the other on the pram's large metal handle. 'I should know how to do it, but no matter how strictly I follow the rules, I just can't get it right. I don't think I'm cut out to be a mother.'

He put an arm round her and faced her. 'Nonsense, Rose, you're a wonderful mother.'

'No I'm not. I'm hopeless. I can't get her to go to sleep at night. She's keeping us all awake, even her grandparents. I can't expect them to put up with it much longer, not at their age.'

'They'll cope. They can sleep all day!'

'But you can't. Oh, I'm sorry, George. I clearly wasn't meant to be a mother or I would have been able to have my own baby.'

'Rose!' He pushed her back slightly and pulled up her chin, making her look at him. 'Why must you always doubt yourself like this?' She could hear a hint of annoyance, of impatience in his voice. 'You *are* a good mother. You are always patient with her, even when she's being a little tyke.'

She pulled away from him. 'But I'm a fraud. I don't think I can love her.'

'Give it time, Rose. That's what you told me the Karitane nurse said last week. Give it time and she'll stop crying.'

She looked under the pram hood again and sighed. 'I can't love her when she cries all night long.'

'But you will, don't worry Rose. You will. The Karitane nurse told you not to worry about the sleeping. That babies learn. Our baby is just a slow learner, that's all.'

But Rose didn't believe him. *She* was the slow learner. She was the one who was at fault. Why couldn't she form a close bond with her baby? Why was she holding back?

Every time she held her close to feed her with the bottle, every time she picked her up to change her nappy or to show her the shiny green leaves turning in the wind on the camellia tree or smell the winter sweet in the front garden, there was something preventing her from giving herself completely to Katharine.

Joan had also told her to give it time. Joan, who'd gone through three years of nursing training with Rose, had adopted a baby too a few years ago. She'd never admitted it at the time, not to anyone, she'd said, but it was months before she'd been able to feel anything more than mild interest in her daughter Lily when she was a baby.

'She felt like a wee stranger in our home,' Joan had said over afternoon tea while Katharine slept by the clock on the veranda just outside the door, under close observation by Lily, who was clutching a large rag doll.

'I think I'm just tired,' Rose said. 'I'm sure it will be a lot better when I've had a good night's sleep.'

Joan smiled. 'I wouldn't set too much store on that. Lily slept like a lamb.' She put her cup down and pushed the door to the veranda further open, studying the pram with the sleeping baby and its attentive guardian, before turning back to Rose. 'It's just the suddenness of it all, that's my belief anyway. You don't have all those nine months to think and breathe the baby as it grows inside you. You just get a phone call and suddenly there's a baby waiting for you to take home.'

Rose joined her in the doorway and together they gazed at their daughters until Lily noticed them and interrupted their thoughts.

'Little Katie's waking up, Mummy.'

Rose tiptoed over to the pram. Katharine was stirring but her eyes were closed. 'I don't think so, Lily.' She held out her hand. 'Come on, come inside. She needs her afternoon sleep.' Lily took her hand and followed her. 'At least,' she added, turning back to Joan, 'the Karitane nurse says she does.'

'I wouldn't take them as gospel,' Joan said. 'They're so full of rules. You don't have to do everything they say, you know. Besides, some of it's quite contradictory to what they taught us at the hospital.' She returned to her seat and picked up the picture book Lily had been looking at earlier and handed it to her. 'Here you are dear, have another look at that.' Lily obediently took the book and settled herself on the floor to read.'

'I wish I was back there now.' Rose picked Lily's rag doll up off the floor and held onto it. 'It was all so simple then. We did as we were told. And we had such fun.' She sat down again, in clear view of the veranda door, and picked at the doll's woolly hair.

'Didn't we? We're both wives and mothers now but it still feels like nursing at times – cleaning up bottoms and soothing upset people, only they're a lot younger!'

'But I always felt in control then. I was wearing a uniform. I was trained for the job and I was confident that I knew what I was doing. Now I've got absolutely no confidence at all. I don't seem to know anything.'

'Perhaps you should wear a uniform.' Joan grinned. 'Seriously, I don't think you should worry. You're doing just fine …'

'When we were living in Te Kuiti it was so easy. All I had to worry about was whether the meat was tough, the strawberries were ripe, and if my morning tea sponge was as light as the other bank wives'. Having a baby seemed such a wonderful idea, like it would complete the picture of perfection. If only I'd known.'

Now gone forever, that earlier life was like a country idyll – there had always been time to gossip at the greengrocer's or take tea at Paton's; life was so simple when the biggest disaster was overcooking the marmalade or letting the weeds grow in your front garden.

Leaving the King Country had been bittersweet, with so many farewell parties she couldn't believe there was anyone left to say goodbye to. Their photos had been in the paper twice and Ailsa Craig had reported once again that 'a sumptuous supper was enjoyed by all'. But however sad she felt to be losing good friends, she had been buoyed by the knowledge that soon she was to have a baby. The Department had promised.

Joan stood up. 'You wouldn't have done anything differently.' She made for the veranda door and peeked through it. 'Look at what you've been blessed with – the most beautiful baby you could wish for, and she's all yours.'

'As long as I pass all the tests.'

'What tests?'

'You know, the way they check up on you. If I don't do the right thing, the Karitane nurse might report me to the

Department.' She poured Joan another tea, adding a thin slice of lemon.

'Surely not? I never thought that would happen.' She took the tea off Rose and put it on the tiny table beside her armchair.

'That's the impression I got from that Mrs Lowe who was here. Remember I told you?'

Joan nodded. 'Yes, we've all had the inspectors.'

'She said the Karitane nurse would keep an eye on me.'

'But that's just to make sure you're coping.'

'And to make sure the baby's putting on enough weight and you're doing everything they say you have to do.'

'You and Katharine would pass with flying colours. She's bonny.' Joan picked up her cup and took a sip.

'Not last time the nurse came.' Rose poured herself another tea and added lemon. 'According to her, Katharine wasn't putting on nearly enough weight. She quizzed me about how much Karilac I used in each bottle, how I mixed it, as if I was putting her on short rations.'

'If you're using Karilac, Katharine should be fine. It's a recipe for a chubby baby. Have you tasted it? It's full of sugar, it's so sweet.' Joan pulled a face then put down her cup again.

'I don't have much choice, really. I've got to use Karilac, and I've got to get more of it into Katharine so the next time the nurse comes she's the right weight.'

The nurse from Plunket was due the following week. Rose dreaded the moment when the scales would come out and the drilling would begin again about Katharine's consumption of the sickly formula. It was bad enough having to use the powdered evaporated milk, bad enough not being able to feed her herself, without having to mix up sugary cow's milk four times a day.

~ ~ ~

The following morning there was an unexpected knock at the door. She could tell who it was by the colour of the coat visible through the small panel of opaque glass on the top section of the front door: the Grey Invader had returned.

'Good Morning, Mrs Stewart,' she said brightly when Rose opened the door. 'How is it all going now you have baby home?'

Rose put on her most cheerful face, wishing she'd dusted, trying to remember what state the laundry was in. Had she covered the nappy bucket after dropping this morning's one in? She been just about to fire up the copper and start scrubbing so the disinfectant, baking soda, bleach and vinegar could work its magic. She prayed there was no lingering smell.

She showed Mrs Lowe through the kitchen where she sterilised bottles and prepared formula; then the laundry, where thankfully the lid on the nappy pail was firmly shut and the lavender oil she used in the rinse was sending out a faintly pleasant odour. The baby bath, propped in the corner, caused only a brief nod of approval. Once she'd been into the nursery, where Katharine was snuffling through her morning sleep, the Grey Invader seemed to want nothing more than a cup of tea in front of the electric fire in the upstairs living room. Rose wondered if this was where the inquisition would start and was glad George was at the bank in town and wouldn't interrupt or act defensively.

'I'm sorry, Mrs Lowe, if I'd known you were coming I would have lit the sitting room fire,' she said as they climbed the stairs, Rose bearing the tea tray. 'It's far too cold in there this morning.'

'I wouldn't want you to go to any trouble on my account.' Mrs Lowe took the proffered seat by the heater.

Rose poured the tea. 'What can I help you with?' She passed a plate of peanut brownies and perched on the edge of the chair opposite.

'Baby seems settled.'

'Yes. She sleeps well in the daytime.'

'And at night?'

'Well. . .' Rose didn't want to admit to any difficulties. She wanted Mrs Lowe to think of her as the perfect mother, on top of it all, confident and at ease. She hoped Katharine wouldn't wake before Mrs Lowe left, so the inspector wouldn't see how terrified she was of dropping her baby while changing her, of stabbing her with a nappy pin, or getting the formula wrong when mixing milk for her bottle.

'Not a good sleeper then?'

'No.'

'Could you fetch me baby's record book, please?'

Rose had been dreading this moment. But there was no way out of it. 'Certainly. It's just inside the nursery door.' She fetched the book and handed it to Mrs Lowe, perching on the chair again as if it were filled with knives.

Mrs Lowe thumbed over the pages – only the first three bore the notes from the nurse's three visits – seeming to expect more.

'Katharine Margaret, born March the seventeenth, six pounds eight ounces,' she read. She thumbed over the page again. 'And last week I see she was ten pounds nine ounces.' She paused.

Rose was certain she was in for a telling off.

'That seems perfectly satisfactory.'

'It does?'

'Yes. Why? Aren't you pleased with that?'

'Well no. That is, I don't know. The Karitane said that she wasn't putting on enough weight.'

Mrs Lowe, uncharacteristically, snorted. 'They always say that at Plunket. I think they want to have a nation of chubby babies force fed every four hours – except, of course, after ten p.m. Karitane babies are trained to be so regimented they could form an army. It's simply shocking!' Mrs Lowe thrust Katharine's little brown book on the table where it landed with a loud thwack. 'Personally, I've always had my doubts about all that. I suppose they told you not to feed her in the middle of the night either?'

'Yes.'

'And have you?'

'No. Of course not.' Rose could see where this was heading. The Grey Invader was testing her. 'I've done everything Truby King says, I promise you.' She hoped fervently that Mrs Lowe wouldn't ask to see his book.

Two nights ago, when trying to get Katharine to settle, yet again with no success, she'd become so upset at the persistent crying she'd picked up *Feeding and Care of Baby*, opened the window, and thrown it out. As if pleased, Katharine had almost immediately stopped crying, which had come as such a relief Rose had gone straight to bed and forgotten all about the book until the morning. It wasn't until she was hanging the nappies out on the line that she'd seen the book lying there, its cover wrinkled and the outer pages more than a little lumpy. Even when it had dried, it was still badly misshapen.

'And baby keeps crying, right on into the night?'

'Yes. The nights are difficult, it's true.' Rose tried not to let Mrs Lowe see just how difficult, keeping her face as expressionless as she could.

'You wouldn't believe how many young mothers say that to me. I hear it all the time, you know. And do you know what my advice is?'

Rose shook her head, no.

'Ignore Truby King. Throw the book away!'

Rose thought she was joking and laughed.

'No, Mrs Stewart, it's no laughing matter. I'm perfectly serious.' While Rose sat there stunned, unable to think of a word to say, Mrs Lowe picked up her purse, clicked it open, and produced a shiny new copy of the book by Dr Benjamin Spock, *Baby and Child*. 'Have you seen this before?'

'No. I've heard of it though.'

'You'll find its advice is almost completely the opposite of what you've been told so far. But if that's not working for you, then I dare say there's no harm in giving this a try. I'll leave the book with you.'

'Thank you. That's very kind …'

'Nonsense, it's part of my job to make sure baby is doing well.' Mrs Lowe snapped shut her handbag and stood to go. 'I don't know how many of those books I've given to young mothers these past few months. But they do seem to work.'

After she'd gone, Rose ran back upstairs and, without stopping to pick up the tea things or check on Katharine, she opened the book.

'You know more than you think.' The opening words stunned her. How could someone say that to her, when she clearly didn't know the first thing about infant care. She read on and the more she read, the more a glimmer of hope beamed across the room all the way to the nursery door.

Could she give Katharine a bottle whenever she wanted one? Even in the middle of the night? Could she let her go to bed when she was sleepy and stay up when she wasn't? Was this the answer to all her difficulties?

A small cry came from the nursery, followed by another, just a whisper of a cry, but Rose knew it would soon become more persistent.

She didn't look at her watch. She didn't worry about the tea things or making Katharine fit into her schedule. She went straight to the baby's room, picked her up out of the crib and held her.

'Good news, my darling,' she said. 'I'm allowed to pick you up when you cry and feed you when you tell me you're hungry.' Katharine snuggled into her and stopped crying, nuzzling her mother for milk. 'And best of all, the book says I'm allowed to cuddle you. Well guess what? I'm never going to stop.'

~ ~ ~

On her first birthday, Katharine – or Katie as she was known by now – was to have a party. Rose invited the little girl next door, Vicki-Jane, who was almost exactly the same age; fifteen-month-old twins Keith and Kathy from around the corner; and of course her parents and the aunts. George's parents had been invited too, but never ventured far from their farm in Nelson and had declined.

Rose would never forget the day George drove her all the way from Christchurch to meet his father for the first time, long before the War, long before they moved to Wellington.

His father had gone as far south as he was prepared to travel, arranging to meet them at Stanley Brook Hill. They'd arrived first and waited beside the car in the chill wind.

George's father pulled his truck over to the side of the road; it was a long time before he got out.

'Should we go to him George? Is he waiting for us?'

'No. He'll come when he's ready.'

So they'd waited until C.T., as he was known, casually pushed open his door, clambered from the cab and strolled over. He said nothing. Just looked her up and down then said brusquely, without even a smile, 'You'll do.' To her astonishment, he held out a banana. 'Here, you must be hungry. Have this. But save the skin. I want it for the pigs.'

Dutifully, she accepted the banana and ate it while he and George talked about sheep. Looking back, she realised that was the longest conversation she and her father-in-law ever had.

It was a relief the reticent C.T. and his wife Margaret had declined the party invitation; their presence would have put a dampener on the day.

Ever since that roadside encounter, Rose had been more than a little scared of George's father. George, for some reason, detested him. She'd asked him once why that was and would never ask again. The look of pure hatred that crossed George's face was so frightening she'd not mentioned C.T. since. All she could do was garner clues from his childhood stories, from his discussions with his brothers Leslie and Trevor. The picture they painted was of a father so strict and authoritarian his sons had gone out of their way to be the exact opposite – to treat their friends, their wives and ultimately their own children with respect, kindness and, as often as they could, with laissez faire.

Of his mother, George said nothing, leaving Rose to guess that she had lacked – or had been deprived of – the spirit to stand up to her husband. Margaret had not been invited to accompany him on the journey to Stanley Brook Hill and Rose's wartime wedding had been such a hurried affair, with just her own mother and father and a few Christchurch friends as guests, that George's parents had declined to attend. So Rose had yet to meet her mother-in-law. Katie's party would be another opportunity missed.

Rose knew she'd gone overboard planning for the party, but she was determined to celebrate having made it through the first year – and, though she barely admitted it, she wanted to show everyone she could be as good a mother, a better mother even, as 'real' mothers who had given birth to their own babies.

She'd certainly come a long way since those early months when Katharine refused to sleep at night. Thanks to Dr Spock – or really thanks to Mrs Lowe – Katie had gone to sleep almost straight away as soon as Rose had introduced a late-night feed. She'd written a thank-you note to the Lady Inspector and on her third and last visit just a month ago, Rose almost felt like she was entertaining an old friend – even though she was still dressed from head to toe in grey. For a moment, she'd seriously considered inviting her to Katie's birthday party.

The party was postponed to the Saturday afternoon, so George could be there. The day was fine and warm so she and her mother decided to hold it outside, with the aunts and her parents seated on the veranda and the toddlers and their parents outside. She overheard George becoming involved, as he often did, in a serious discussion with his father-in-law – this time about the Mayor, Mr Macfarlane, and whether he was devoting enough time to the city when he was away in Wellington part of the year being a member of Parliament.

Rushing past on her way to the kitchen to collect the birthday cake, Rose paused for a moment behind George, intending to ask him to light the candles, when she noticed his left leg – the one shortened an inch when so badly broken by the encounter with a Wellington taxi – twitching uncontrollably. George, still embroiled in his discussion, was pushing down on his left knee, his knuckles white with the effort, but to no avail: the leg continued to jiggle up and down as if powered by an electric motor.

'Are you …?' She stopped herself. He wouldn't want her drawing attention to it. She continued on her way past, balancing the cake over to the low table she'd laid with a white linen cloth.

Her mother brought Katie over and the aunts gathered around. Vicki-Jane was lifted down, protesting, off the rocking horse presented that afternoon by Great Aunt Doris and carried over to the table. The twins toddled over, their mother close behind. With the little ones gathered expectantly around the cake, the full presence of the adults was required.

'Come on Jim, you're missing the birthday cake,' Doris called to her brother-in-law. 'You too, George, come and see your daughter blow out her candle.'

The two men got up from their chairs and stepped down off the veranda onto the paved terrace. There was a cry and Rose, lighted match in her hand, saw George's leg crumple under him as he fell to the ground.

'Are you all right, old chap?' Her father was right beside him, offering him a hand up.

'I'm fine. My leg just gave way.' George tried to stand but Rose could tell his leg was causing him pain. 'No, I'm fine,' he repeated as her father then Aunt Doris tried to help. George had that stubborn look on his face. She knew better than to intervene.

Slowly, George walked towards her, pretending nothing was wrong. But, almost imperceptibly, his left leg was dragging slightly along the ground. Nobody else seemed to have noticed.

That evening, they gathered around the piano, Katie clutched firmly at her grandmother's side. Rose played and George sang, in his fine tenor, *Where e're you Walk* and it seemed impossible to believe it had happened. They looked the picture of a happy family, the image of contentment; the rosy glow from the coal fire lighting a halo at the back of Katie's dark curls; George's voice strong and true, without a quaver in it; the song a tribute to love:

'And all things flourish, and all things flourish,

Where e're you turn your eyes.'

She put all her effort into the accompaniment, feeling a deep surge of love for her husband as he sang on. Was there something wrong with him? Was it linked to the episode in the car on the road out of Te Kuiti? Or was she just being silly? She'd asked him, after the party, after all the guests had gone home, but he'd brushed it off.

'It's nothing,' he'd said. 'My leg's fine now. Must have pinched a nerve.'

The song finished and she looked up at George, who'd picked up the music sheet and closed it.

He smiled reassuringly. 'There's no need to worry Rose. I'm just fine.'

Chapter 4.

Christchurch. 1987

Rose heard the front door slam; the string of attached cowbells clanged in Swiss arpeggios.

'Where are you?' Kate called.

'In here.' Rose's back was sore from holding George. She'd parked herself on the floor behind him, propping him from the waist up to prevent his head from jamming against the bedside cabinet. He'd fallen at an awkward angle so she'd lifted his upper torso to keep him upright while dialling Kate's number on the phone.

'He's come down again,' she'd said when Kate answered.

'That's okay Mum, I'll be there in ten minutes.'

Rose thought she heard the trace of a sigh. 'Sorry to get you out in the middle of the night.'

'It's no problem. I hadn't gone to bed yet anyway. I'm a night-owl like you, remember?'

It had been more like twenty minutes, actually, but Rose was used to being patient.

'Sorry, Kate,' she said again as her daughter entered the bedroom.

'It's my fault,' George said. 'Sorry, Katie. You're a treasure.'

'Don't apologise, you two. It's no problem.'

Kate held her father while Rose stood up, then the two women manoeuvred George up off the floor, using the fireman's lift Rose had taught her daughter years earlier. His falls usually happened when Rose was helping him out of his chair and into bed or, less often, when transferring him from his armchair into the wheelchair, and Rose was aware her calls for help were becoming more frequent.

Sometimes, to save Kate coming out, or when Kate was at work, she'd called the police and two constables had arrived – usually after a long wait – to scoop George off the floor. She couldn't believe the speed and apparent effortlessness with which they hoisted him up on the bed, shaking his hand, patting him on the back, and departing with a sympathetic smile for Rose.

'I bet you were a front-row prop,' George would tease them – even once when it was a policewoman. She'd taken it well, but Rose had told him afterwards he'd have to think of something new to say in future.

Up into the chair he went, then across into bed, his thin, powerless legs dangling uselessly as they transferred him.

'Thank you, Katie,' he said while Rose fussed with the bedcovers and pillows. 'I don't know what I'd do without you.'

'That's all right, Dad. Just don't get any heavier, okay?'

Rose knew there was no chance of that. George had developed what he called 'a soul above food' and, though appreciative of her cooking, rarely asked for food to be brought to him. Often she would come home after being at work or out on one of her day-long tramping trips to find his sandwiches untouched. At most he'd drink the tea out of the thermos and eat a piece of sultana cake she'd left beside his chair; when she commented, he genuinely didn't seem to have noticed.

'I've been busy talking to Charlie,' he'd say of one of his old bank colleagues from up north who'd moved to Christchurch and often visited, or 'I was so engrossed in the crossword.'

Mostly, she knew, he would have been sound asleep, nodding off in his chair, waking, watching a bit of television, nodding off again, answering the phone, nodding off again. His days were measured by the ticking of the mantelpiece clock and the flickering of the midday television news, sending him into a somnambulant reverie that was interrupted only by interventions from Rose, from friends and the weekly home help.

'Can I get you a cup of tea, Dad?'

'No thanks Katie. I've got to watch my waterworks.' He smiled and pointed at his tummy hidden under the floral chintz bedspread. 'No fluids after eight p.m. Your mother keeps a close eye on me.' He patted the covers. 'Here, sit beside me for a minute and tell me about yourself.'

'George, it's eleven o'clock at night.'

'I know, I know, Rose. But it'll only take a minute. Won't it Katie?' He smiled hopefully at his daughter. She never said no.

Kate plumped herself down on the side of her mother's single bed and tucked her feet up on her father's bed opposite. Rose ignored her black boots.

Kate started to tell her father about work and being given weekend shifts, which made child-care easier because her husband David was at home.

Rose still disapproved of her daughter going to work so soon after having her baby. Little Amelia was only one when Kate had started back as a reporter for Radio New Zealand.

'It's only part-time, Mum,' she'd reasoned. 'We need the money. Besides, I don't want to drop my career. I've spent all these years getting a name for myself in journalism, I don't want to throw it away.'

'You know I'd be happy to take her more often.

'You've got more than enough to do.'

And Kate had snorted when Rose had pointed out that *she* stayed home with her.

'That's what women did in those days. But not any more,' she'd said.

'But I was out of the workforce all those years and I was still able to get back in, no trouble. Just a bit of retraining …'

'But that was nursing. Nursing isn't the same as journalism. You stay out of it for a few years, nobody's heard of you any more. And the technology's changing so fast. I can't just stay at home. I've got to keep up or I'll be unemployable. I'm doing some freelance writing in my spare time just to keep my name out there.'

'You don't have any spare time.' Rose had often noticed how tired her daughter looked.

'At night when Amelia's asleep, I can type up stories. That new magazine, *North and South,* you know, the one I did the cover story for their first edition. . .'

'Yes.' Rose remembered the cover when it came out the previous year with her daughter's name on it and how proud she'd felt at the time.

'They've asked me to be their South Island writer. They're commissioning me to do a lot more.'

Rose plumped George's pillow then sat down beside him facing Kate. 'I heard you reading the news on Sunday morning,' she said. 'You sounded very chirpy for that time of the day.'

'I'm enjoying it. But I'm going to have to brush up on my Maori. My pronunciation's letting me down. They're putting me on a training course – so that must mean they want to keep me on.'

'You've got a great voice for the news.' Kate was so unlike her. She couldn't imagine ever having the courage to talk into a microphone knowing the whole country was listening.

'I'm getting used to five o'clock starts. Amelia had me well trained when she was little.'

'And how is little Amelia?' George's eyes lit up.

'She's all go. I took her to Sumner today with her friend Sophie and they played in the shallows and made sandcastles while David and I just lay on the blanket and read our books. It was bliss.'

George beamed. 'I remember we used to take you to Sumner when you were little. You used to make the best sandcastles of them all.' He turned to Rose. 'It was always much warmer there than further up along the coast. I'd like to go again one day. Rose – do you think we could?'

'Yes, of course. But we wouldn't be able to go much further than the promenade with the wheelchair.'

'I don't think even you could get him across the sand, Mum,' Kate said.

'Never under-estimate your mother, Katie,' he said. 'She can move mountains … and quite possibly sand dunes too.'

'We'd better let Kate go home now,' Rose said, aware of the time. 'We've kept her up long enough.'

Kate stood and gave her father a kiss. 'Good night, Dad.'

'Good night, Katie.'

Rose followed her daughter outside to the front door and stood in the hallway, her fingers touching the door handle. 'Thank you.'

Kate picked up her jacket off the hallstand and started shrugging it on. 'I worry about you, Mum. He's getting too much for you.'

'I'll manage. He's no trouble.' She let go the door handle and stepped further back into the hallway.

'But he's getting harder to move around. He used to be able to stand and balance on his frame, but now he can't even do that.'

'Some days are better than others.'

Kate stopped fiddling with her buttons and touched her mother's arm. 'How are *you*?'

'Oh, I'm fine.' Rose patted her daughter's hand. 'I'm hardly ever home, it seems, but George never complains.'

'It's not Dad I'm worried about. You'll wear yourself out.' Kate dropped her hand and faced Rose front on.

'I'm fine.' There was no other choice. She wouldn't let them put George in a home. She fingered the photos on top of the carved camphor chest, which contained the family treasures – Kate's baby clothes; Brownie Talbot, Kate's favourite soft toy, straw protruding from his paws; her grandmother's intricately embroidered linen; and her own wedding dress – not the white one she'd always wanted, had designed, but the blue, fitted dress she'd had to substitute quickly when war and George's injury had intervened. It was still wrapped in newspaper from their wedding day in January 1940.

'It must be getting time for you to take it a bit easier, that's all. Perhaps you should give up nursing all those old people at Woodchester?'

'I have thought of it, but I enjoy it. It's only weekends.'

'Don't you think it's all a bit much for you? I mean, Dad takes up such a lot of your time, and you have to do everything around here.'

'Nurse Maude gives me Mrs Chisholm once a week to clean the house.'

'But she spends more time talking to Dad than cleaning.'

'She's a good cleaner. And you know your father. He does like to talk.' Rose grinned. 'He had the Mormons this morning. They started looking desperate after half an hour. They hadn't managed to get a word in edgeways the whole time.'

Kate laughed. 'That'll teach them to come knocking. You'd think he didn't have anyone to talk to the way he goes on.' She rested her hand on the door handle.

'That's what everyone thinks. But no matter how many visitors he gets, he never runs out of something to say.'

'Now you're changing the subject again, Mum. Look, I know it's good for you to get out of the house for a bit and have a break from Dad, but Woodchester isn't much of a break is it? I mean, you're looking after frail old people there too.'

'Your father isn't old.'

'Well he's not young.' Kate fiddled with the cowbells attached to the door handle, clanging one of them against the door. 'You're going to have to, sooner or later.'

'I know.' Rose sighed and picked up the framed photo of her mother and father on their wedding day from among the other family photos on the camphor chest. She stroked the top of it absent-mindedly. 'I'll have to give it up soon. I'm surprised they haven't said something already.'

She'd feared the subject might come up last month at Woodchester after she'd tried to change the seating arrangements at dinner time. In the four years she'd been there, it had seemed so silly that all the men sat together at one end of the dining room and all the women at the other. Last month, she'd decided to mix them up. She'd drawn up a carefully constructed seating plan – the slow eaters could sit at one table, the deaf at another, the politically affiliated at another. The women had loved it. But the men had thrown her dark looks and had muttered unhappily. The following night, the men rebelled and had effectively gone on strike, refusing to come into the dining room and asking for dinner in their rooms. Word would have got through to Matron for sure. But she hadn't said anything and Rose had certainly not mentioned it to her.

She often thought back to her days as a pinkie at Public, when she'd told her fellow pinkies that one day she would be Matron. And now, here she was, Matron of a residential hospital and nursing home – at least Relieving Matron at weekends, which was almost the same. It might have come at the end of her career, when she was around retirement age and after a long break from the workforce, but she was happy to have achieved her goal at last. She knew she'd have to give it up soon, that she couldn't keep going much after seventy – but she didn't feel old.

Rose put down the photo and grinned at her daughter. 'There's plenty of life in the old girl yet. It's the tramping keeps me young. Only three weeks to go and I'm off on the Queen Charlotte Walkway.'

'I don't know where you find the energy.'

'Joan says I've got an extra battery.'

'Well she's right. All my friends say you're a role model. Now, I really must go.' Kate turned the door handle then stopped. 'Where did I leave my keys?'

'You're always losing your keys.'

'I'll try the bedroom. That's the first place I went when I arrived.'

'Careful George doesn't trap you again.'

Kate turned back, smiling as she disappeared into the bedroom.

Looking after George had formed a bond between Rose and her daughter, intensifying the close relationship that had developed gradually, tentatively as Kate emerged from her tempestuous teenage years. The arguments, the name-calling, the intense loathing in her eyes when she looked at Rose, it had been so bad she and George had sent Kate to a psychologist. There must surely be something wrong for her to be so angry, to hate her mother so much, to make her life so miserable. But the psychologist had explained it wasn't unusual behaviour for the teenage years, especially for an adopted child. 'Children of this age are obsessed with their identity and ego,' he'd said.

Meanwhile, Kate had raged against the psychologist, against being made to see him against her will. She was even more distant and wilful.

Kate was fifteen – rebellious, rude, feisty fifteen. Rows with her mother became increasingly frequent.

Rose would never have spoken to her mother the way Kate spoke to her. Her father would have got out the cane if she had, the threat of it being sufficient deterrent alone. But Kate didn't care what she said or how hurtful it was, and the language she used was execrable – Rose never thought she'd hear such words uttered in her home.

George remained silent while the battles raged around him. Sitting in his armchair in front of the flickering new black-and-white television, he must have heard everything but he never took part.

Rose could only guess at the awfulness of his years in the Pacific training heavy artillery at Japanese planes, years that he never discussed with her, nor with anybody. Those years must have taught him hard lessons about fighting wars: ever since, he'd been a peacemaker, he refused to take sides.

Fifteen years in a house with two women, particularly two women at the opposite ends of the hormonal spectrum, easily persuaded him the best course of action for as peaceful an existence as possible was to retreat to the sidelines while Rose was left to fight her battles alone. His refusal to take sides used to infuriate her.

It was during the worst row she and Kate ever had that his impartiality brought her to breaking point.

'I can't stand this any longer.' She stood in the doorway to his study, arms folded, her voice raised higher with each word. 'You just sit there and don't say anything. The least you could do is stick up for me when she's screaming at me like that.'

'But Rose, she doesn't really mean it. She's . . .'

'Did you hear what she called me?'

'Well, I . . .'

'A dried up old bag. That's what she called me. And you just sat there and agreed with her.'

'I didn't agree. I didn't say . . .'

'No, you didn't say anything. You never do.' Rose ran into the bathroom, banging the door shut behind her.

She splashed cold water on her face, bathed her stinging eyes with a facecloth and sat on the edge of the bath for a long time, trying to calm herself down, before unjamming the bathroom door and retreating to the kitchen.

The argument had started when Kate wanted to go to the movies with some friends in Sumner – an hour and two buses away – and complained she wouldn't be able to see the end of the movie if she had to catch the last bus home. Rose had refused to compromise, which according to Kate, meant she was paranoid.

'Nobody else's mother is as mean as you. Every body else is allowed out after eleven,' Kate said.

'I don't believe that for one minute.' Rose gripped the paring knife she was using to cut vegetables for dinner.

'You never believe anything I say. I hate you!' Kate's eyes flashed.

Rose could feel herself start to burn with mounting anger. 'That's a terrible thing to say.' The paring knife slipped from her grasp.

'I hate living here,' Kate shouted. 'I wish I'd never been born.'

'I wish we'd never chosen you.' Rose clamped her mouth shut as soon as she'd said it, but it was too late to take it back. She thought of the tiny baby she'd brought home from Essex

Hospital, so filled with joy and expectation. How could that tiny baby have turned into such a monster?

Rose put out her other hand in a gesture of surrender. 'I'm sorry, Kate. I didn't mean to say that.'

'I bet.' Kate had shrugged her off. 'You're not my mother. You never were.' Her gaze was searing. 'I really hate you!' she screamed as she fled back up the hallway to her room. The door slammed behind her.

Stunned, Rose returned to the study where the television was still flickering but the sound turned way down. George was writing down some numbers while looking at his watch.

'What are you doing?'

'Timing you,' he said, adding up the numbers. 'You've been arguing for over an hour and a half so far.'

Rose felt herself boiling over. 'How could you?' She stood in front of him, furious. 'You're doing it again. Just sitting there, not taking sides, not backing me up. Did you hear what she said? She said I'm not her mother.' Just repeating it made her feel like breaking down, like crumpling in a heap on the floor and giving up entirely. What was the point?

'She didn't mean it.'

'She did. You should have seen the look in her eyes.' The hatred of the moment burned into her brain. 'You shouldn't let her get away with it, you should tell her to apologise instead of sitting there with your stopwatch timing us. It's … it's…' She was so angry she could hardly speak.

'What do you expect me to do? It won't help if I get involved.'

'It would help *me*! You should be sticking up for me, George.'

'It sounded like it was Kate who needed sticking up for that time round.' His mouth was in a tight line.

Rose knew the warning signs of his rare temper but she ignored it. 'What do you mean?'

'I heard what you said. You could hear it all over the house – the neighbourhood probably. You said you wished you'd never . . .'

'Don't repeat it,' she cried. 'It was bad enough the first time.' She sat on the chair opposite George's and looked out the window. 'She knows just how to wind me up.'

'That's no excuse, Rose, and you know it.'

She turned and faced him. 'I'd like to see what you'd do if she called you names like that and was so vile to you. *You* wouldn't put up with it.'

'I would like to think I'd turn the other cheek. That's what you should do.'

'Oh, it's all very well for you, Mister High and Mighty, sitting there on your throne and pretending you're above all that. But someone's got to run this place. Someone's got to stop her staying out half the night. You've got no backbone, George. You never did have. It's got nothing to do with your condition either. Long before you got multiple sclerosis, you would wriggle out of confrontations and sit on the fence.'

'I say, Rose, that's hardly fair.'

'You're supposed to be the man of the house. Well, it's about time you started. Because I'm sick of making all the tough calls.'

George picked up his pen and waved it at her. 'Then you should stop being so strict on her.' His voice was getting louder with every word. 'What does it matter if she stays out one night at her friend's place? It won't kill her.'

'I might have known you'd take her side when it came down to the wire.' Rose could feel spittle around her mouth. 'Now I know why you never stick up for me.'

'I'm not taking sides, Rose. I'm . . .'

'You are. You're sticking up for her and not me. That's all the gratitude I get for everything I do for you.'

'Rose, I can't take sides . . .'

But she could hear no more. She leapt out of the chair and fled to the kitchen where she sat at the table, shaking with rage. How dare he side with Kate? After all the care and attention she lavished on him, struggling to help him shower in the morning, helping him dress, taking him breakfast, baking him muffins for morning tea, lunches, dinners, getting him back into bed at night – there was no end to it, day after day. And what thanks did she get? Instead of backing her, he'd abandoned her.

Along the end of the corridor, Kate's record player started up, breaking the silence, music booming through the closed door: 'Hey, Jude…' Rose had never liked the Beatles. They were noisy and uncouth.

A cold nose nudged at her hand, lying in her lap.

'Tess. You've come to stick up for me.' The little snub-nosed King Charles spaniel had left George and come to her, which was quite something. Normally Tess remained on George's lap or in her basket at his feet. She fondled the dog's soft floppy ears. 'At least you care about me.'

The dog trotted over to the pantry and looked expectantly at the door. She wanted her dinner.

With a deep sigh, she stood and fetched the dog biscuits out of the cupboard, doled out a handful into the dog bowl and sat down again while Tess began to crunch through her dinner.

Not even the dog was on her side.

She sat there, staring unseeing out the window. The Beatles were telling her not to carry the world on her shoulders. What choice have I got? she felt like shouting. *Hey, Jude* ground on to the end then silence. Soon afterwards, Kate's door opened and moments later she appeared in the kitchen, bearing an overnight bag.

'Where do you think you're going with that?' Rose couldn't help herself. After battling for so long, she wasn't giving up now.

'I'm going to Sumner and I'm staying the night at Barbara's.'

Rose jumped up, hurried over to her daughter and stood beside her, holding herself steady on the fridge. 'You can't do that. Her parents are never home and her older brother is always having parties. You told me that yourself.'

'You can't stop me. I'm going.' Kate brushed past, her backpack knocking against Rose's shoulder.

'I *can* stop you, and I will. You can't go.'

'You're not the boss of me. I'm old enough to live my own life. I'm not a child any more.'

'You are, actually. You're not sixteen yet. And that means I'm your legal guardian. You're not going out tonight.'

'I'll leave home then. If that's what it takes, I'll pack my things and go live with Barbara. Her parents won't mind.'

Rose felt herself losing control. She started screaming at her daughter, words just coming out of her mouth unbidden. She was so upset, she had no memory of what she'd said but it had the effect of impelling Kate back to her room, the door slamming behind her again.

Kate didn't go to Sumner. Some time later, she came out of her room for dinner. They ate in silence, the news blaring to make up for the absence of conversation. When he finished eating, George lined up his knife and fork in a neat line on his plate and pushed it to the back of his knee tray.

'Come here, please. Both of you.'

Kate looked up at him quizzically. Rose knew Kate would take her mother on anytime, but she rarely argued with her father. She went to stand beside George.

'Rose?'

Reluctantly, she put her plate down on the side table and joined them, standing on the other side of his armchair, keeping her distance as much as she could. She was in no mood for silly games.

'I want to congratulate you both.' He took hold of Kate's hand with his right hand – his good one – and raised it high in the air.

'Rose?'

Rose suspected she knew what was coming and wasn't happy. She refused to hold his hand.

He ignored her avoidance. 'You're the champions.' He was smiling with that puckish gleam in his eyes Rose knew so well. 'You've broken your own record.'

'Why, what do you mean?' Kate looked grim.

'Two hours and forty-eight minutes,' he said, grinning.

'What?'

'You two were arguing for precisely two hours and forty-eight minutes. That's an all-time record.'

'How do you know?' Kate had stopped scowling.

George let go of his daughter's hand and pulled out his writing pad. 'It's all here.' He showed them his spidery scrawl – even harder to read than Rose's own writing since his multiple sclerosis had become so advanced – and there it was, a list of times: stops and starts, with the end of the final round underlined several times. 'Total, two hours and forty-eight minutes.'

Kate folded her arms tightly, scowled again and stomped off down the hall to her room but this time didn't slam the door. Rose silently gathered up the dishes and retired to the kitchen, still angry with both of them.

She'd never forgotten that awful evening and she'd never said anything like that to Kate again, no matter how much she provoked her.

'You okay, Mum?'

Rose smiled at her daughter, so different now.

'Of course. I'd better get George settled for the night.'

'You never stop, do you?'

'I often wonder how you fit it all in too, you know.'

'Everybody does that nowadays, Mum. Every woman, anyway. I must be a chip off the old block. Now, I really must go.'

'So you are.' Rose laughed and kissed her daughter goodbye. 'Thank you.'

As she closed the door she looked across the brightly lit courtyard to the old family home beyond, the family home she and George had brought Kate up in until they'd had to build a wheelchair-accessible house in the footprint of the old asparagus patch.

A chip off the old block? That was one of the best things Kate could have said. She nursed that thought as she prepared George's hot-water bottle, gave him his pills and climbed into bed with a book. Was Kate really taking after her? Even though she wasn't flesh and blood, did it mean the time spent nurturing and supporting her daughter through all those difficult teenage years, through births, deaths and marriages, did it mean Kate was really hers? Perhaps she was.

Chapter 5.

Christchurch, 1987

Rose wiped away tears from slicing onions, resisting the temptation to give in and shed real tears. She'd promised when George was first diagnosed with multiple sclerosis that she would never feel sorry for herself and she wasn't going to start now just because she was under a bit of pressure. Over the years, she'd watched the degenerative disease eat away at his nerves and slowly remove the mobility in his limbs. It had been as hard for her – the carer, whose job it was to provide unflagging support even when she felt like giving up – as it had been for him. In some ways, his comparatively placid and peaceful nature had made his acceptance a little easier. Rose often wished she could be as patient and uncomplaining.

Hastily, she julienned carrots and celery, set three eggs to hard-boil, and made a roux for Kate's favourite comfort food: fish pie. She was way behind already: George had to be shifted from his study into the living room, the study needed tidying, the table to be set, her tramping pack and lunch things were still scattered around the kitchen, and the dog was dancing beside the bench waiting to be fed. At this rate, the pie wouldn't be ready until well after seven and her granddaughter Amelia would be fractious with hunger.

You *will* try to do everything at once, she told herself sternly. You should take note of Kate and slow down a bit.

Easier said than done, though, if she was to have her own life occasionally. It was the tramping trip that had made her late. The walk on the hills with the Over Forties Tramping Club had taken longer than expected because Nellie had hurt her knee coming down off a stile and their usual fast pace had slowed considerably after that. Tramping in the fresh clean air up there, where Rose could look out over the plains to the snowy Southern Alps and across to the Pacific Ocean – it tended to clear the mind and sweep away the distress of dealing daily with George's disability.

It was another half-hour before the pie was in the oven and she could turn her attention to George.

He was asleep in his chair, unaware that they were running late, oblivious to the scattered newspapers and journals around his side-table.

'Time to go into the other room,' she said loudly to wake him.

He gave her one of his glorious smiles. 'There you are Rose. You've caught the sun today. You look radiant.'

'Thank you George. It was a lovely day,'

Tess jumped onto his knee and licked his nose.

George laughed with pleasure. 'You're worth a thousand GPs, Tess.' The dog nuzzled into him then turned round twice and settled in his lap. He absentmindedly stroked the dog's brown and white fur.

'Time for you to move, George. The family will be here very soon.'

George never complained, never protested at being hoisted in and out of his wheelchair, never let his gradual deterioration get him down. Or at least, not that she knew of. He'd always kept his darkest thoughts to himself.

Rose adjusted the canvas cradle under George, hitched the four corners onto the hoist and turned the handle to raise him high enough to clear the arms of the chair and settle him back down in the wheelchair. Success. Since the hoist had arrived, she'd not once had to call up Kate or the police to scoop George off the floor.

Once he was settled on the sofa with the dog and his crossword, Rose gave the study a quick tidy, scooted into the bathroom to clean herself up then the bedroom to get changed out of her tramping clothes. But she'd only just tossed the thick rugby socks and mud-caked trousers into the wash-basket when she heard the familiar clang of the cowbells on the front door.

'Hi Mum, we're here.' It was Kate calling from the hall.

'I'll be there in a minute. You go on in.'

'Grandma? Where's Grandma?' Amelia called out. A second later, the four-year-old was in her bedroom flinging herself round her knees.

She picked her up and hugged her then set her down again. 'Grandma's changing. She'll be ready in a minute. You go and see Grandpa and Tess.'

'Why have you got those funny green tights on Grandma?'

'They're for tramping. I wear them so my legs don't get cold'

'They're funny.' Amelia giggled. 'You look like Kermit the frog.'

Rose laughed. 'So I do. My tramping buddies would like to hear that.'

Her granddaughter took off again and Rose soon heard the sound of George's laughter in the living room.

Quickly, she peeled off her Kermit tights and slipped on her navy trousers and tartan blouse; then a hasty dab of powder, a scrape of lipstick and squirt of White Linen perfume before hurrying into the living room to greet Kate and her husband.

'David's got our contribution for tonight,' Kate said, giving her mother a kiss.

'I'll take it through to the kitchen, if you like, Rose.' David held out the Country Road bag weighed down by its contents.

'Goodness, I wasn't expecting anything.' She led the way into the kitchen.

David picked up a dish and put it on the bench. 'That's from Kate. She says apple crumble is your favourite.' Next he fished out a bottle of champagne. 'Kate has some good news.'

'Really?'

'You get the glasses and I'll pop the cork.'

'Is it a …?'

'No! Don't say a word.' David held two fingers up to his lips. 'Wait for Kate.'

Rose went through into the sitting room where Amelia was entertaining her grandfather with her latest toy, posting moulded shapes into matching holes around a plastic sphere, and Kate was sitting next to him on the high-winged sofa, smiling. Rose did as instructed and extracted four champagne flutes from the mahogany chiffonier, placed them on the silver tray on top and waited for David to pour.

'So, what's the news?' she said when everyone had a glass.

'We're having another baby,' Kate said, beaming. 'At last.'

'That's wonderful.' Rose and George both laughed. 'Congratulations!'

They each held up their glasses in a toast and took a sip.

'Real French champagne,' Kate said. 'I'd better make the most of it. The new advice is not to drink when you're pregnant.'

'We'd better be careful then. It's been quite a journey getting here.' David gulped half his glass. 'Boy that tastes good.'

'Hey, what's the hurry?' Kate held up her glass. 'It'll be good for you to join me in abstinence.'

'Really?' David examined his glass then swallowed another mouthful. 'I suppose it wouldn't hurt.'

'Maybe it's a boy this time,' Kate said.

'Maybe it's twins.' Rose knew her daughter had been taking fertility pills. After it had taken such a long time to produce Amelia, Kate had said she was going straight back on them. She was getting too long in the tooth for having babies, she'd said, and wanted to move the next one along.

Kate had never been patient, never been one to sit back and wait for something to happen; ever since she was a child, she'd known how to boss people around to get her own way, to push things along so they fitted into her timetable. And people let her do it. Rose had often chided herself for letting her daughter take over, but such was the force of her will, it seemed impossible to foil her.

Where did that strong will come from? Not from herself, surely? Maybe it was the birth mother, Elizabeth. Maybe she'd been a determined young woman too. She'd often wondered what had become of her, after she'd given her baby away. Had she remarried? Had she gone on to have a family of her own? She hoped so, for her sake.

'Twins would be too much for me at my ripe old age.'

David looked aghast. 'Me too.'

'Are we going to have two babies, Mummy?' Amelia stopped posting the coloured wooden shapes into the hexagonal box, jumped down off the couch and ran to Kate, climbing on her lap. 'I want a baby brother *and* a baby sister.'

'One at a time!'

'Oh I don't know.' Rose grinned.

Kate pulled a face.

'Now, I must go and check on the fish pie.'

'My favourite, Mum, you spoil me. Can I help?'

'No, you stay here with Grandpa. You can set the table in here though. We can use the fish knives and forks.'

As soon as she'd said it, she wished it unsaid. Those damned fish knives and forks. Antiques, made of bone and sterling silver, a gift from Aunt Doris, they'd initially been intended for Kate as a wedding present but then Doris decided Kate's husband wasn't good enough for her – or nice enough to Doris – and had given them to Rose instead. There was no present for Kate. Doris didn't even come to the wedding, which Kate pronounced a blessing. Rose was inclined to agree with her.

She was like that, Doris, changing her favours on a whim, becoming thoroughly vindictive and even downright nasty when she decided she didn't like someone – often for a minor infringement like being born Catholic, or failing to agree with her on the choice of Prime Minister.

Rose had been on the receiving end of her rudeness more than once. Right up to the day she'd died, Aunt Doris had borne a grudge against her for some unknown slight and had left half her estate to some very distant relative in Dunedin who'd had very little to do with her – except kowtow from a distance – and the other half to Rose, her closest relative in all ways. Rose would like to say it wasn't the loss of half the estate that hurt – but it was. It would have made all the difference in getting the care for George that she needed. There wasn't a lot of money involved – but there was even less after half had gone to the southern interloper and there had been too little to buy the electric wheelchair and hoist, let alone provide a part-time nurse for extra care. Rose was finding, in her advancing years, that the constant attention he required was exhausting. Not that she would ever admit it to Kate.

Kate had been furious at Aunt Doris's slight to her mother and never wasted an opportunity to show it, even now.

'Oh, the Great Aunt Doris memorial fish knives and forks,' Kate said sarcastically. 'Honestly, Mum, of all the domestic implements man has created I would have to say bone-handled fish knives and forks would have to be among the most useless. I mean, what possible . . .?'

'I know, I know,' Rose soothed. 'Sorry I mentioned them. Put out whatever you like on the table, as long as we can eat with it.'

She retreated to the kitchen with her glass of champagne; she didn't want David polishing it off. She'd grown fond of David over the years – it had taken time after his cavalier treatment of Kate when they'd first gone out together – but he'd proven himself a caring husband, a good provider and a doting father. And he was kind to George, listening to his endless theories, debating politics and current affairs. But he did have a fondness for the drink.

Pulling down the kitchen blinds against the chill twilight, she flicked a wry smile at the reflection of herself in the window. Aunt Doris had a lot to answer for. The fish knives and forks were only a tiny part of the problems she'd caused.

Ever since she'd come to live in Christchurch Doris had become increasingly difficult, holding her wealth – diminished though it may be – and her antiques as an enticement for her family to be nice to her. One false move and you'd be cut out of her will. Kate used to say she'd been disinherited so many times she'd forgotten whether she was in the will or out – and she'd stopped caring.

But that hadn't stopped her and Kate from swooping down on Doris's house the day after she'd died – and the day before the distant relative from down south made her own swoop north – to collect those treasures of Rose's mother that had fallen into Doris's hands. She remembered the glee with which she and Kate had made the raid, and the snippy comments from the southern imposter, who'd inquired the next day after every ring and bracelet, every piece of bone china, even the ugly ormolu clock, as if it were the last treasure of Tutankhamen. What amused Rose, even now three years on, was the incredible detail the imposter knew of such things when she'd visited Doris in Christchurch just the one time. It was Rose's belief she'd carried out an inventory of the place – of all the drawers and cupboards – every time Doris had gone to the bathroom or after she'd retired for the evening.

The fish knives and forks had been on her list.

After Doris died, Rose had tried to give them to Kate. 'She's dead now. She can't take them off you any more.'

'You can keep them, Mum. Doris isn't my real family anyway.'

Which had hurt even more than Doris's unending rejection of her daughter.

She hardly thought about it these days, about Kate being adopted, being from another gene pool. It was more than thirty years since Rose and George had signed that piece of paper promising never to tell Kate about her origins, promising to keep her birth mother's name a secret and pretending, whenever Kate had asked, that they didn't know the woman's name. She'd almost forgotten the awful feeling of guilt each time she'd denied Kate the truth about her origins. Kate hadn't mentioned it for a long time. But she obviously hadn't forgotten.

Rose often wondered how Kate would have turned out if she hadn't adopted her. Sometimes she thought her daughter wasn't like her at all, and sometimes she could see similarities – and not just in the blue eyes and brown hair, even though Kate had dyed hers auburn these past ten years. The similarities were more in her behaviour – always busying herself, never sitting still for long, making sure her diary was crammed with appointments. And her optimism. Rose felt she could take some of the credit for that at least.

They'd made sure Kate had always known she was adopted – when she was about four, as soon as they thought she could understand, they'd told her. Rose remembered buying a distinctive pale orange and green-covered book, *The Chosen Baby*.

George would settle in his favourite armchair in front of a blazing coal fire in the living room, sit his daughter on his knee and read aloud, pointing at the orange and green pictures, answering Kate's questions about her own adoption.

'Did you come to a hospital like that and pick me out?'

'Was it because I had blue eyes like you and Mummy?'

'Would you still have adopted me if I didn't smile at you?'

'Was Vicki-Jane adopted too?'

And when George had patiently answered and managed to turn all the pages, it was always the same:

'Read it again, Daddy,' she'd say as soon as George closed the cover. 'Again please.'

And George would open it up and start once more at the first page: 'Once upon a time . . .' and tell for possibly the hundredth time the story of Mr and Mrs Brown and how their baby Peter and, after a few more years, his sister Mary, were adopted into a home where they were wanted and loved.

The Chosen Baby seemed to have satisfied Kate's thirst to know her origins long after it was consigned to the bookcase and replaced by other books at her bedside – *Swallows and Amazons, Ballet Shoes, The Incredible Journey*.

It wasn't until she'd turned thirteen that she wanted to know more, that the simple explanations in *The Chosen Baby* failed to suffice. That was the year that she first demanded to know who her 'real' mother was.

All her teenage years she kept asking, writing letters to her mother – with no address to send them to – throwing tantrums over not being told the truth and trying to find out for herself. Rose had felt like a criminal at the time, denying her daughter the one thing she most wanted to know, and she still felt bad about it to this day. But the Social Security Department had insisted it be kept a secret. She and George had signed a deed promising that's what they would do. It was part of the deal, part of the price they'd paid for being given Katharine for keeps: they could tell her she was adopted, but no more.

And now it looked as if the secret was to be revealed and Kate would be able to find out for herself. Rose had seen the stories in the paper about the law change. Undoubtedly Kate would have seen them too, but she'd never said a word.

Should she give Kate the piece of paper, long buried in George's deed box, the birth certificate containing her daughter's original name – the name her birth mother had given her – as well as her mother's and father's names?

She couldn't. She and George had made a promise. And it wouldn't be right to expose the birth mother to scrutiny after all these years, risk ruining her life, whatever that might be. What if she had a family of her own? She might not have told her husband or her children. What then? Rose couldn't be responsible for that. Or what if she had gone on having relationships outside wedlock?

When Kate was a teenager, Aunt Doris used to say that Kate came from 'bad seed' – that she had inherited her mother's genes for promiscuity and would do nothing but give the family a bad reputation. Rose half feared she was right as she watched her daughter chase after boys every time they went to the beach, to the skating rink, to the rugby. Kate was incorrigible, managing to transform her perfectly respectable clothes into something that made her look like she had no self respect, made her look just like her friends, who hitched their skirts up above their knees, teased their hair in a matted pile on top of their heads, and stuffed cotton wool inside their bras to make A-cups into a triple-C.

Rose remembered that Saturday afternoon when Kate was thirteen; she'd driven past the ice-rink on her way to visit her old friend Joan and there, in the carpark, was Kate and two of her school friends, skates hanging carelessly off their shoulders, looking much older than their years, talking to a group of boys gathered around a large white low-slung car. She'd been so surprised, she'd driven around the block and parked on the other side of the street, far enough away to remain unseen but close enough to see what was going on.

The boys were smoking. They'd offered the girls a puff and Kate had taken the cigarette, held it up to her lips then puffed out a plume of smoke towards the boy who'd given it to her. Rose had been so outraged she almost leapt out of the car, rushed over the road and plucked it from her daughter's fingers. Almost.

When Kate handed the cigarette back, she leaned over and gave the boy a kiss.

That's when she noticed Kate was wearing lipstick and the jersey she had on was not the same jersey she'd left home in just after lunch. This jersey was tight, black and polo-necked. Even under her jacket, her chest was fully outlined. Rose couldn't believe it was her daughter.

'You mark my words,' Doris had said, 'that girl's heading for trouble. Her mother was nothing but a tramp, and now the daughter's taking after her. You shouldn't let her behave like that.'

~ ~ ~

The Adoption Amendment Act was passed and still Kate didn't say anything. It wasn't until after James was born that the subject came up. Rose was visiting her daughter and new grandson at the Women's Hospital, carrying camellias and rhododendrons from the garden. Kate was alone, sitting up in bed reading a magazine.

'Where's my new grandson?' Rose said after she'd kissed her daughter.

'He's away in the nursery. They seem to think I need a rest.'

'And so you do. You make the most of it.'

'I know, I know. There won't be much sleep when I get home with him.'

'I'll just be a minute. I'll find a vase.' Rose was half-way out the door.

'No, don't. Not yet. There's something I've got to ask you.'

'What is it?' Rose had a sense of dread. By the look on Kate's face, something serious had happened.

'The results came back from James' heel-prick test today, and they said he tested positive for cystic fibrosis.'

'What? Surely not?' Rose sat down hard on the big high-sided nursing chair next to the bed.

'Yes. They said not to set too much store by it yet, that it's only a preliminary result. They've taken another blood sample and are doing more tests over the next few days.'

'Well that's something.'

'But Mum, I have to know . . . Kate put her magazine down and pushed herself to sit up straight. '. . . if there's any cystic fibrosis in my family. It's important.'

Rose wilted under her stare. She knew perfectly well just what Kate meant by 'my family'. She didn't mean Rose and George, or her parents Amelia and Jim. She didn't mean the taciturn C.T. and his wife Margaret. She meant her own birth mother: she who could not be named. And her birth mother's family, whoever they were and whatever their state of health.

There was a long silence.

'I'm going to have to track her down now. You can see that, can't you?'

'I'm not sure I . . .'

'Whenever a doctor's asked me "Do you have any of these diseases in your family's medical history?" I've never been able to answer it. And it's always bugged me. But now it's of vital importance. I've got to find out what's in my genes, because now it's affecting my children's genes and it's just not fair on them. I need to know what the past can tell me about my baby's future.'

'Of course.' Rose felt utterly defeated. There was nothing she could do now to stop it. The rollercoaster ride she'd always dreaded was about to begin – the rollercoaster that she'd been told twisted and turned and looped back on itself whenever anyone tried to find their birth family.

She'd talked about it with Joan over the past few months, ever since the first reports had appeared in the newspaper about the changing law. Both Rose and Joan had agreed they would never bring up the adoption law changes with their daughters; they would wait for them to broach it. And neither girl had.

Now Rose realised that had probably been foolish, that she'd had her head in the sand and of course the issue hadn't gone away.

'Will you help me find her?' Kate asked.

'Of course,' Rose repeated numbly. She would have to support her on the path to discovery, or at least pretend she did. Much as she loved Kate, she wasn't sure she could ever welcome the search taking place. What if she lost her to her birth mother? What if Kate found she liked her birth mother a lot more than she liked Rose? The woman would be a lot younger than her, for a start, and probably a lot more with-it. She'd probably have her own family, the brothers and sisters Kate had always wanted. She'd go off with them and Rose would never see her again. That's what had happened to one of the old ladies at Woodchester. Her adopted daughter had found her birth mother and had little to do with her adoptive mother for years afterwards, only coming back to her when her birth mother had remarried.

'Don't look like that, Mum.'

'Like what?'

'Such a long face. Anyone would think I was going to rush off with her and never see you again.'

'Well, I was thinking that, yes.'

'Don't be so silly. You've been my Mum for over thirty years. I'm not going to run off on you now.'

'I suppose not.' But Rose didn't feel convinced.

~ ~ ~

A few days later, when Kate was back home from the hospital, further tests came back to say that James did not have cystic fibrosis.

But Rose had given it a lot of thought.

Soon after the test results came through, she copied the relevant details from her daughter's original birth certificate onto a piece of paper.

'I wanted to save you the bureaucracy of having to ask for it officially,' she said as she handed it over.

'Is that my original name?'

Rose nodded.

'It's nice.'

Rose didn't like the sound of that, or where it might be heading. If Kate thought her original name was 'nice', did that mean she'd feel that way about everything connected with her origins, including her mother?

'Underneath is the name of your birth mother and father.' But she could tell Kate had already seen that. She was holding the photocopied piece of paper as if it were the Holy Grail. She took a seat at Kate's kitchen table and traced her finger along the groove in the polished rimu.

It was a while before Kate spoke. At last she said quietly, 'Thanks Mum.' She came over and gave her a hug. 'I don't expect it's easy for you.'

Rose decided she might as well be honest. 'No.'

'I'll show David.' Kate left her in the kitchen and carried the piece of paper reverently away to the nursery where David was changing James' disposable under the watchful eye of Amelia, never far away from her baby brother.

~ ~ ~

In the spring Rose marked her birthday by retiring from her weekend duties at Woodchester, farewelling the elderly patients with difficulty – she felt they had become part of her life, even though George and Kate expressed little interest in them. And now she found her days longer, her patience with her husband more sorely tested; she felt confined, tied to the house and to George, even though she knew he would never have wanted her to feel that.

One morning, a little over a month after giving up her job, she was awoken early by George calling across to her from his bed. Raised on large, solid chocks of wood, the single bed was high enough to facilitate her washing and handling him on and off the mattress, but its height meant he seemed to tower over her when she was lying in the bed next to him.

'Rose. I say, Rose.'

She struggled to wake up. 'Yes, dear, what is it?'

'I'm afraid I've had a bit of an accident.'

She knew exactly what that meant. Before she could stop herself, she said 'Oh no, not again.'

Then the smell hit her. Her nursing training, followed by her time changing nappies when Katharine was a baby, had taught her not to gag. No matter how bad the smell, she would always cope.

It wasn't the smell that got to her. It was the knowledge that for the fifth morning in a row, George had messed himself and she would have to start her day not with a hot shower and breakfast over the morning paper but cleaning up faeces, washing him down, changing then scrubbing down the sheets and his pyjamas, and doing two loads of laundry all over again.

And this morning she was supposed to be tramping with her friends from the Over Forties Tramping Club. If she was to meet them at the foot of the hills at ten, she would have to get George cleaned up, make his breakfast and get him into his day-chair before half past nine.

'I won't be a minute.' She eased herself out of bed, hurried to the bathroom and relieved herself then stood in front of the bathroom mirror, staring at her reflection in despair.

The face staring back at her looked years older than she remembered seeing before. Her fly-away hair was sticking out in a frizzy halo; her usually rosy cheeks were wan. What had happened to the radiant young woman from Te Kuiti?

She wanted to run. She couldn't stand it any longer.

Suddenly, as if propelled by an unknown force, she was striding down the hall to the kitchen. She grabbed the car keys off the rack, opened the garage door, backed the car out, turned down the drive and sped away up the road. Where to go? The only person she could think of was Joan. Joan had nursed her husband through cancer until his death at a comparatively early age. Joan would know what to do.

Turning out of their street onto the main road was always difficult; at this hour of the day, to turn right to reach Joan's, crossing over the busy early morning flow of traffic into town required precision timing. Rose was finding it hard to concentrate and missed several opportunities. A car behind her honked impatiently.

She couldn't do it.

Slowly, she pulled over to the side of the road, waited for the following car to get onto the main road then u-turned and drove the few hundred metres back home, parking the car in the garage, its door still wide open.

She sat there, unable to move, her hands wrapped around the top of the steering wheel. She was a nurse. A trained nurse. She could never run away from a patient in need of nursing. Those three years of training, learning the devotion required to her duty, the importance of the patient and of meeting their every need – what did she think she was doing? What would Matron say? Images of the late Miss Widdowson flashed into her mind – the stern-faced stickler for the rules, whose regime at Public had taught her everything she knew, not just about medicine and treatments, but about care of the patient, about putting the patient first. Miss Widdowson would never countenance running away from a nursing task because it was too hard, because she was sick of it.

Suddenly, Rose felt incredibly calm, as if she were watching herself through the car windscreen. She didn't feel like Rose; she wondered if perhaps she'd gone mad, if this dissociation she was experiencing was the first sign she was losing her mind. Or was she simply coming to her senses?

Calmly, she opened the car door and got out, walked through the garage door to the laundry, picked up the paper towels and bath towels, cloths, disinfectant, washbasin, apron and a clean set of George's underwear off yesterday's pile of clean clothes and marched herself down to the bedroom. The sight of George, lying helplessly in his own mess made her weak with shame. How could she do this to him?

'Where've you been, Rose? I thought you'd driven away.' George looked away. 'I thought you'd left me.'

She struggled with the guilt threatening to overwhelm her. She wanted to apologise, to confess, but that would only make George feel worse. 'No, George, I wouldn't do that to you.' She blushed at her duplicity. 'I just had to move the car to get something out of the garage. You know how crowded it is in there.'

'I don't do this on purpose, you know,' he said quietly, still looking at the closed curtains. 'Do you think I do? Do you think I can help myself?'

She shook her head. 'No, of course not,' she said brusquely. 'I'm sorry about the delay, but I'm here now. Let's get started, shall we?'

Covering her nightdress with the blue plastic Harrods' apron, Rose approached George's bed and, from then on, didn't allow herself to think about what she was doing until it was over and George was sitting in his chair, dressed, his razor in his good hand as he set about shaving in front of the magnifying mirror on his tray-table. He remained cool, distant. She understood; he wasn't a fool.

The washing machine agitator marked time in the adjacent laundry as she sat at the kitchen table and thought about what she'd done – or nearly done. She decided to ring Joan and confess.

Joan tried to soothe, to minimise the offence. 'You're making a mountain out of a molehill, old girl,' she said. 'We've all wanted to run away at times.'

'But I actually did it. I got to the end of the street…'

'And then you turned round and did your duty,' Joan said. 'Tell you what, I'll pop round for a cuppa this afternoon and we can…'

'I can't,' Rose cried. 'I'd love to talk to you, but I'm going on a tramp today. In fact, I've got to be off very soon or I won't make it.'

'Then I'll be round at half past five when you're back from your day trip,' Joan said firmly. 'You can pour me a gin and we'll talk.' Then, before Rose could protest, she was saying goodbye and was gone.

Hastily, Rose laid out everything George would need for the day while she was away. No need for his pickle bottle any longer now he had a catheter, but there was still his lunch to prepare, just the right amount of tea in the thermos flask, the paper, phone, pens, notepaper and other paraphernalia he needed to occupy his day. Each time she took something to him, he turned away and occupied himself with the radio, the newspaper, anything he could find. She was relieved; she was still upset – at herself and at his condition. As the multiple sclerosis ate away at him, so it was eating away her freedom and her enjoyment of life.

She could work it through when she was out in the fresh air on the hills – because she was determined to go.

But with eleven of them out tramping together there was always someone wanting to walk beside her and talk; she hardly had a moment to herself. But the dread she'd expected to feel returning home at the end of the day was gone; the claustrophobia she'd feared had vanished. Feigning cheeriness, pretending nothing had happened that morning, she breezed into George's study and launched into an account of the tramp, filling the air with anecdotes and reported conversations until the tension between them loosened.

Then Joan arrived with both gin and tonic and took Rose off into the other room for a private discussion, suggesting Rose talk to the doctor about the selective colostomy surgery that many people with long-term MS underwent to solve the incontinence problem.

'And you should be able to get a nurse,' Joan said.

'But we can't afford one.' She thought bitterly about Aunt Doris's inheritance and how there hadn't been enough to pay for a nurse to help her – not even three mornings a week.

'No, not a private nurse. You should qualify for a district nurse.'

The next day, Rose phoned the doctor, who applied to Nurse Maude and, before too long, nurses were rostered to visit every morning, even weekends, to get George up, washed and dressed. There were no more early-morning escape attempts.

Rose still experienced frustration, anger even at George's dependence on her. But she made sure she got out of the house at least once a week to tramp the hills – the daily nurse visits made her mornings a lot easier – and for three weeks every year, she could go on longer tramps, staying overnight while George went into respite hospital care.

She still missed Woodchester, the men and women she'd befriended there and the sense of purpose to her day. At Woodchester, she could make a difference to the lives of forty-two frail and ailing people, could bring a smile to their faces, could give them comfort when their children failed to visit and could return dignity to their day if they soiled themselves. She missed the routine, the gratitude, the camaraderie.

She imagined it must have been the same for George after he gave up work – worse even. After twenty years working for the bank, most of that time in the cavernous ANZ banking chamber in Hereford Street, he would have been desolate having to give it up while still comparatively young at the age of fifty. But he'd never said, had remained stoic and cheerful, as he always did in adversity. He had inherited his father's ability to say nothing, especially when something was really troubling him. Stubbornly, he refused to be drawn, even as the years passed; as if giving up work in your prime was something everybody did.

At first, though, the loss of the daily bus trip into town with his packed lunch and the interaction with his colleagues would have scarcely been noticed, because they'd travelled the world – their one and only OE, as Kate called it.

They'd both known the trip had to be taken then while George was still comparatively mobile. Within a few years, the doctors had warned, his mobility, along with a lot of his physical functions, would go. They were both in their late fifties and were both novices at travelling. George's service in the Pacific had been the only overseas travel; Rose had never been out of the country. This was to be their one and only chance to see the world. So Rose took unpaid leave from the hospital and embarked with George on a four-month trip to all the places they'd dreamed of going.

She'd managed to get George on his two walking sticks almost anywhere an able-bodied man could go – up the lift in the Eiffel Tower, into a boat underneath the Niagara Falls, into a plane over the Grand Canyon; they'd got tipsy on ouzo in Greece, eaten snails in France, stayed in Florence Nightingale's house in London, surveyed the field of Waterloo in Belgium and, in Pennsylvania, the site of Lincoln's Gettysberg address (which George could still recite in total – however useless his limbs might become, his mind remained fully honed), kissed the Blarney Stone in Ireland, visited countless Roman ruins and English castles. In Scotland, George had come down with a fever. She blamed the hectic schedule for exhausting him; until Scotland, he'd been fine. He was admitted to the Royal Edinburgh Infirmary for six weeks while they checked him over; to fill the time, she'd worked at Jenner's department store behind the glove counter.

The Infirmary's diagnosis had been the same as twenty years earlier when George's multiple sclerosis was discovered. But there was one bit of good news: there would be occasional periods of remission, such as at that time, when they'd travelled the world.

Returning home had been hard. It was as if he'd used up all his extra energy while away because within weeks, George's MS had regressed and his mood with it. Unusually for him, he was grumpy and tired and Rose put it down to grieving for his old way of life, his daily routine at the bank, the numerous people he came into contact with there, the stimulation that had nourished him.

She'd tried to make up for it by inviting his friends around, by keeping him occupied with his hobbies, his banknotes, his American Civil War books. After a time, his humour returned. Rose kept herself busy tramping, making George's life as comfortable as she could and looking after baby James on the occasional weekdays when Kate was called into work.

~ ~ ~

It was on one of those days, when Kate came in from work to pick up James, that she thrust a letter into Rose's hand. They'd gone into the spare room, where James was asleep in his carrycot.

'This came in the mail today.' She looked unaccountably guilty as she handed over the envelope, as if she should be ashamed of something.

'What is it?'

Kate went over to James' carrycot, checked him then looked back at her mother. 'It's a letter from my birth mother.'

Rose drew in her breath and steadied herself on the dresser.

'I wrote to her a few days ago. I didn't want to worry you, in case I never heard back. But she's written this.'

Rose let go the dresser and studied the envelope. A Wellington postmark. Smooth, rounded, nicely slanted, neat handwriting. She opened it and looked at the letter – much neater handwriting than her own, which Kate often complained was almost impossible to read. Good spelling.

'Are you sure you want me to read this?'

'Yes, Mum, of course.'

November 25, 1987.

Dear Katharine

Well, that was certainly a bolt out of the blue getting a letter from you. Luckily I have a strong constitution and made a quick recovery, and decided to reply quickly to you and perhaps find some answers for both of us after all these years. I have often wondered what became of you and now I know.

First you must understand that when I was a girl it was not the accepted thing for anyone to keep what they called an illegitimate baby. I was not given a choice like they are today and was whisked away to a home for unmarried mothers in Christchurch where I waited for the birth of my baby. Afterwards we were not allowed to see the baby or even hold her, and were not allowed to make contact with the baby's family. It seems cruel and heartless the way girls were pressured into parting with their babies. We were told we would be giving a childless couple the chance to become parents and the child would have a better upbringing, which is possibly true, but of course the blood tie is terribly important.

I didn't put a veto on my name because I didn't think you would want to find me, but I suppose I subconsciously wanted to know what had happened to you anyway.

I lost contact with your father when he discovered I was pregnant. It's not that he was a bad person but he wasn't ready to carry the responsibility of a family. I don't know what became of him. He was tall and good looking.

In a very strange coincidence, the day your letter arrived, in the same post I received a copy of "North and South" magazine with two articles by Katharine Stewart in it. I imagine that must be you?

It is all right for you to write to me here - my husband Steven knows about you. However, I have never told my children. I have a son and a daughter, who were born two and four years after you were, but I ask you to please respect my privacy as I'm not ready to tell them yet.

Do you come to Wellington sometimes? I would like to meet you but can't really leave town without questions being asked.

Liz'.

'Goodness, Kate, she wants to meet you.' Rose handed the letter back and smiled at her daughter, feigning enthusiasm. She knew how badly Kate had wanted to meet her birth mother, had wanted to discover her true origins, but Rose felt only dread.

'Do you think I should?' Kate took the letter and held it in front of her, as if finding it hard to believe it real.

'You've wanted to meet her all your life. Surely . . .'

'I know. But now it might be about to happen, I'm scared.'

She put her arm round her daughter, trying to muster the support she didn't feel she could give. 'She's got two other children now. You've got siblings.'

Kate returned a wry smile. 'I've got a brother and a sister. Just what I've always wanted – but they don't even know I exist.'

'I dare say you'll get to meet them eventually, when Liz is ready to tell them.'

Kate looked doubtful. 'She doesn't sound too keen.'

'Put yourself in her shoes for a minute, Kate. She's had a huge shock, hearing from you after all these years. She needs time now to work it through.'

'Do you think I should tell Dad?'

'Of course. Why wouldn't you?'

Kate looked down at the carrycot where James was still fast asleep and didn't answer.

'Come on then.' Rose couldn't understand Kate's reluctance to tell her father. He was a complete softie where his daughter was concerned. She took Kate's arm and led her to the study.

George couldn't find his reading glasses and then took an eternity to read the letter while Kate stood fidgeting and Rose perched on the side of his chair, helping interpret the handwriting.

'I see,' was all he said when he finished.

Kate stood there expectantly, clearly waiting for him to continue.

Rose said nothing.

It was James who broke the silence, starting to whimper from his carrycot in the spare room.

'I'll have to go,' Kate said quickly, glancing out the door then back at her father. 'What do you think of the letter Dad? Isn't it exciting?'

George looked thoughtful. 'It may be exciting for you. I know you've wanted this for a long time, Katie. But you must spare a thought for your mother. You can be sure that she will be terrified of losing you now.'

'But Mum,' Kate turned to her. 'I would never do that. You'll always be my Mum.'

Rose tried to manage a smile.

'Honestly, Mum.'

James' whimper had turned into a full-throated wail.

‘I’ll have to take him home for a feed.’ She looked torn, as if she didn’t know whether to comfort her baby or her mother first.

Rose could have helped her, could have said ‘Don’t worry, dear, I’ll be fine’, and Kate could have left reassured. But she couldn’t do that. She felt unusually lifeless; not even James’ piercing cries could rouse her.

Kate disappeared out the door and the wailing abated. Moments later she stood in the doorway holding the carrycot and its whimpering, wriggling baby.

‘I’m sorry, Mum. But I’ve got to go. I’ll call you later. Okay?’

‘Yes, you’d better go.’

‘Bye, Dad.’ Kate put the carrycot down for a moment and kissed her father.

Rose stood and followed her to the front door.

‘Bye, Kate.’ She let Kate kiss her without responding, not because she didn’t love her – she loved her daughter beyond reason – but because she simply couldn’t. If she said anything, she knew she wouldn’t be able to hold back tears of the rejection she felt so keenly.

She watched her daughter splash through the puddles on the drive, which was littered with rose petals scattered ahead of the earlier southerly blast. As soon as she heard the car engine start, she closed the door. The cowbells clanged mournfully.

Part 3: Kate

Chapter 1.

Christchurch. February, 1987

The peach palette of the obstetrician's waiting room was getting on Kate's nerves almost as much as the crying baby in the nearby pram. In a half-hearted attempt to bring peace, the mother gently pushed the pram to and fro. The crying reached a crescendo.

Amelia put *The Hungry Caterpillar* book on the floor and looked up at her mother. 'What's the matter with the baby?' The question came out just as the baby gathered breath for its next burst, so everyone in the waiting room could hear.

The room was full, all the chairs occupied by women with babies, women without, heavily pregnant women and women probably wishing they were heavily pregnant, plus a couple of uncomfortable-looking husbands. One smiled at Amelia. The mother of the crying baby looked even more harried.

'Maybe he wants a feed,' Kate said quietly in response.

'Are we going to have a baby too?'

'I hope so. One day. Now go back to your book. I think we're in for a long wait.'

Amelia picked up *The Hungry Caterpillar* and turned the pages. She had yet to learn to read but Kate had read it to her so often Amelia knew the words off by heart.

The woman next to her continued to rock the pram gently. The baby continued to cry. Kate caught a glimpse of a red screwed-up face.

She picked up a magazine and thumbed through it, barely seeing the pages of skimpy summer fashions as the baby's cry pierced through her conscience, unearthing memories of the last time she'd seen this specialist. She'd been in hospital, her legs spread wide on the narrow steel operating table, the unmistakeable darkened blood pooling between her thighs. Another baby lost.

Mr Sissons' fertility drugs had worked only too well: two pregnancies in two years, followed by two miscarriages. She could get pregnant, but she couldn't keep them. And now she was waiting for her six-monthly check-up so he could see if she was fully recovered and should continue trying.

What was wrong with her that she couldn't have babies as easily as most women? It wasn't David's fault; the doctor had soon determined he was, as David had proudly put it, 'as fertile as a ram at rutting time'. He'd also determined her egg production was erratic and had speeded it up with drugs. But the babies weren't hanging in there for much more than the first trimester before ejecting themselves from her womb. And nobody knew why.

'It just happens, sometimes,' the doctor had said six months ago in the recovery ward. 'To some women more than others. I'm sure you will carry to full term soon.'

But David was as dispirited as she was. The fun in 'practising for a baby' had evaporated, the twinkle in his eye had disappeared. And she could hardly blame him. Who could be expected to fancy a wife whose sole interest in sex was procreation? He'd endured the temperature-taking and the silly rituals she went through to try to conceive. He'd put up with the cries of rage when she got her period. He'd had enough, and had said so.

Why was it so hard? It didn't used to be.

She remembered the 1970s, when she and David had been going out together for just over two years, when Great Aunt Doris first cut her out of the will because David was Catholic and that was apparently tantamount to him having horns and a forked tail. About that time, she realised her period was long overdue, her breasts felt sore, her symptoms mirrored those in the medical books lining the Women's Page library at work: she suspected she was pregnant.

David Price, she knew, was 'the one'. They worked together at The Press, they socialised together at the pub at tea time and later at the Media Club until the wee small hours, they slept together in David's grungy bedroom in his grungy flat. He was clever, he was funny, he was tall and attractive – even with his thinning long hair and thick gold-rimmed glasses – he had a photographic memory for facts if not for appointments, he seemed to know everyone, and he was an intrepid reporter, never scared to ask the difficult questions, much more fearless than she was when faced with reluctance or a downright refusal to answer questions.

The trouble was David didn't know he was the one, and didn't seem to think she was the one for him. He broke up with her once. She winkled her way back with him again. He broke up a second time. A third time. She got the message.

That was when she realised she was pregnant.

That was also when she realised she wasn't ready to be a mother, especially not on her own. She had not long made it into the reporters' room at The Press, having served an apprenticeship writing captions and filing photos in the Illustrations Department. She still had to complete her MA thesis. And, when that was done, a friend who worked on the Women's Page had asked her to travel overseas next year to take the traditional OE working holiday in London.

A baby was out of the question, especially a baby whose father wasn't ready for commitment. She didn't even feel she could tell David she was pregnant, not now that they'd finally, finally, finally broken up. She was ashamed of herself for being so foolish thinking it didn't matter that she'd only just started back on the Pill. The packet had warned her it didn't work straight away. She was also ashamed at proving Great Aunt Doris right: she *was* no better than her mother. History had repeated itself. Despite the Pill, Kate had fallen into the same pregnancy trap her mother had twenty years earlier and there was no escape. Abortion was illegal. If she had the money, she could fly to Australia and have an abortion there. But forty-six-dollars-a-week wages made no room for an airfare across the Tasman, let alone an expensive private procedure.

She'd gone back through the books in the Women's library. But there was nothing there. She'd found references to what the books called old wives' tales, like drink a quart of gin while sitting in a hot bath. So she'd tried it. Or at least as much gin as she could swallow before becoming so maudlin she'd flooded the bath with her tears then so nauseous she'd had to climb out of the bath and throw up into the toilet.

Knitting needles were another suggestion, but after stealing her mother's number eights, she'd chickened out and returned them unused.

Driving fast over bumpy railway lines didn't work either, not even on her Vespa.

As a last resort, she'd tried swallowing a month's supply of the Pill. She had it on good authority that always worked, so one night in desperation she popped the lot out of their blister pack and forced them down, finishing it off with a slosh of gin for good measure. She'd felt very ill and dizzy, but a week later, still no period and her breasts felt even tenderer when she put on her bra.

She didn't expect much from the doctor, she knew the law. He was sympathetic but said that his hands were tied: 'If you can't afford to go to Australia, I'm afraid there are no other options.'

A few days after seeing the doctor, her period arrived: thick and glutinous, darkest red, clinging to the pad in sticky blobs. She cried with relief at first and then with grief: surprising unbidden tears of crazy grief, mourning for a baby she hadn't wanted. Was it an early miscarriage? It was gone, that was all that mattered then.

Now it was different.

Why did she keep losing her babies? Was it in her genes? Clearly her birth mother didn't have that problem, keeping her through to term. Was there something in the chemical cocktail of her DNA that meant she wasn't supposed to be a mother more than once? Would Amelia bear the same fate as her own – to be an only child?

'Mummy, I want to go to the toilet' Amelia interrupted her thoughts, performing a confined tap dance on the peach carpet.

'Right.' Kate looked around and saw the sign. 'Come with me.'

When they came out again, she went up to the desk. 'I'm sorry to trouble you, but I'm going to be late for work if I can't get in soon.'

The receptionist studied her list, looked at her watch and smiled insincerely. 'Sorry Mrs Price but Mr Sissons still has one other patient to see before you. If you'd been here on time…'

'I know. It's okay.'

It wasn't okay, being late for work. The boss was lenient, but she had an interview booked for half an hour after she started and she had to pick up the recording equipment and read the research notes as well as walk to the theatre where the interview was taking place.

She'd been late for the obstetrician because Amelia had held her up trying to decide which dress she wanted to wear. By the time she'd changed twice then discarded the smocked dress her grandmother had given her in favour of a pink frilly tunic and even pinker leggings, there were only five minutes before their appointment and no time to drop her off at day care. She hadn't raised her voice at Amelia to get a move on, no matter how late they were. There was something about her firstborn that prevented her from getting mad, even when Amelia was really naughty.

From the moment she'd been born, emerging at six pounds thirteen ounces and letting out an astonished wail in response to the paediatrician's robust tap on her bottom, Amelia had unleashed in Kate an unfamiliar wave of emotion that engulfed her completely. The sight, the touch, the closeness of her baby – the first flesh and blood she had ever known – sent a shockwave all the way down to the bowels of her being, making it almost impossible to breathe. Her throat had been dry, so dry she felt she would choke; her arms had ached with the sudden weight her daughter had become.

'Mrs Price?'

'That's you Mummy.'

'Ah. Our turn.' Kate wasn't used to being called by her husband's name. Keeping her own name had put her in the same category as 'Women's Libbers' and leftie dissidents but she didn't care and remained Kate Stewart – except with the plumber, the electrician and the gynaecologist.

She gathered up her bag and *The Hungry Caterpillar*, took her daughter's hand and pushed the door into Mr Sissons' consulting room.

'Now, let's see,' he said when they were seated, Amelia bright-eyed and expectant on a buttoned leather chair. 'Your test results came through on Monday, Mrs Price. Everything is as it should be. There don't appear to be any after-effects.'

'That's good.'

'And you are pregnant. Is that what you were expecting?'

'No.' She took a deep breath. 'No, I wasn't. I didn't think it would be so soon.'

'You obviously don't have any problem conceiving now you are on the medication.'

'It's keeping the baby that seems to cause the problem.'

'All I can advise is for you to take it easy. Not too much rushing around.'

'No. I'll try.' She would have to make some changes this time. Cut back on work maybe and keep Amelia in day care a couple of days so she could rest. But would she? Kate hated sitting still for long.

'Mummy, will you keep the baby?'

'I hope so.'

'Then why did you say it was a problem?'

'I'll tell you later. We'll be finished here in a moment.'

'So, Mrs Price, do you have any history of pregnancy loss in your family.' He looked down to study his notes.

'No, I . . .'

'Oh, I see you were adopted. I don't expect you will know.' He peered at her over the top of his reading glasses, as if studying an unusual specimen.

'No I don't, I'm sorry. I know nothing of my family background. My birth family, that is.' How much longer would she have to go on apologising to the medical profession like this? She hated it when this happened. She hated not knowing.

'Mummy, what's adopted mean?' Amelia said when they got outside the rooms.

Kate explained.

'Am I adopted?' Amelia looked worried.

'No you came out of Mummy's tummy, like our next baby will.' She hoped.

~ ~ ~

As soon as Kate hit the newsroom, she phoned David and told him the good news: they would be having a baby in November. He didn't sound as elated as she'd expected, but excused him for being surrounded by nosey colleagues who would undoubtedly tease him mercilessly. Or, more than likely, he'd be so engrossed in the story he was writing that nothing – not even a baby announcement – would distract him. Sometimes Kate wondered if David – with his single-minded focus, his ability to block out all distractions and research something to the nth degree – was more than a little like her father.

Next, she phoned the theatre manager and apologised that she'd be a few minutes late, then gathered the tape and her notebook, flicked through her research notes and took off down the stairs and out into the street for a fast walk to the Court Theatre.

Her mind should have been on the writer of the next play the theatre was producing; usually she was much better prepared, would have studied the bio in detail and looked him up in the station's archive. But all she could think about was the baby she was carrying and why David hadn't been more enthusiastic. Was it because he didn't want his colleagues to know? Or was it because he was scared she'd lose it again? She couldn't blame him for that; she was worried too. But she had to block it from her mind. The doctor had told her to try to relax, not to get stressed or anxious, to think positive thoughts.

Kate made herself think about the job she was about to do. Rick Davidson was acting in his own play *A Trap for Young Players* and was apparently an engaging and lively interviewee, full of quotable quotes and one-liners. He'd be sure to come up with an ideal sound-bite, the news boss had said.

The fast walk to the Arts Centre made her breathless but she continued into the foyer where Jeff Farnsworth, the play's director, was waiting at one of the café tables. She waved; she'd met Jeff many times. He stood up as she approached.

'Sorry I'm late,' she said, trying to breathe normally without much success.

'Don't worry about it. Rick's running late too. He must've known.'

'That's good.'

'Would you like to do the interview here?'

'It's a bit noisy, with people at the ticket office.'

'Right. We can go backstage. It's quiet there. Would you like me to show you through? The box office will tell me when he's here.'

'Okay, I'll . . .'

'Sorry I'm late Jeff,' said a deep theatrical voice right behind her.

Kate turned around. The voice belonged to a man a few years younger than her and not much taller. His beard was as neatly trimmed as his manner, clipped and impeccably polite, but there was a warmth to his smile, as if he were teasing her ever so gently.

'You must be Kate Stewart. Please excuse me for keeping you waiting. I didn't realise the theatre was so far from my digs.'

'That's no excuse at all, you slack bastard.' Jeff clapped him on the back. 'You'll be late for your own funeral.'

Kate laughed. 'It's okay. I was late myself.'

'Don't let him get away with it. Make him suffer.'

'Just don't ask me any tough questions. I don't know any tough answers.'

'I hear you're an old hand at radio interviews?'

'It's those rounded vowels. He picked them up at Radio New Zealand.' Jeff imitated Rick's speech.

'No?'

'Yes, I'm afraid so,' Rick said, putting on an upper-crust accent. 'All that training in received pronunciation – that's what people used to expect on public radio. Of course, anything goes now.' Here he imitated a broad Kiwi twang.

Kate adjusted the heavy tape recorder strapped to her shoulder, turned it on and held out the microphone while her subject was on a roll. 'How did you make the move to the theatre?'

Rick adjusted his features into a suitably serious expression. 'How did I move to theatre? Very gradually. I don't like being poor. But after I got a lucky break on *Gloss* I had to give up radio. I miss it terribly of course.' He pulled a face.

Smiling at his wry humour, she put the heavy tape recorder down on the theatre café's table and sat down beside it, inviting Rick to join her.

'You sure you're okay to do it out here?' Jeff looked around the foyer. The box office queue had died down; it was comparatively quiet.

Kate nodded. 'I'd hate to stop him now he's warmed up.'

'Warmed up? You make me sound like a corpse coming to life.' He imitated a ghost spooking her, holding his arms high in front of him.

She laughed then continued on, asking him about his career, his family, his play. The interview lasted for nearly twenty minutes and revealed he had a partner but no children and was involved in writing for and acting at a new experimental theatre in Wellington. At weekends he earned the rent by doing DJ filler-stints on Radio Windy. His play, *A Trap for Young Players*, was semi-autobiographical, he said, in that it followed a group of young actors rehearsing *Macbeth* who were plagued with bad luck. 'The curse of Macbeth comes to play in every sense,' Rick laughed. 'It's more of a comedy than a tragedy.'

She had more than enough for a short item for local news and for a longer piece for the weekend arts programme. As he answered her questions, cracked jokes and continually put himself down, she had a feeling she'd met him before.

'How are rehearsals going?'

'Gangbusters,' Jeff said.

'Terrible,' Rick said at the same time.

Jeff laughed. 'You're way too sensitive for your own good.'

'It's no fun watching your lines disappear. You spend hours thinking them up and getting them down on paper and – phht! – Jeff dispenses with them at the stroke of a cheap Biro.' Rick was looking pained. 'I know a lot of writers who've died in the aisle when their play goes into its first rehearsal.'

'You'll thank me for it on opening night. Less is more, you know.'

'At the rate you're going, Jeff, there won't be any lines left.'

'Then we can mime it. The critics will love it.'

'I don't think so.' Rick pulled a face. 'I'm taking that red pen off you tomorrow.'

~ ~ ~

Back at the station, Kate quickly edited the tape and wrote the intro, filed it and started on the next story for the day. But she couldn't take her mind off the visit to the specialist's. She got up from her desk, crossed the newsroom to the corridor and headed for the tearoom. It was empty. Taking her time over the tea, lost in thought, she felt her tummy, wondering where the baby would be exactly, hidden away in there. She smiled for a moment. She was pleased, of course she was. But she was also terrified that it would happen again. Did miscarriage run in her genes? What else was she harbouring in her veins, what else was pumping through her heart and brain that could affect her babies' lives?

Perhaps it was time she found out. Perhaps it was time she started another search – an official and entirely legal search this time – for her birth mother. What if she were prone to heart attacks, high blood pressure, varicose veins? Could her children inherit cancer genes, diabetes, arthritis? Maybe there was a thinness gene hidden away there if only she could release it.

She'd often wondered about her origins; she'd often tried to find out who she really was, where she came from. But because it was illegal to know the name of your birth parents, because it was a dark secret and anybody who wanted to unlock that secret was made to feel guilty, criminal even, she recalled resorting to almost criminal means.

She had just turned seventeen. Fuelled by an intense unhappiness of being constantly at war with her mother, she'd left home, got a job, gone flatting and gone to university all at the same time. Perpetually broke, she'd spent almost every waking minute working – at university or at her job – and failed miserably at both.

The job was a grinding thirty-seven-and-a-half hours a week at the Social Security Department, a forbidding, old, dirty cream stone building in Hereford Street. It was the only job she could find that allowed up to eight hours a week off to nip down the road to university for lectures.

After just a few months, she'd discovered that the Social Security Department, which was responsible for paying unemployment and sickness benefits to people who were mostly unemployable (in an age when unemployment was one per cent), held a whole basement full of records that would most probably include information on the origins of her birth.

She smiled at the memory of the callow fellow - a whole grade higher than her on the public service scale – she'd fallen for, unrequitedly, who unwittingly showed her how to gain access to the basement files. As protocol demanded, she'd filed a requisition for permission to descend into the bowels of the building to conduct a search for some specific information. Permission was granted.

The ancient lift only went so far, jolting to a stop with a rebound so fierce she thought they'd hit the basement floor. Around the corner from the lift well, steep narrow concrete steps took her down to a long corridor, lit by three dim bunker lights housed in wire cages, as if they might try to escape and take the light with them.

Pulling the key out of her pocket, expecting a policeman to jump out any minute and arrest her for illegal entry, she cautiously approached the steel door, hesitating for a moment, thinking perhaps she should go back before she was found out.

She pushed the key in. It didn't fit.

She'd been set up.

Then she noticed another key hanging lower down on the chain. She tried it in the lock. It fitted. She turned it, twisting it hard until she heard a click and the door swung open, its hinges creaking eerily, as if she were in a Zombie movie. The undead would be behind the door waiting to attack.

She could feel her blood pumping, could hear it rushing to her head. She froze: could move neither forward into the vault nor back up the stairs where the fusty departmental air was a lot easier to breathe.

Ahead were row upon row of steel-braced wooden shelving units containing stack upon stack of brown card-covered files, each with a number and a code.

Could she do it? Where to begin?

To the left, high up near the ceiling, a shaft of light was pouring through a tiny opaque window. To Kate, it was a beacon, pulling her forward, granting her entry. She stumbled forward, unsure of herself, puzzled by the codes on the files. John, the man she fancied, the man who'd revealed the secret of the departmental tomb, hadn't told her the codes were this obscure.

She walked along the rows, checking the numbers, looking for something alphabetical, something with the year of her birth, something she might realise.

She hadn't counted on the system being smarter than she was.

If her birth records were there, they weren't in any recognisable format and there was no possibility of searching all the files – there were thousands and thousands of them.

She retrieved the file she had the code to then took off, her heart still thumping, hurriedly locking the door and returning to the stairs, riding the clanking scary lift to her floor, stopping by the toilets on the way to recover, to stand for a moment behind the locked door then to wash her hands, her face, get rid of the dust and the subterfuge that had held so much hope.

A day or two later, her supervisor called her into his office and asked what she thought she was doing down in the records where she had no need to be. The requisition, he said, had bypassed him, which was entirely against the rules. The file she'd used as a pretence for entry was superfluous to requirements.

Cornered, she'd confessed.

She'd been so embarrassed she couldn't remember what happened next; the following day she received a memo to say she'd received 'a note' on her employment file and warning her not to try anything like that again.

Within six months, she'd left for the illustrations department of The Press where the files were almost as dusty and inaccessible as in the public service and where she was still allowed time off for lectures.

Chapter 2.

Wellington. Mid-1988

Kate strode along the Oriental Bay promenade trying to walk off the remains of the Ansett omelette anchored in her tummy like a paperweight. She was in no state to contemplate lunch. Yet she wanted to make a good impression. How pernickety would she look if she refused anything to eat? She could see her mother feeling obliged to pick away at her lunch, embarrassed to be eating when her daughter wasn't; or worse, her mother would feel she should go without too. And what sort of a lunch would that be?

Poor Mum. She'd made it perfectly clear that she didn't want Kate to see her birth mother; that she was scared of losing her, that was what had happened to other adoptive mothers she knew. Better to wait until the meeting was over, see how it went and maybe then tell her. Or maybe not.

She watched two seagulls fighting over a piece of bread, screeching at each other as if their life depended on it. Would she be caught in the middle like that? Tugged at by two women who didn't know each other, probably never would, each claiming sole right to her affections? The fat seagull won. The smaller one ran to the water's edge and pecked at a piece of seaweed as if he didn't care then ruffled his feathers. The sun glinted off the water behind him, making Kate shade her eyes.

Her mobile phone rang loudly in her bag. Dragging it out by its stiff little aerial, she lifted it to her ear, stretching her hands to reach around its girth and looking up and down the esplanade, hoping not to draw attention to herself. She hadn't quite become used to it yet, it was so obtrusive, shouting 'Look at me' to anyone in the vicinity, but it had cost her boss $5000 and he'd given her a list of instructions to look after it and ensure nobody tried to run off with it.

'I'm only giving it to you so you can track down those MAF scientists you need to film,' Larry had said. Larry was the producer on *Science Express*, the TVNZ programme Kate was reporting for. 'It's been like herding cats to sort out who's who there. I don't want you to miss out. But don't you dare lose it.'

How anyone could lose something so big and heavy she didn't know, but she was as conscious of the programme's budget as Larry was, and so she treated the new-fangled gadget with the respect such an expensive high-tech brick deserved.

The call was from David.

'How did it go with your mother?' he asked after they said hello.

'I haven't met her yet. I'm just about to go into the café now.'

'Oh, sorry, I thought you were meeting at twelve.'

'No, one.' Of course David would forget the meeting time; he was lucky to remember what day it was sometimes. Just like Dad. He was so wrapped up in his job at *National Business Review* chasing people he called 'commercial hazards'.

'Did James go off to day-care without kicking up a fuss today?'

'Yes. Like a lamb.'

She laughed. 'Typical. It's only me he plays up for.'

'I'll have to work on that. We don't want him to become a Mummy's boy.'

'Not much chance of that.' She laughed. 'Look, I'd better go. These calls cost a fortune and the battery runs out in no time.'

'I bet you feel as cool as Madonna with such a fancy piece of technology to play with.'

'I feel like a dick, actually. People are staring at me. I've got to go.'

Kate took one last look at the waterfront – across to the tall concrete buildings climbing from the harbour up the hill, around past the port to the big white ferry docked at its berth and back again to the stony beach, the sentinel Norfolk pines, the row of houses and cafes along Oriental Parade. Nerves were making her heart race.

Now or never.

She plunged across the road, ducking traffic, and entered the café before she could change her mind. It was she who'd asked for this meeting, who'd written the first letter, who'd been crying out to meet her mother. And now she was tempted to run back out the door and forget about the whole thing.

There was nobody in the café matching her mother's description of herself: short, wavy brown hair, not exactly slim, wearing a navy jacket and a cornflower blue scarf. Her own looks, her favourite colours.

She went in further and scanned the far corners. Not there. Perhaps her mother had chickened out?

Steeling herself, she slid into a seat near the window, picked up the menu and studied it closely. Salads. Quiche. Fish and chips. Fancy burgers. Toasted sandwiches. Too much choice. No appetite. She put it down and stared out the window. That's when she noticed a woman in a blue blazer and pale blue scarf hesitate outside, turn back the way she'd come, pause, and return to the café, stopping in the doorway then continuing on in.

This must be her mother. The mother she'd dreamed about all her life, the first grown-up she'd ever seen who shared her DNA.

She didn't look much like the Hapsburg princess she'd dreamed of.

She didn't look all that confident.

She didn't look much like Kate. But then, she was nearly twenty years older.

Who did she look like? There was a vague familiarity. Kate couldn't quite put her finger on it; maybe she'd met her somewhere, somehow, before.

The woman looked around. Kate stood up and waved then hurried forward.

'Thank you for coming.' She'd rehearsed what she was going to say; that wasn't it. It just slipped out, responding to the fear in her eyes. Was it fear? If not, it was close. She tried to make herself more relaxed and welcoming, less nervous, less apprehensive.

'Look at you,' her mother said. 'You look just like my sister.'

They embraced. It felt odd, artificial. This was her mother. Yet she didn't feel like flesh and blood. She was a stranger. They were both strangers.

'Do I?' Kate forced a laugh. 'I've never looked like anyone before.'

They sat at the table, awkward, uncomfortable.

'I'm so glad you said you'd meet me,' Kate said. 'I wasn't sure if you would.'

'To be honest, I wasn't sure either.' Her mother pushed her glasses on top of her head – just like Kate did – and studied her. 'I'd buried you so deep in my past, I didn't know if I could face it again.'

'I'm glad you did.' Was she glad? She didn't think so. Not yet. 'I was going to say "Mother" but it doesn't seem right, somehow. What should I call you?'

'Just call me Liz.'

'Okay Liz.' She laughed nervously and tried to think what to say next. 'Did you have trouble finding a park?'

'Oh, no. I don't drive. I never have. I caught the bus.'

'You don't drive? That's unusual.'

'I tried once. My husband Steven tried to teach me. But I was hopeless. I haven't driven since.'

Kate was just about to say that Mum drove and she was seventy, but stopped herself just in time. 'I couldn't survive if I didn't drive,' she said instead. There was a moment's pause. 'I don't know where to begin.' She smiled nervously. 'There's so much I want to ask you.

A waitress hovered behind.

'Shall we order first?' Liz picked up the menu. 'I'll have a quick look.'

Kate looked for something light. 'I think I'll have the pumpkin soup, please,' Kate said to the waitress. 'And a glass of lime and soda.'

Liz put the menu down and looked relieved. 'That sounds good. I'll have the same.'

As soon as the waitress had departed, Kate started on her list of questions.

She learned that she had a whole new family – well, half a family, on her mother's side – a new aunt and uncle, a brother and sister, a niece and lots of cousins, all completely oblivious to her existence. She learned that there were artists in the family, writers, poets even; according to her mother she was related, somewhat distantly, to the poet John Masefield and his cousin the playwright Christopher Fry. She learned that she had every chance of living to a ripe old age, that there was no history of heart attacks or blood pressure, or diabetes, or asthma, that the women in the family who weren't struck down by cancer lived to a ripe old age.

'Cancer?'

'Yes, there's a lot of cancer, I'm afraid,' Liz said. 'Your grandmother died of cancer, and my sister Jilly died of leukaemia when she was just eight years old. I've only got one sister now, Penny. She's quite a bit younger. You'd like her.'

Kate didn't know what to say. She'd never thought of getting cancer, never had a skin check or a mammogram. Maybe she should? Or maybe the cancer genes had been overridden by her father.

'What about my father? Do you know if he had any health issues?'

Liz pursed her lips. 'No. I don't know anything about his background. He was a tram conductor and he seemed healthy enough; he was a runner, very fit. That's all I know.'

Kate didn't like to probe. There was a steely fix to her mother's eye that discouraged further discussion. She already knew his name from the information Mum had produced. If she wanted to know more, she'd have to find him herself.

Her mother started fiddling with a locket around her neck. Oval-shaped, silver, with a finely detailed pattern etched on its face, the locket seemed to act some form of stress relieving distraction for Liz.

'That's a pretty necklace,' Kate said, hoping to draw her out.

'It was my grandmother's,' was all she would say.

Their lunch arrived and the subject changed ever so subtly from the past to the present. Liz asked about Kate's family.

'I've brought photos.' She pulled out an envelope and flipped a series of family photos onto the table, picking up the one on the top.

'That's Amelia. She's four and at pre-school. And James is just nine months. He's home with his grandmother today.' She knew that was stretching the truth, but didn't want to admit to having him in day-care while she worked part-time. Her mother might not approve.

Liz smiled. 'They're lovely.' She held the photo closer then picked up the next one on the pile, of David and the kids. 'But I can't see any resemblance to my daughter Jessie or her wee girl Emily. I think they look more like their father, like David.' She turned the photo round so Kate could see. 'Don't you think?'

'They do.' It was true, everybody said Amelia was the spitting image of her father. But James looked different, more like her.

'Have you got any photos of your grandchildren?'

Liz produced several photos from her bag. 'I brought these to show you. This is Jessie with baby Emily – she's getting on for two now. She was born in London when I was over there.'

'Did you go over to be with Jessie at the birth?'

'Yes.' Liz hesitated as if she was about to say something else, but didn't.

'Your first time in London?'

'Yes.' She toyed with her soup spoon. 'But I was glad to get home. I didn't like it much.'

That was a surprise. Kate couldn't imagine anyone not liking London.

'And you said you had a son?'

'Yes, Richard. I've got a photo of him somewhere. Let's see. I hope I didn't forget to bring it.' She delved in her handbag. 'It's of Richard with his wife Kim. It should be here somewhere. They got married just before Christmas. Lovely wedding. Jessie couldn't come back for it, not with a new baby, but she's promised to come back to New Zealand later this year.' Liz looked pleased. 'I love having my family around me.'

Kate didn't seem to be included in that. It was perfectly understandable, she told herself, especially when you've just met your mother for the first time. You couldn't expect her to embrace you into the family just like that.

All her life she'd felt an outsider, not belonging to her adoptive family, no matter how nice they were, she never felt she was one of them; but she didn't belong to Liz's family either – they didn't even know she existed.

She'd wanted to say about the baby, Emily, that she looked just like Amelia at that age, but it was as if Liz didn't want to know, as if she were denying any possibility of genetic similarity.

'Ah, here it is.' Liz produced the photo from a side pocket in her bag.

Kate couldn't believe it. 'That's Rick!'

'Yes, Richard.

'Oh God!'

'What? Do you know him?' Liz was looking alarmed.

In that instant, Kate realised she couldn't admit to having met Liz's son before, to knowing who he was. Liz was so fearful of her family finding out about her shameful secret, she'd be horrified to discover her son Richard had already come face to face with the secret personified.

'No. He just looked familiar, that's all.' He did too. She'd seen it in him when they'd met. Something she recognised, something about his laugh. She'd thought it was because he'd been on television, because he was familiar to the thousands of people who'd seen him in their living rooms every night on *Gloss*. Now the puzzle was solved: his familiar laugh was an echo of her own.

She should have realised Rick was Liz's son. Not at the time she met him – she didn't know her birth mother's name then. But she'd discovered Liz's married name a month later, in March last year, during the search at the births, deaths and marriages registry. The surname Davidson and Rick's home town of Wellington, both should have been a give-away. How ironic! All this time she'd been trying to trace her mother and her brother had already been introduced to her, been interviewed by her, without her knowing.

She hadn't seen him since that time she'd interviewed him, when she'd gone to the opening night of his play *A Trap for Young Players*. But he'd been on a high, celebrating with the rest of the cast; she'd only said a few congratulatory words before he was lost in the opening night crowd around the theatre bar.

The review had been guardedly positive, which was quite something for the theatre critic. She remembered the gist of it: 'this well-known television actor has made a credible transition to the stage', he'd said, adding somewhat sniffily that Rick had written the play himself, as if that ought to be held against him, while praising its theatricality. Kate had seen Rick's name mentioned since then in television roles, and had heard his play had been picked up by another theatre in Auckland. She wondered if his mother had seen it when it premiered in Wellington before coming down to Christchurch.

'What did you say Rick, er Richard, does?'

'He's an actor. He was on television you know, in *Gloss*.'

'Yes, I remember. Did he act on the stage too?'

'Yes, I think so, but I've never seen him. I don't like going into town and the theatre – I don't like crowds. But he was good in *Gloss*.'

Liz took the photo out of Kate's hand and passed over another. 'Here's Richard and Kim again with all of us at Christmas.'

They went through more photographs, tracing back the years to when Liz was a teenager.

'This is me when I got my first job.' She held out a black-and-white photo of a young woman in a long winter coat, low-heeled brogues and a smile so direct and confident Kate hardly recognised her. But she did recognise the teeth, the overbite and the chin, pointed slightly – Dad called it elfin. And the way the wavy hair refused to be tamed into a fringe.

'I've got a photo of me at that age too,' she said and flicked through her pile until she found the one of her taken in her mother's back garden, standing on the lawn in a psychedelic mini-dress.

'You do look nice.' Liz held it next to the photo of herself. 'But I don't see the resemblance.' She picked out another photo of a girl in a school uniform. 'That was just before I had you. When I was sent down to Christchurch.'

Kate took it and saw the same familiar features that Liz didn't – or didn't want to – see. 'Was that a difficult time?' She knew it was a redundant question, but she didn't know what else to say.

'Mostly it was. I was very homesick. And lonely.'

'What about when I was born?'

'Even lonelier. I wasn't allowed to hold you. You were taken straight from me.' She lowered her eyes and seemed transfixed with the sugar bowl, picking up the spoon and playing with it, swishing the sugar from side to side then spooning it up, holding the spoon aloft and letting a few grains trickle back into the bowl.

Kate felt suspended, like the spoon. Another grain fell, like sand in an egg-timer, measuring the gap in the faltering conversation.

Liz had said in her letter that she'd not been allowed to hold her daughter. But hearing it out loud somehow made it very real. She looked across the table at her; Liz was showing no emotion, just a slight quiver of the lip and flutter of the eyelids gave her away. You couldn't read her eyes; she was still staring at the sugar bowl, even though she'd put the spoon back inside it. Kate reached out and touched her mother's hand and felt a slight recoil, or was it a tremor? 'I can't imagine how that must have been.'

Liz didn't reply.

There was a brief moment then when Kate thought she might be able to make a connection, to break through her mother's reserve and shyness. But her mother's hand lay motionless on the table. She waited a moment longer, in case Liz turned her palm upwards and grasped her hand, until it became embarrassing. She withdrew her hand and returned to her soup. Suddenly it was unappetising. She didn't want any more. Putting down her spoon, wiping her mouth with the paper napkin, she tried to think of something to say, to cover the awkwardness of the moment.

'My daughter starts school in July,' was all she could think of.

Liz smiled. 'I remember when it was your fifth birthday wondering how you would like going to school.' She looked out the window. 'I thought about you on all your birthdays. I tried sending you a card once. I got in touch with the hospital where you were born. But of course, they wouldn't tell me anything.'

Kate knew just how that felt. She smiled back. 'I used to think about you a lot too. Wonder what you were like.'

Liz laughed. 'I'm afraid I'm not very interesting. I've not done very much at all. Not like you.'

'I'm sure that's not true. Tell me what you do.'

Liz recounted her life through her husband's and her children's lives, and Kate learned more about the likes and dislikes of Steven Davidson than she really wanted to know. She learned about her sister Jessie, who'd worked in an art gallery in London 'right up to the birth of her baby' and who'd switched to managing a fitness centre part-time now her second baby was one. She learned more about brother Richard – more than he'd told her himself. Liz was proud of his role on *Gloss* but didn't say anything about him writing plays. Maybe he hadn't told her? Maybe she didn't want to know? But she added that he played saxophone in a big band at a night club at weekends and grew hydroponic salad greens in his back yard, selling them at a weekend market. Kate wondered why he'd kept that to himself at the interview. She would very much like to ask him.

'Do you think I'll be able to meet him? Or Jessie when she comes back?'

'Heavens no, not yet.' Liz looked aghast. 'I'm not ready to tell them yet. One day, maybe. But I couldn't now.'

Kate was annoyed. What was it about her that her mother was ashamed of? What harm would it do for them to know? 'Why is that?' she said.

'I haven't been well, you know. The doctor says it's depression. He's put me on medication, but I still don't feel right. Getting a letter from you, well …' She tailed off.

Was she trying to lay the blame for her depression on Kate? Had the letter, the first contact from her firstborn in thirty-six years, reawakened the shame and the anxiety she'd buried all that time? It was entirely possible. Kate should have realised that her mother would be shocked, possibly seriously upset, getting her letter. Her mother's depression was more than likely Kate's fault.

They talked some more, but she could tell that the meeting was as good as over. Kate paid the bill for two – 'It's the least I can do,' she said out of guilt – and they swapped photographs, picking the ones of when they were teenagers. Kate studied it one more time before putting it in her Filofax: the image of a mother that looked just like her at that age but refused to acknowledge it.

Just as she was going, her mother called her back. She was picking at the strap of her handbag, looking anxious. 'I really don't want my kids to know,' she said. 'It would be too much for me now. I just ask you to wait a while. One day I'll tell them. Okay?'

Kate hesitated. She wasn't sure she could agree to this.

'Will you promise me not to tell them?'

Kate thought for a moment. Now that she'd met her mother, she realised that the key to finding her identity, to knowing if she fitted in with her mother's family, lay with her siblings.

'Please Kate.'

Liz was fiddling with her locket again, twisting the fine silver chain with such an intensity Kate feared it might break.

She nodded, reluctantly. 'I won't tell them.'

She would wait.

~ ~ ~

Kate had booked a late flight home, leaving plenty of time for whatever the meeting might have led to. If her mother had suggested seeing her brother or coming home with her, she'd been ready. But now, as she watched her mother's sagging navy shoulders depart down the footpath towards the bus stop, she was relieved there'd been no other family involved. Relieved and disappointed. The way things had gone, a family reunion was out of the question.

If only it had been different, if only her mother was vibrant, like Mum. Even though she was twenty years her senior, Mum could run rings around her mother. Mum would say *carpe diem*, seize the day, and she'd live each day as if it were all that mattered, rushing around in her little red Honda Civic looking after Dad, after the dreaded Great Aunt Doris before she'd died, after any sick or lonely soul she knew. But Kate didn't think Liz had *carpe-d diem* for some time. How she ever got herself over to London was beyond imagination.

Having thought this day would bring her face to face with her identity, she found instead she had even less idea who she was. She'd thought meeting her mother would provide the answer. But instead it raised the same question: who was she? She knew one thing for sure: she might bear physical similarities to her mother but their personalities were dead opposite. Her quiet, shy, unassuming mother, who refused to allow herself any emotion, who lived her life through her family but wanted to deny her first daughter's existence: where did Kate fit in with that?

She hadn't expected this. She'd expected … what? Fireworks and starshells; resonance and recognition: to find someone she looked just like, someone who thought like her.

There was an undoubted physical resemblance, even if Liz didn't see it. But their way of thinking was worlds apart. If their genes were the same, their spirit was quite different.

What about Mum? In many ways, Kate felt she was more like her. Not just the blue eyes and brown hair – the only physical similarities they shared – it was more than that. She had the same seize-the-day impatience to be getting on with things, to have lots of friends and experience as many cultural and social events as she could fit in, to be determined to make a difference and be stubborn if anyone tried to stop her.

Perhaps she was an amalgam of both her mothers? Nature *and* nurture: a product of both.

But the harsh reality was that Liz didn't want to acknowledge even a physical resemblance. What similarity Kate had found had been brushed away; she was beginning to doubt if it had been there at all.

Kate walked into town and wandered round the shops in a desultory way, not in the mood to buy anything but with nothing better to do than try something on. But nothing seemed to fit, everything looked wrong. The trousers made her bum look big; the shoes made her feet look like paddles; the earrings were too dangly; the lipstick drained colour from her face.

Reaching the end of Lambton Quay, she crossed the road to where her father had been hit by a taxi forty-eight years ago, just before he got married: the same government buildings, probably the same busy traffic – such an innocuous stretch of road, but so dangerous. And so damaging for Dad. The doctors had said, years after his diagnosis when more was known, that the shortening of his left leg by an inch that day, its failure to heal, followed by poor conditions in the tropics when he'd been stationed in New Caledonia during the War, would most probably have brought on multiple sclerosis.

She stood for a few moments beside a bus shelter and watched the traffic whizz by. Someone was trying to cross the road, jaywalking, ignoring the crossing lights. She wanted to call out, warn them of the inherent risk this spot held. But in an instant, they were across and the traffic continued to roar past, erasing the footsteps from the road.

Crossing carefully at the lights, she climbed the hill to Parliament Buildings to see if her friend Vanessa in the Minister of Tourism's office had time for a coffee. But she was in a meeting.

Suddenly she felt very tired. James had woken her at five in the morning wanting a feed and had then refused to settle, so there'd been no more sleep. She'd expressed more milk to join the store in the freezer and got ready for the day. Now she wanted nothing more than to get home to David and the kids, tell him all about her day over dinner, fall into bed and go to sleep.

Except what was there to tell? Would she be honest and tell the truth: that her mother was a bit dull, that there'd been no connection, no great burst of emotion or mother-daughter bonding? That it felt like a second rejection? Or would she maintain the myth? The myth she'd clung to since she was a teenager, the myth that her mother was someone special, someone to be celebrated.

The biggest lie she'd ever told was that her mother - her birth mother – was German royalty, a countess, a Hapsburg princess. She was thirteen; in all other ways honest, forthright and generally regarded as a good girl. She always had been; she had to live up to her status of being special, the chosen one. With such a reputation, she thought she'd get away with it.

What on earth had she been trying to prove?

She knew she wasn't the only angst-ridden, pre-pubescent girl wanting to distance herself from her mother, wishing she came from a family far away, a family connected to the world of glamour, wealth and fame, a family removed from her own ordinary, humdrum, small-town existence.

But German?

She blamed it on Hardy Kruger. At thirteen, he was her heart-throb. Square chin softened by a dimple, with slicked-back blond hair and eyes unbelievably blue, he was the archetypal Aryan. Drafted into the German army during the War, his film career cast him many times as the archetypal Aryan soldier, inducing her to become a temporary war-movie aficionado – as long as Hardy Kruger was in the movie, she'd see it. But it was his starring role in Howard Hawks film *Hatari!* with John Wayne that spurred her on to join New Zealand's Hardy Kruger fan club.

She'd seen that movie eleven times. She'd entered all the colouring competitions, cut his photo out of all the magazines she could find, even nicked a poster from one of the movie theatres and hung it on the wall directly beside her bed. Every night as she lay there waiting for sleep, she'd been helpless under the unmoving gaze of those over-enlarged grainy eyes.

So when Vicki-Jane had asked, 'Who *is* your real mother then?' the answer was already fully formed.

They'd been talking about mothers. And because Kate had rowed with her mother that morning about whether she'd be allowed to stay the night at Vicki-Jane's and because her mother had won, Kate was in need of revenge.

'She's so Victorian,' Kate had said. 'She's no idea how things have changed.'

'She never lets you stay out late.'

'*She* thinks it's late.'

'What, ten o'clock? That's not late.' Vicki-Jane wasn't a face-value kind of friend. She liked to probe, to stir things up.

'I know. She just doesn't get it. I tell her everyone else is allowed out. It's so archaic that I'm not allowed to stay the night.'

'Maybe she knows you better than you think?' Vicki-Jane's eyes twinkled with amusement.

'How could she? Anyway, she's not my real mother.'

There was a moment's stunned silence.

'What?' she said eventually. 'Are you adopted?'

Kate nodded.

'I never knew that. I always thought your mother was, you know, your real mother. She looks so like you – brown hair, blue eyes.'

Kate winced. Whenever anyone said that, it made her mad. As if matching a couple of physical traits could make you belong.

'Mum says that's because they selected babies as close to their adoptive parents as possible in those days, so they'd fit right in.'

Fit right in. She'd been chosen because she had the same colouring, but she'd never felt that fit.

'How long have you known?'

'That I was adopted? Oh, as long as I can remember. Mum and Dad said they told me as soon as I was old enough to understand.'

'And did you ever wonder where you came from?'

'I have for years.'

The distinctive apricot and sea-green coloured cover of *The Chosen Baby* book her parents used to read to her at bedtime every night flashed before her eyes. She could see it quite clearly, the toddler clambering across the bars of his cot, puffy white clouds in the background, his eyes searching distant skies for happy-ever-after. And inside, the same green and pink toddler standing in a cot, arms raised, being picked up by a beautiful woman with dark hair and an apricotty-pink face. Behind her was a handsome young man of similar hue. Why were the colours so garish? Perhaps the paintbox of time had duo-toned the idealised illustration of the perfect family. But all along, she'd known she was the green and apricotty-pink child in the cot; all along she'd known how lucky she was to have been chosen by her Mum and Dad to live with them and her grandparents in a big house with stairs to climb and lots of toys to play with. All along, she'd accepted that was where she came from – that she was chosen out of a book.

'So did they tell you about your mother?'

'No. But I met her once.'

'You met her? Really? What was she like?'

'Very pretty. You know, blue-eyed like me, but blonde. She was German.' Kate was on a roll. There was no going back.

'German?'

'Yes, German. She had an accent. She'd come out to New Zealand just to find me.' She took a deep breath and continued. 'She told me she was a Hapsburg princess.'

It had seemed so right at the time, hardly a lie at all. The moment she'd said it, she believed it to be true. Vicki-Jane was understandably incredulous.

'She can't be.'

'Yes. That's what she said.'

She couldn't remember what happened after that. Vicki-Jane had brought it up again several times and Kate had quickly learned what a good memory you needed to be an accomplished liar. The more she said, the more mired she became in ridiculous detail, detail she couldn't substantiate. She'd looked up Hapsburg in Encyclopaedia Britannica and soon realised princesses were a bit thin on the ground. But she'd ploughed on. Too late to take it back, to admit she'd made it all up.

Why had she done it? Until her teens, she'd been a goody two-shoes and had never, that she could recall, told a lie. But puberty seemed to change all that. She'd lied about her birth mother; she'd lied about going out with boys because as far as Mum was concerned, they didn't exist; she'd lied about going to flute lessons when she biked off instead to hang around Boys' High with her school-friend Trisha; she'd lied about going to school when she'd been in Cathedral Square milk bars looking for boys. What was the matter with her? Vicki-Jane never bunked school or hung out with boys – unless they were horse-mad like her. Vicki-Jane would never lie to her mother like that or to her employer, like Kate had done at the Social Security Department.

Deep down, Kate knew that the fable of the Hapsburg princess came from some part of her being that needed to belong, that needed the touch and physical acknowledgement of her own flesh and blood. Just to know who her mother was, a name, something real she could hold on to, a photo maybe, to know if she was still alive, something tangible that could fill the lifelong emptiness and end her search.

She couldn't remember exactly when she'd first thought about finding her mother, when she'd first wondered who she was. She *could* remember Mum telling her how brave her mother was giving her up so Kate could have a better life.

'Better than what?'

'Better than she could give you.'

'But why?'

'Because she wanted you to have a better life.'

And so it went, round and around, without Kate ever gaining much of a clue about the reality of it.

She could also remember asking if her mother was allowed to have any more children and if she'd be allowed to keep them next time. Her best friend Vicki-Jane had a brother and she'd wanted one too. In fact, she'd wanted to go one better: she'd wanted a sister. Vicki-Jane didn't have one of those.

Just a month older than her and living right next door, Vicki-Jane had been her closest friend since she was two. They'd sat next to each other at primary school and often walked there and home again together, chipping away at the icy puddles with heavy brown lace-up shoes on wintry mornings, snapping flowers from gardens and scattering the petals along the footpath in the summer.

By Standard Three, Mum had become exasperated. She'd seen the pair of them as double trouble – twice as naughty when they were together, getting lost in the thick bamboo, shooting at each other with home-made bamboo bows and arrows, and wading across the shallows to the tiny island in the middle of the Avon River.

If they weren't in the park, they would be up on the garage roof, shooting arrows down from their home-made fort, or down the back of their neighbouring quarter-acre gardens, trampling around the vegetables and climbing the many trees.

Some days, they'd climb over the back fence and trespass in the neighbouring high school grounds, burrowing in the huge dirt piles to make tracks and bridges for their toy trucks and cars, hoping the caretaker wouldn't tell them off and send them back home. Mostly he didn't.

But they got into trouble at primary school in other ways, for talking in class and passing notes to each other, and to other kids as well. Vicki-Jane was a 'bad influence', Mum said. The solution, Mum decided, was to take Kate out of primary school a year early and send her to the girls' school next door, the one where they'd been playing in the dirt pile.

Luckily for her and Vicki-Jane, their parents rarely spoke. They were chalk and cheese: Vicki's parents were horsey, racing, duck-shooting, whiskey-drinking types; Kate's had never been to the races or touched whisky in their lives. Without knowing it, Vicki's parents had decided the very same thing. The girls' initial despair at being parted during school hours soon turned to joy when they discovered they were both bound for the same school at the same time. Their parents were less than thrilled.

Vicki-Jane had been like a sister – better than a sister, really because they were the same age and their interests were mirrored. They fought like sisters too from time to time, but there were too many things to do together to sulk for too long.

It wasn't until they arrived at the new school, made new friends and drifted apart that Kate's yearning for a sister began. She thought of making one up. But after Vicki-Jane, no imaginary sibling could be as much fun. Besides, one imaginary family member was more than enough to keep tabs on.

Making stuff up about your origins, she'd since learned, was what the adopted child was prone to do. Which made a neat parcel of predictability out of that spontaneous lie about German royalty. She still felt warmth flush into her face whenever she thought of it.

Her children would never know that longing, would never need to pretend they had another, better, family somewhere else. Amelia and James were her flesh and blood. She remembered the shock of the heel-prick test when she and David feared they harboured cystic fibrosis in their DNA, and the guilt she had felt for not even knowing if that could be possible. That guilt had been the impetus for tracking down her mother and finding out if there were any genetic surprises lying in wait. Like cancer.

She knew she should take more care of herself, take things easier, not get so stressed over trying to do too much; she'd read somewhere that stress was supposed to raise your chances of getting cancer. And she knew she should lose a few pounds. But how? She couldn't think of anything that she could cut out to remove some of that stress - she couldn't give up work because they needed the money to help with the mortgage – and she had no free time to get to the gym.

She made herself a promise to eat the sort of healthy stuff everyone was telling you was good for you – good for losing weight and good for staving off diseases like diabetes and cancer. She would stop drinking. If David could do it so could she. He'd announced on New Year's Day that he wasn't going to touch another drop and he'd been true to his word. She'd heard that alcohol could lead to cancer; why tempt fate? She would read up about the foods and vitamins that were supposed to help prevent cancer, take some tests even. Before her resolve weakened, she marched herself into the nearest bookshop and browsed through the lifestyle section, checking out tips, buying the one that seemed the most sensible. With that resolve ticked off, she found a café and ordered a pot of English Breakfast. While she waited for the tea, she looked in her bag for something to do and found her Filofax. Flipping through to today's date she found the piece of paper she'd ripped from her teenage diary and smiled as she opened it. She'd meant to show it to her mother at lunchtime, to tell her how all her teenage diaries were dedicated to her – by name. Mum had told her, long ago, her birth mother's name.

'All I know is that her name was Elizabeth and she was from Wellington. I can't tell you anything else.'

'Can't tell me? Or won't tell me?' Kate had said when she was old enough to feel angry at being denied her birthright. But it didn't matter what she said, whether she tried to wheedle it out by being nice, or needle Mum into shouting it out in desperation, she never found out her mother's surname.

So she started each entry: 'Dear Elizabeth'.

While she waited for her tea, she started to read:

'Dear Elizabeth

'I wanted to be different and write a diary without writing to anyone in particular, but it was so impersonal – when I felt alone there was no one to share things with – and so I am writing to you. I have never met

you, but somehow that makes it better; I don't know your tastes or morals and so I don't have to worry about offending you. Besides, I know that being my mother you will understand all that has happened, is happening or is about to happen. Unless your callousness in disowning me extends to the present and you don't care what I do. But even then I should forgive you.

It is to you that I owe my life. To you and no one else this book is dedicated.

Your author and daughter,

Kate.'

She smiled as she refolded the page and put it away. How prim and proper and pompous she sounded. Prissy even.

'Your tea.' A smiling young woman deposited a slightly dented silver teapot, milk jug, sugar bowl, china cup and saucer on the table and departed, swinging the silver tray.

'Thank you,' Kate said as she left.

She poured the tea. It was weak and watery and a stray tealeaf swirled around, following the trajectory of her spoon. She watched it slowly sink beneath the surface, still swirling clockwise on its way to the bottom.

Chapter 3

Wellington, August 2010

It was happening at last. Kate couldn't believe that in just a few minutes, she would meet her brother and sister for the first time. Her mother had promised she'd tell them the week before to give them plenty of time to absorb the news then her daughter Jessie would pick Liz up from home and take her to Liz's sister Penny's place in Plimmerton.

Her letter set the appointed time. She would be there.

At exactly half past three, Kate parked the rental at the kerb and pressed the bell beside the tall rimu front door of a sleek, well-designed, almost new two-storey house overlooking the sea. The strong smell of salt and seaweed underlined the sound of waves crashing on the stony shore. To the side of the entranceway, she caught a glimpse of the bay under a dappled sun as the southerly clouds scudded across the water.

A woman, who was even shorter than her and perhaps five or six years older, answered the door.

'Hello. You must be Kate.' Her smile, welcoming, genuine, revealed teeth just like Kate's, the same overbite, the same lips. The fringe, the glimpse of a streak of grey hair along the parting line, the chin, the neck – it was all hers. Even the eyes, though a different colour, looked the same, the loose skin over the eyelid, the glasses tucked on top of her head.

It was like a genetic mirror had been held up to each of them.

There was a long silence while they both took it in.

For the first time in her life, Kate had come face to face with her reflective self. Suddenly, she felt a strong sense of connection.

'Yes. I'm Kate. Kate Stewart.' She smiled and held out her hand then let it drop; it seemed inadequate. Instead, she stepped forward and held out her arms. 'You've just got to be Penny.'

They embraced.

Kate rubbed her stinging eyes with the back of her hand. This was almost too much.

'There's no doubt you're Liz's daughter.' Penny invited her in with a gesture and Kate followed.

'Liz told me her sister was much younger. I had no idea just how much younger though.'

'Yes. She was twelve when I was born.'

Kate did a quick calculation. 'So that means you must be just six years older than me.'

'Oh my God, you two are so alike.' A woman, slim, pony-tailed, maybe in her early thirties, had come around the corner into the entrance hall and stood there looking at them, open-mouthed.

Liz and Kate both laughed.

'You even laugh like her.' The woman held out her hands in an exaggerated shrug. 'This is so spooky.'

Kate stopped laughing abruptly and put her hand to her mouth. Could this be true? Was it possible she could laugh just like someone she'd never met? People who grew up together often spoke the same way, used the same inflections, the same words and phrases, the same tone. But there'd been no chance for her to copy Penny's laugh. This must be what it was like to be part of a family that looked like you, sounded like you, laughed like you; was this where she belonged? And if she and Penny were so similar, what would her brother and sister be like? Even more similar?

Kate studied the young woman. She didn't see a likeness to herself at all and she was far too young to be her own half-sister. If it wasn't her sister. Where was she?

'This is my daughter Michelle,' Penny said, touching Michelle's arm. 'She's an architect and works in town, but she wanted to come and meet you.'

Kate put her arms around Michelle lightly then studied her. She didn't look much like Penny.

'Mum never told me about you until last week,' Michelle said. 'It's come as a bit of a surprise.'

'I expect it's been a surprise to you all.'

'It certainly was,' Michelle said. 'I'll leave you two to talk. I'm off to the kitchen to make the tea. I promised Mum I'd look after you both while you get to know each other. You'll have a lot to talk about.' She disappeared down the passage and Kate soon heard a tap running and teacups rattling.

'It wasn't such a surprise for me,' Penny said, looking back at Kate as she led the way through to the lounge. 'I found out about you some time ago.'

'You did? How?'

'My brother Jerry knew. He'd known all along, it turned out. He overheard our parents talking about Lizzie after she'd been sent away.' Penny stopped walking and turned to Kate. 'Typical Jerry. He was always sticking his nose in. And once he knew, he couldn't help ask Mother if it was true. But she swore him to secrecy and he only told me after the Adoption Law changed. He said he was worried you might turn up and thought I should know.' Penny paused in the hallway beside a long splashy, boldly-coloured triptych taking up most of the wall.

'A few years after you were born, when Lizzie was having Jessie, he asked her, as only Jerry would, if it was a boy or a girl. She tried to pretend it hadn't happened, but then she realised Jerry knew. "A girl," Lizzie said. And she told him the name she'd given you: Felicity Frances Hamilton.' She smiled broadly and put an arm round Kate's shoulders. 'Welcome to the Hamilton family, Felicity Hamilton.'

Kate gasped. It was the first time anyone had called her by her original name.

'Thank you.'

They continued to walk slowly down the hall, Penny with her arm still around Kate.

'Jerry found some letters Liz wrote to you when she was still living at home. She got a job for a couple of years until she got married and she must have felt your loss very much during that lonely time. I remember Jerry coming round to visit one day with his baby son and watching Liz cradle him in her arms like she didn't want to let him go. I didn't know at the time, of course, but she would be missing you terribly then.'

'But I never got any letters.'

'No. They were never sent. Jerry found them when he was cleaning out our parents' house after Father died. There was such a jumble of things in boxes in the attic and that's where your letters were. Tied in a pink ribbon in an old shoebox with Lizzie's diaries and photos from school. Jerry said they choked him up That's quite something for him. He's a real rugby head, your Uncle Jerry. A man's man. I don't think I've ever seen him cry.'

'You don't know what I would have given to see them when I was a teenager. I wrote a diary to my mother – to Liz – every night.'

'I expect she would have liked that.'

Penny led the way into a vast, arched lounge with a sweeping view across the sea to Mana Island. Sun was streaming through the window highlighting the steel grey carpet and the fat charcoal cane chairs and couches arranged to capture the view. Bright aqua and sky blue cushions and a large sea-coloured oil painting highlighted the marine theme.

It was a lovely room but it was empty. Where was Liz? Where were her brother and sister?

'Is my mother here?'

Penny looked uncomfortable. 'No. She couldn't make it.'

'But she was going to bring her kids. She said she was going to tell them about me and I could meet them.'

'She never told me that.' Penny looked even more uneasy. 'She said it was just her you were expecting; she didn't say about Jessie and Rick.' Penny paused, looked out to sea then back at Kate. 'She must be scared of telling them. She must be terrified of the shame she was made to feel when she was pregnant with you – the shame of disgracing her family and herself. She's put that shame into a box and screwed the lid down tight, and now she feels it slowly escaping again and threatening to envelop her.'

'But people don't feel like that any more. Her kids wouldn't want her to be ashamed.'

'I know. But we can't possibly understand what it was like for her then. The legacy of that time is that she doesn't want anyone else to know. She found it hard enough telling me about you, asking me if I'd see you instead.'

'She chickened out,' Michelle said matter-of-factly as she came into the room. 'She does that sometimes.'

Michelle was carrying a tray of cups and saucers, a teapot and milkjug. She set it down on the coffee table and started pouring the tea. 'Mum wanted to do it properly. She's been baking.' She indicated a plate of plump almond biscuits.

'I'm impressed.' Kate accepted her tea with milk and selected a biscuit. 'Thanks Michelle . . . and you too Penny.'

Penny laughed. 'It's nothing. Hopefully it's better than the supermarket.'

'Okay, Mum, I'm off now. I've done my bit.'

'Won't you stay for a cuppa?' Penny asked.

'No. I came to meet my new cousin and now I'm going to leave you two in peace.'

After saying goodbye, Michelle returned to the kitchen and a few moments later Kate heard the front door close.

'Let's sit down.' Penny gestured to one of the chunky charcoal cane chairs and sat in the other.

Kate perched on the edge of the seat and put her bag on the floor.

Penny started pouring the tea.

There was a moment's awkward silence before Penny said 'I can't believe that you . . .' and Kate said 'Isn't it funny how you and I . . ?' and they both laughed, that same warm, hearty chuckle – the one Kate's kids gave her such a hard time about.

'Don't sit next to Mum at the movies,' Kate's son James would say, 'especially a comedy. You can hear her laugh all over the theatre.'

And her daughter Amelia would dig her in the ribs at the funny bits in *101 Dalmatians* and wriggle down in her seat and cover her eyes with embarrassment.

Kate waited for her aunt to go first.

'I was just going to say I can't believe that I've found someone else who looks so like me.' She handed Kate a cup and studied her closely. 'I mean, you look like Liz in so many ways, but she's quite a few years older than you – and me. With my other sister Jilly dying young, and Jerry looking much more like his father, I haven't experienced this before.'

'Me neither. It's funny isn't it? It's the first time I've seen anyone else behind my face.'

'You look like your sister too, in some ways. Have you seen a photo of her?'

'Yes, when she was in England.'

'Goodness, that was years ago. 'I'll show you the family photos.' Penny set down her cup on the coffee table, picked up an album nearby and opened it at the first page of sepia-coloured photos. 'Look at these.' She pushed the album towards Kate revealing an array of individuals and family groups from what appeared to be the early part of the twentieth century.

'That's your grandmother, my mother Helena Hamilton, when she was younger. They always used to tell me I looked like her and now I can see that you do too.' She let go the album and looked up at Kate. 'You know, my husband Graeme didn't believe it. He thought you must be making it up, that you were a con-woman, trying to muscle in on the family fortune.' She snorted derisively. 'As if there was one.'

'Oh?' Kate picked up her cup and took a sip. Making it up? Her ability to tell fibs had long gone.

'Lizzie doesn't know Graeme knows now. I haven't told her. I never told her I already knew either, and neither did Jerry. But as soon as Lizzie asked me to come today instead of her, I just had to let Graeme know about you turning up at long last. You're family, for heaven's sake.' She smiled and patted Kate's arm gently. 'Graeme'll see how foolish he's being as soon as he claps eyes on you. There's no doubt at all you're one of us.'

'One of us? You don't know how much that means to me.'

'How did you find Lizzie?' Penny was pointing at a photo of Liz in the album and looking at her questioningly. 'Did you have to search for a long time?'

'I've been searching all my life.' Kate realised this sounded a bit grandiose and laughed. 'But I only made headway after the law changed in the mid-eighties and it became legal to search. There's a standard letter you write, in case someone else reads it. I think Liz must have wanted to get the letter, deep down, or she would have put a veto on me. You know, put an official ban on me finding her.'

'And that was, what, twenty years ago? She put you off meeting your brother and sister all that time?'

'I promised her I'd wait until she was ready to tell them. But she always had an excuse. And when she got sick, she said it would be too much for her, make her worse. So she never told them and I kept my promise,' Kate said.

'She thought no one knew about you. There've been so many times I was going to tell her I knew. When she was really depressed, I was going to talk to her about it. I thought it might be the cause of her depression, keeping something like that inside her all these years, especially since the law changed, and not being able to talk about it with anyone. But it's hard to get inside her protective shell. She pushes you away when you try to get close. Just changes the subject. She didn't used to be like that when I was little. But she's done it for years now.'

'She seems to be a very private person.' Kate took another sip of tea then bit into a biscuit, catching the crumbs before they fell to the floor.

'She's shy in public.' Penny turned the page on the album. 'Not like our mother. Helena Hamilton was always having people round for her National Council of Women meetings. But Lizzie used to hide upstairs, even when she was old enough to be introduced around. She's not good in crowds or with new people, so she avoids going out as much as possible.

But when she's just with family, she can be the life and soul. Her family is everything to her.'

'Mine too.' Kate's strong sense of family – even if she didn't look like any of them – had been instilled by both Mum and Dad. Mum had continued to run round for years after the dreaded Great Aunt Doris who was Mum's closest relative, while Dad spent as much time as he could with his brothers, his nieces and nephews, even when they lived out of town. She remembered long hot summers on her Uncle Leslie's farm, endless sundowners with Uncle Trevor – while Dad nursed a single sherry for hours – and Christmases with cousins in Golden Bay.

Penny nibbled on a biscuit then said, 'What was it like, meeting Liz for the first time?'

'Not at all what I expected.' Kate put down her cup and thought about it for a moment. She couldn't tell Liz's sister the truth – that they hadn't got on. 'She told me about her family and showed me some photos.' Kate thought for a second then ploughed on, figuring it would all come out sooner or later. 'It was the weirdest thing, but when she showed me a photo of your brother, Rick, I realised I'd met him before.'

'No!' Penny laughed incredulously.

'Yes.' Kate smiled. 'He'd written a play called *A Trap for Young Players*. They brought it to Christchurch and I got to interview Rick for radio.'

'I suppose in New Zealand, there are sometimes very few degrees of separation between us.'

'They say this country is just one big village.' Kate shrugged. 'She also told me about the family's medical history, and especially about the cancer gene that seems to lurk everywhere.'

'My sister Jilly, my aunt and eventually my mother – they all died of cancer.'

'It was a worthwhile warning for me,' Kate said. 'A few years after I met Liz, I took myself off for a mammogram, just in case. I think I must have been about forty. They say you should start having tests at fifty, so I'd never have bothered if

I hadn't learned it was in my genes.' Kate picked up her cup and took a fortifying sip. 'And there it was – a tiny lump at the base of my left breast.'

Penny gasped.

'I'm fine now,' Kate attempted a reassuring smile. 'I had a mastectomy and a replacement at the same time, then chemo – the works. It was a long time ago.'

'I'm so sorry it had to be you.' Penny gazed out to sea for a moment. 'I got breast cancer too. Just a couple of years ago.'

Now it was Kate's turn to draw in her breath.

'Like you, I went through all the treatment and, like you, here I am today.'

Their tea went cold while they shared treatment experiences and reflected on how different things might have been if it hadn't been detected at such an early stage.

'Does Liz know?' Penny asked.

'Yes, I wrote to her when I found out and thanked her for the warning. It probably saved my life.'

'She never said. But then she wouldn't; she wanted to keep you a secret.'

'I was hoping the secret would be out in the open now, that everyone would know.'

'She's made a start with me. I'll see if I can push her to tell the kids.'

The sun was casting an orange glow through the living room when Kate realised how late it was. They'd been talking for nearly three hours without noticing the time passing, as if they'd known each other all their lives. Kate had to go. She was supposed to meet her friend Vanessa for dinner in Courtenay Place – an arrangement she'd made in case she suffered a similar disappointment to the day she'd met her mother – before catching the last flight home. It was just as well she hadn't planned on an inaugural dinner with her siblings – that would have to be another day. Because she *was* going to meet them, she was sure of that. Penny had promised – well, at least she'd said she'd try.

'They ought to know about their sister Felicity,' she said then caught herself. 'Sorry, Kate. It's funny, I've always thought of you as Felicity. I can't get it out of my mind.'

Driving along the motorway back into town she made the resolve that somehow or other she would get to know her brother and sister.

She'd always been stubborn. David once said, when she was hounding him to fix the bathroom door – a job he'd put off for weeks because she suspected he didn't know how to do it – that she was one of those irritating people who just never gave up. 'You're like a dog with a bone,' he'd said.

As she coasted down the gorge road, she got out her bone and began to gnaw at it.

There had to be a way to make it happen. She'd been asking Liz for twenty-three years to tell her kids, to let Kate meet her siblings. What if Liz never told them? It certainly seemed that was the likely outcome. From what Penny had said, Liz would keep avoiding the issue, change the subject, put it off as long as possible – forever if she could.

What was so frustrating was that she'd already met Rick. She could just pick up the phone and tell him the news. And it wouldn't be that hard to find her sister Jessica through official records. Maybe that was what she should do. Just tell them. Write them both a letter and let them know she existed.

And yet – she had promised her mother she wouldn't tell.

She decided to leave it a bit longer, to give Penny a few weeks to see if she could prompt Liz to make the move. And if she still wouldn't budge, a letter was the only alternative.

Her mother was proving an enigma. She wanted to be able to understand her, to stand in her shoes and find out what it had been like all those years ago – and what it was like for her now. But how to get through to her? They were like chalk and cheese. They might look alike, but their personalities came from different worlds.

Would she have been more like her mother if Liz had kept her instead of adopting her out? What *would* she be like? She'd often wondered.

There was no Domestic Purposes Benefit when she'd been born, no support system for women who decided to keep their own babies, which accounted for the fact that so few did. Even a cheap Cuba Street bedsit would have been beyond her mother's means with a baby and no means of support.

Kate knew she'd been lucky; she'd enjoyed not quite a silver-spoon existence but certainly a silver-plated one. Not that her parents were wealthy; they'd had to go without so she could have extras like music lessons, ballet classes and swim school. And how had she rewarded them?

Kate wasn't proud of her teenage years. All her childhood, she'd been compliant, a chameleon, adapting to her adoptive family to prove that she fitted in – she genuinely believed she might be sent back to wherever she'd come from if she wasn't a good girl. But in her teens, she'd broken free and rebelled. It was as if she'd been holding it all back, waiting for the right moment.

She blamed it on hormones. One day, she'd woken up to a moon crater of acne across her freckled face and a constant sense of pent-up fury winding her up so the only possible reaction was to explode. That's when the war had begun.

Poor Mum. She'd given her a terrible time. As if she hadn't had enough to worry about with Dad deteriorating slowly. Pity she hadn't been able to see it through her mother's eyes at the time; she mightn't have been such a cow.

For the first year or two, the arguments were comparatively low key – that is, you wouldn't have heard them on the other side of the street – but by the time she'd turned fifteen, they were epic.

Once upon a time Dad would have taken more control and given her the strap for bad behaviour, but she was too big for that at fifteen – and besides, he'd never have been able to catch her.

He used to. But she'd become more cunning as he'd become less mobile. She remembered the autumn when she was thirteen and in big trouble she'd been able to hide in the overgrown asparagus patch in the back garden. Guilty of wading through the river in its deepest part, almost up to her neck, with Vicki-Jane and her brother Michael, and coming home not only very late but also very wet, she hadn't needed to see the belt in his hand to know she'd be in for it.

The asparagus bed took up a large rectangle down behind the tall privet hedge where a neat vegetable garden was filled with all the greens any normal girl detested: broad beans, Brussels sprouts, silver beet and, every year, a seemingly inexhaustible supply of asparagus.

The first week or two, Kate would happily eat the spears of asparagus that Mum carefully turned to mush on the stove but after that, it started to lose its appeal until, as the end of the season approached, it made her literally gag.

It was long after the season was over, when the remaining spears had grown to over three feet high and surrounded themselves with a thicket of lacy fronds of greenery, that she'd run into the middle of the asparagus bed, pushing through the swathe of tall stems, to escape the stinging pain of another hiding. Hidden by the thick growth, she'd remained undiscovered, slowly drying out under the warm afternoon sun, occasionally worried that Dad might set a match to the whole bed, like he did every autumn to burn off the dried tall fronds. She imagined being chased out of her hiding place by tongues of flame, like the rabbits she'd seen once in a *Movietone News* trailer fleeing from a farmland fire.

But Dad had given up his search. It was nearly dinner time, when the hunger pangs outweighed the fear of Dad's leather belt, before she ventured back inside.

She couldn't remember his reaction when she finally reappeared, but she could remember that the punishment for the crime had long been forgotten and the strap returned to its dressing table drawer.

She didn't hold any grudge against Dad for the strap; it was what fathers did in those days. When Vicki-Jane and she had compared notes, she'd been grateful her father was so merciful and that he got the belt out so rarely.

The belt had long disappeared by the time that record bout of two hours and forty-eight minutes began. When it was over, she suspected Dad was so relieved that he could hear himself think again – and hear the television news – that retribution was the last thing on his mind.

She couldn't even remember what the argument was about, its epic duration having acquired more significance than the actual row itself. She remembered an impasse that must have come about the two-hour mark when Mum had gone into the study with Dad and closed the door firmly behind her. She recalled raised voices – most unusual between her parents – and her mother coming into the kitchen quite some time later, her eyes red, her manner quite distracted. But Kate hadn't had the sense to leave it there; she recalled threatening to leave home and her mother had gone ballistic. She still felt bad whenever she thought of it, not the least because it was just one of many similar rows when she'd said vile things to her mother she later regretted but never said so, and never apologised. And now it was too late; Mum had died last year.

As she descended Transmission Gully, Kate looked across the harbour towards Wellington – the sea now comparatively calm and blue under a clear sky with only occasional scudding clouds. She'd waited long enough. She decided she would confront her mother; she would demand to meet her siblings. If Liz wasn't prepared to tell them, she would.

~ ~ ~

But it wasn't that simple.

She wrote to Liz, telling her how disappointed she was that Liz hadn't kept her word and told her children. She delivered her ultimatum.

Liz didn't reply.

Kate didn't know what to do. What if her letter had tipped Liz over the edge? What if Liz had been admitted to hospital again? What if the unthinkable had happened and she'd died?

Then the earthquake happened. Magnitude 7.1 on September 4, 2010 in the early hours of the morning, waking Kate up and throwing her and David out of bed. Immediate family was all that mattered. Followed by extra demands at work, additional shifts, people's heartrending stories to be told. Injuries were reported, but no deaths. Timing had been everything – most people were asleep in their beds and out of harm's way.

Once the phone was back on, among the many callers checking if she was okay was Penny. Kate learned that yes, Liz was at home; yes, Penny had encouraged her to talk to the kids; no, she hadn't heard from her since. She promised to give her sister a reminder.

Weeks slipped by. China, glasses, photo frames, the TV set – so many smashed things to be photographed for insurance then replaced, so many family treasures lost forever, so many things now to be fixed on shelves with Blu-tack in case there was another big quake.

There was the usual rush into Christmas, family to be accommodated, presents to buy, celebrations to be arranged, including the annual family Boxing Day party at her home.

It was the big aftershock that day that became the turning point for Kate. Although not one of the biggest aftershocks, it was shallow and centred not far from Kate's home; and she was in the kitchen at the time getting ready for the party. But instead of terrifying her, this earthquake made her mad.

Boxing Day was when the Stewart family got together to talk about their year and catch up on how all their kids were doing. Every time they got together though, Kate would feel the odd one out, the ugly duckling. Her cousins were all tall, striking, with a beautiful bone structure, cheekbones, hipbones even. Kate couldn't remember the last time she'd seen her hipbones. Two of her cousins had been international models – they still looked gorgeous, they still towered over her. Next to them, Kate never felt she belonged. Even though her cousins were possibly the nicest people alive, even though they always included her, treated her as one of them, she still felt a fake. It wasn't that she didn't like being with them, it was just that she didn't feel she deserved it.

With Penny she no longer had that odd-one-out feeling. With Penny she almost felt she belonged. She could almost believe she was 'one of us'.

Boxing Day was a turning point. It was the day she decided she simply had to meet her brother and sister and persuade

Liz to tell the rest of her family about the daughter they never knew she had. She wasn't going to be kept a Hamilton family secret any longer. Maybe it was the effect of the constant aftershocks, maybe it was all the champagne. It soon became evident that the earth moving throughout the annual family get-together had been all the reason everyone needed to get thoroughly sloshed. Another aftershock? Grab the wine bottle to stop it falling and pour another glass of bubbles. She'd been glad to have her family around, glad she wasn't on her own every time the house twisted and shook and the glass doors rattled on their hinges. After all the wine, she could almost believe she looked as good as her cousins.

~ ~ ~

Later that week, as soon as the library reopened, Kate sat down in front of all the electoral rolls and looked up the names Liz had given her years earlier. It took longer than she thought, but at last she found the addresses of her two siblings.

Back home, she got out her laptop and wrote – and rewrote several times – two letters. It then took her over a week – and a raft of New Year's Resolutions – to pluck up the courage to post them.

Christchurch

January 5, 2011

Dear Jessie

This letter may come as a bit of a surprise to you but I can think of no other way to do this but to write and tell you that your mother, Liz Davidson (nee Hamilton), is also my mother.

I was born on March 17, 1951, at Essex Hospital Christchurch. Soon afterwards, Liz had to give me up for adoption, as was the custom at that time. Since then, I have had a very happy life (with, of course, its ups and downs) and have tried to make the most of every day. My adoptive parents loved me deeply and gave me everything they could.

However, they never hid from me the fact that I was adopted and I always had a hankering to find out who my birth mother was and whether she had her own family. Over 20 years ago, I traced Liz and wrote to her. Not long afterwards we met, in Wellington. We exchanged photos, memoirs, stories, and we have kept in touch since at Christmas time.

She told me she had two further children, and a little bit about each of you. I have often asked if I could meet you but she has repeatedly said she couldn't cope with that yet and asked me to wait. In 2000 I was undergoing chemotherapy for breast cancer and it occurred to me then, and has occurred to me since as I get older, that I didn't want to die without giving it my best shot to meet you. I wrote to Liz and asked her again but she refused, saying she wasn't well and it would be too stressful for her. She said she might be up to it some time in future. I didn't die, as you can see, and have made a full recovery, but the desire to find you lingers on.

In the last few months, I've asked her again. She said she would do so and even arranged for us all to meet. But it never happened.

This time I don't feel able to hold back. I would very much like to meet you, even if just only once. I know it will be very difficult for you and may take you some time to come to grips with this, and I will understand if you don't reply immediately.

I have lived in Christchurch most of my life, have a husband and two adult children.

I haven't included a photograph at this stage as I felt it might be a bit much all at once. However, I'm happy to send one if you like. I have seen a photo of your mother when she was young and there is quite a resemblance with photos of me at a similar age. I don't know what you look like, so I don't know if there is anything in common.

I will be in Wellington in February and March and could meet up with you then if you are up to it.

I have also written to your brother Rick, whom I met once many years ago through my work without knowing he was my brother. I have found you all from the information Liz gave me, plus looking up the electoral rolls.

I don't know whether Liz is frail or simply afraid of the repercussions, but if it would be too stressful for her to find out that I have told you about me, you may choose not to tell her I have contacted you. I suspect that is what she would prefer. If you want proof without going to her, I could supply it.

The next step, if there is one, is up to you.

It had seemed so easy when she had left home that morning to drop the two letters in the box on the way to work. But poised in front of the narrow grey slit in the Post Office wall, Kate's arm suddenly felt weighed down with lead, sending a message to her brain that allowing the envelopes to be bitten off and swallowed by the postal flap was possibly not the right thing to do after all.

She was being entirely selfish. That she knew for certain. She had written the letters – almost exactly the same, apart from an acknowledgement to Rick that they had already met – in self-centred fulfilment of her own desire. But what if her siblings didn't share that desire? What if meeting their unknown sister was the last thing they wanted? What if her surprising news tore the family apart?

It was this last possibility that made her hesitate on the footpath, envelopes poised in front of the letter box.

'Kate, fancy seeing you here.' It was one of the insurance brokers she'd befriended covering earthquake recovery issues.

'Good morning, Philip. Collecting your mail?'

'It's a daily ritual now I have to work from home. Empty the mail box and pick up an espresso next door.' He waved a thick pile of large envelopes. 'You looked like you were frozen on the spot.'

'Oh, no. Just posting some mail.' She thrust the letters into the box and it snapped shut behind them. She heard the soft rustle and thud as they hit the bottom. Too late now. They'd gone.

Writing then posting the letters was one of the hardest choices Kate had ever made. It was even harder than telling Mum twenty years ago she'd met her birth mother.

'You could have told me before you went,' Mum had said quietly, plucking at the blooms on the winter sweet in the vase on the dining room table.

'I didn't want to hurt you.' Kate shifted in her chair.

'So why tell me now?'

'I'd have to tell you sooner or later.' She took a deep breath. 'And I wanted you to know that it wasn't the big event I'd always expected. If anything, it was a bit of a disappointment.'

She looked across at her mother, who continued to fiddle with the flowers. After a moment, she looked up at her daughter and smiled thinly. It was hard to read the look in her eyes, but a shadow of relief seemed to cross her face.

'So what was she like?' Mum said at last.

Kate thought for a moment. She should have prepared an answer; she had no idea what to say. It had seemed so easy, telling David; he'd laughed with her at the anti-climax after Kate had yearned so long for the reunion to occur.

But telling Mum was different. She knew that Mum had dreaded this moment – she'd said so often enough. This was Kate's chance to set her mind at rest. She put her coffee mug down and fiddled with the last piece of muffin on her plate. Mum made great muffins, each time a new flavour, trying out a recipe she'd cut out from the paper or a magazine.

'She wasn't like you at all,' she said at last. 'Or like me. Although I think she might look a little bit like me.' Kate reached down and patted the cocker spaniel nosing around her chair looking for muffin crumbs.

'So what was she like?' Mum prompted again.

'You've got so much energy, Mum, you're always on the go, always doing something – usually to help someone else – and I feel you've made me that way too. But Liz – that's what she calls herself, not Elizabeth – she seemed so passive, so lacking in energy or drive, she seemed to have no confidence in herself. I wouldn't be surprised if she was suffering from depression.'

'Oh, I'm sorry to hear that.' Mum looked surprised and a little relieved. 'You know, that's not how I pictured her at all.'

'You pictured her?'

'Yes, I've always had an image of a confident, almost forward young woman who would end up doing very well for herself, who would pick herself up and have a career.'

'She said she worked in a draughtsman's office for a while tracing plans, but she never got much beyond tracing other people's work and left as soon as she got married. She never went back to it. Not like you.'

Rose smiled. 'Did she say anything about her other children?'

'She doesn't want me to meet them. She made me promise not to tell them until she's ready.'

'Oh Kate, I'm sorry,' Rose put her hand out to cover her daughter's and gave it a comforting squeeze. 'That would have been like closing the final gap for you.'

'But the incredible thing was that I'd already met my brother, Rick – she calls him Richard – I met him once when I interviewed him, and I never knew.'

'That's so sad. You didn't know at the time, and now you're going to have to wait a whole lot longer. What if you meet him again through work and Liz still hadn't given you permission to tell him?'

Kate had already thought about that. 'To tell you the truth, I'd be torn. I don't know what I'd do. I've thought seriously about wangling an interview with him somehow. He's got plays coming out every few years and it's only a matter of time before one of them comes to Christchurch.'

'Would you say something? Would you let him know?'

'I'd be very tempted.'

But it had never happened.

Three days after posting the letter she got a call from her brother Rick. She was sitting in the lounge watching *Sunday Theatre* with David and James, who was back home while studying Business at the Polytech. Amelia was in Auckland, where she'd been working in marketing for ACP magazines since graduating just over a year ago.

Kate recognised the voice immediately – the rounded vowels, the range of expression, dropping to that deep bass resonance mid-sentence.

'Hello Rick,' she said.

David picked up on it immediately; his eyebrows shot up and his mouth opened in a wide grin. He mimed a high five.

She grinned back, trying to hide her nerves, and took the phone through to the dining room

'Your letter came as a huge shock,' he said. 'We had absolutely no idea.'

'I'm sorry it was so sudden like that. But I didn't know how else…'

'No, it's fine, really, in fact it's a bit of a relief.'

'It is?' This was unexpected.

'Yes, you see, Mum's been so sick these last few years, hyperventilating, really in a bad way. She had to go into hospital for a while and she's been taking medication for depression ever since. I've been sure there's something behind it, something that's been causing it. I was so worried, so sure there was a cause, I asked her not long ago was there something she hadn't told us? Something in her past that was upsetting her, perhaps? But she said no, nothing. And then your letter arrived. I was so relieved to learn about you.'

'I'm sorry she's been upset. And I hope this doesn't make it worse. She made me promise not to tell you. She said she'd been unwell and just couldn't cope with it.'

'I knew as soon as I read your letter. Mum started getting sick right about the time when the Adoption Law changed and when you came back into her life.' Rick laughed. Laughed! 'At last we know what's behind it all. And we can start to deal with it, to help her through it.'

Kate swallowed. Was she really the cause of all this pain?

'I'm sorry I …'

'No, stop apologising, it's not your fault. It's just wonderful you've turned up at last. I think you may be the answer to all her problems.'

Would he tell Liz? Yes, he said, but possibly not for a while. He'd talk it through with Jessie, and with his Aunt Penny, his mother's younger sister.

They talked about getting together, 'meeting again now I know who you are' and about Jessie's reaction. She'd been less enthusiastic than Rick; having not met Kate before, she didn't know if she could believe her, and she found it even harder to believe that her mother could have had a past life involving an illegitimate baby.

As Rick talked, Kate could understand perfectly how Jessie felt. She would find it equally impossible if someone had announced out of the blue they were her sister or brother. She knew of innumerable people it had happened to, and it hadn't always gone well.

It was funny talking to this man who was now her brother. It felt like she'd known him all her life, like she could confide in him, tell him how it had been all this time not being able to talk to him, not being able to break her promise.

They ended the conversation at thirty-eight minutes and twenty-two seconds, according to the phone display, after swapping email addresses and agreeing to meet soon.

'That was a marathon effort.' David switched off the television when she came back into the lounge. 'Did it go well?'

Kate couldn't stop grinning. 'Very well.' She didn't know what else to say, where to begin. It was too big to put into words.

'Do you think you'll get to meet him and your sister soon?'

'I think so. My sister, Jessie, she's not so keen. But Rick says she'll come round soon. She just needs to take it in.'

'Can't say I blame her.'

David patted the sofa next to her. Kate sat.

'Are you happy now?'

'Happy? I suppose I am. I mean, I'm worried about Jessie, about whether she'll come round, and about Liz, and what she'll say when she finds out when I've broken my promise. But for now, yes, I'm happy. I've found my brother. I've wanted to do that for twenty years. Now all I need is to meet him, and my sister.'

'I'm pleased for you,' he said, extending his arm across Kate's back and giving her a hug. 'I know you've wanted this for a long time.'

'Grandpa would be pleased too,' James said.

'He would?'

'Yes, he used to say you'd never feel complete until you found your original family.'

'He said that to you?'

'Yeah! Course. He liked to talk, you know.'

Kate nodded. She knew.

'I asked him once about you being adopted,' James continued. 'I think it was when you had breast cancer and were talking about it being in your genes from your mother – your other mother. Grandpa said there was a part of you that was missing, and that would only be restored once you found the family that you belonged to originally.'

'I can't believe…'

'He said he always wished he'd been able to help you with that. He'd be happy you've found them'

'I can tell him next time I see him.'

'It's his birthday soon.'

'I'll tell him then. I'll put flowers on his grave and tell him all about it.'

Kate didn't mind saying it out loud. Talking to her father while she stood under the drooping cherry blossom at the back of the cemetery seemed to ease her mind. A problem shared, as they say. Not that she imagined her father talking back. She wasn't into that spiritual reincarnation sort of stuff. But he'd always listened, and somehow she felt he still did.

David gave her shoulders another light squeeze. 'He'd like that.'

Chapter 4.

Mid-2011

'Hey sis! Where've you been all my life?' Rick was standing in the Circa Theatre foyer grinning, shifting from foot to foot, then started moving towards Kate while calling her name. The heavy door banged shut behind her as she hurried across the foyer and hooked her arms around his shoulders, feeling the soft leather of his figure-hugging motor-bike jacket. It slipped through her fingers, releasing that wonderful animal smell. She suspected she would remember this moment, the feel of this smooth leather and breathing its pungency for the rest of her life.

'I should have recognised you the first time we met,' he said. 'How could I not see that? You look just like my mother looked twenty years ago.'

'Do I?' Kate stood back from Rick and studied him, fingering her hair self-consciously. 'I don't know if I look like you though. You're different somehow.'

'That's what they all say. I think I'm a throwback to my grandfather rather than my mother.' He stood profile on and pretended to preen. 'What do you think? My grandfather was a handsome bugger.' Then he laughed, a hearty, deep-throated husky chuckle, not at all like Kate's. 'Come on, let's go over to the café and order a coffee.'

They ordered and sank into the deep leather settees facing the waterfront.

'A sunny, calm day,' Kate said. 'Wellington Harbour looks so beautiful when it's like this.'

'It's *always* like this in Wellington,' he said, grinning.

'That's what you all say here.' She paused, unsure whether to refer to her letter so soon. 'I want to thank you for taking this all so well. I didn't …'

'No, thank *you*. You're the best thing that's happened to us for a long time.'

Kate took a moment for that to sink in then said, 'But what about Liz?'

'Penny and I went to talk to her last week and she seemed fine with it. In fact, she seemed quite relieved to be able to talk about it at last. I didn't think she was going to stop.'

'What did she say?'

'She talked about being sent away from her home, how lonely she felt in Christchurch, how the time dragged by until at last you were born, then she wasn't allowed to even hold you. She said she's never forgotten that moment when you were taken away and she never saw you again.'

Kate swallowed. She'd often imagined what that must have been like for Liz, but couldn't even begin to understand. 'What else did she say?'

'She told us about your father, that he was good looking, swept her off her feet so fast she just couldn't say no. He was tall, sporty, she said, and he looked so handsome in his uniform, she just went along with him. She said she had no idea what she was doing, what he wanted her to do. She said she'd talked about 'it' with her friends, but when it came to it, she had no idea what 'it' was, what was expected of her. She was under the impression she'd be able to do 'it' with her pants on.'

'That's incredible.'

'Penny and I weren't expecting that at all. It was like the floodgates had been opened at last and out it came in a rush.'

'Was Penny shocked?'

'I don't think so. She told me she'd known about you for years. '

'Yes, she told me that when I met her.'

'She said she'd been thinking of telling me and Jessie but didn't ever find the opportunity. I think Penny's quite glad the secret's out.'

A waitress brought their coffees.

Kate pulled hers towards her, picked up the spoon and played with it.

Rick poured a finger of sugar into his black coffee and stirred it. 'I hope I haven't upset you,' he said.

'What? No, I …'

'I didn't mean to go into all that detail about what Mum said. Certainly not so soon after we met.' He lifted the spoon out of the cup and set it down. 'I don't even know how you feel about all that. It's so personal.' He picked up his cup and blew across it, fixing her with his eyes. 'I was going to say "I don't know what came over me", but I do know. It's you. It's like I've known you all my life. I just feel so comfortable with you, like I can say anything….' He tailed off.

'So do I.' Kate felt close to tears but made sure they didn't spill. She didn't want him to think her emotional. Instead, she sipped her coffee. It was hot and burned her tongue. The tears came closer to spilling.

After that, they couldn't stop talking. An hour flew by, two, three. The waitress brought more coffees and a flask of water, then tea with carrot cake. They talked about everything – their partners, families, family traits and foibles, their work and their hobbies, their favourite movies and books, plays and music.

And then it was time to go – Rick to record a radio commercial, Kate to meet her friend Vanessa. By then, they'd agreed there would be a family reunion at Rick's place as soon as it could be arranged to get everyone there – everyone from Kate's family as well as his.

'I'm sorry Mum isn't still with us. She'd have loved to be at the reunion,' Kate said as she hugged Rick goodbye.

'It won't be family without both your mothers,' Rick said.

Kate's Mum had died nearly two years earlier from a massive stroke in her ninety-fifth year. In some ways, Kate was glad she wasn't still around. Sure, she'd have been pleased that Kate was finally meeting up with her family; Mum had listened patiently for years to Kate's complaining about how long it was taking. But Kate doubted that she'd want to come to the reunion. She was frail and a plane trip might have been too much for her; besides, the Hamilton family wasn't her family and she'd have felt like an intruder. 'No, you go dear, then come back and tell me all about it,' Kate could imagine her saying.

Mum would have hated the earthquakes too. Her church, the rose window in the Cathedral, the Provincial Chambers, most of the beautiful old buildings she loved were all coming down. If the stroke hadn't killed her, grief from the earthquakes would have.

Kate missed her every day, missed the ease with which they could share thoughts, feelings, and news both good and bad; missed the comfort of a mother's understanding; missed the security of her love.

There was another mother now, but she hardly knew her. They'd met only once. Liz knew nothing of the policeman in the nursery, the two hours and forty-eight minutes, the shared effort of picking up her Dad off the floor time after time, the search for identity. She couldn't know; she hadn't been there.

~ ~ ~

The taxi dropped Kate in front of Rick's unpretentious, neat weatherboard villa in Karori just a few minutes after two-thirty. As David paid the driver, she gathered the bunch of daffodils she'd brought for her mother off the back seat, stepped out onto the kerb and looked around at her family – her husband David, relaxed, in jeans and a jacket, not at all concerned about what lay ahead; her daughter Amelia, a bit of an Aucklander now, after five years working in marketing and living across from Eden Park, sunglasses pushed back on her head, her long brown hair sleek and loose. She was dressed to make an impression in tight black jeans and high black boots, as sophisticated as her twenty-eight years would allow. And towering over her, James, twenty-four, as casual as his father, swapping his trackies under protest for jeans and a t-shirt without any holes. He'd managed to change a shift to get the day off – much harder now that jobs were so hard to come by.

'Right then,' she said, 'it's all …'

'Yes, Mum, we know,' James interrupted. 'It's important to make a good impression.'

'Relax, Mum,' Amelia said, taking her arm. 'It'll be fine.'

She smiled and let herself be led up the path.

Rick answered the door and ushered them into the lounge.

His family – her family – lined the room, taking up every available space, sitting on sofas and the arms of sofas, on chairs, and standing in the corners. At the far end, centre stage, was Liz, perched on a dining chair, holding court. For a few moments, as she stood back from the doorway in the hall, there was a tremendous racket, everybody talking at once.

But the second Kate came through the door, there was a sudden hush. Jaws dropped. Eyebrows rose.

Liz held up her hand in recognition.

'I guess there's no doubt you're Liz's daughter,' someone said and suddenly, laughter erupted and people started talking again.

'I'll introduce you around,' Rick said.

Kate met Rick's partner Kim; hugged her mother and shook hands with her husband Steven. Further round the room Penny took over from Rick and Kim, who disappeared into the kitchen to make the tea, and introduced Kate and her family to her Uncle Jerry, his partner Celeste and his adult daughters – her cousins Angela and Sue.

As she made her way round, Kate kept glancing at Liz, their eyes occasionally meeting, until at last she stood in front of her.

'These are for you, Liz.' She thrust the daffodils into Liz's hands, bent over and kissed her cheek, aware that this was the first time she'd seen her in over twenty years. It hadn't been a deliberate absence; meeting again had simply never been suggested, by either of them, not in any of their many letters. So they hadn't.

As she quickly studied her mother, she was shocked to see how much older she looked, but then, of course, so would Kate after twenty years. Liz's hair was now completely grey; Kate suspected hers might be too, if she ever let it return to its natural colour.

Smiling, Liz lifted the daffodils to her nose and breathed in spring. 'You shouldn't have.'

Kate introduced her husband and children and Liz commented on how nice they looked then asked if they were the same age as her grandchildren Emily and Johnny.

'I'm not sure, just a couple of years,' I think.

'Do you know if Jessie's here yet?' she asked Liz. She'd looked for Jessie as soon as she'd come into the room and realised she wasn't there; had hoped she might be in the kitchen helping.

But her mother didn't know if Jessie was coming and suggested she ask Rick.

She stayed with Liz a little longer and talked about Liz's family, how she'd been looking forward to meeting them. She waited for a reaction, but there was none. She thought Liz might tell her off, might remind her of the promise she'd made to keep the secret. But Liz didn't mention it. She didn't say much at all, but Kate could see that she was relaxed and happy, quite the opposite from the way she looked when they'd first met in the café on Oriental Parade. The anxiety, the stress, the fear of what might happen when her family found out the truth were nowhere in evidence. Did Liz know Kate had reneged on her promise and written to her children? Rick had emailed that he and Penny had visited Liz and told her they knew about Kate; Penny had told Liz she'd known for a long time. From Rick's report, Liz had carried on as if she'd expected it to happen, as if she already knew.

Maybe Liz need not know Kate had been the catalyst. Maybe she no longer cared.

Not for the first time, Kate wondered if she should have contacted her siblings years earlier.

She excused herself from her mother and led David and her children into the kitchen to find Rick.

'You never know with Jessie,' he said, spooning tea leaves into a large teapot. 'She said she was going to come, but then she said she might be late, might not make it.'

'Is she cross with me for writing the letter?'

'I don't think so. Maybe. I don't really know.' He shrugged and pulled a face.

The doorbell rang. Rick looked relieved. 'Hopefully that's her,' he said, leaving the tea to Kim and hurrying to the front door.

Kate followed him, gesturing to David and the kids to stay close.

'Hey, Jessie, you're here,' he said, opening the door. Standing on the front porch was a woman, taller than her, much slimmer, more athletic, the same strong wavy hair, the same eyes, same chin – pretty much everything the same, only thinner and a seven or eight years younger. Behind her were a slightly tubby, bearded man and two young adults, presumably their children.

'May I introduce your sister to you,' Rick said grinning broadly at Kate. 'Jessie, this is your sister Kate. Kate your sister Jessie.'

They laughed at the irony of sisters meeting for the first time so late in life, but their laughter was awkward, stilted. They embraced lightly, still reticent.

'Come in, everyone, come in,' Rick said and the hallway was suddenly too small.

Kate introduced her family and they, in turn, were introduced to Jessie's husband Michael and their two adult children, Emily (who was working in IT like her father and bore a striking resemblance to Amelia), and Johnny (who was finishing a web design degree at Polytech). In the crowded hall, everyone stood close together, slightly awkward, smiling uneasily.

Rick suggested the younger family members go into the dining room. 'You can watch television, use the computer, whatever you like. Johnny knows how to get everything going.' Then he herded Jessie and Kate into the living room. 'You two will have lots to talk about,' he said, steering David towards the kitchen. 'Come on, the men can get the tea.'

Kate stood beside Jessie inside the door, uncomfortable, not sure of what to say.

'Look at you two,' Penny said. 'You look just like sisters.'

Unsure of herself, Kate paused. Did they? What would Jessie think of that? She was a bit scared of Jessie – she seemed to be the one who didn't want Kate around, who felt that Kate was an intruder. But there was no sign of reticence on Jessie's face now. She was smiling at her Aunt Penny. At that moment, she linked her arm through Kate's and together they walked into the room. Someone started to clap. Soon everyone was clapping. Kate could feel herself going red, her face flushing with either embarrassment or pleasure – or both.

They approached Liz.

'Hello Jessie,' she said. 'Kate was worried you weren't coming.'

'You never told me I had a sister.' Jessie kissed her mother on the cheek then looked back at Kate and winked conspiratorially.

'No I didn't.' Liz grinned, her eyes sparkling with mischief.

They talked to their mother for a few minutes then Jessie took Kate's arm and led her over to the only vacant corner.

Kate could see David in the doorway watching her; he shook his head, gesturing for her to go, indicating he was about to talk to Liz's husband, who was hovering behind his wife, seemingly lost among strangers.

'Mum won't say it, but she's really happy about us all getting together today,' Jessie continued. 'She's been looking forward to it ever since Rick told her.'

Kate smiled, relieved. 'I was worried how she'd take the news about me.'

'I think she's relieved it's out there. I saw her the next day and she looked so happy – much happier than I've seen her in years. Once she realised nobody was laughing at her or pointing the finger, or telling her what a terrible thing she'd done, she was fine.'

Kate kept smiling, reassured by this, but also uncertain. What could she say to a sister she'd only just met? Who'd been reluctant to accept she existed?

'And how's it been for you? It must have been quite a shock.'

'It hasn't been easy. I couldn't believe it at first. I just couldn't believe that Mum would ever have done that – you know, before marrying Dad. She always seemed so straight, so upright, so fundamentally ordinary. But once Penny said she'd known about you for years, well, I had to accept it.' She stood back from Kate and studied her. 'And then it dawned on me, I've got a sister. I always wanted a sister.'

'So have I,' Kate said.

They looked at each other, tentative, wary, not sure about this new status then suddenly, at the same time, burst out laughing.

'It's so weird, isn't it?' Jessie said as they hugged each other tightly – so different from the light embrace of earlier.

After that, they couldn't stop talking, making up for the years apart. They talked about their childhood, their favourite toys and beachside camping holidays, discovering both their parents had favoured pop-top caravans for getting out of town, photography, and spaniels for pets. They talked about schooldays, about being in the school musicals and plays, and about falling in love, about having children and the perils of OE. It was some time after the arrival of afternoon tea that their intense conversation was brought to a temporary halt.

As she and Jessie talked, Kate had noticed out of the corner of her eye Rick and Kim handing out cups and mugs and the four children had been press-ganged into passing the vast array of baking everyone had brought – almond biscuits, pieces of citrus slice, spiced apple cake and miniature cup cakes covered in pink and white icing and decorated with blue forget-me-nots. Kate kept on talking.

'Come on you two,' Rick interrupted, guiding them both towards the coffee table. 'Everyone's waiting for you.'

As soon as Kate approached the table, Kim lit a candle on one of the cupcakes. 'That's to celebrate your arrival,' Kim said. 'Your first day with us. I made them myself.'

'Happy birthday, Felicity Frances.' Penny raised her cup.

Everyone was smiling.

Kate didn't know what to say. She glanced across at Liz whose half-smile belied the tears in her eyes. She smiled back. 'Thank you everyone.' That's all she could think of. They were looking expectant, as if she should make a speech. Words wouldn't come. She swallowed. And swallowed again. 'Thank you,' she said again, then picked up the cupcake and went to blow out the candle then paused. She held it out to Liz. 'Blow it out with me,' she said. Together, she and her mother blew out the candle then she unpeeled the paper case, broke off half the cupcake and handed it to her mother to eat. There was applause and a camera flash. Holding his new camera in one hand, James arranged the two of them to pose for a shot, which set off a whole line-up of family shots, from the entire family gathering, using a timer, to smaller groups, including the four younger family members and finishing with mother, daughters and son.

The tea had gone cold. Rick and Kim went back to the kitchen to make more.

Kate watched James showing his new cousins the photos of themselves on the back of his camera. 'I'm going to put that one on my Facebook page,' James said.

'Can you email it to me?' said Johnny. 'I'd like it too.'

'You can friend me,' James said.

They disappeared into the dining room again to look at each other's Facebook pages on Rick's computer.

David called her over to where he was still standing in front of the fireplace with Liz's husband Steven.

'Listen to this,' he said.

Steven shuffled on his feet, looking embarrassed.

'Tell her what you were saying just a moment ago,' David prompted.

'I was saying how nice it was to see Liz's children happy together – all three of you,' Steven said.

'He was watching you and Jessie in the corner talking and putting your arms round each other and laughing together, and Liz was watching you too and smiling.' David touched her sleeve affectionately.

'Yes. She's having a good day.' Steven seemed reluctant to say more.

Kate smiled, took his hand and thanked him.

'You're monopolising the guest of honour, Steve,' Jerry said, coming up behind her and steering her away to one side where his partner, Celeste, was standing.

She figured Jerry must be in his seventies; Celeste would have been mid-fifties.

Jerry looked more like Rick than Liz.

'I hope the Hamilton family isn't overpowering you,' Celeste said. 'They can be a bit like that.'

'Only a little bit,' Kate said.

'She'll get used to it,' Jerry said. 'She's one of us now.'

He explained that he'd read several letters that Liz had written to her in the year after she'd returned home from Christchurch. Each one had started 'Dear Felicity' and had been gut-wrenchingly sad, he said. 'So I still think of you as Felicity, even now I've met you.'

'Maybe I'll have to change my name.' She laughed dismissively then wondered if perhaps it might not be a bad idea after all.

'Don't knock it,' Celeste said. 'I have.' She explained that she'd joined the wiccan community some years ago and chosen a new name. 'I know Jerry's daughters think I'm nuts,' she looked at him and smiled self-deprecatingly, 'but I don't care. But I won't bore you with the details. You can come to one of our meetings and see for yourself if you like.'

Kate gulped. She knew nothing about wiccans – had always imagined them like the witches in Macbeth huddled over a boiling urn of frogs' blood, pond scum and bat droppings. But Celeste wasn't wearing a pointy black hat and an enveloping long black cloak; she was dressed much the same as everyone else in jeans and a colourful tunic. 'Maybe I should. I might learn something.' She smiled encouragingly and realised she meant it – she just might go.

Jerry called over his daughters, Angela and Sue who, Kate guessed, would both be in their forties.

Sue looked a lot like Jessie; Angela was taller, more finely featured, more like Rick.

'I expect Celeste's been telling you about her other life,' Sue said, pulling a face and giving her stepmother's arm a squeeze.

'Come on, don't give me that.'

'It's okay, I suppose, the wiccan world.' Sue said. 'Probably the most fun you can have when there aren't any men around.'

'We're going to leave you two to catch up on the last sixty years,' Celeste said, steering the other two women away.

'Sixty years? Shouldn't take long!' Jerry turned to Kate and suddenly looked very earnest. 'I'm so relieved you've turned up at last,' he said, looking straight at her. 'I've been getting more and more worried about Liz these past few years. I suspected she'd be worried about you turning up after they changed the Adoption Law, but of course I couldn't say anything. It was a taboo subject with her; she simply closed down at the very mention of the Act and the law changing. When she found out I knew, that was pretty bad. She wanted me to promise not to tell Penny or her children, but I refused. I said I'm not getting caught up in all that, making everyone feel guilty and ashamed. I tried to get her to see reason, to believe that no one thinks like that any more. But she wouldn't listen. She wouldn't discuss it any further.'

'Did you ever think of telling her children?'

'Oh yes, many, many times. Especially when they were older. But then I'd see her looking so sad and I just didn't have the heart.'

Kate didn't like to think of her mother being sad; it felt like it was her fault. 'Has she always been sad?'

'Mainly these past twenty or so years, since the Adoption Law changed. I think she was terrified it would all come out and she'd be exposed.'

'It's all out now, though.'

'Yes, at last. And look how good she is. I haven't seen her so happy in years.'

Kate smiled, savouring the moment. Each time Liz smiled now, she would feel a little less guilty for being the cause of her grief.

She asked him if he'd ever met her birth father, if he knew anything about him, but Jerry said no, Liz had never brought him home and had never spoken of him.

'I wasn't supposed to know about it, of course. But she never spoke of having a boyfriend at the time. She kept him a secret. Until she had to confess to Mother, of course. But I only found out about that after Father died and I discovered her letters to you. She told you everything.'

'Except I never got to read them. Do they still exist?'

'I don't know. I gave them back to Liz. She never said what she did with them.'

He told her about the Liz he used to know, when they were both at school – about her likes and dislikes, her schooldays, her favourite books and her dolls, her love of helping in the garden and swimming at the beach, her first job at the draughtsman's office and how she gave it up to get married and start a family.

'I always thought she had it in her to go a long way, to have a real career. But she never had a chance to get any further than the bottom rung of the ladder.' He sighed. 'That's what women did in those days.'

'It's all changed now, thank heavens.' David joined them by the fireplace, holding the mantelpiece with one hand, his mug of tea in the other. 'I can't imagine how we'd cope on one income.'

'I'm sorry, I've been neglecting you.' Kate touched his arm.

'I'm fine. I've been talking to Jessie and her husband Michael.'

Angela came up to Jerry and offered him more tea.

While they were talking, David bent down and whispered in Kate's ear. 'Michael's not that keen on you. I thought I'd better warn you. He reckons you'll upset Liz and make her condition worse.'

'Oh? Did Jessie agree with him?'

'She didn't seem too worried. But Michael was quite rude. He doesn't like you at all.'

Kate looked across at Jerry, who was still talking to Angela, and lowered her voice. 'I think Michael's a bit odd. He came up when I was talking to Jessie and interrupted, as if I wasn't there. He seemed a bit geeky, you know, with that posh accent. And totally lacking in the social skills.'

'Well he is a computer nerd.' David glanced around, checking they weren't overheard. 'I wouldn't worry about him. You can't expect everyone to accept you straight away.'

Kate could see Michael out the corner of her eye talking to Rick. He seemed to have Rick cornered and was berating him about something. 'I think I'll keep away from him,' she said.

Over the next hour or so, Kate made sure she spoke to everyone else she hadn't already met, including Johnny and Emma, as well as those she had. She spent more time with her mother and Penny. It was then, with just the three of them together, Penny and Kate kneeling beside her chair, that Liz talked about how it had been after Kate was born.

'After all that labour, after all that pain, they just took you away from me,' she said. 'I wasn't allowed to hold my little baby.' And she said it in such a sad, little-girl voice that Kate thought she was going to cry.

Stealing a look at Penny, she could see her lip trembling. Kate took her mother's hand. 'I'm here now,' she said and felt a faint squeeze in return.

Liz was briefly distracted by James and Johnny laughing loudly through the double doorway into the next room. 'Look at that,' she said, indicating towards the two boys. 'The next generation. I wonder what they're up to.'

'I'll go and see.' Kate stood and went through to the computer, where the boys had found a mutual friend on Facebook. Amelia and Emily were sitting at the dining table deep in conversation; it seemed to be about their jobs.

'Everything all right in here?'

Amelia looked at James and rolled her eyes; James and Johnny grunted 'Yeah.'

'Good. It'll be time to go soon. Half an hour maybe.'

There were protests from all of them. She returned to Liz and Penny and reported back.

Jessie and Michael left first, followed by Jerry and his family. It was time to go. She asked Rick to call a taxi and – her offer of help with the dishes quickly declined – talked to Rick and Kim until it arrived.

Rick smiled at Kate's profuse thanks and said it had all been worth it to see his mother smiling.

'She didn't say much though,' Kate said. 'I thought she might say something about how you found out about me and about us all being together now.'

'She wouldn't do that. She's never said much, never really shown much emotion. I can remember when we were little, she was quite demonstrative, she'd give us a hug occasionally. But once we were at school, no. She's always been very buttoned up.'

'That must have been hard sometimes.'

'It was. When I was a bit older, I used to look at her and try to understand why she was like that. Jessie would be upset about her boyfriend and Mum just didn't respond. She'd tell Jessie she'd soon get over it. Same with me. But now I know what Mum has been through, I can understand why she was always holding herself back.'

'Hopefully that's come to an end. Look at her now.' He indicated through the hall door into the living room where Liz was surrounded by family, still holding court, beaming happily. 'We should have done this ages ago, sis,' he said.

~ ~ ~

In the back of the taxi, squashed on either side, James and Amelia competed to tell Kate about their cousins. After the detail of their work, studies, likes and dislikes, she asked if they had discussed how they came to be related.

'Of course.' James did an eye-roll. 'That's why we were there.'

'Yeah, we talked about it, but not for long.' Amelia turned her eyes from the passing streetscape to Kate. 'It wasn't a big deal, really. We mostly talked about our families and work and how weird it was we looked a bit like each other.'

Kate smiled. All those years Liz had protected her family from finding out about her illegitimate daughter, living in fear of being shamed once again – and they didn't care. 'It wasn't a big deal,' as Amelia had said. All they cared about was having new cousins who looked a bit like them, who had interests in common.

James turned on his smartphone and tapped its face a few times. Kate could see his Facebook page come up on the screen. 'Oh mint. Johnny's put his photos up already.' He held it up to his sister. 'You and Emily. Peas in a pod. And look, she's as short as you are.'

~ ~ ~

There was a text from Rick on Kate's mobile. Rick was in regular contact, often by text – though not as often as Jessie, an inveterate texter – and had also emailed several times since the afternoon tea party a month earlier.

'Just home from Sunday with Mum.' The text said. 'She cracking jokes now better than ever. Doc taken her off medication. Yay.'

Kate was so thrilled she phoned him.

'Hey, sis,' he answered.

'Hey, bro.'

They both chuckled.

'It's unbelievable, eh? Mum's started reducing her medication. The doctor says she'll be off it completely in a month or less. We're all over the moon.'

'Did he say why?'

'No need for her to be on it. It's obvious, isn't it? Now the family all knows about you and she can see we're all fine with it, she's no longer weighed down by all that guilt and shame, she's free.'

'You really think that's it?'

'Of course. You little ray of sunshine. Mind you, we're not going to tell the doctor why she's so much happier. I don't think she's quite up to telling everyone about you yet.'

'No?' Kate teased.

'Well if you want to come and live up here, I guess everyone would see for themselves.' He laughed. 'Oh, by the way, Johnny was here with Jessie at the weekend. Did you know Jessie's kids and your kids still hook up on Facebook?'

'Still? I wondered if they'd stay in touch. Funny how a couple of generations on, things can change so much.'

~ ~ ~

It was Cup Day. The New Zealand Cup was running at Riccarton Racecourse; many of her friends had dressed up, borrowed hats bearing long curling feathers and swathes of netting, and headed off to the races in a show of support for Christchurch, still reeling a year on from its first big earthquake. Kate had turned down invitations to the members' stand and even a ticket to a hospitality tent. She wanted to stay home.

David took the hospitality pass and the binoculars and persuaded James to drive him to the racecourse. She had the afternoon to herself.

All year, she had been meaning to go through her mother's things, but the time had disappeared in earthquake repairs, family activities – there were two families to keep her busy now – and work. She'd promised herself that she would spend the holiday weekend going through the boxes of papers, photographs, ornaments and treasures they'd saved from her mother's house before selling it.

Cleaning out the house had been a mammoth task, taking trailer-load after trailer-load to the tip, removing the mountain of stuff her mother had hoarded in the garage, the spare bedrooms, the attic and in the seemingly endless line of cupboards and drawers. Kate hadn't realised what a hoarder Mum was until she'd come to clean it up.

'I'm doing a drawer every week,' Mum would promise when Kate commented on the state of the garage, or the cardboard boxes full of photos.

'I don't even know half those people,' Kate would say, fingering the sepia portraits of grim-looking men and women posing around ornate high-backed chairs and potted palms. 'You have to write their names on the back.' But Mum never did. It pained Kate, but she had to throw most of them away. What was the point of keeping photos of stern, stiff-collared men and unsmiling women you didn't know? There was no one left to identify them; all Mum's friends had died years ago.

On the Thursday, before the bank closed for the holiday weekend, Kate went into her parents' branch and asked to access the deed box her father had kept locked away ever since she could remember. She'd heard Mum and Dad talk about it often enough but had never seen it and had never thought to ask her mother in her later years what was in it. It seemed rude, somehow, to bring the subject up, as if she were admitting she knew Mum might not be around much longer and should therefore hand over the means to retrieve whatever was in it. Besides, her parents seemed to have coped perfectly well without accessing it in years, so she'd assumed that whatever heirlooms were hidden inside couldn't be of much value or use.

Originally, Dad had kept the deed box in the vault of his employer, the Union Bank. When it was taken over by the ANZ Bank, he switched the deed box over to the ANZ vault. By the time Kate retrieved it from the small suburban branch where her parents had transferred their accounts there was no vault, just a back room with a complicated double-key system that only the manager knew how to unlock.

It took a very long time – while the counter queue grew increasingly longer – for the teller to retrieve the box. She arrived through the code-locked door with a large, dented and heavily scratched metal box and hefted it onto the counter with a dull thud. On the lid above a wire handle was written her father's name: Geo. E. Stewart. She turned the key and lifted the lid. On the underside were etched the words 'Union Bank' and inside was a heavy brown manila envelope.

She picked it up and opened the flap. Sheaves of paper seemed to be all it contained. She tugged at them, holding the envelope sideways. Along with the papers, several metal objects fell out, scattering across the counter – a gold and onyx seal for stamping hot wax on the back of envelopes, and several gold and silver fob watches and chains, some in cases, some open-faced, with a dial of roman numerals.

'Will that be all?' The teller looked questioningly at her and Kate realised she was holding everyone up.

'I think I'd like to take these home and go through them.'

'Whatever you want. You're welcome to look at them here. I can give you a room.' She indicated towards a row of offices on the far side of the room.

Kate didn't want to sort through her parents' treasures in a glass-fronted office where everyone could see her. 'Thank you, but no. I'll take everything home.' She signed on several dotted lines and the teller took the deed box away.

What would Dad say? All these decades he'd kept his precious belongings locked away in a bank strong-room and here she was casually planning to take them home with no security at all. He'd be horrified.

As she walked out of the bank with her envelope of treasures, she found herself mentally explaining to her father that she was going to be home all weekend, she wouldn't let them out of her sight, and she'd sleep with them under her pillow – even the pocket watches.

There was no time to go through everything that evening, with guests for dinner and a messy house to be cleaned first. But, true to her word, Kate buried the envelope under her pillow, flattening the collection of watches so she could get a good night's sleep. The next morning, she forgot all about it.

As soon as David departed for the races, she started to sort through the boxes of her mother's things, methodically making piles – things to keep, things to give to someone who would appreciate them, things for the hospice shop, things to throw away. But every new box held a treasure of memories, papers to be scanned, a pile of diaries too tempting to put down, photos that held meaning, books she recalled from her childhood that couldn't be parted with.

The apricot and green cover of *The Chosen Baby* appeared in the middle of a pile; she had to put down all the other books and read it. 'Once upon a time …' and she remembered Peter and Mary who held their arms out to be taken home and loved by Mr and Mrs Brown. If only it were that simple. She could see Dad pulling her up on his lap and reading it to her beside the fire and how she clamoured to hear it again and again. It had made her feel safe, somehow; it had made her feel wanted. *The Chosen Baby* went into the 'things to keep' pile.

It was only when she stopped for a late lunch that Kate remembered the manila envelope under her pillow. Dad would have been dismayed. How could she forget something he'd set so much store on? It was, of course, still there.

She sat on the duvet cover and tipped the contents of the envelope out, scattering them across her side of the bed, papers falling in a lop-sided semi-circle, watches, seals, brooches and bracelets dropping in the middle of the papery arch like a golden anchor. Kate gasped. Treasure indeed. She picked up a chain bracelet, feeling the silky slipperiness of the gold links; a child's solid gold bangle, broken at the join; a baby's gold name brooch engraved 'Rose'; a Masonic seal; a gold and another silver fob chain; a pearl ring; a cameo brooch; a piece of polished greenstone set in a gold brooch mounting. She'd had no inkling about the jewellery.

Then she noticed a dark embossed case still in the bottom of the deed box. It must have been lying under the envelope. She pulled it out, opened the clasp, and smiled. Lying on a bed of white satin were six gleaming antique silver, bone-handled fish knives and forks – the ones Great Aunt Doris had refused to give her at her wedding and Kate had refused to accept from her mother after Doris had died.

Kate gently closed the lid, carried the cutlery case into the dining room and placed it in the top drawer of the chiffonier next to the other silverware where it belonged. Mum would be smiling.

Returning to the bedroom, with the jewellery still scattered across the counterpane, Kate started to sift through the papers. To her surprise, she found several documents from a Masonic Lodge. At the bottom of several pages was her father's signature above his official title: secretary. They were dated 1948. There was a family tree compiled by her father in

1992 to mark the 150th anniversary of his grandfather's arrival in Nelson Bay. And there was a pile of marriage and birth certificates dating back to 1818 with the names of people – presumably her ancestors – she'd never heard of.

Right at the bottom was a cream envelope, marked with age.

She opened it and extracted a pale blue legal document.

'New Zealand to wit,' it said. 'In the Matter of Part III of the Infants Act 1908: Order of Adoption under Section 16.'

It was her adoption papers certifying that her parents had 'fulfilled all the conditions and requirements of the said Act and the rules made thereunder relating to the adoption of children', and that the Stipendiary Magistrate, whose signature was unreadable, was 'satisfied of the several matters of which by the said Act' he was required to be satisfied.

There was still something in the envelope. She pulled out a thin piece of paper, brittle and browned at the edges, so thin it was almost transparent.

BIRTH CERTIFICATE

Name: Felicity Frances Hamilton
Date of Birth: March 17th 1951
Place of Birth: Christchurch, New Zealand
Mother: Elizabeth Cecily Hamilton, Clerk
Father: Peter Raymond Williams, Tram Worker
Dated this 30th day of June, 1951

DSS

There was an official stamp on the bottom right corner and the initials DSS – Department of Social Security.

Kate let it drop on the bed next to the other papers and rubbed her forehead with her hand. She had to sit down. She found a space on David's side of the bed and fingered her original birth certificate – such a small and insubstantial piece of paper to be carrying such significance.

It had taken sixty years for it to come to light.

Even though Rose had been prepared to pass on the names on the certificate to Kate when she'd asked twenty years ago, she had kept her word to the Government department.

From the time Rose and George had promised that Stipendiary Magistrate not to tell, they had kept the Adoption Order and her birth certificate locked away in the far reaches of a bank vault where nobody would ever see them, not even the person whose arrival into the world the birth certificate announced.

Kate stared at the small scrap of paper. She had arrived, she thought. This is me.

Chapter 5.

Christchurch. 2011

There is an email from Shakespeare in my inbox.

I click on it. The other emails can wait. Shakespeare@paradise.net.nz has news.

'It's for aspirational purposes, you understand,' my brother Rick explained when I asked him why he chose such a pseudonym online. 'I'm sure if the Bard were alive today, he'd have been a huge fan of all that technology can offer.'

I still smile when his emails arrive, and not just because of the tagline. I still find it hard to believe– a new brother and sister, a new family I only met a few months ago yet feel like I've known all my life.

Rick's email is reporting on his search through birth and marriage records for my birth father – a search I would have had to travel to Wellington to make.

'I've just had an email from Shakespeare,' I call out to David, who is changing out of his work clothes in our bedroom across the hallway.

'So how's your new bro?' David appears at the door to the spare room where we share a computer and a desk in jumbled disorder.

I look up from my laptop and smile. 'Rick's been to the Wellington library. He says he's got writer's block and decided to go sleuthing to see if he could find out anything about my father. He said it might give him an idea for a play.'

David grins. '*Much Ado About Nothing* perhaps.'

'More like *Love's Labours Lost*.' Turning back to the screen, I show him the email. 'He's scrolled through the Wellington papers and found the birth records of my father. Now I know he's for real.'

'What? Did you think he was a fabrication? What would that make you? A changeling?' David's eyes are smiling at the joke.

'Sometimes I wonder.' Taking my hands off the keyboard for a moment, I look up at David. 'Of course he must have existed, or I wouldn't be here. It's just that, with tracking down my birth mother and her family, my birth father was pushed into the background. I never gave him much thought once I knew Liz's story. He seemed like the bad guy who ran off on her. But since I've met the rest of Liz's family, I'm curious to solve the other mystery – my birth father.'

'I often wondered if you would do that. No matter what he was like once, he's probably quite different now. Could be even more brothers and sisters for you to find.'

'Could be.' I look up at him. 'Can you handle any more family?'

'Can you?' He grins and a questioning eyebrow shoots up.

'Good question.' I open two pdf attachments and settle on the first, which lists births. 'Here it is. Peter Raymond Williams. Born July the twenty-first in 1928 in Wellington. That means if he's still alive, he'd be eighty-three. I wonder if he is.' Further down the page, there's a scanned marriage record. 'In February 1953 he married Margaret Jean Symonds. That means he got married the same year as my birth mother. How about that? A couple of years after they created me, they'd each moved on enough to marry someone else.'

'No looking back. Can't say I blame them.' David studies the screen. 'Rick is doing a great job of sleuthing for you. You're very lucky.'

I flick up and down the page, studying the lines of names. 'He says he loves doing this sort of thing. It's like a detective story.'

'I can understand how he feels. It's *just* like a detective story.'

'Not so much a who-dunnit as a "where-is-he-now"?'

'And is your birth father still alive?' David asks, stepping back from the desk.

Returning to Rick's email, I scroll down the screen. 'Rick doesn't know. The cemetery records for Wellington haven't got him listed as deceased, but of course he might have left town long ago and be alive and well anywhere.'

'What about the electoral rolls?'

The second attachment is a scan of several photocopied pages. I scroll down to W. 'Yes, there he is.' As I stop to read, David leans over my shoulder. 'He was listed as a tramways worker until 1958 and after that it looks like he became a grocer at the top end of Willis Street somewhere. That's all we know.'

'It's a pretty good start. Rick should have been an historian.'

'It's a pity Dad isn't still around,' I say, 'he was passionate about history – especially family history. He would have known just where to look to see if Peter's still alive.'

'I'm not sure he'd want to find a second father for you. It might make him feel a bit redundant.'

'It's funny, you know, I've left it so long to even begin looking for him. But I'd be sad if he wasn't around any more, if I'd left it too late.'

David goes to the doorway then turns back to me for a moment. 'You'd better get a move-on then.'

'Yes, sir.'

'I'll get dinner soon. James is already asking when it's going to be ready.'

'You should tell him to get it himself. Sitting about all day studying, he needs to get off his chuff. It's not as if he can't cook - he's great when he puts his mind to it.'

'He's inherently lazy like me. It's in the genes.'

'Nonsense. He's been learning by example. Genes are all about what your arse *looks* like, not whether you have the energy to *get off it* or not.'

David pats his bum and disappears.

Turning back to the keyboard, I Google my birth father's name. Rick's already done that, but I might be able to do better, using some of the investigative journalism tricks David's taught me on the Companies Office website and the online databases accessed through the library. Soon, I have a company file with a list of directors and one of them is Peter Raymond Williams. It's a grocery importing and wholesaling company, which makes sense. If my father was a grocer, he could well have gone into grocery supplies. Tracking back through the company records, I see he could be comparatively elderly, which would fit; he was a founding director and the company has been around a long time. There is a real possibility it could be him – there can't be too many Wellington tramways men from the 1950s with the same name, surely?

The company directory lists the directors' addresses. His is in Miramar.

I Google-Map his house, but there are no photos along his street so I click on the satellite button and find him on Google Earth. I can't help but smile to myself at the ease with which such sleuthing can be done now. Not all that long ago, I'd have to spend hours at the Companies Office then take a trip to Wellington and drive up and down his street for the same view I'm looking at in my own home now: a big single storey house with an orange-tiled roof perched high on a hill overlooking the sea. A steep cliff below the house drops down to a winding road and a rocky shoreline. He must have a spectacular view of the harbour, almost out to the heads to the south and all the way over to Eastbourne to the north. I move the arrow to see further along his street; his house is surrounded by equally sizeable homes, many with decks hanging out over bush-clad sections all facing out to sea.

I can just picture him in there with his wife, tall and slim, her greying hair cut short, spiked up on top of her head, dangling silver earrings, her flowing multi-coloured tunic hanging over black straight-leg pants, striding into the living room in black, low-heeled sandals, bringing plunger coffee and shortbread at ten. My father will be sitting at the window, his business papers on his knee, ignoring the work he should be doing, staring out the window at the ferry steaming by. His hair thick and white, his face lined and weather-beaten, he'll have a far-away look in his eye, thinking of . . .

Not of me, that's for sure.

On the nearby bookshelves will be framed photographs of sons and daughters in school uniform, at university graduation perhaps, grandchildren at the beach, playing sport, family gatherings at Christmas.

The Google-Earth cliff-top house is comforting to visit; it makes me feel at home.

But it isn't my home. I close the page to rid myself of the image. There are other emails waiting to be read.

I click on one from my daughter Amelia: 'Got a promotion today after a good performance review. More money! Well, not that much, but every bit will help pay for the car to get its warrant. I'm going to be in charge of the customer relationship web campaign. Will look good on the CV next year in the UK.' The rest is about all the stuff she's selling on TradeMe to save money for the big OE and how her boyfriend is getting on studying for his Chartered Financial Analyst exams.

The remaining emails can wait, I decide. Returning to the one from Rick, I read it again and click back to the Companies Office website. Is there a phone number for my father? I scroll through the company's information. There is a global email address: admin@capitalimports.co.nz. Perhaps if I try various iterations of Peter's name, an email might get through:

From: felicity.price@xtra.co.nz
Sent: Tuesday, November 15 2011. 5:30 p.m.
To: Peter.Williams@capitalimports.co.nz;
Subject: Missing Pieces.
Dear Peter,
I was watching a programme on Prime TV called *Missing Pieces* about people searching for lost family. It has prompted me to write to you as it is possible you are the missing piece in my life.

On the other hand, I may have the wrong person and if so, I apologise for disturbing you.

I was born on March 17, 1951. My mother was Lizzie Hamilton.

I have led a fruitful and largely happy life and, if you are my birth father, I would like to thank you for giving my life to me. If you would be amenable to meeting me, I would like that very much and would welcome an email in return.

Yours sincerely

Felicity Price

I add my mobile phone number at the end, read it through several times then, before I change my mind, press 'send'.

Beyond the laptop, a silver-framed photo of my mother and father on their sixtieth wedding anniversary makes me feel like I'm cheating on them. What would they think? Mum was keen for me to meet my brother and sister and the extended family beyond them but she died before it happened. She never knew the joy it brought, which I regret – because she would have revelled in that joy vicariously and taken it as her own.

She was wary of me meeting up with my birth mother, though, and I suspect she would feel the same about my birth father. What about Dad? What would he think? Dad would never be drawn on any of it, not with me anyway. His comments to James suggest he wouldn't be worried.

But Mum and Dad aren't around any more and some part of me, some stray piece of DNA looking for a home, still wants to find my birth father.

A deep-throated low-revving engine rumble and a split second later, another aftershock. For a few seconds, the house judders, the window rattles, my desk jolts away and back again. It ends with a slow roll. The light swings but doesn't flicker.

'Four point three,' David yells from the kitchen.

'No, a shallow four,' James calls out from the lounge.

They'll find out on Geonet in a few minutes.

It's a measure of how accepting we are now of this seismic swarm that, instead of rushing for the doorway, we wager with each other over the magnitude – with increasing accuracy.

It's a measure of how accepting I am of my new family – and they of me – that my brother and I join forces to track down the man who lured our mother into the Karori Pavilion almost exactly sixty years ago.

Unsettled by the aftershock, I stand up and go into the hall where there's a line of family photos – Stewart family, Davidson family, Hamilton family. I beam from their midst, the ugly duckling in some, the swan in others. Where do I belong? Where do I fit in?

It no longer matters. What matters is that, for a while, I have stood in the shoes of both my mothers and come to understand them a little better.

~ ~ ~

Rick's not an effusive sort of guy. He saves his most expressive moments for the stage. I travel to Wellington for one of our increasingly frequent meetings – in Christchurch and in Wellington. When he introduces me to the bandmaster of his big band, I am expecting his usual reticence.

I'm listening to them play at the Front Room nightclub, enveloped with the crowd in the big brassy sound of multiple saxes, trumpets, trombones, amped up keyboards and guitar, when suddenly the encore is over and Rick is at my table looking for a drink.

'It's my shout,' I say, 'the least I can do after being so well entertained.' I call the waiter over and order a beer.

He's telling me about the band leader, how he writes most of the music, how people ask for his tunes by name, when the man himself comes over.

'This is my older sister, Felicity.' Rick is standing up, beaming.

'I didn't know you had two sisters,' says the band leader.

I stand up too, shake his hand, congratulate him.

'Aha, that's because Felicity arrived fully formed as a sister just a few months ago.'

So of course we have to explain it. Then Rick says, 'It was like we've always known each other, like we grew up together.'

The band leader is clearly impressed: he perches at our table and studies me. 'Can she play the trombone?' he asks then laughs.

'The flute actually,' Rick says.

'You want to audition?'

'You're joking, right?' I laugh and shake my head. 'I haven't played for years. I'll leave it to the experts.'

Then Rick says, 'She's a writer like me too. And now my sister Jessie has the sister she always wanted instead of a bossy brother like me.'

I hug him.

'Not that Felicity isn't bossy at times,' he says punching me on the arm and grinning. 'She's one of us now.' He looks at me, still grinning. 'You are, you know – you fit right in with our lot. You have from the moment we met.'

Kate sat back in her chair and ran that round in her head a few times. It sounded good. Penny had said something like that too.

~ ~ ~

I'm sitting in the Addington Coffee Company waiting for a friend to arrive. This place has become the city's business hub since the earthquakes. Some days, like today, you're lucky to find a seat let alone a table to yourself. I've taken a table outside, trading off the chill easterly against the early summer sunshine.

My mobile rings.

'Is that Felicity Price?'

'Yes.'

'This is Peter Williams.'

Suddenly my heart shoots up into my throat and starts banging against my chin. That name. It's him!

'Oh.'

'I was delighted to get your letter.' Everything stands still. The coffee stops swirling in its cup, the crowded café goes quiet. 'You sound a lovely person and I would like to think I could be your father, but I'm afraid I was born just ten years before you were, so I'm sorry it can't be me.'

My heart starts beating again. The coffee swirls. The noise in the café is intense.

I collect myself back together, tell him I'm sorry too and thank him for calling.

'Good luck with your search,' and he's gone.

Author's Note

My most heartfelt thanks to members of my two families – my husband and children, both of my mothers, my new brothers and sister and their families, my aunt and cousins and other members of my new extended family – who have both allowed and supported me in my quest to tell this story, no matter how painful or difficult it has been to revive memories that have lain buried for many, many years.

Adoption was my birth mother's only option at the time and there is no doubt that her choice, while bringing her years of regret, gave me a very privileged life. Adoption has a lot going for it.

But under the old adoption law, the decree for absolute secrecy undeniably caused both of my mothers and me – and everyone involved in the closed adoption triangle – an inexcusable amount of grief. Its amendment in 1986 to allow adoption records to be opened has at last brought these dark family secrets into the light - with varying degrees of resolution.

I would also like to thank my IIML tutor Damien Wilkins and all my classmates, without whom this book would not have been possible.

"The Chosen Baby" by Valentina P Wasson, and illustrated in pale apricot and green by Hildegarde Woodward, is available for sale on Amazon.com.

Made in the USA
Monee, IL
14 May 2020

30944101R00177